NEW LIGHT

NEW LIGHT

Annette Gilson

BLACK HERON PRESS

ISBN-13: 978-0-930773-77-9
ISBN-10: 0-930773-77-2

Jacket art and design by Sarah Sandman

BLACK HERON PRESS
POST OFFICE BOX 97656
SEATTLE, WA 98145
www.blackheronpress.com

one

I saw my first vision in St. Louis, Missouri, on the patio outside Boris Alexander's apartment. At the same time, inside, half the Washington University medical school partied on, getting drunk or stoned or laid. Not me. I got to have my mind-state altered without even raising a beer bottle to my lips. I was the chosen one, right? Out of a clear sky the night was suddenly altered for me—the stars rubbed themselves against my body, and Houdini came to me from out of the dark. I saw the world in a way I couldn't explain. I've since quit trying.

Contrary to what you might expect, seeing a vision is a physically demanding experience. After it's over you're left exhausted, especially if it's the first vision you've ever witnessed. That's why it's not good to have one at a party. By the time I came back in from the patio, Boris's Welcome to Spring bash was over, and Boris himself was crashed out on the couch. But I was lucky; Houdini stayed with me, out there on the roof top, after the vision spent itself. He was solicitous and kind, cradling me against him until I recovered. When it was over and I was myself again, he left. I became just some woman at a party. I was no longer in need of his attentions.

Boris's building is located in St. Louis's Central West End. It's tiered like a wedding cake at the top; his apartment, on the 14th floor, occupies the first of these tiers, and has attached to it one of the building's huge corner patios. It's a garage-like expanse three times the size of his apartment, a crazy amount of space for anyone in a city. It must've cost his father a fortune. But it was worth it: guests were invariably intimidated or impressed by the view, and it made a great party venue. It also made a great platform for visionary transport. Only the eastern edge is bordered by the apartment building; on all other sides the patio opens onto empty air beyond the railings. You can stand and look north, south, or west, and feel like the whole of St. Louis is laid out before you. The wind roars past and if you close your eyes, you can see yourself, very small, high above the earth.

It was about eleven when I first wandered from the dining room out into the night. At that point the vision was still hours away. The volume of the party was turned up high; there were shouts and laughter coming from the far end of the patio where a crowd of people were dancing beneath the stars. Boris wasn't among them. In fact I hadn't seen him in a while—sometimes he liked to pretend he was just another guest at his own party, disappearing for minutes and then more minutes and then more, then turning up wanting to know what he'd missed. Since I was an out-of-towner and didn't know anyone anyway, I didn't mind acting as recording angel. I had the necessary detachment.

At that moment the vastness of the open night was inspiring excess. One of the dancers, a pretty, shapely woman, had stripped down to her underwear. The other women in the group, looking cumbersome in their clothes, continued to move half-heartedly to the music, glancing from her to the men whose eyes followed her every sway expertly. Her best move was an Egyptian kind of thing, palms together over the head, with steady undulations of the hips. She'd had lessons or practised by herself in front of the mirror; you could see by the concentrated precision in her face that she knew what every movement looked like. She was hardly aware of anyone else. Then a fat man picked up her dress. He began to dance with it, holding it up before him and sliding it sinuously across his chest and belly. This startled the woman; she grabbed the dress out of his hands and pulled it over her head. The men booed and she turned her back on them. She crossed the desolate zone of concrete between the group of dancers and the partiers inside with remote face, as though she were walking in sunshine down a wooded path.

I stood back to let her go by, stifling an impulse to congratulate her. The people milling around on the patio looked lost now, as though she'd been the spirit of the dancing night, present among them unrecognized. After being ignored, mocked and derided, the spirit of the dancing night finally got fed up, put her clothes on, and went back inside. Leaving the men wilted and politically incorrect, the women put-out yet inexplicably saddened. They had all relinquished that sense of possibility that is so vital to parties, and didn't think to try to propitiate the offended spirit.

The preceding tells you more about the angel doing the recording than the people out on the patio. Truth be told, people in St. Louis know how to invoke the god of parties. As a matter of fact, there was a pleasing tension in the air at that gathering, an edgy buzz underneath the laughter and voices. The aura of expectation made people glance lingeringly at one another, before taking the plunge or moving on through the crowd. You could feel it in the air. The hesitation, the inability to act on impulse I just described—that was all me. I was still in observer mode. I'd been in St. Louis only a week; I didn't have a feel yet for the city or for the Midwest. I couldn't enter in.

I have a theory that explains this. I believe the spirit travels on foot. I didn't feel grounded yet because part of me was still wending her way westward from New York, vaguely following the exhaust trail my used Toyota had churned out behind it. Therein lies the danger of jetting off to some tropical island for a weekend. You fly down to Barbados for two days, zip back, and you're home before your soul has made it as far as Maryland. I don't mean to say that the soul is pedestrian and incapable of unearthly transports. Only that it's honest. It earns its passage.

And yet, despite my lack of spontaneous participation at Boris's Welcome to Spring party, the truth is I left New York on impulse, after living there for three years. Maybe I was still stunned by the grandiosity of that gesture, still trying to fathom its meaning for my life. After all, it was only a week and a half earlier that I stood on the sidewalk by Morningside Avenue, looking down at the park spread out below me. I remember thinking, my God, it's the end of April and there's barely any green on the trees. It wasn't that spring was late that year. No, I thought, in New York springtime is meted out according to income. If you were wealthy the sun shined and the grass flourished. Though Morningside Park was on the edge of Columbia's airbrushed community, it belonged to the darker streets and pinched lives that lay beyond the wall.

Then I looked back at my neighborhood and decided that the poverty of springtime wasn't selective; it had infected the whole city. Everything around me seemed reluctant to open up. Nothing offered itself to the eye. Cars edging along the street looking for spaces, pedestrians passing with their chins in their collars, even the sidewalks leading up to the doors of buildings seemed to exist half-heartedly. The overcast afternoon hovered between daylight and the fade toward dusk. The city resisted any agent—weather, time of day, time of year—that might translate it into a place its inhabitants wouldn't recognize. And so I was trapped there, in the literalness of that moment. I had become a part of it, and like it, suffered from that failure of the imagination.

Three years in New York isn't a long time. Everything is in constant motion around you. You assume that you're moving too. And in a way you are. City life is a constant negotiation. You're confronted with so much that lies beyond the imaginable, in people, buildings, and random events—layers of past amid relentless concessions to the present; collisions of culture and temperament. You don't need imagination in a city. At any rate, you don't notice its lack.

Four days later I had quit my job, packed up, and bought a car. I drove straight through to St. Louis, and a week later Boris threw a party to formally welcome the spring and me.

I left my post by the patio door and headed down the hall to the bathroom. En route I had to squeeze past a cluster of raucous med students, tall, wearing blue scrubs, smiling with set jaws, who deliberately blocked the way. At first they wouldn't move; then one said something about my ass and they parted to inspect me. I turned the hall corner and collided with a man coming from the other direction.

Caught off guard (my shoulder square in his sternum), the man froze the way a cat will when it's startled. He stared at me without expression, yet with disconcerting intensity. His eyes had a slight slant and his cheekbones were prominent and angular.

I looked at him, he looked at me, and I remembered a trip my family took when I was a child. We had pulled off the road into the parking area of a look-out point. I stood on the sidewalk staring out at the Grand Canyon. The wind was fierce. My mother leaned against the station wagon, hugging herself in her jacket; my father stood by the hood, looking at her, his jaw hard. Their expressions frightened me. I turned back to the view. The metal of the sign describing what I saw was cold, as was the wind, but the sun felt warm on my face. Before me, the earth fell away.

The recollection shimmered briefly, then the face of the man standing before me seemed to refocus, just slightly, the way a rock-face shifts when water is poured over it. I thought his expression changed in some imperceptible way, but maybe the sudden thrust of memory had caused it to blur. I took a good look at him. He had a long nose, pronounced Slavic cheekbones, a full mouth. He was a little taller than me and took up room in a broad-shouldered way, as though he were used to having people move over for him. His hair curled around his ears. He reminded me of Baryshnikov in his thirties, only with rougher features. But it was the feeling of his eyes on me that I remember best. There was something invasive in his stare. Then, as though I'd imagined it, the look was gone. He nodded and stepped back to let me by.

I nodded too and moved past him. The whole thing could have been choreographed. It took only a few seconds. But in the bathroom I found myself contemplating my face in the mirror. He was attractive, but it wasn't that. The curious shift in expression seemed enigmatic; perhaps I was associating it with my memory of the Grand Canyon. My reflection frowned back at me. I made it blank, trying to recreate the look on his face. When I came out of the bathroom there were four people waiting.

I went back to the patio. When you don't know anyone at a party, it's good to have a view. A strong wind hit me in the face as I stepped outside, and I walked against that pressure to the far railing, opposite the remaining dancers who had begun to drift into private groups of two and three. I could make out the big dipper overhead, though the stars were slightly swollen with haze. The night felt like summer. I looked out over a quiet street lined with tall buildings.

I didn't call my parents to tell them I was leaving New York; I just dropped them each a postcard saying I'd call them from the road. When I arrived at Boris's I sent off a couple more postcards. I couldn't face talking to them. I knew exactly what they'd say. My father would warn me that I couldn't expect him to fund my irresponsible lifestyle; while my mother would tell me I didn't know what I was getting myself into. Sure, the wandering life seemed glamorous from the outside, but I had to believe her that it wasn't. Both speeches would be irritating, though my mother's would be harder to take. Sometime in the last few years she had decided it was imperative that I Succeed. She wanted me to get into the corporate world and show them that I was Somebody. Don't follow my example, she kept saying. She'd had affairs with salesmen, used car dealers, stockbrokers, even one wealthy computer software designer. Boyfriends were for her like jobs were for me. Each one vanished forever once the glamour of the affair ended, and she, and I, moved tirelessly on.

But she wanted me to play by the rules. If I succeeded, it would be a vindication for her. It would be proof that the Martins, though they had money and connections, didn't have everything. It didn't matter to her that if I did succeed my father's family would claim that success as their own. But it did matter if I failed, because it would be her failure. They would blame her. I avoided talking to her in part because I felt I was letting her down, but more because I was embarrassed for her.

My father didn't embarrass me. After the divorce he sewed himself up like a child making a paper valentine with a border of yarn stitching. The child prefers a card whose edges are all sewn symmetrically to one that opens and declares I love you. He married a tall, heavy woman with excellent social skills who managed things for him. As for me, he decided I took after my mother and would never amount to anything. But even so, he went through the motions, asking what my game plan was and what kinds of skills I could claim for myself. I told him I was looking into computer training. He got excited about dot.com companies and offered to send a check if I enrolled in a course.

After talking to my father, part of me always admired my mother. I knew she'd use me to get revenge on the Martins if she could, but at least she was willing to fight. It wasn't easy either—she had to defy them just to walk down the sidewalk feeling okay. That's why it was important to her that I succeed. It wouldn't matter then that she'd never see any of them again (except when she showed up, uninvited, at the odd funeral). Her victory would forever alter the world of privilege that had caused her so much suffering. She believed they would then concede that she had been the only real human being at all those gatherings, all those years, while they had been monsters, sharpening their fangs in their Back Bay lairs. And so she would vanquish their smug condescension to a woman who—she knew they knew—was smarter, but helplessly more exposed, than they.

Maybe she was smarter, in a quirky, useless way, but she knew none of the rules, and her abilities were emotional and intuitive, not tactical. They matched her earnestness with their mock-earnestness and she fell flat, and knew it. She felt outwitted. It was terrible to watch, especially because I was included in it all. They condescended to me as an extension of her. My father hid in his role of the new-barbarian corporate executive, and was as humiliated as she was, in his own way. But they each suffered alone.

I abandoned the patio with its view of citynight and streetlights and went back inside to get something to drink. In the kitchen I found the dancing woman, now standing by the refrigerator drinking a beer. She ignored the murmured comments made by men who leaned against the countertop across from her, expectancy on their faces.

"I wouldn't have had the guts," I blurted, surprising

myself. She glanced at me with fast eyes. Then she shrugged. "Believe it or not, I wasn't doing it to show off." Her voice was flat. "I was going with the moment."

She tipped the bottle back and drank, then looked at me again. In that same flat voice she said: "What's the difference between letting yourself go because it feels right—with the wind and the music and the open sky and the stars—between that and being an exhibitionist?" For a moment the flatness in her voice disappeared and was replaced by a flutter of something exalted. She tamped it back down and gestured toward a man who continued to grin at her unpleasantly from across the room. "That guy over there said if I needed to show someone what I've got, he'd watch." She looked at him for a moment with cold eyes, then shrugged.

"It's probably all he's good for," I said, smiling.

She just looked at me. "How do you know Boris?" she asked.

I explained that we were roommates at Vassar and hadn't seen each other since graduation.

"Oh, you're his friend from college," she said. Her manner was instantly transformed. She smiled warmly. "I'm Lisa. I heard you were here—I just got back into town yesterday." She smiled again, now apologetic. "Listen, I'll see you later. I have to go find my boyfriend. He always disappears when I take off my clothes."

She left the kitchen, and in the other room I saw her stop to talk to Boris, who had reappeared. He came into the kitchen and gave me a smile. "I hear you met the other Elizabeth. Come on. I want you to meet Ty."

He led me to a group of black men getting high in the living room. "This is Beth," Boris said. "She just came in from New York. Thomas, John, Ty." He accepted the joint from John, took a drag and held his breath for a moment, then added, "Among their other occupations they're in a very good band called the Three-Tones." He expelled smoke with the words and offered me the joint, then lifted it to his lips again when I shook my head.

I didn't know if the name of their band was meant to be a reference to skin color. Thomas had glossy black skin the eye is pulled into, becoming, like light itself, absorbed by the color's depth. Ty's skin was the rich dark brown of chestnuts. John was the lightest of the three.

"Boris, you know, he has excellent taste," Thomas said in a rolling Caribbean accent. He smiled charmingly, presenting the comment to me as a compliment. His flirting reminded me of a man elaborately doffing his hat to a woman. Another era.

"He does have good taste," I agreed. "In New York throwing parties is a lost art. Everyone's there to be seen. When you introduce two strangers they square off suspiciously, trying to decide if they should flatter or ignore each other."

Boris took another drag, smiling, and passed the joint to Ty, who handed it on to Thomas. "Oh, we've heard about New York," Boris said.

"Your party has possibilities. You can feel it. People are willing to be interested in each other."

Boris exhaled again. "It's not people's willingness I rely on. It's their desire to be seduced. Persuade me to do what I can't admit I want."

Thomas smiled at me. "I admit to everything."

Throughout this exchange Ty had been watching me. Now he said, "What brings you to St. Louis? Aside from the possibilities."

I smiled. "I came to see Boris."

"In search of her past," Boris said.

I nodded. "He's the only person from college I'm still in contact with."

"No ties?" Ty said. I looked at him and he smiled. "It's okay. These days it's hard to sustain things. Too much happens. Too many gaps to explain."

A woman came up to Thomas and they started conversing in French. John sidled off and Boris said he had to check on the beer supply. He kissed his fingers to us in farewell. We watched him weave through the crowd.

"How do you know Boris?" I asked.

"We work together. I just finished my master's in neuroscience. For now I'm still working in the lab."

"For now?"

"I start med school in the fall. At Wash U."

"Impressive."

He shrugged. "I like the idea of being a doctor. I don't know if I'll like being a doctor. That's why I'm doing the MD/PhD program. I can always retreat into research." He smiled again. "I'd like to work with people. If I can sustain it."

There was a pause and I glanced out at the crowd. Out of the corner of my eye I saw the man I'd collided with in the hallway. I turned so that I could see him better but by then his back was to me.

"What made you leave New York?" Ty asked.

"Oh, a lot of things," I said vaguely.

He waited and I realized he expected a real answer.

"God. I don't know exactly. I'd been there for three years. One day I thought, what the hell am I doing? I've worked in five different restaurants; I go out and get drunk with people I barely know. I decided it was time to figure out what I'm doing."

"And have you figured it out?"

"I just started. Won't it take a while?"

He gave me an odd smile. "Only you can say."

We looked at each other.

"It's not just the three years in New York," I said

lightly. "Your average troubled adolescence, then Vassar. Boris will tell you what that was like. We weren't exactly driven to find our future careers."

"You think a career will answer your questions?"

"No," I said. "But my parents do."

"What do they think of this trip of yours?"

I laughed. "I don't know. I haven't talked to them about it."

Ty studied my face for a moment, then nodded in silence.

"What?" I said.

But our conversation was interrupted just then by Boris, who returned with a woman in tow. "All the separate strands of my life are being woven together tonight," he said, and introduced us to Sarah, a tall, slender woman in her late forties. At first I didn't realize how old she was—the shining blonde hair and lithe body led you to expect a younger woman. She moved with slinky grace and men turned around to watch her. Then they realized she wasn't twenty and recoiled. From their expressions they seemed to think she'd played a trick on them.

Boris was talking about the striptease on the patio. "We won't see Lisa for a while. Not till after she gives up on Tony. Why she even bothers with him is beyond me. After tonight he won't speak to her for days."

"Most men don't want women to enjoy being looked at by other men," Sarah said, looking at me. "They want to be envied, but it's a transaction between men. The woman is supposed to remain passive."

"It's not even like she shows it *all*," Boris said. "He's envied even more because they see how sexy she is, but the mystery's still *intac*ta."

Sarah slipped her arm around Boris. "You two used to be roommates?" she asked me. I nodded. She asked how I liked St. Louis, why I'd left New York, what I hoped to do. When I hedged she talked about herself. She made the conversation seem natural, with a deftness I distrusted. The signals she gave off made me nervous: the politely interested tilt of the head, the prompts coming on cue, the almost invisible work of sifting and ordering as she searched for the category that fit me, and topics that would draw me out.

"I've known Boris since he was a teenager," she said. "I knew, even then, that he was an interesting person. His mother and I are friends. Have you met Marie?"

I had met Boris's parents several times at Vassar. They didn't like each other, and only came to visit him as a couple once. Alone, James Alexander was no more talkative than he had been with his wife. Marie, on the other hand, became much funnier and livelier without her husband. She took us shopping, made sushi, and insisted that we do no homework while she was there.

My unhelpful responses couldn't have satisfied Sarah's curiousity, but Boris told me later that I too was interesting. Based on what, I wanted to know, but Boris told me I was prejudiced.

"You always get like this. You resent the social instincts of the rich. You think they have it easier than everyone else."

"Don't they?" I asked.

"Of course they do. That's why they're the rich. But those instincts are a burden once you leave that sphere."

"If you leave."

"If you leave," he agreed, "you spend your life overcompensating. The point is, Sarah's not rich. When she and her husband divorced, it turned out he didn't have as much money as everyone thought. His reputation is his income. Or is it his income is his reptuation? Anyway, he's a mentalist. He travels around giving shows and conducting seances.

Can you believe it? She did all right; I mean, she's not broke. And now she's the ex-wife of a mentalist. That's much better than being the wife."

Across the room I spotted the man from the hall again. "Boris," I said, when Sarah paused for a moment, "who is that?" Sarah blinked, and after the brief interval it took to digest the slight, started up a conversation with Ty. Boris leaned in to follow my line of sight.

"Oh. That's Harry. Just the kind of man you should avoid."

"Why?"

"He's weird. Kind of intense. He's been working at the med school for the last few months. No one knows his story." He shrugged dismissively. Boris had a distaste for people whose intensity threatened to overwhelm his own. I insisted. With reluctance he told me what he knew.

The man's name was not Harry, but Houdini White. "Harry" was Boris's little joke. He was a consultant who'd been moving back and forth between psych, a few of the neuroscience labs, and several other departments. Boris said he was *supposedly* facilitating inter-department collaboration through some kind of research project. Someone said he was Hungarian, that his mother had christened him Houdini because his grandmother loved the great escape artist. Boris didn't believe it, but he did admit that he admired the invention.

"Still—what the hell is he doing?" Boris exclaimed. "If you press him he'll tell you something about experiments on the effects of a new designer drug on the acetylcholine system. But I mean, *what*? No one I know is working on acetylcholine."

"You're talking about Houdini?" Ty said then, turning toward us.

Sarah looked from Boris to Ty to me. "Harry

Houdini?" she said.

"If he is working on acetylcholine, that would explain why he's down in the sleep lab," Ty said. "Acetylcholine modulates dreaming in the brain."

"Harry Houdini's brain?" Sarah said with a smile. Boris explained.

I was having a hard time concentrating on what Boris was saying. I felt off balance, almost like I was drunk, though I'd decided not to drink that night. I listened to Boris and realized that I could also follow three other conversations going on in the groups of people around us. I was becoming increasingly conscious of the bodies pressing in, the many voices swirling like smoke, the air thickening. I heard Ty say that Houdini was also involved in the psych department's hypnotism studies. Boris claimed that the whole schtick was part of some elaborate suggestibility experiment, with the entire staff as the subjects.

I surveyed the crowd as though compelled. The voices and laughter seemed to simmer in a murmuring soup of unspoken desires, resentments, fears. It was getting hard to breathe. "This is ridiculous," I muttered.

"What is?" Boris asked distractedly.

I finally saw him standing by the front door. As my eyes focused on the elusive Houdini White, the act of looking became suddenly pleasurable. I gazed at him, transfixed, until some small part of me began to panic. I barely managed to wrench my eyes away. I turned my back to him through sheer force of will, and then I could *feel* Houdini there, behind me.

It was strange and oddly familiar at the same time. I tried to ward off the feeling by focusing on Boris. I tried to remember the conversations I'd had earlier. With a nervous clutching fear I attempted to conjure up New York. But I felt walled off from everything, as in one of those photographs by Bellocq where the head of the female subject is scratched out. All you can see is her dress or lacy undergarment or naked breasts. The furniture and carpets and wall-hangings are luminously vivid in their elegant black and white tones, but the room is haunted by her absent presence. That's how I *felt*.

As I stood there with my back to him, I could visualize the space between Houdini and myself perfectly. It ached with possibility, like the distillation of being that emanates from a theater's empty stage. My sense of myself, each nerve-end of consciousness, arced up toward him, burning invisible pathways through the air to connect us. I couldn't help myself. I turned back. I had to see him.

He knew.

He mingled with the crowd as though seeking camouflage, and people unconsciously edged away from him, their faces troubled by dreamy unease. He stood near some men and women talking by the glass coffee table, and after a moment the group broke apart. Each person glanced uncertainly around, then drifted off to the kitchen or bathroom. Houdini watched them scatter, then moved on.

I glanced back at Boris again, and he and Ty were both watching me. Sarah was gone.

"He's aware of you too," Ty said.

"You don't know that," I said, my voice high-pitched and panicking. Ty didn't seem surprised. Boris was silent.

"No, I don't know. But I feel it." Ty looked at me steadily and for a moment I thought he was going to kiss me. Instead he looked away, and said in a casual voice, "Sometimes you sense things about people." He switched to a black dialect. "Everbody ride they own train. But sometimes you get off at the same station."

He turned then and made his way through the crowd across the room. When he came up to Houdini he stopped and shook hands with him. They went through the motions of polite talk. I watched them and discovered I felt nothing. No curiosity, no concern. There was no room for anything but the overwhelming presence of Houdini, and the strange tingling in my skin.

I fled to the patio. Or perhaps I should say: the waiting vision called me forth.

Outside was space. A huge figured expanse of buildings, lights, night sky. The pressure instantly vanished. I took deeper, measured breaths. My skin continued to tingle but it was pleasurable again, not suffocating.

No one was dancing now; the patio was empty. I walked forward into the dark open expanse. The wind was stronger than it had been earlier and made the Christmas lights Boris tacked up tremble. I went to the far railing and looked out over Kingshighway, the park stretching west to my left. Downtown was to my right with the Arch rising up like a metallic shadow.

I felt exposed there, leaning on the railing facing north, with the city wide open all around. Overhead the big dipper was still faintly swollen, while here and there a scattering of pale city-stars gleamed fitfully through the haze. The lights in the streets below burned pink and white and orange, and the traffic glared in ripples of red and white along the interstate.

My skin felt like it was pulling away from its bed of muscle and blood. The electric feeling that combed my body grew more intense, even though I was calmer out there on the patio. The whole night seemed drenched in inevitability— the dark haze of sky, the wind in my face, the intimacy of Ty's look, and the draw I could still feel, out there on the patio, to Houdini. It was as though I knew him, as though there was something between us already. I had only to admit to it, as Ty said, and everything would become clear. At the same time that I felt this, I also felt humiliated by it, like it was wrong, like I was giving in to a romantic fantasy.

I held onto the painted rail, face into the wind, and just like in a romance, he came up from behind me. He put his hands on the rail beside mine. It occurred to me that I should feel surprised. Instead I looked up at the sky and realized it was packed with stars, brilliant ones crowding out countless fainter others. All I could feel was the immensity of light, the burning beauty there. There was panic but it was somewhere small and distant inside myself. I said carefully, not sure what it would be like now to speak: "There are too many stars." I waited but they continued to crackle and hiss. I said: "No city sky could be this bright."

He looked up, considering, turning around to make a full scan. He looked back at me. His being there was a simple fact. He seemed to accept what I said in the same way.

"I'm not kidding," I said. It was as bright as noon on a cloudy winter day. The stars pulsed and roared dully like the steady background volume of surf when you're at the shore. Houdini's face was lit up—I could see every nuance of expression, every shielded thought. It wasn't that he didn't believe me. He was oddly sympathetic. "There are too many stars." I repeated. "Tell me what you see."

"Not that many," he admitted. He looked down at my hands and I realized I was holding on as though I were about to fall. I tried to relax my grip but I couldn't. "You're okay," he said gently.

"No I'm not. I'm not okay." I looked up again. I could *feel* the stars now. The tingling in my skin grew stronger. It wasn't unpleasant but it was terribly distracting. Beside me Houdini seemed to burn darkly. I wasn't afraid, but the palpability of the huge open space of city and sky was now too much to take in. "I can't hold on," I said, not sure what I meant. He put his arm around me gingerly and I felt a rush of dark weight and strange weightless burning. His presence partially shielded me from the expanse overhead.

"I'm not drunk, I swear," I said. "Jesus Christ. I feel like I'm going to fly out in all directions."

Houdini didn't comment.

"I dropped acid when I was a teenager and it was nothing like this. It doesn't feel like a hallucination. I just—oh god." It wasn't vertigo—it wasn't even hard to speak. I didn't feel disoriented. I felt exactly like myself, except that I was faced with a huge volume of sensory information steadily rushing in. As though I could hear and feel and see with unbearable acuity. When I spoke, the words came out effortlessly, and the wind seemed to cradle our voices next to us for a second before carrying them away.

He didn't move, just held me steadily. I felt as though my expansion outward could carry us both into the pulsing night. I'd bear Houdini upward like a wave, and then he'd fall away, crash to the street.

"I don't think it's chemical," he said. "Not drugs anyway."

"How do you know?" I demanded.

His face was level with my own and for a moment our eyes locked. I almost let go of the railing. It was sexual, but it was also a strangely intellectual sensation, graceful, the way dancing feels intelligent, especially when you're in perfect synch with the music, or your partner, or the ecstatic night. I looked back at the crowded sky and shimmer of restless starlight. That tingling felt safer.

"It's a kind of entropy you're experiencing, isn't it? But believe me, you aren't really coming apart."

"How do you know what it is?" I couldn't feel suspicious of him, even though the burn of his presence was dark and obscure. He was unreadable, but I was impervious to danger.

"It'll probably be over soon," he said, trying to be reassuring.

"How do you *know*?" I repeated. I tried to pull away and he drew his arm back. The empty surge I felt was awful. I shut my eyes and he steadied me again.

He had to make an effort to master his reluctance. He explained briefly. "I'm studying the phenomenon. It's happened to other people too. When I saw you in the hallway, I wasn't sure—there's a look people get as it's coming on and I thought I saw it in your face." He hesitated again. "Is it still as intense?"

I looked at the brilliant sky. The space around us seemed to have contracted slightly. The external world was less intrusive now.

"A few minutes ago you couldn't have pulled away like you just did," he said. "Usually, when it's this intense, it doesn't last that long. Here, sit down." He guided me so that I crouched down, and when I felt the roof beneath me, hard and solid and real, I finally let go of the rail. My hands were two clutched fists I couldn't unclench. I felt as though I'd been holding on for hours. I put my head on my knees. Houdini held me against him as the world returned to itself and my skin shrank to wrap muscles and blood and bone. I was too exhausted now to question him, and he seemed content to sit in silence.

The Visionary Company

To claim that my vision earned me a place in the company of American mystics would be silly. What I am is a kind of fringe character, she who was visited by the vision but lacked the faith of the mystic. But although I don't see myself as a visionary, having the vision did affect me. I mean aside from the fact that it brought me to Houdini's attention. It introduced a mystery into my life, just when I'd run out of belief in such things.

But from a more practical perspective, the vision gave me a new perspective on American history. I used to think that our forebears made that months-long Sunday morning trek across the Atlantic to go to the church of their choice—and arrived cured of their dreams. That is to say: they *landed*; they resolved themselves into an immensely pragmatic people who got down to the business of ekeing out a living from the wilderness. But I understand it differently now. Our history is riddled with people who spent their lives pursuing the invisible world that hovers just beyond this one. Many of them put the can-do side of their temperaments to work building mystic communities. There's a flair to that. One detects the stubborn insistence on having it all.

Over the past months I've been reading about them. I have a few favorites. There's Anne Hutchinson, a leader of the colonial Antinomian movement. She was brought to trial by the ministers and governor of Massachusetts for condoning heresy, and pronounced "like Roger Williams or worse." Kind and intelligent and much loved by many of the Massachussetts colonists, she "acquitted herself well" in court—and was duly banished. How did she envision herself, as she stood there in the courtroom, calmly defending her belief in justification by faith? It took courage and self confidence. I imagine Anne would insist it took something else as well, something that didn't come from inside Anne. After they kicked her out she went first to Rhode Island, where Williams had established a democratic, religiously tolerant colony, then to New York. She established her own community, believing as she did in "the paramount authority of private judgement"—something we take for granted now, but which, then, was regarded as radical and incendiary.

The historian's pages smell like mildew; the elegant phrases that describe Anne's defiance seem at once incantatory and impregnable. Like other secrets of the past, even the sensibility that framed those words has disappeared. And in part, this is what draws me, makes me keep on reading. I am compelled by the mysteries that glimmer in the background, the sense of something lost, a thing that is vital to our knowledge of ourselves.

But, predictably, it's also seduction that I succumb to. Many of our visionary ancestors were outrageous and power-mad, their ardent desire for another world igniting all sorts of other hungers. I know their longing. I stood on the patio and felt my body raked by stars—and now I turn the crumbling pages of library books, or wander into bars, where I listen to the imaginations of the quietly drunk, that are after all a kind of vision quashed.

John Noyes is one of the black sheep. He founded the Oneida colony, inaugurating a form of free love there. It was hierarchical sexual liberation, in that the older adult members supervised the sexual activity of the younger members. That meant that the elders of Oneida got to satisfy their lust for the younger members freely. A primary tenet of the community was the practice of sexual continence, so as to ensure that the prolific sexual interchange didn't starve out the colony. Children were produced only by those unions that had been declared acceptable; of course, Noyes fathered the most. All this is fascinating, but what really gets me is the group's law against falling in love with one person. It was seen as a kind of sexual selfishness; lovers who spent too much time together were no longer permitted to see each other. Did this bizarre set-up evolve out of some fear of intimacy on Noyes's part? And how did the younger members feel about being chosen by the elders for sex, and being unable to refuse a liason? While, secretly, their hearts ached with unpermissable love.

There are so many of these figures in our history, who shared in common the ability to organize the chaos of their followers' lives into a demented kind of order. Some of them, like Robert Owen, founder of New Harmony, were charismatics more than mystics, their social experiments a search for heaven on earth, rather than an attempt to leave the earth behind. Others were severe ascetics, like George Rapp, who sold Harmony to Owen and brought his followers east to establish a new community under the name of Economy. Rapp's repudiation of the sexual instinct was so extreme, he was said to have castrated his 28-year-old son for violating the group's voluntary abstinence pact.

They matter, these visionaries. All believed they had the calling and the power to reinvent the visible world. They trusted in the purity of the transformative vision. William James said: "The world suffers human violence willingly. Man engenders truth upon it." They lived by this.

three

When the vision ended and the stars grew distant and hazy again, I remained, half-crouched on the gritty roof, a hollowed-out creature, exhausted and small. The metal mesh that protected roof from empty space was a grid of dark on dark; beyond, shining through the windows of buildings, abrupt lights scorched the night.

Houdini and I sat in silence. I can't explain what either of us experienced because I was beyond language, beyond linear coherence. I sat there and saw myself strangely, as though I were a piece of quartz I kept turning in my hand, fooled by the illusion of translucence into believing I could see into its bright center.

I said that I left New York on impulse. But there on the roof I saw that it wasn't impulse. I left because there was nothing else for me to do. I'd used up everything I had. Which meant that Ty was right, I couldn't sustain anything. Not even my friendships with Dan and Kevin.

I'd been in New York almost a year when I met them. I had just finished a depressing shift at El Mariachi, an upscale Mexican place on the upper East side where the waitresses vamped between tables as though they were on the catwalk. For months I'd been on the verge of quitting, but the money was so good I kept postponing it. The tall, slinky women I worked with resented my presence: I'm taller than average, in pretty good shape, and fairly attractive, but I'm not slinky. I couldn't understand why Johno, the owner, hired me in the first place.

Neither could he, once he realized his mistake. It didn't make sense. It violated the cardinal law of table-waiting in New York, the first thing any server learns, which is: restaurants type you. As an aspiring waitperson, you will be able to work only in those parts of the city for which the class-latitude of your appearance and demeanor qualify you. If you're hip you can work down in the Village or Soho; if you're clean-cut and liberal you can work on the Upper West side. If you're a smart-ass but fast on your feet you'll make it in the financial districts; there is some cross-over here with the Upper East side, but for that area you also have to look expensive, and be willing to kiss your way through serious shit for your money.

For some reason I was an exception to this rule. By the time I left the city I'd been on the Upper East and West sides, in Rockefeller Center, down in the East Village, and finally at Bart's, an expensive place near Macy's. I even did part-time work during the holidays as a caterer for a pretentious outfit down near the Fulton Fishmarket. In the beginning I prided myself on this ability to get hired anywhere. But after toughing it out at El Mariachi for two months (my third job), I realized that I was cursed. Johno didn't know how to deal with me, so he pretended I wasn't there. The other women managed their resentment toward me by applying a lacquer of slick politeness to every interaction.

One Thursday night, during what would turn out to be my last shift, I was feeling nauseated as usual by the unguentary, self-congratulatory atmosphere: the young Wall Street brokers boasting of their million-dollar portfolios and six figure bonuses, the waitresses who leaned over them with expensive cleavages and model-smiles as they served Mexican fondue. At the service bar, as Jake put up my round of Coronas, Sabrina, Johno's star waitress (she who—it was said—administered pre-shift blow-jobs and always came out licking her lips), ordered eight Cuervo Gold strawberry frozen margaritas.

"You think you're better than us because you went to

Vassar," she said suddenly, as Jake squeezed limes into the mouths of the beer bottles. I stared at her. "Oh, don't give me that innocent above-it-all crap," she spat. "If you knew how to use it you would." Something in Jake's face flickered slightly—Jake who never smiled—and he turned away to make her drinks.

When I got off at two a.m. I left the restaurant and started to walk. I was too agitated to go back to my hallway bedroom between the two violinists (heavy practicers and light sleepers). I hadn't realized Sabrina and the others hated me as much as I hated them. From Lexington I went east, then down Second Avenue. I came to a bar called The Drum. It was so crowded inside that people spilled out onto the sidewalk. The crowd's hoots and laughter rose and fell with the fluting accents of the Irish. The whole place looked like it had been brought over, brick by plank, from Erin's green shores.

This was how I discovered that a section of the upper East side had been colonized by the Irish. I was trying to pass between bodies on the crowded sidewalk, when I found my way blocked by two men.

"Sure and you're lookin' a bit lost, the wee lass walkin' alone at this time o' night," said the older of the two, who was bearded and good-looking and in his forties. "Surely she's lookin' for somethin', is my guess. Would you be willin' to settle for second best then?"

Dan, the instigator, admitted later he'd deliberately thickened his brogue to charm me wi' the magic o' the old country. He didn't have to work on me for long. He elbowed his way into The Drum and presented me as his American sweetheart. I put my arm around him obligingly and he pulled on his beard with mock-distress. Everyone around us laughed. His friend Kevin, who was also bearded but had a harder body and a more self-conscious manner, followed. He was taller than Dan, my age. "He's a charmer, that one, make no mistake," Kevin confided loudly, so that Dan roared out, "Now look, the younger one is after her, I always say: trust no one."

By the end of the night we were quite drunk. Dan leaned in: "You know we're normally very successful at ensnaring unsuspecting American girls."

"This is no exception," I insisted. "I'm ensnared; I suspect nothing." He declared then that they would get me a job as a waitress at the restaurant where they worked, to rescue me from the hell of El Mariachi.

"The waitresses don't give blow-jobs, but one time I came upon one of the strippers hired for a private party in the upstairs men's room," Dan said with a straight face.

Kevin groaned. "A terrible pun," he said. "Tell us you didn't really avail yourself of the young lady's services."

"I've never paid for it in my life," Dan said with a smile at me.

We established a routine over the next year and a half. Bart's was famous in the late nineteenth century as the favorite spot of actors and playgoers, when the theater district still hovered around 36th Street. Gradually theaters moved uptown and Bart's became part of the past rather than the present. You walked through the front door, with its awning and tile-inlay doorstep, and found yourself back in time. Clay pipes that had been smoked by customers over the years lined the ceilings; the Lincoln and Lilly Langtry rooms were done up in velvets and brocades; the bar gleamed with more tile and the high polish of mahogany and brass.

Some nights, after our shifts, we'd end up at The Drum, or downtown at McSorley's. The drinking would have begun with enthusiasm at Bart's, but by the end of the night it sometimes changed tone. Dan would stand up and say mournfully, "Oh, if I were the young man," then salute us blurrily and wander out of the bar, leaving Kevin and me alone. In this way, as often as not it was Dan who decided which nights Kevin and I would spend together. Once he left, the night was over. I think in a way we felt obligated to have sex because he envied us so.

But for the most part it was fun with Kevin. I liked him. He came to New York after winning a green card lottery. He had no intention of settling in America; he had a law degree from Trinity and was planning to start up a practice in Dublin. But when he won the lottery he decided to take an extended vacation, taste a life he'd never get to lead again. He worked as a bartender and at the same time studied for the New York bar exam. That way, he explained, if his practice wasn't successful in Ireland he'd have something to fall back on. It also gave him a reason for being there, one he could hand his parents and grandfather.

It was an exotic vacation, living in New York among Irish expatriates like Dan. And then there was me. Sometimes when we were talking Kevin's voice cramped up; he gasped audibly for breath, as though being near me squeezed the air out of his lungs. At first I thought it was a kind of asthma, until I realized it never happened when he talked to anyone else. I think, even though he knew he was leaving, he entertained some kind of fantasy about the two of us.

About a year after I'd started at Bart's, I moved into a living room on Morningside Avenue. My bed was ten feet from the couch, cordoned off by a tent-like series of hanging blankets, a bit like the wall of Jericho in *It Happened One Night*. It was a marginal improvement over the hallway with its competing violinists. I assured William Brixton, whose place it was, that I wouldn't spend much time there, which seemed to be why he let me move in. I got a lot of flack from Dan and Kevin for moving in with an Englishman. Dan shook his head and said to Kevin that I was sleeping with the enemy. Kevin didn't find that very funny.

One night I brought Kevin back to William's apartment. (It was always William's apartment; I never felt at home enough to claim title.) We squirmed noisily on the bed together, lit up by streetlight that shone through the shadeless window. After we'd uncoupled and lay there in a vague embrace, he fingered the blanket wall. "I couldn't do it," he said after a moment.

"Do what?" I asked.

He turned over to face me. "I'm sure he wants to sleep with you. A lovely woman in his own apartment, and he has to listen to her having sex with another man. I couldn't do it myself."

I laughed. "He prefers figs to pomegranates," I said, quoting a line from a Pasolini movie that Boris and I had loved in college. Kevin didn't understand. "He's gay," I explained. "I mean, he's not out, but it's clear." I laughed again. "What is it about me and gay men? My roommate in college was queer too."

I stopped laughing. Kevin was staring at me with shock and disgust. I asked him if he was kidding, and he turned over and didn't say anything else that night. We didn't talk about pomegranates and figs again, and I didn't bring him back to William's apartment.

I have no idea how Kevin felt about me after that. Things were strained between us, but we didn't talk about it. Then one night, a couple weeks later, the two of us were sitting in the main barroom after closing out. Dan was behind the bar; he had another half hour before he got off. He filled two glasses with Guinness and set them down in front of us, then drew a small one for himself.

"The hymn to what's gone is the most mesmerizing of emotional fugues," I declaimed, mock-serious, raising my glass.

Dan drank down his Guinness before meeting my eyes. "What are you saying, Beth?"

"Take the three of us," I said. "When we're each living somewhere else we'll see this time as a beautiful, poignant period in our lives. We'll see each other as parts of ourselves we've lost. Fragments of our own souls. But in truth, we're just looking to get plastered."

"I'll drink to that," Dan said and drew himself another glass.

"No, it isn't that people glorify the past," said Kevin, the Gaelic-speaker who had once demonstrated several stiff-backed Irish dance steps for me on the corner of 6th and 38th at three a.m. "It's just that as time goes by they understand the things that've happened to them better." He hummed the opening bars to "I Wonder What's Keeping My True Love Tonight," a song he sang sometimes in bed, when we were too drunk to screw. I respect the Irish and their unabashed sentimentality, now that I've learned what a powerful tool it is. In the next breath he announced, looking not at me but at Dan, that he was going back to Ireland.

The news took me by surprise. He had his ticket; the arrangements were all made. No warning. But I was even more surprised by how hard Dan took it. He froze behind the bar, his glass to his lips. Recovering, he drained the glass and wiped the foam from his beard.

"So you're going back then, Kevin," he said. As exiles they weren't friends so much as fellow citizens of an Ireland that exists only in the US. When Kevin said he was returning it was as though he had been transported magically to the real Ireland, leaving Dan the empty shore and the haunted green fields.

Dan couldn't go back. He never said exactly why, only let on vaguely that it was political. His sentence was permanent, and Kevin's return reminded him that he wasn't a young man out on a spree before settling down. He was sick of the exile's life. He had been a teacher. I couldn't imagine being afraid, as he was, of losing your job in a bar.

I tried to console him in the weeks after Kevin left. He had catapulted into depression; I joked with him that in this, as in everything else, he was not a cautious man. I told him he couldn't compare himself to Kevin, who was essentially conservative. Even Kevin's wild period had been carefully managed to appear legitimate. "You have to be who you are," I said. "You're the rebel."

"No," Dan said. "Not now. I was a different man then."

His depression mellowed eventually. He regained his sense of humor, but there was still something wrong. Things weren't easy between us anymore. Now when we walked into The Drum, and Annie and Patrick and the others broke off their jokes and with one will stretched silence as taut as a bedsheet, Dan simply looked away. I refused to go anymore. "You know they don't like me," I said to him. "It can't be fun for you either."

He said, cheerfully mournful, "It is though. It's the compensation I get for never having gone to bed with you. They all think we've slept together, and that's almost as good."

Our patterns changed. We stopped staying out late. Maybe I was avoiding the inevitable scene when he tried to take me to bed and I refused—or didn't refuse. I don't know. But one evening it felt like it used to. He was working the service bar, I picked up the drinks from him, we joked and flirted. After work we headed uptown and stayed out till four in the morning. We went back to his place.

It was too late, and we'd had too much to drink, to do more than kiss sloppily in the doorway. He said something slurred about wanting me for so long, and I let my head fall to his shoulder and admitted to having been scared of him that first night, when we met in front of The Drum. The power of the attraction, I said blurrily. He pulled me into the living room of his tiny apartment and I sprawled onto the couch. He stood over me swaying and I shut my eyes because he was making me dizzy.

I woke up a few hours later to stifling heat and the radiators clanking away. For a moment I thought someone had really been banging at the door. A grey, sickening light came through the window. The radiators continued to knock and I got up. On my way to the bathroom I passed his bedroom. The door was half open; Dan lay naked on his bed.

I'd always thought him a handsome man. I liked the grey-black of his beard; I liked how he lowered his chin to pierce me with his gaze, then bit his lip and nodded. It was very sexy. But I woke up on the couch; he was in his own bed. I stood looking at him in that hung-over, baleful state, my body overheated and my mouth parched.

He lay there, arms and legs splayed awkwardly, as though a giant had flung him down on the bed. There was grey in his pubic hair and on his chest, and his stomach sagged to one side. His penis was a small, shrivelled thing. Maybe it was seeing him naked. Maybe I felt that neither of us really wanted it. A sudden suspicion that we were both playing at desire, that we were afraid to see what would happen if we stopped making jokes and tried to make love. Afterward, I didn't regret that it hadn't happened. All my sexual imaginations of him became drenched in the early sorrow of that morning.

I quit Bart's not long after the night I spent at Dan's. When I told him I was leaving he said something about everyone needing a change. I think I expected him to have more to say. I couldn't tell if he was relieved or sorry to see me go. He looked at me, and I simply didn't know.

I sat in huddled misery, on the roof above a city that was not New York, with Houdini's arm around my shoulders. There we were, sitting in tar grit, both of us silent. Maybe, like me, he was trying to fathom the vague darkness. Maybe he too just noticed lights burning in the top two floors in the tower across the street; and saw, further east, more towers skulking at the fringes of the hyper-real burn of streetlights, which simultaneously granted and took away life in the darkness.

The physical contact—his body against mine—was frail and tenuous. I didn't want to move. I felt that he had sensed what this vision had done to me, just as he'd sensed it coming on. I wanted him to understand what it meant to have him there, beside me. I wanted him to know how grateful I was at not having to face the darkness alone.

Houdini removed his arm from my shoulder. The night air was chilly on my neck where his body had touched mine. He avoided my eyes as he stood.

I tried to remind myself what the vision had revealed to me, that the wooden walls of my mind were hinged like shutters and could be thrown wide to reveal fantastic views on every side. But as Houdini turned to survey the nightscape of subdued city, even that was gone. It had vanished, like everything else, through my carelessness and inattention. I got to my feet too.

"You knew it was happening," I said in a croaky voice. I cleared my throat. "Before I did."

He looked at me, then turned his gaze to the buildings that surrounded us. He seemed reluctant to commit himself to words. When he finally spoke his voice was strangely muted, so that I couldn't hear him. When I asked him to repeat what he said he glanced back at me. He cleared his throat.

"I said, entropy. But more than just a vision of it. As though you were simultaneously the primal matter of the universe, and yourself, a woman standing on the deck of an apartment building."

four

Sunlight burned on the black paint of the railings. The fringed
flaps on the white umbrella made a slapping sound in the
wind. Boris frowned at all the brightness and pulled the brim
of his hat down until it rested on his sunglasses, then clutched
his coffee mug with both hands. I wasn't hung over, but the
world of roof and buildings—luminous and wind-scrubbed
as it was, buoyed up by the sounds of weekend traffic—still
seemed flat. Even in sunlight, with the slanting shadows of
morning darkening the street that ran along the west face of
the building, and the bright green space beyond where the
park sprang up in lush defiance of Kingshighway—this world
was not as persuasive as last night's murky vision-universe.

"And he claimed he *knew* it was coming on," Boris
said again.

"That's what he said."

Boris pursed his lips and contemplated. He'd been
crushed when he discovered I had had a vision, right there on
the patio of his apartment, and he had missed it. He insisted
I could've let him know somehow. How, I wanted to know.
He said I could've paused in my visionary ascension just
long enough to appear to him in astral form. Just for a
moment. He would've taken it from there.

"And he really didn't hit on you?" Boris said again.

I shook my head and smiled.

I was meant to hear the edge in his voice, muted
though it was. Joking laced with reproach, the faint accusa-
tion that sexual relationships would always take precedence
over our friendship. The inescapable hierarchy of desires. It
began in college when we'd bring lovers home for each
other's inspection. After the fun was over and the men had

left, Boris and I would talk about our respective nights, rate the conversation, the sex, the sincerity level. At those moments we were more intimate than any lovers. But after a while it changed. In our senior year there were some men I wouldn't bring home. I'd come back to the apartment the next morning alone, and whoever it was would remain a mystery to him, much more threatening than any real man. It wasn't jealousy, exactly. It was that there was suddenly distance between us. There was something we hadn't shared.

Now those imaginary college betrayals seemed silly—displaced fears of being adult, a reluctant acceptance that there was no absolute loyalty, no perfect friendship that would protect us from the world. It wasn't sex anymore that distanced us; now it was something much more real. Three years I lived in New York. I never called him. I did write, a number of times. But I couldn't talk to him. He knew me too well. He would've forced me to face myself.

I know he understood. But that's not always enough. He even forgave me, but that too isn't always enough.

So the gap remained, and we skirted it. The fact that I came to St. Louis counted for a lot. We slipped with remarkable ease back into our old routines—food shopping, watching movies, cooking meals. He understood that I had come to him. Even so, underneath he was still upset. Because, of course, it wasn't just about me. Over the last three years things weren't so great for him either.

Like me, Boris had been planning to live in New York after college, but instead he ended up moving back to Missouri. His father insisted: it was a kind of arms-for-hostages deal and Boris was the hostage. After he came out in high school he was estranged from his family for years, especially from his father, who had made a lot of money and looked forward to founding a midwestern dynasty. Boris had ruined his dream. By sophomore year in college he and his father had made an uneasy peace. In the emotional equation they worked out, Boris was required to move back home.

The uneasiness of the new peace didn't go away. In the three years since graduation Boris had tried on four different careers. He worked as a technician in a physics lab at Washington University, did a stint in an architectural firm, spent a semester in a master's program back at the University (choosing as his specialty the American literary Renaissance, of all things), and finally got the job in the med lab he had now, plugging monkeys into a wall. He liked working with the monkeys, even though it was sad. He said he was on long-distance with his own mortality.

All this I could understand. What I couldn't fathom was Boris's emotional response. Whereas I threw myself into sexual relationships over the past three years to avoid facing the emotional wasteland, Boris cut himself off. He claimed it was because he was terrified of getting AIDS, but it was more than that, as he well knew. "You mean moving here might have had something to do with it?" he said, wide-eyed. But it was serious. He said he didn't even know how to go about being intimate again. That's why my abandonment had been so cruel. He had friends here of course, but we'd lived together for two and a half years. I knew him.

We ate leftover pizza and I tried to evoke the vision for him. "It felt like I was being taken over. I stood and looked out over the street, then up at the sky. My body was expanding. I could feel the stars."

Boris didn't say anything. He went musingly over to the far railing, then called out: "Here?" He flung his arms out to the sky.

Inside, the phone rang.

"Maybe it has to do with why you left New York," he said as he headed inside to answer it. "Lisa would say it was like the planets coming into alignment. You, that guy Houdini, meeting here. Chance or fate?" He flourished his hand above his head dramatically, to mime the receiving of inspiration.

When Boris stuck his head through the doorway a few minutes later, it was to announce in a perplexed voice that he had just buzzed Houdini up.

It wasn't clear to Boris or to me why Houdini came there that morning. When Boris opened the door, there he was, standing silently before us in the hall. He didn't offer an explanation, didn't attempt to be polite. He just studied each of us in turn, then asked if he could come in.

Boris and I looked at each other. The whole thing was pretty weird—we both felt self-conscious suddenly, like we'd been caught doing something wrong. Boris gestured Houdini in. My heart was still beating fast, but as we stood in awkward silence I felt annoyance start to overlay my perplexity. I watched Houdini take in Boris's retro '60s decor as though he'd never seen it before. He didn't bother to explain why he was standing there, staring; his only concession to polite form was a bag of pastries he carried in one hand.

Boris decided to find the whole thing amusing. He took the pastries from Houdini and ushered us out to the patio, saying, "Wait, it's coming to me. You aren't sure why you're here. A vision directed you." Houdini looked at him without answering.

We breasted the bright morning of the patio and sat down. Houdini gazed out at the park, at the congregations of tiny trees displaying thin coats of uncertain green. Even the sunlight seemed to quail before his ferocious gaze. Part of me was amazed at his balls, coming uninvited to Boris's apartment without apology or explanation. But part of me was fascinated. He felt no compulsion to speak. There was no pretence at polite conversation. He didn't care what we thought of him.

"How do you feel this morning?" he asked me finally, fixing me again with that gaze. The directness of the question caught me off guard; I glanced at Boris instead of answering. Houdini followed my eyes to Boris and frowned at him for a moment before turning back to me. "No after-effects?"

I laughed uncomfortably. Boris said, "What happened out here last night? Beth said you knew. How?"

Houdini's eyes slid back to him and he gazed at Boris in silence. "I mean it," Boris said, uneasy and defensive. "How did you know?"

Houdini looked out over the park. "I study the neurophysiology of brain states." He looked back at Boris. "Corporate research and development."

No, I thought, not Baryshnikov, in spite of the high cheekbones and the Slavic mouth. Houdini no longer resembled a man who burned for the body's sensual self-discipline. He was pragmatic now, matter-of-fact, even cold. He said: "Since the '70s big corporations have been interested in something they call potential enhancement. They've managed to co-opt a number of New Age techniques—transcendental meditation, motivational seminars, visualization, astrology. I do visions. To answer your question, that's how I knew."

Boris opened his mouth to speak, then shut it and looked at me instead. I was silent too.

"My company is a big multi-national," Houdini continued, off-handed in a deliberate way. "Pharmaceuticals are their major interest, but they've bought up a number of subsidiary concerns. What I do for them is complicated. You could say I develop new motivational resources. That's what I'm working on here, at the med school."

"Visions," I said flatly. "You study visions."

Yet he was serious. He wanted us to believe that he

specialized in visions. That he was paid by a pharmaceutical company to understand the brain chemistry of the vision state. When I smiled ironically he leaned forward. It was true, he said, whether I believed it or not. We had to forget our preconceptions about corporate culture. Businesses were mainstream only as long as it was profitable to be mainstream. He told us of yearly seminars in New Mexico, attended by representatives from GM, IBM, AT&T, designed to help businesses use esoteric phenomena like the occult, Hindu mysticism, and metaphysics to become more competitive. These days that kind of crossover was commonplace. Companies were willing to tap any resource to increase productivity.

He explained that his company had given a lot of money over the years to the med school. Investing in research and the future, they called it. And so when Houdini needed to do specialized lab work Wash U gladly took him on as a visiting researcher. Houdini found himself enjoying this break from the corporate world. Pure science was a luxury he hadn't enjoyed since grad school. He assured us that of course he liked what he did: as a scientist and executive he was given free rein in his work, as long as it showed positive results. He never had to worry about funding or peer review. But it was nice to be back in an environment where research was conducted for its own sake.

Boris was no longer amused. He was critical of the ties between the school and industry and observed with distaste that Houdini's company had bought him research facilities. Houdini nodded. Annoyed, Boris looked at me.

"So you came over here to explain this to us," I said. Houdini pursed his lips and looked suddenly very Slavic and arch. I wondered whether the Hungarian story Boris had related was true. He crossed his legs, as though deciding something.

"Think what a multi-national corporation could do if they were able to induce visions in people."

He smiled. It was a cold and unpleasant smile, but again I got the feeling that he meant for it to seem so. Neither Boris nor I replied. What would we have said? Houdini looked from my friend to me as though disappointed we hadn't criticized him. The umbrella flapped and shifted in the wind; the sun shone from higher in the sky and caught the edge of the table nearest Boris, creating an inch of burning white. Houdini himself, leaning back in his chair, was head and shoulders in sun. The light burned in his dark hair until he sat forward again, his forehead unclenching beneath the gentle hand of shade.

"There's a group in southwestern Missouri who call their community New Light. They used to be based in California. I plan to go down there."

Boris looked from Houdini to me, a look of disbelief dawning on his face. "You're going down to some New Age community to research their visions?" He started to laugh. Then he stopped. "You claim you're researching visions, and you just happen to come to my party and meet Beth, who is promptly overtaken by a vision herself?"

Houdini looked at Boris steadily, then back at me. He shifted in his chair, noticed the bag of pastries sitting on the table, pulled out a cruller. He broke it into pieces and laid these on the table. He looked at us and shrugged. "It defies explanation."

Boris stood up abruptly. He was suddenly very angry. I understood how he felt—it was quite possible that Houdini was making fools of us. But as I looked up at Boris I realized that, unlike him, I wasn't angry. In fact, I was intrigued. Boris met my eyes in silence, waiting for me to echo his frustration, then said pointedly, "I'm getting more coffee." I watched him cross the patio. I didn't follow him in.

Instead I looked back at Houdini.

He turned his eyes away from me and out at the park again. The wind blew the fine dark hair into a fan on top of his head and he frowned, looking out toward the west. Then, in a quiet voice, his eyes still focused on the distance, he said that he was sorry. I blinked. He added, "I hope you understand. I don't want to invalidate your experience."

He didn't look at me, but he didn't have to. I did understand. I felt the thing I'd felt the night before, a kind of mysterious attraction, overwhelming, dangerous. He told me, with a flicker of a glance, about the purpose of his work. To understand the brain's processes. To penetrate the strange world of consciousness. He claimed that there are things we know without knowing how we know them. Our lack of understanding didn't make them less true. As he spoke, I believed he understood my vision in a way I myself could not.

In other words, I wanted to believe him. He looked me in the eye. His own were so dark, the pupils were indistinguishable from the irises.

He sensed my hesitation. "You know what I'm talking about." Voice low. "You felt it too."

I looked out over the park, then nodded. "You just appeared. I was aware of you. Before I went outside."

I sensed rather than saw him lean forward. "Yes," he said. "I was aware of you too."

There was a long pause. He continued to stare at me, I continued to stare out at the park. Then I felt the pressure of his gaze removed. He was frowning down at the crumbs and pieces of cruller on the table, some new emotion brimming up behind the fixed scowl. What had just happened? I felt a moment of panic, as though he had tried to communicate something to me and I had failed to receive it.

He looked up at the ribs of the umbrella's white

canopy, then over at the building across the way.

"A good hypnotist can size up a person's susceptibility to being hypnotized in a few seconds. In minutes they can pick out of a crowd the people who will fall into the deepest trances."

I was taken aback. "Are you saying you hypnotized me?"

"No." He frowned. He allowed himself to look at me again and my stomach fluttered. "I just meant that maybe I've become attuned to this vision phenomenon, after working with it for so long. Maybe I sense its latent presence." His eyes on me were sharp, to see if I believed him.

It was all too much to field. I made my tone slightly-mocking. "And the fact that I was going to have a vision drew you to Boris's party?"

"Across time and space," he replied calmly. "That's what these people believe."

Faith

Who was Houdini White? It's a question I ask myself now, looking back at that Saturday morning after the vision, when Houdini came to see me at Boris's apartment. He'd behaved so differently the night before. The two of us stood on the patio facing into the wind, while my body was wracked by stars. Afterward, once the sky had coldly withdrawn, he held me against him, protecting me. The moment didn't last long, but it had happened, it couldn't be erased. Yet it seemed as though it had been erased—the man who stood in Boris's hallway the next morning was someone different. That Houdini was cold and aggressive—until he inexplicably turned again. Was it simply that he wanted to confuse me? Or did he shuck off the corporate mask to make me soften, sucker that I am, and look into his eyes, yearning to understand what it was that connected us. It was inexplicable, I felt. It was overpowering. And oh, it was seductive.

But who was he?

There is another way to consider these questions. One could ask why the witness to my first visionary trance was the purported namesake of the legendary Harry Houdini. Coincidence? My Houdini just happened to be named after a man who was known in his time as the arch-skeptic, the exposer of mediums, the debunker of spiritual cons? And then, as he pursued his PhD just happened to become interested in New Age phenomena, with the result that he was currently on his way to a visionary colony called New Light?

On the strength of these ambiguities I have added Houdini White's symbolic progenitor to my list of mysterious and compelling visionaries. It's all part of my attempt to make a believable narrative out of the experiences I had with

Houdini—a narrative that coheres, that explains. But I want more than explanation. I also want to understand how these experiences matter, how they fit within a larger framework. Which framework? That's another question.

I should state first that Harry Houdini was not just a skeptic who exposed more fake mediums than anyone of his time. He was actually obsessed with the world beyond this one. Was that why Houdini White chose the name, if indeed he did choose it? He knew that Harry Houdini was driven to pursue charlatans relentlessly because he wanted so much to find a medium whose powers were real? Is this the message Houdini White intended to convey?

I like Harry Houdini. I like his fierceness. The death-defying stunts, the dramatic escapes, the burning gaze. He was loved throughout Europe and America because of his charismatic defiance of those universal laws that bind the rest of us. In some spectacular, dangerous way, he was free of them. He was a fraud, he assured us: but an honest fraud. The magic was not really magic but hidden skill. And therein lay his magnificence. He enchanted us with his unearthly abilities, and at the same time assured us there was nothing enchanting or unearthly in anything he did.

But of course it's important to remember that he was compelled to perform those spectacular feats. The nightly escapes from handcuffs, chains, straightjackets—these weren't just smoke and mirrors. I mean they didn't have that lightness of tone. To Harry they were terribly serious, and not because there was danger involved. Each stunt was born out of his terror of being trapped by life. Haunted by fears of death and poverty, he proved again and again that he could escape any constraint that humans could devise. His prowess was the magic formula. And so he issued challenges to audiences all over the world, daring them to find a way to hold him.

He strove always to outdo himself, and the stunts became wilder and more dramatic. But in 1913 the nature of his defiance of death changed. His mother died suddenly while he was performing in Europe. Harry collapsed when he heard the news, and for the rest of his life he was bereft. He became obsessed with trying to reach her, to go beyond the grave. In his desperation to talk to her again he consulted medium after medium, all of whom claimed they could contact Cecilia Weiss.

Maybe that was the source of his vendetta against the spiritualists. Maybe he thought that the fake mediums were contaminating his attempt to contact the Beyond with their bad faith. Or maybe he just wanted to believe that it was possible to cross from one world to the next, and searched for a true medium who could help him do this. When he discovered the falseness of their claims, he exposed them with the ruthlessness of the true believer. And left behind him an endless line of fakes.

All these things must have made Harry Houdini fascinating to Houdini White. Harry was the skeptic who believed in his own myth, the believer who refused to be seduced by his own longing for proof. So perhaps it was appropriate to have the legend of Harry Houdini, like the ghost of defiant desire, surround my ascension into the hyperreal world of visions. There I was witness to things I couldn't understand; I was faced with motives and desires that were inscrutable to me. None of it made sense, but it didn't matter. Houdini was my ascending star, and the world gave way before his imagination.

six

The members of New Light—or Visionaries as they called themselves—seemed to be the object of that passion I had sensed obscurely burning in the scientist Houdini White. Or, if not the Visionaries themselves, then the visions to which they dedicated themselves as a community. It seemed incredible to me that your belief in visions could be so great, you would drop everything to go live on a farm in southern Missouri. What happened once you got there? Did you forge a new life, dedicated to the hiss and burn of stars against your skin? To the feeling of your body expanding impossibly fast, lifting up and up into the night sky, carrying you away from everyone you had ever known—Boris and his friends, Kevin and Dan, even Houdini himself? Leaving behind the known world and plunging forward, into something completely new.

Before he left Boris's that Saturday morning, Houdini invited me to meet him later that night at a bar downtown called The Way Out Club. He was rendezvousing with a woman who knew the Visionaries and had been to their community. He was hoping to persuade her to take him to New Light. I thanked him for the invitation and said I'd think about it.

"You'll think about it," Boris said with a snort as I closed the front door. He stood in the doorway to the kitchen, scowling, his arms folded across his chest.

"You're back. You didn't get to say goodbye to Houdini."

"I can't believe you let him do that."

I sat down on the couch. "What?"

"Oh right. Don't feign innocence, Beth, it's so not

you. You encouraged him. You ate it up, all wide-eyed and breathless."

"Boris," I said, making my voice sound reasonable. "Put yourself in my position." His eyebrows shot up and I said, "No, I mean it. I was out there on your patio last night. Something happened to me." I leaned back on the couch dramatically. "He knows something about it."

Boris attempted cool disdain. "He was playing you."

"I know." I was equally cool. "I know it and you know it. And he knows that we know. So does it matter?"

Boris grabbed a trash bag from the dining room table and shook it out, saying, "Something happened to you all right."

I watched him gather up beer bottles. I refused to let the conversation simply end like that. I got up and stood before him, my own arms folded, as Boris dropped bottles into his bag, the sour, acrid smells of beer and cigarette butts filling the air. Finally he looked at me, letting the bag clink and settle on the floor.

"And what if he made it happen? What if he slipped something in your beer, or what if he had some little science fiction device in his pocket, he pushes the button, beep, you see visions."

I laughed. "Nobody else saw a vision. You were standing right next to me."

"Or what if he's just conning you?" Boris frowned. "You had this vision, and suddenly he's a vision researcher."

"You said he works in the med school. Doesn't he?"

"*Yes.* But that doesn't mean he's not a pathological liar. You're not going to The Way Out Club by yourself to meet him."

I didn't say anything.

"It's some weird hippy psychedelic bar in a shitty part of town. You're not going by yourself."

"You're coming too?"

He gave me a defiant look. "Yes, I am. And I'm calling up Ty and Lisa and Sarah too. We'll sit someplace where you won't see us. We'll keep an eye on you. We'll make sure he doesn't use his vision device to drag you off and do something horrible to you, while you're convinced you're seeing angels."

I went over to him and put my arms around him. "My hero," I said.

We drove down separately. The bar was located on a seedy corner of Cherokee Street; as Boris had said, not a nice neighborhood, but easy to find. You walked inside and were hit by a wave of sound: garage-band rock, laughter, a swarm of voices. Teen-aged hippies swayed in the door leading to the band room. A row of older men and women dressed in worn jeans and t-shirts sat at the bar; they looked me over as I walked in, then went back to their drinks.

I scanned the room. On the walls hung posters for horror movies from the '50s and '60s, featuring fainting, half-naked women and monsters with bloody knives. To the right of the entrance was a play corner. Inset shelves above a table and chairs, crammed with Life, Candyland, and other board games I remembered from when I was a kid. Houdini was sitting in the last booth.

I went over to his table. He looked at me, not quite smiling, but not quite not smiling either. Two beers sat on the table before him.

"Where's your friend?" I asked, leaning toward him so he could hear me over the music.

"She's not here yet. Sit down." He gestured with vague invitation toward the cushioned bench across from him. "I bought you a beer," he added. I realized with surprise that he was trying to be cordial.

I slid in opposite and we looked at each other without speaking. I didn't bother to ask how he knew I'd come. It felt very strange to be seated across from him. It was strange first because, in a loud bar crowded with Goth girls in ripped tights and leather, and schools of swaying hippies, the very idea of visions seemed ridiculous. But it wasn't just that. As I sat across the table from Houdini, I felt the same oppressive awkwardness you feel on a first date. I glanced up at the Monster from the Black Lagoon, dripping cartoon sludge from amphibian shoulders, then out at the patrons again.

He leaned forward. "You have no context for what you experienced."

The look he trained on me was intense. He was different once again, neither the man who'd talked flippantly that morning of corporate research strategies, nor the one who said gently that he didn't want to invalidate my experience. This was a new tone. "You have no context," he repeated. "That's why I came to you. Aside from the fact that it was a remarkable coincidence. My research, your vision."

I looked at him warily.

He said: "Have you ever heard of chaos theory?"

No, I hadn't heard of chaos theory. I'd been waiting tables in New York, hanging out with Irish expatriates and out-of-work performance artists. We were all busy expressing ourselves. Still, I wished I could have said: oh, *chaos*— knowingly, as though that explained everything. He was a man obsessed with scientific myth, my tone would imply, someone who wanted to supplement History with a road map, one composed of esoteric mathematical theories. In actual fact I said nothing. Across from me Houdini moved his beer bottle to the exact center of the table and began his lecture.

Chaos, I learned, is a mathematical way of dealing with disorder. It does things linear mathematics can't do.

Houdini said it's used to chart random systems, like the weather or the population of tuna along the eastern seaboard. Once scientists found the ordering principle in a system, they could then predict what would happen within it. The system's chaoticness was only appearance; a complicated order lay beneath the surface. The theory was first proposed in the '60s; by the early eighties a lot of researchers had become interested in this idea of secret patterns lying within seemingly random systems. It had become trendy among scientific circles; you could gauge how progressive a scientist was based on his or her receptivity to chaos theory.

But of course Houdini wasn't interested in the normal applications of the theory. He wanted to use it to understand human history. To unfold a mythos as complex as any Greek or Hindu pantheon.

"Over the last few hundred years there have been lots of movements like New Light," he said, pressing down on the tabletop with flexed fingers. "They look random, but they may actually form a pattern."

As I said, it was a lecture, though an impassioned one. He gave me the example of Mesmer in France. Mesmer, he said, is called a charlatan, yet he discovered hypnotism, set off a social movement that had profound effects on Parisian life in the late eighteenth century, and is now recognized for laying the foundation for Freud's early work. "He's a crackpot, right?" Houdini said. "Go back to the social setting. Mesmerism swept France ten years before the Revolution. It challenged the social hierarchy. Mesmer's sessions were very popular with the wealthy, yet working people also attended them. The wealthy were outraged by this proximity to the lower classes, but Mesmer believed in equality. So the question is, did Mesmer's work influence the course of history? Among his followers were a number of revolutionaries." Houdini sat back, both hands clenching his beer bottle as he listed names: Lafayette; Jean-Louis Carra; Jacque-Pierre Brissot.

None of those names meant anything to me. I told him it sounded impressive, and I was impressed, by the intensity with which he made his case. This didn't satisfy him.

"All right, closer to home," he said. "Take the nineteenth-century spiritualism movement in this country. More charlatans, pretending to be mediums who communicated with the beyond. But these fake mediums got people interested in the idea of another world. They claimed that people could see this other world now, not wait till they'd crossed over. They said it was scientifically verifiable."

"The mediums believed in science?"

"The spiritualist image of the afterlife was very different from traditional religious ones. Science, mysticism, it's all thrown together. Okay, so more mediums surfaced, and then Mme. Blavatsky appears on the scene, queen of mediums, head of the Theosophical society, very influential both here and in Europe. She claimed that the world was entering a new era. Her Golden Dawn. Blavatsky's followers believed in the possibility of a new world, one whose laws weren't the same as ours. Writers, artists, doctors, politicians—a lot of big names were influenced by her doctrines. Yeats, Isherwood, Conan Doyle, Huxley; Kandinsky and Mondrian; Gandhi, Nehru. The range of her influence is incredible."

But that wasn't all. In fact, Blavatsky's group weren't just mystics, they were social and political radicals. Blavatsky moved the headquarters of the Theosophical Society to India, where the organization became part of the national independence movement, helping to prepare the way for Ghandi. And in England it was affiliated with the labor movement. The spiritualists' attempts to reinvent the way people saw reality had reverberations in the political and scientific life of the time, and continued to affect people over the years. In Germany the Nazis adopted elements of theosophy. Today New Agers have recycled many of its doctrines. A surprising number of people continue to believe in the psychic phenomena Blavatsky helped to popularize, everyday joes as well as doctors, physicists, and psychiatrists.

Houdini insisted that all these effects could be manifestations of chaotic patterning. But to see chaotic pattern, mathematicians have to use an equation that isn't plotted in real numbers. I didn't understand that, and he said that it was a symbolic solution, a function of higher math. He told me it was like going from Euclidean to non-Euclidean space. You solve the equation in an imaginary dimension, then you translate the solution back into real numbers. The solution to the chaotic patterning is only available in imaginary space, but that doesn't mean it isn't real in our dimension.

He was leaning forward, hands cupping the solution he'd carried back from the imaginary realm. "It's the chaotic effect. It doesn't matter if spiritualism itself is a sham, just like it doesn't matter that you solve for the chaos pattern in imaginary space. Both map out patterns in the real world."

All this information was overwhelming at first. I glanced around the room, wondering if the whole thing was some elaborate put-on, yet another performance, like that morning. I had no way to evaluate what he was telling me—I didn't know much about spiritualism, let alone chaos theory, imaginary space, and the host of other things he brought to the mix. I didn't know that in the last few years chaos theory really had become a hot new paradigm, one that spun off all sorts of esoteric theories and imaginings of the world, some a lot more bizarre than the one Houdini was outlining. I thought the whole thing sounded crazy.

But in a way it didn't matter. As he leaned forward,

gripping that beer bottle, there was something irresistible about him. I felt a faint flush, a residue of our interlude on Boris's patio. I was glad for the dimness of the bar because the memory rose up in my mind like a flame, burning my cheeks.

We sat there a while longer. Houdini answered my questions with surprising patience, told me about his doctoral dissertation in cognitive psychology, and explained how he became interested in exotic mathematical theories. He said that his postgraduate work in neuroscience had encouraged him to think across disciplines. This was what led him to a job in the corporate sphere.

"So which is it?" I interrupted him, as suspicion flared. "Are you studying the visions so that you can search out history's invisible patterns, or to make money selling them to a corporation?"

It brought him up short. His face closed; instantly he became remote. It was as though I'd thrown a drink in his face.

"Neither," he said finally. "Both." He smiled oddly. "Whichever you prefer."

I was going to ask him what he meant by that, but he glanced at his watch and put his hands flat on the table. "It's time for me to meet my contact. Your friends, by the way, are in the garden out back."

And with that he disappeared down a crooked back passageway that led to the phone and the bathrooms.

The music coming from the band room was loud, heavy on the bass. I would have to fight my way through the mass of swaying bodies to find my way to the garden. I didn't move.

I didn't know what to think. Whatever it was Houdini did, he was good at it. I couldn't say he challenged my beliefs, exactly—more like he infiltrated my sense of how the world worked. He talked about things I'd never heard of— chaos, the roots of New Age spiritualism, Mesmer's hypnotic power—and made me feel like my previous notions of history were a child's crayon drawing. But the thing was, chaos and spiritualism were just the surface. Maybe it wouldn't have mattered what examples he'd produced for me. Maybe the power to disorient lay in Houdini himself.

A big man sitting at the bar got heavily to his feet and moved toward me. He wore a grizzled beard and a worn flannel shirt that strained across his chest and stomach. He asked if he could buy me a drink. I thanked him but said I was meeting some friends outside. He didn't believe I was meeting anyone, but when I asked him the way to the garden he pointed toward the band room silently.

The garden was a courtyard of pebbled concrete crowded with people. With the door closed the music retreated to the background, and a cool wind blew from the west, cutting through the humid night air. Beyond the milling bodies was a ring of tables surrounded by a tall wooden fence hung with jalapeno pepper lights. Potted palms waved their fronds, making the lights wink on and off. For a moment, as I looked around at the strangers talking and laughing, I felt I'd stumbled onto one of those places you're always looking for. Where things can happen. Candlelight flickered on the tables, small torches stung the darkness with slanting flames. It was the kind of place you would come to alone, knowing that, at any moment, something important might be revealed.

I made my way through the crowd toward Boris and the others, who were sitting at a table in the corner. I was struck by how happy they seemed. Boris and his friends made an odd group, yet they were complete, self-contained. Boris was leaning forward, saying something scandalous to judge from his expression, while Sarah shook back her short blonde hair, laughing in protest. Ty, sitting beside Sarah, was more reserved. He listened, an undercurrent of thoughtfulness always present, like a sharper, colder layer of water beneath the sun-warmed surface. Beside him Lisa leaned forward and said something that made them all laugh, while Sarah put her hand to her chest as though to claim modesty.

"Beth," Boris said, still laughing as I came up. The others turned, smiling up at me. Boris patted the chair beside him. "You haven't been kidnapped."

"No. But thanks for keeping an eye on me."

"Houdini saw us come in," Lisa explained. "You should have seen Boris and Sarah pretend not to recognize him. I went over and said hi."

"She blew our cover on purpose," Boris said.

"We haven't come to a consensus on strategy yet," Ty said drily.

They asked me what Houdini had talked about. When I tried to explain to them about spiritualism and chaos and Houdini's search for a pattern, there was a short silence, during which the laughter and the voices of the people at adjacent tables washed over us. Boris and Sarah exchanged looks. Ty's eyes flickered from them back to me, but he didn't speak. Only Lisa came to my defense.

"Why is that so weird? He's a scientist; he's studying visions. He needs to know about their history. You guys are so judgmental. This chaos stuff could be real."

"If you were a scientist, would you meet Beth in a bar to talk about your work?" Sarah asked.

"Why not? It's what he studies. He doesn't care where he is. And he was meeting the woman. Right?" Lisa turned to me.

"That's what he said." I heard the uncertainty in my voice and glanced over at Boris. He fixed his gaze on the candle in the center of the table.

Ty looked at Boris thoughtfully, then asked, "Does Houdini make you uncomfortable, Beth?" I saw Sarah sit up, ready to pounce.

"You work with him," I responded, ignoring the others. "Do you trust him?"

Ty ran a thumb along his bottom lip absently. "He's a legitimate researcher. But I don't see why he has to go down to this community in southern Missouri."

"This is my point," Boris put in.

"He thinks there's a pattern," I said. "He thinks there are historical forces being played out."

Ty considered this.

"And why exactly does he need you?" Boris demanded.

"I don't know," I said. "The vision, the fact that he came to your party, and there I was." I glanced at Ty again. "Maybe he thinks there's some connection."

"There has to be a connection," Lisa said. "It's too wild. You can't ignore it."

Sarah sat back with theatrical outrage, looking incredulously from Lisa to me. "I can't believe you're taking any of this seriously." She made a show of reining herself in and continued with condescending kindliness, "Beth, people used to come from all over the country to see my ex-husband. They believed in his psychic abilities. He's compelling, and he's a good performer. But it's not just performance. He was convinced of his right to tell people what reality is."

"Houdini's not exactly the same league as your husband," Ty said wryly.

"He calls himself Houdini!" Sarah snapped.

Boris nodded. I could tell he felt vindicated by what Sarah said. I felt my face burn behind the cover of candlelight.

"Beth," Sarah continued, "it's easy to fall into. John

and I were married for fifteen years. I was with him for three years while he did the mentalist routine. It's seductive. But after a while I started asking questions. His version: I got into that women's rights business." She laughed with sudden annoyance. "Don't get me wrong. He's a charming man."

From Sarah's expression I guessed that she'd been more frank than she'd intended. Her marriage to John—who was quite famous among certain circles for his ability to read minds, contact the dead, and remind the living of desires they'd forgotten they had—was one of her more useful credentials. The marriage had become a vehicle for her own notoriety. It allowed her to show off her exotic affiliations and at the same time ridicule her ex. Her candor had been inadvertent, and now she crossed her legs and looked at Boris. "You tell her," she said.

But at that moment Houdini emerged from the crowd. Behind him, as though caught in his wake, was a woman with a delicate, wistful expression. Her hair fell down her back in a long tangle, and she held her flowing dress and scarves against her body as though they would protect her from the gauntlet of carousers standing around the cement patio.

There was an embarrassed silence as the two of them came up to us, the woman gazing around the table with wide eyes, then back at Houdini.

"This is Karen," he said. She touched him tentatively on the arm. "I'm sorry," he said. "This is Glass." He introduced Boris and me, and I introduced the two of them to Sarah and Lisa.

"I still use Karen for the phone," she said as Houdini brought her a chair. She sat down beside me. "You know, because it's not a real encounter. But when I'm with people my name is Glass. I'm fragile right now."

No one spoke. Glass looked around the table, then back at me.

"Houdini told me about your vision. I wanted to meet you. I think stars signal a great capacity for transcendence."

Though she was familiar with the language of visions, Glass was not a Visionary herself. She told us that she had been to New Light once, visiting her friend Alia, who'd moved to the community seven months earlier. Glass said that Alia had been going through hard times in St. Louis: bad jobs, bad boyfriends, no direction. The community had helped her. Glass herself also lived on a commune, called East Wind, which had been established in the Ozarks in the '60s by disenchanted hippies. The two women had gone to grade school together, but had fallen out of touch until they ran into each other at The Way Out Club over Christmas. When they found out they were both living in communes in the Ozarks, they realized their lives had been running along parallel courses. They were destined to be friends again. Glass had gone to see Alia in February. "It's a slow time when you're living on a farm. People get edgy from being cooped up. Sometimes you need to get away." She smiled sweetly.

Their appearance had changed the mood at the table. In spite of Glass's charm, Boris had gotten angry all over again; he wouldn't even look at Houdini. Sarah on the other hand could hardly take her eyes off him. Houdini seemed not to notice either of them. He listened attentively to Glass, his face gentle and encouraging. He was the picture of politeness. Privately I was astounded. I had been convinced earlier that he had no sense of social behavior, no awareness of how he appeared to other people. I had found the idea satisfying in an ironic way: the psychologist who was hopeless in social situations. Yet there he was, kind and modest-seeming. He even smiled as Lisa, sitting beside him, leaned across him to touch Glass on the hand. "I think what you're doing is so cool," she said. "You guys are like architects. You're designing a whole new world."

Sarah raised her eyebrows at that. "Tell me, Glass," she cut in smoothly. "You said you've never had a vision. Could you have one if you joined New Light?"

Glass looked at her soberly. "It doesn't work that way. You don't join because you expect something. You're called."

"Sarah doesn't get that," Lisa explained. "She's a consumer; she wants to be sure she gets something for her money." She flashed Sarah a defiant glare.

Sarah looked at Houdini pointedly. "Oh, I'm sure I'm not the only one."

Glass followed Sarah's eyes with an uncertain expression. Nervously, she said to Lisa, "You see, Beth didn't expect to have a vision. It came to her. It's not a spectacle. The visions are part of each person's spiritual journey."

Lisa nodded but Sarah cut in. "Yes, but what are they? How do people get them?" She glanced at Boris and checked herself, modulating her voice to nonchalance. "Think about it from Beth's point of view. How does she know these New Light people are on the level?"

"Are you going to New Light?" Glass asked me in surprise.

I laughed and told her it was the first I'd heard about it.

She frowned. "How did your vision direct you, Beth?" When I looked at her blankly, she said, "Didn't the vision leave you with a desire? Some kind of direction to move in?"

There was silence as everyone looked at me. I didn't know what to say. Boris and the others waited expectantly, and so did Houdini. I looked away from him, to Ty. But the vision came back in all its vividness anyway; for a second I felt the rush of stars. Then it was gone and I was left embarrassed by the incongruous feeling of authenticity, there in the cement garden.

I admired Glass's perfect simplicity. She waited, and

when I didn't speak, she shook her head.

"You need to find out, Beth. You need to pay attention to it. A vision is a serious thing." She touched my hand. "You're splitting off. Part of you is existing on a very intense spiritual plane, dwelling in that Reality, while the rest of you is ignoring it. That's dangerous. Bad things can happen to you. In splitting off, you disconnect your spiritual self from your everyday self. Your higher self isn't there to watch over you."

"And so, what?" Sarah cut in again, leaning forward. "She should turn to Houdini for guidance? He'll make sure that she doesn't 'split off,' as you say? Please."

Glass looked at me thoughtfully. "Maybe you should go to New Light."

Everyone—except for Houdini and me—started talking at once.

"Beth can't go to New Light," Sarah said, raising her voice over the others to confront him. "The idea is absurd and you know it."

"I agree," Houdini replied.

Sarah blinked. After a moment she gave the slightest of smiles—a look of appreciation to a partner for a well-played hand of bridge. The look seemed to annoy Boris.

"So you came over to my apartment this morning to tell Beth about New Light because you *don't* want her to come with you," he snapped.

Houdini stroked the hard edge of his chin thoughtfully. "I considered it, but it's not a good idea. As Glass would say, Beth has to find her own path." He shrugged and said to me, "It was the coincidence that threw me. I thought there was something more to it. You know what I mean. The suggestion of a pattern."

"We never talked about going to New Light," I said.

"Don't listen to them," Lisa said. "They're jealous.

Nothing like your vision has ever happened to them." She turned to Glass. "Sometimes when I'm dancing I feel this wild sense of exaltation. Like I'm being touched by something. Maybe I should check out one of these communes."

"Lisa will convert the visionaries into whirling naked dervishes," Boris laughed. "I can see you now. But sweetheart, your thing is anarchy, not community. You wouldn't go for all the rules, even if they did let you take off your clothes."

"The Quakers used to walk around naked all the time," Lisa said defensively. "They were taken over by the Light. The spirit moved them."

"I think it was a different spirit," Boris said.

Sarah was still studying Houdini with an intrigued expression. "So, Houdini. Are you planning to be a participant observer down at New Light? What's the psychiatrist's equivalent for going native?"

Houdini smiled easily. "I think it's better not to remain detached."

"That must be a professional liability," Sarah murmured.

"If I were you," Lisa said to me, "I'd want to find out how the vision was directing me."

"Lisa, Houdini is of course a very charming and interesting man." Sarah flashed him a small ironic smile. "However, he is not the kind of man one can simply go off with."

"Why not?" said Lisa flatly.

"He can't be trusted. Can you?" Sarah said to him. Her smile widened.

"No," he said simply. "Sarah's right, I can't be trusted."

"Why not?" Ty asked. The question sounded different coming from him. Houdini looked to Sarah.

She crossed her arms over her chest with annoyance and leaned back in the chair. "Why?" she said archly, looking at Houdini. "Don't be coy." Houdini was silent and she turned her eyes to Ty. "Because it's a game, and if Beth doesn't know how to play she'll get hurt."

"Oh, it's no game," Houdini said. Sarah frowned. "It might be to you, but it isn't to me." He turned to Ty. "Why should any of you trust me? You don't know me."

Ty nodded, whether in assent or simple acknowledgement of his words, I didn't know. He looked at me.

It was my turn to eye everyone at the table. I cleared my throat. "But what about my vision?"

"What about it?" Houdini said.

"You've researched what's going on in the brain," I said lamely.

Houdini shook his head. "Nobody knows for sure how these things work. People have been having visions for centuries."

"Why don't you just ask him if you can go with him," Boris said to me bitterly.

"Boris is right, Beth," Sarah said. "You don't know him. It wouldn't mean the same thing to you."

I ignored them. I looked at Ty but he was silent. When I looked again at Houdini, he regarded me impassively.

"You wanted me to come," I said to him. I shrugged. "I'll come. I promise I won't trust you."

Houdini lifted his beer but he didn't drink. "You *want* to come. Against the good advice of your friends."

As he looked at me I felt again the flavor of something dramatic and inexplicable. In for a penny, in for a pound, as my mother used to say. I decided I might as well play up my gesture of self-offering for all it was worth. Sarah leaned over to Boris and said something in his ear and they both looked at me like I was about to jump off a ledge. Lisa bit her lip. Ty turned his eyes back to the candle flame. Suddenly I laughed. Glass looked at me uncertainly.

Houdini didn't know how to read my laugh. He added, quietly: "You should realize then that I do have to trust you."

I managed not to laugh this time. Everyone was so intent and concerned. I looked at Boris, who was frowning at me, arms crossed over his chest. I reached across Lisa and touched his hand.

"I'm sorry, Boris. I'm being directed."

seven

But when I woke the next morning I wasn't so sure. The memory of the vision was less persuasive. It still burned in a cloistered part of my mind, among other exalted ideas of myself that didn't get a lot of airtime. But I also remembered Ty's expression as he stared at the candle in the glass bowl, and Boris's fear that I was going to shoot into orbit again, and maybe not talk to him for a few more years. So when Glass called to tell me that her friend at New Light said we could come down the following Friday, I hedged. As the week wore on, I became less and less certain.

Boris worked on me. He didn't trust Houdini, and on Monday night he reminded me that I had a tendency to fling myself into relationships with weird people, mistaking the tension caused by emotional dysfunction for incipient sexual or spiritual connections. I admitted I was having second thoughts. He leaned back in his chair dramatically, hand to forehead, then grinned and made an effort to rein in his elation.

"I know why you were attracted to the idea of the visions, Beth. We all want something like that. But Houdini's out to prove something." He rose to clear the platter with the remains of the scampi. "You know what it is?" he said, pausing in the doorway. "You're like Boy Wonder or Batgirl. You're there, doing your part to fight against the forces of evil. But is it really your fight? I mean, did Batgirl ever get her own TV show?"

"I'd rather be Cat Woman," I said. "At least she got a good costume."

He wanted me to think about what I would do next, so that I

wouldn't fall back into old patterns. He offered to help me find an apartment in St. Louis if I wanted to stay. I said I'd think about it.

Now that I knew I couldn't go, I had to tell Houdini. I delayed calling him for several days. I couldn't face him. On Wednesday Boris said that Sarah wanted to have coffee with me. He told me I needed to get out of the apartment while he was at work. I laughed.

"You mean you want her to remind me of all the reasons I shouldn't go down to New Light. I know those reasons, Boris. I'm just not ready to deal with Houdini yet. I think I need to work up to it."

As a compromise I asked him for Lisa's phone number. Boris was pleased, but I could tell he felt hurt on Sarah's behalf. He poured a pot of boiling pasta into a strainer and stood back from the steam cloud that rushed upward from the sink.

"She's actually really interesting, Beth. Don't judge her too fast."

"I'm sure she's interesting. She wouldn't feature in your collection otherwise."

Boris stirred the sauce, tasted it and made a face. He added some vodka and nutmeg and stirred with a flourish when I raised an eyebrow. "She likes you," he continued. "She thinks you're unusual. She told me she found you difficult to place."

He was playing on my vanity. "Yeah?" I said in my cool, sly voice. "Does Ty like me too?" Boris gave me a look as he handed me a glass of wine.

And so, the next day, Tuesday morning a little before eleven, I drove down to Soulard, the old section of the city where Lisa lived. I passed abandoned projects and street after street of beautiful old buildings that were boarded up and falling apart. St. Louis is younger than the northeast, I know, but to me it feels older. New York is hyper-modern, despite its age and its layers of history. Buildings crumble before your eyes, but you still feel the future pulling you forward. In St. Louis the past is the stronger pull. Even the construction of new buildings and bridges seems antiquated, as though each attempt to move into the present becomes belated before the gesture has been completed.

But in Soulard the past actually thrived. The streets were narrow, lined with brick sidewalks and buildings, all carefully maintained. There was a courteous, restful quality to the eighteenth- and nineteenth-century townhouses. Lush gardens glanced out from the spaces between them. Lisa and I were meeting at a place called The Venice Cafe. I turned onto Russell and parked. Lisa was waiting for me.

The Cafe announced its alternative status in the staccato lettering of its name and the riot of colors and textures decorating its exterior, all signaling trendy discordance. It clashed proudly with the residential stateliness of the area. We walked in through an entranceway glittering with mirror-and-tile mosaic, into a mausoleum of kitsch. "Don't worry," Lisa said as I looked around at the stuffed monkeys in cages, the huge gilt shark hanging from the ceiling entwined with ribbon, the dyed feathers, Barbie dolls and artificial legs. "We'll go out to the garden."

We sat at a wobbly plastic table, underneath an ailanthus crookedly straining for sunlight. Lisa didn't look good. There were bags under her eyes and she seemed irritated. She held her hand up until the waitress saw her, then sighed and looked around with a dissatisfied air. The garden was quite big: trees and potted ferns and uneven bricks where the trees had disputed for land over the years. By the iron fence that closed us in, rhododendron and lilac bushes, the first budding, the second in bloom.

I told Lisa I wasn't going to New Light. She gave a

disinterested nod.

I didn't have many close friendships with women. I know what that says about me, but there you are. I said Soulard looked like a cool place to live, I asked her how she was, I told her I would probably be getting on the road again in a week or so. Then I sat there and felt awkward. A busboy set glasses of water before us and turned away, and Lisa and I watched as the table rocked gently in his wake. Water splashed and pooled on the plastic surface.

"I'm sorry," I said. "This is your day off. I'm sure you had other things to do."

"Me? No." She shrugged tiredly. "I was up all night. Tony and I got into a fight."

The waitress came and we ordered coffee. Lisa nodded to someone behind me and I turned around to see Sarah coming toward us. "It was Boris's idea," Lisa said in a low voice, grimacing in Sarah's direction. I liked that she was physically unable to disguise how she felt.

Sarah sat down with us breathlessly. She didn't mention Houdini. I decided that was worse than if she had. She looked amazing too, whereas Lisa and I were both wearing jeans and shapeless t-shirts. Sarah had on a grey silk blouse; a Mexican bolero jacket of black and white cotton, decorated with Aztec-looking buffaloes and cranes; black capri pants that showed off her perfect figure. And Italian boots. She saw us looking at her outfit and waved one hand dismissively. "When you're my age you have to dress."

"Not with a body like that you don't," Lisa said dryly.

Sarah smiled at her. "Only you can pull that off."

She announced she was buying us lunch. "It's the least I can do," she insisted over our protests. She smiled again. "Seeing as I'm crashing the party."

"Boris wants Beth to move here," Lisa said. "We're supposed to help convince her. I didn't get any sleep last night. It's up to you."

Sarah raised her eyebrows, still smiling, and as the waitress stepped up to hand us menus, transferred the smile to her. We listened to the specials and watched her depart. Then Sarah looked at me seriously .

"Why don't you stay, Beth. To be honest, I'm worried about Boris. He takes too much pleasure in being morose." She glanced down at the menu and mentioned that the portabella mushroom sandwich was very good.

"Maybe if you stay you'll have another vision," Lisa said.

Sarah flashed her an arched-brow look. "That Houdini business is over." She smiled at me. "You need to settle down. Find out what you want to do."

She sounded too much like my parents. She glanced down the menu, letting her fingertip rest beside the rosemary chicken and arugula salad. And suddenly I felt depressed. Maybe I did need to find out what I was going to do with my life. Across from me Lisa sat with her chin in her hand. "It's easy for you to say," she told Sarah resentfully. "You don't have to *do* anything."

I looked at the two of them and down at the menu in my hands. I felt a curious rumble inside me, like far-off summer thunder, and thought that I was hungrier than I realized. The rumble grew embarrassingly louder, so that I let the menu fall to the table and clutched the flimsy armrests of my chair.

My sense of perching at a plastic table beside the rough trunk of an ailanthus was becoming vague, for lack of a better word. I felt my substance dilating, going wide and thin, *disjecta membra*. Really it felt as though I were being spread with a gigantic butter knife, back and forth, thinner and higher, higher and thinner, in danger of becoming stuck up there in the tedium of stratosphere, above the blue lid the sky becomes in summertime. It was not a pleasant sensation. The convex curve of the sky below me was an impossibly big and hazy barrier; it hung there like a huge diaphragm wedged into the horizon's cervix. I hovered above it like a doomed spermatozoon.

Dimly I saw Sarah nod, heard her admit that she found Houdini interesting. I also saw the image she kept hidden from herself in the depths of her mind: she flung him down onto a boulder draped with a bloody fur, slit his clothes with a crude stone blade she held in her teeth, then nuzzled him like a hungry calf. I had no time to be alarmed by this picture. In an explosive rush I felt the rest of my conscious self hurtling upward, leaving nothing but dull body at the table. I became aware of the broad expanse of city below me, spread out between ribbons of lead-colored riverwater. I saw the profile the city kept hidden from human eyes. It lay coiled below me, its true form revealed: that of a slumbering, marvelous beast.

Thin straight lines of avenue and street cross-hatched its back. Its glittering hide was patched and pocked with buildings, the green fungi of parks, and fine bristles of streetlights, stoplights, telephone poles. Its patterning was beautifully corrupt, almost ascetic in the self-mortification it described. The slow pulse of traffic in its veins; the austere skeleton described by the architecture of its residences; its exhaust-darkened breath. From the lid of the sky I looked down upon a primitive, magical animal, which stirred in half-waking recognition, then turned over and went back to sleep.

I had the taste of ash in my mouth. My earthly self sneezed.

"All right," Sarah was saying across the cafe table, her voice becoming clearer as the clanking of scales faded out. The stinking spurts of steam from the monster's nostrils dissipated, and I could see again.

"All right," she said again in an annoyed tone of voice, and I was back in the molded plastic chair that made my jeans stick to my skin, with uneven bricks lifeless beneath my feet. I saw Lisa automatically check out the guy who sat down at the next table. Everything was normal. Nothing had happened.

Sarah was leaning forward. "I admit that," she said. "You're right. And he's attractive. He's mysterious. If I were you I'd be tempted too. But my god, Beth. You can't just go down there. You don't know him. You don't know what could *happen*."

I formed what I hoped was a knowing half-smile, trying to piece together what I'd said. There was a brief silence as the three of us looked at each other.

Finally Sarah pursed her lips. "So," she said. "You're going down to New Light with Houdini." Underneath the annoyance, only a shadow of envy.

"I think you're right," Lisa said to me, awarding Sarah a passing glance of happy defiance. She grinned at me. "What are you going to tell Boris?"

Directions

That's the mystery, right there. That's how it appeared to me.
What I thought I wanted to do, what I said to Boris, Lisa,
Sarah, myself—all that was irrelevant. Consistency was irrelevant. I was in the hands of something large and powerful. I
was squirming in its sweaty grip. Call it what you like—the
inexplicable, the inevitable. It had me.

And anyway, after announcing, in the midst of a
vision, that I was going to New Light, I felt that it would be
bad form to back down.

But I have to say that it was strange, that second
vision. It was nothing like the first. There I was, floating
above that vast daytime sky which, if you don't like the
diaphragm metaphor, could be likened instead to the plastic
lid on an economy-sized tub of Blue Bonnet margarine. Rather
different from the sensual rapture of the patio nightsky. And
the flavor of the second revelation was different too—it felt
overwhelmingly ironic. Its cool, detached emotion didn't
leave me feeling directed, to use Glass's term, nor did it
promise much capacity for transcendence. Instead, the vision seemed to be commenting on the idea of visions. It was
a reflection on the nature of the visionary experience, a kind
of meta-vision. I couldn't decide if it was mocking the idea of
Beth Martin as mystic, or if it was the equivalent of a visionary slap on the hand administered because I hadn't taken the
first vision seriously enough. I didn't know what to think.
But I didn't let that stop me. When I got back to Boris's I
called Houdini. I left a message on his machine telling him I
was ready.

nine

The next Monday I had breakfast waiting for Boris. At 7:30 he shuffled into the kitchen in his cotton robe, his chin glittering like it'd been rolled in crushed glass. He accepted the coffee I held out to him.

I had folded a paper hat and put it on his plate, and without a word he sat down and placed it on his head. The pancakes steamed as I set them before him. I poured him a glass of juice and shook a multivitamin out of the bottle, then slid into the chair opposite.

He reminded me to call him regularly from New Light. I promised I would. He told me I didn't know what I was getting myself into. I agreed. He said that he had half a mind to take his vacation and come down with me. I was silent. "Oho," he said, "you don't want me along."

"Boris," I said.

He nodded as though he had made an irrefutable point and put a wedge of pancake in his mouth. "You think I'm mad at you," he said, chewing. He patted the paper hat on his head. "I'm not. I have to tell you what I think, just like you have to do what you have to do."

"Oho," I said. "You wouldn't want to come anyway."

At a little before nine I pulled up in front of Houdini's apartment building. He was waiting outside, a dufflebag slung over one shoulder, and I was surprised to see how ordinary he looked, neat and compact in his jeans and white Oxford. The slanting light of morning glared off the curving shoulders of cars and Houdini squinted as he crossed the street in all that brightness, with a fleeting expression of ferocity.

We followed the directions Glass had given him to

her sister's place down on the south side. Block after block of two-family houses built of mustard brick, crammed together on one-way streets lined with cars. Not a tree in sight. Houdini stayed in the car while I went up to the front porch. The screen door hung open so I knocked tentatively on the inside door, then jumped when a child shrieked one house over. Her window was only a few feet from where I stood; I heard with perfect clarity a woman shout down her screams, and the slaps administered.

Glass came to the door after a few minutes. She looked tired and smiled wanly at me. "My sister and I always fight when it's time for me to leave," she said, closing the door behind her. She had only a small flowered bag which she shrugged onto her shoulder in answer to my offer to carry it. As we walked out to the car she set each foot down carefully on the dun-colored sidewalk, the green of her toenails glittering defiantly in the dust-colored sunlight. Houdini waited with one hand on the car door.

"Do you mind if I sit in back?" Glass asked him. She crawled in and cradled her bag in her lap, looking out the window attentively as though the car had already started to move.

We took highway 44 out of the city and in twenty minutes had left the St. Louis suburban sprawl behind. We entered a country of trees and farmland. Birds arced over fields, cows flicked their tails as they gazed at us idly. Glass rolled down her window to let the wind take her in the face, and told us that being in the country was good for her chaka. But she admitted that it was St. Louis rather than cities in general that bothered her. Her childhood self was in ascendance there. Each time she came back, that self fitted itself over her like another skin. "Identity is a part of the landscape," she explained. At East Wind she was a different Glass. Each of us

trailed previous selves behind us like so many breadcrumbs.
"What about when you're down at New Light? Do
you have a self there?" Houdini asked. In the rearview mirror
I saw Glass regard him warily.

"I've only been there once," she said.

"I just wondered whether their spiritual philosophy
affected you. You know. Whether you could feel it."

Glass looked out the window again. She said she
didn't fully understand their philosophy. There was an awkward pause. Then she added: "On the phone Alia said she's
happier than she's ever been."

The drive took most of the day. We left 44 for a smaller state
highway whose north and south vectors traded off a passing
lane like people drinking from a bottle. At one point we were
stuck for fifteen minutes behind a truck full of hogs until the
passing lane reverted to south-bound traffic. Eventually we
turned onto a winding back road hemmed in by trees. Glass
kept watch and told me where to turn, eagerness entering her
voice. After a while our road ran out of pavement, at which
point she announced we were driving along New Light land.

At a break in the trees there was a drive. Glass told me
to turn there and I slowed. The car lurched over rutted earth.
A sign read "Pleasant View Farms."

The drive snaked through hilly land for half a mile.
The new grass in the fields on either side threw long rippling
shadows; copses of trees marked the edges of fields with long
columns of thin shade, the adolescent leaves not yet robust
enough to cast the deep shadows of summer. The slanting
rays of sunlight lit up the tremulous green; it was the golden
time of afternoon.

We drove through a landscape of trompe l'oeil. The
hilliness of the land confused perspective; buildings appeared and disappeared as we crept along the winding dirt

drive. A young forest climbed a hill to our right, while on our left, against a grassy rise, stood several prefabricated structures and some trailers that had taken root. Beyond these, the roof of a big barn was visible. Beside the barn's rustic solidity, the flimsier buildings seemed grafted onto the landscape. Then the drive curved around and the centerpiece of the place came into view: a large farmhouse glowing pale lemon in the late sunlight. It was Houdini who saw the woman in the long purple robe watching us from the porch.

I parked next to a tractor in the sandy lot. A path led across a small patch of field to the farmhouse. We walked single-file; Glass went first, then Houdini; I brought up the rear. The long new grass brushed our knees and no one spoke.

When we reached the porch the woman, thin-faced and severe-looking, didn't smile. "The Mother is waiting for you," she said severely, and went in.

Glass and I glanced at each other. She looked as unnerved as I felt, which made me feel a little better. Houdini started up the stairs and she and I followed him. The three of us stood blinking on the threshold to the dim hall.

Inside a match sputtered and flared. The woman's thin face seemed to float like a mask above her dark robe as she touched the flame to the wick of a candle and placed it in a sconce on the wall. That was when I glanced with surprise at the wall opposite. A human eye stared down at me. Beside it a snarling feline leapt into clarity, its muzzle vivid, the rest of its body hurtling dimly from the heights; beyond it, a vine climbed sinuously into the dark. As the woman lit more candles I realized that the lefthand wall of the hallway was one long mural. It was too dim to see any of the images clearly, but the scenes were fantastic and strange. Bosch, Rousseau, Ernst, translated by New Light's focusing lens. There were monsters and metamorphic women, plants that looked sentient, animals that seemed about to spring onto the hall rug. Matters of scale and perspective had been deliberately distorted so as to jar the viewer.

The woman knocked at the last door at the end of the hall, then disappeared inside.

"Who's the mother?" I whispered.

"Their leader," Glass replied, glancing nervously at the image of a man staring in perplexity at his penis, which was metamorphosing into a spear-like vine. She turned her back on the mural and hugged herself.

The thin-faced woman in the robe came out again, half-closing the door behind her. "You may go in." We started forward but she drew Glass aside with a touch on the arm. "You're to come with me. Alia is preparing dinner."

The brilliant room we entered was a shock after the dark hallway. Sunlight shimmered through gauzy curtains that hung fluttering in the open windows, and stained-glass hangings transformed the afternoon's slanting rays into patterns of colored light. All the chimes in the room swayed with a confusion of tinkling silver sound, while curls of fragrant smoke wafted from silver elephant incense burners. Scattered all about were candles, some lit, some not, the flames glowing like little eyes in the golden light of afternoon.

It was overwhelming. My gaze moved drunkenly from object to beautiful object. Walls were laden with tapestries and brocades; mirrors bordered their mysteries with tile and bits of glass. And yet all of this was backdrop; small artillery in the sensory arsenal. What dominated the room was the Mother herself.

It was hard to guess the age of New Light's leader— mid-forties perhaps—a compact, alert-looking woman with plump features and powdery skin the hue and texture of rose-colored flour. She wore a white robe braced with a sparkling gold harness that gave her an indefinable air—I think now she was going for a mix of the Greek goddess Athena and the Indian Maya—wisdom and illusion. She seemed to shimmer before us like an exotic spirit, and at the same time commanded the room like a great impresario.

She smiled serenely at us.

"You must excuse me." She unbuckled the gold harness and shook out her robe. Her voice was apologetic but crisp. "Ceremony is important to our community, but I'm afraid in our isolation we indulge ourselves. The visitor finds the spectacle beguiling, but of course we are not here to pay witness to outward show." She laughed. "The danger of ritual, no? It can obscure the very meaning it celebrates."

She paused as Houdini and I glanced at each other. Then she added, with the flick of a smile, "Yes, well, that danger is the scalpel's blade. Its sharpness allows us to see the living pulse. But we must be careful how we cut."

It was hard not to stare. I made myself look around the room again. Behind the Mother stood a grand, six-foot-high sahib chair, with a high wicker back and elaborate cane flourishes. A tea service was laid out on one of the carved tables that stood between the chair and several low velvet armchairs.

The curtains batted softly at the sunlight. Houdini was about to speak, but the Mother gave a self-deprecating laugh and gestured toward the group of chairs.

"My apologies. I wanted you to feel welcome. Please, sit down."

She seated herself on the wicker throne, this leader of New Light, mistress of exotic frippery and fantastic murals, and poured out tea. Houdini and I sank down and down into the soft armchairs, cradled by wine-colored velvet, and gazed up at the Mother on her seat of pale cane. She held herself very erect. Her face was framed by elaborate rattan flourishes.

Houdini thanked her for receiving us, and said he'd been wanting to come to New Light for a long time. "I've heard a lot about your community and your work with visions."

"We welcome visitors who come to us to learn," she said. Her glance took me in as well. "What is it you want to know?"

Houdini didn't seem to know where to begin. I guessed that she took him by surprise too. The Mother looked from him to me calmly, then sat back in her chair and brushed her throat with musing fingers as she considered us. After a moment she clasped her hands in her lap. She said decisively:

"The visions show us who we are. We seek out the truest parts of ourselves. We have chosen to live apart in an effort to transcend the blindness of the earthly plane."

She looked at Houdini narrowly then, adding: "It's not easy to see who you really are. Especially in a society that gives you so many false images of yourself."

Her eyes flickered to me for a moment, then back to him. Houdini studied her with fascination, his face focused with that intensity I had seen at the Way Out Club. He seemed reluctant to interrupt her monologue.

"Are you here as a seeker or a scientist?" she asked, sounding crafty all of a sudden.

A strange smile broke the stillness of his features. "Can I be both?" he returned.

There was a brief look that passed between them. It lasted a moment only, but it reminded me that each of them knew a lot more about the other than I knew about either. Glass, in asking if she could bring us to New Light, had of course given them information about both of us. And from what I could gather, Houdini had been pursuing the Mother and people like her for years.

"And then there's your friend," she said after a moment, turning her eyes again to me.

Houdini looked at me too. He said, "I met Beth at a party. A strange coincidence: after physically colliding with me, she went into a trance state and witnessed the entropic flow of the universe. It was an unusually intense vision."

The slow burn of the Mother's gaze never wavered.

"One vision?" she asked.

"Two," I admitted nervously. Houdini shot me a surprised look.

The Mother asked the subject of the second vision. I found myself describing the feeling of being suspended above St. Louis, then, in greater detail, the vision of the stars. The whole time I was really speaking, in apology, to Houdini, but his eyes on me as he listened were remote.

She nodded when I was done. "Each vision boarded you like a hijacker. Flew you right out of your normal realm of perception."

"A terrorist image?" Houdini interjected. "You see her visions as a violation?"

"They are exceptional experiences. All visions are," the Mother said. "Just because one acknowledges the visionary nature of an experience does not mean it should be automatically valorized. Some visions are dangerous to the receiver; those I would define as terrorist, to use your word, Mr. Houdini. However, every hijacking isn't a threat. It depends on where they take you, and—if I may extend the metaphor—what political motivations are involved."

She appraised me again in silence. Her grey eyes could shift to a greenish color, like granite reflecting the sea. It was part of the spell being woven. Ancient bard and performance artist; magician and Sunday School teacher.

The Mother shook her head and smiled at me.

"Hijackings. It's not quite right, is it? Part of you felt hijacked, but part of you allowed it to happen."

When I didn't answer she turned her eyes to the window. In a tone that was almost indifferent she went on: "We want to be taken over by something greater than ourselves. To be relieved of the unrelenting ambivalence. Most of us go through life without feeling truly committed to the things we do. We recognize in a vague way that something is missing, but we live with it. Yet sometimes the inexplicable happens. Something changes and we open ourselves to the world."

I knew it was a fortune-teller's trick. The medium tosses out a list of general topics—romance, money, work, friends—then builds on the one that makes you catch your breath. It's all part of the spell, all meant to draw you in. Nonetheless, the effect was real. Her words evoked a familiar ache, the feeling that there was something important I'd forgotten. She paid no attention to me as she gazed musingly out at the spreading branches of a purple beech, and so I let myself sink into the feeling, trying to remember what I'd lost.

I saw a house on a cliff overlooking a curving shore. Peach-colored walls and orange-peach trim; blue sky overseeing the endless lap of water at the narrow beach. I was the young girl following the sand-path down a series of switchbacks to the sea.

It was the Long Island Sound; the house sat on the Connecticut side, perched above sailboats and low-flying gulls. Every morning and night I took walks alone on the slip of beach at the bottom of the cliff. I remembered the salt taste of the early morning air as I came down the path before it was fully light. The sand was cool beneath my feet. I stared out over the water, into the obscure blue distance, listening to buoy bells ringing faintly as they bobbed in the dimness like water fowl. I bent to touch soft waves that changed the shapes of shells and stones. Rings of froth evaporated magically from the iridescent shell-hollows; quartz-veined rocks waited for light to paint them green and red.

A promise had been made to me, there in the obscurity. It was wordless and undefined and belonged to that before-daylight place, when the world had not yet been assigned its shapes, before light banished the shadows into forms of rock and tree and hand, thereby sentencing the world to beautiful limitation. That blue-lit morning had always been with me. I had only to go back there, and I would know the secret again.

The Mother looked at us, blinking. She raised her cup and sipped, and her lips curved in a slight smile.

ten

That first interview with the Mother left me feeling un-
settled. I was tired after the long drive down from St. Louis;
perhaps that made me vulnerable to her theatrical effects.
But I have to admit there was more to it than that. There was
something about her. It made me nervous.

We were met in the hallway by Monica, she of the
purple robe, though she now wore prosaic jeans and a button-up corduroy shirt over her thin, weathered frame. She
led us down the hall without speaking, and I assumed her
silence was part of the performance, to make us reflect on our
interview with the Mother. As it turned out, Monica's silence
was a disapproving one. She didn't want us at New Light.
She was one of a number of Visionaries who were opposed to
allowing outsiders into their community. However, Monica
was also completely loyal to the Mother, who had invited us
to stay. She distrusted us, but she would never question her
leader's judgement.

We passed through a door at the end of the hall into
a large steamy kitchen where dinner was being prepared. It
was hot in the room and several of the men and women
chopping vegetables and stirring pots wore no shirts. They
stared at us as we filed by, as though we were strange
creatures the like of which they'd never seen. I tried not to
stare back. I found myself embarrassed by the bare-breasted
women, though I'd been at plenty of parties with people in
various states of undress. My embarrassment flustered me. I
looked at Houdini instead, who was calmly surveying the
room and its inhabitants. He of course felt no such discomfi-
ture.

In fact, I felt that same odd embarrassment a lot at

New Light, though the feeling lessened as I got used to life at the visionary community. In part I think it resulted from the intimacy of the Visionaries' daily lives. Most of them had been living together for years, and the quality of that life was like nothing I'd ever seen. The public and private realms were not distinct there, or at least were not as clearly demarcated as they were in the world I'd come from. Intimacy— physical, spiritual, sexual. Intimacy and transcendence.

We passed through the kitchen and out the back door. The sun had disappeared behind a small mountain to the west. Birds called from a cluster of trees on the lawn, and more darted from the branches of the huge purple beech tree I had seen from the Mother's window. We descended the stairs into early evening, passing a fire pit full of soft grey ash, walking into the deeper shadow beneath the silver barn I had seen from the road on our way in.

Monica led us across the cropped lawn and down a narrow dirt path that cut north across a field. There the grass was already tall and surged and breathed in the dusk breeze. Monica walked fast, her arms close to her body. She strode on without looking back.

Houdini glanced at me, then called, "Monica, Beth and I want you to know that we're excited to be here at New Light. We're honored that you've accepted us into your community." When Monica didn't reply he said he was especially eager to see their ceremonies so that he could understand the role played by visions in their lives. Abruptly she turned on him.

"The Mother has chosen to let you remain here with us. That means you abide by our rules. You only attend ceremonies if you're invited. You return to your room each night by midnight and also stay there between the hours of noon and one. Do you understand?"

In response Houdini bowed his head formally. When

Monica turned and hurried forward again, he gave me a smile. We followed her the rest of the way in silence. As the dusk deepened she clicked on a flashlight. We passed gardens and a greenhouse, went down a hill, and then saw the lightless building where we'd be staying. Sparrow was the farther of the two barracks-like structures that lay about a mile from the farmhouse, overshadowed by a steeply-rising ridge of forest. The nearer of the two, Kestrel, had lights burning in several rooms. Purple and red cloths glowed in the windows. Monica shone her light briefly onto Kestrel's door and walls as we passed. Painted forms peered back at us through the dark.

I have conflicting impressions of New Light from those first few days. There in the growing dark, as Monica led us forward, the community seemed bizarre and secretive, even dangerous. We passed several one-room huts whose lights braved the dusk faintly, and I wondered what it would feel like to live in a tiny shack in what was really the middle of the wilderness. Later, by daylight, we saw that the farm contained a myriad of structures for housing, from hand-built wooden huts, to dormitory-style buildings, to trailers. The buildings were scattered across the land in cheerful disarray. Many of the single-occupancy buildings weren't hooked up to electricity; they depended on oil- or battery-powered lamps for lighting and wood or kerosene stoves for heat in the winter. I found something oddly impressive in that. People could choose the level of technological development they preferred; if they wanted to simplify their lives, they could. But that night, it seemed to me that Monica was leading us with grim determination away from civilization and the normal world, into an eerie nether land. The blue dusk deepened as we descended into the barracks' valley and the air seemed to vibrate warningly. In the fields on either side of us birds called and swooped with urgency in the vanishing light. Beyond the barracks, where the ground rose sharply and the forest began, the dark reigned absolute.

Every dusk, there at the farm, I felt an echo of that feeling. The sense that a world I had never imagined was about to be born. This feeling was most acute in the barracks, which stood like a lonely outpost on the edge of the farm's cultivated lands. It was there that you were most exposed to the primitive unknown, most vulnerable to the deepening dark that stole out from beneath the trees as the sun retreated. And once the country night had closed in, you couldn't go anywhere without a flashlight, and even with it you could do no more than scratch at the darkness.

But the New Light of day was very different from the nighttime one. In the sunlight it was a working farm, and an industrious one at that. In addition to their gardens and greenhouse, the Visionaries kept chickens and cows, providing eggs, milk, and the occasional chicken dinner. Cats prowled about keeping the mice and rats at bay, and a number of friendly dogs escorted people from building to building. Locally the Visionaries sold seedlings, vegetables, fruit and eggs; they also had a weavery and drying shed. The baskets and wicker furniture they produced, made from native willow and redbud as well as imported rattan, were advertised over the internet. They had their own bakery, laundry, and even a computer center. Actually it was data processing that provided the bulk of their income. They maintained a website that described their community's mission and offered their computing services, competitively priced. Every member was required to spend twenty hours a week at a keyboard, in addition to their other chores.

With all these earthly pursuits, it was easy to forget that the community considered itself primarily spiritual in orientation. According to the Mother, their earthly natures had to be respected before they could approach the spiritual plane. This was really the Mother's function at New Light. She kept them balanced, never letting one side of their nature dominate. She kept them in harmony, and they honored her as the keeper of the sacred beliefs without which New Light would dim. It was she who taught them that each thing must in its opposite reside. That you must court paradox to find the mystery.

Sparrow's interior was vaguely reassuring. The hallway conjured up for me the smell of my father's office—a flat, industrial-building-materials odor. I hadn't thought of that smell for years. A bathroom on one end, then three closed doors on each side of the hall. Monica marched down the corridor to the last door on the right, opened it, and flicked on the fluorescent overhead. This was Houdini's room. She crossed the hallway and opened the door across the way for me. Each room contained a bunkbed and two heavy schoolroom chairs facing each other across a small table beneath a single window. A small electric light stood on each table.

In the hallway Monica turned to Houdini, arms folded, and said there would be a nominal charge. Houdini held out five hundred-dollar bills. Without a word she took them, looked from him to me with grim distaste, then left us there.

Houdini and I glanced at each other, then each turned toward our rooms.

I stood on the threshhold. It was a sterile, musty place. The fluorescent buzz was loud and I turned it off, made my way through the semi-darkness and dropped my backpack at the end of the bed. With the overhead off the field outside was faintly visible, the last light from the fading west hovering in the air. I opened the window to let in the evening. In the soothing silence I could hear the trill of the peepers.

"You had a second vision," Houdini said from behind me, making me jump. He stood in the doorway, lit up from behind by the light from his room. I couldn't see his face. I felt him study me.

"Does New Light fit your chaotic pattern?" I asked, trying to sound ironic.

Houdini contemplated the evasion. "I don't know yet," he said. "I need to see their ceremonies." He crossed the room and sat down at my table and turned on the lamp. As my eyes adjusted to the light I could see that his expression was perfectly serious.

"Is New Light a cult?"

Houdini ignored my question. "How did you feel when we were talking with the Mother earlier?"

"What do you mean, how did I feel?"

"What was it like? Did it seem unusual in any way?"

"Why?" I asked, feeling myself grow wary.

For one moment he was like a snake, a curving continuous line of force, shaking the air around him with his unmoving deadliness. Then the threat and the energy were gone. He sat back, shrugged. "I thought I saw something in your face."

I looked at him closely but couldn't tell if he remembered saying that to me before, when we were out on the patio and my skin was expanding outward like the thin rubber sides of a balloon. It annoyed me. "I didn't have a vision, if that's what you mean."

"Of course not."

He sounded nonchalant. I hesitated, then said, "It was just...strange. I saw this house we stayed in when I was little. It was really vivid."

Houdini nodded. "And what did you feel?"

I didn't want to tell him about the blue morning I'd remembered, when ocean and sky were still joined, when the indistinctness of the pre-dawn had made something in my chest contract suddenly, and then expand with painful yearning. He was looking at me, his mouth pursed. I met his eyes and he turned his own away, to the dark screen beyond the table where night pressed in.

"She knew of course," he said, no longer talking to me. "But did she do it consciously?"

"Do what?" I demanded.

He looked at me; his eyes were appraising, his expression almost arch. "She put you in a light hypnotic trance. She's good."

"She hypnotized me?" I said. Houdini just looked at me. I was going to ask how he knew I'd been hypnotized, but I didn't. Instead I said, "Did you feel it too?"

His face remained remote. "Oh, I'm not susceptible," he said, and again turned his gaze to the night.

Not long after that, Glass and her friend Alia appeared in the hallway and tapped at the open door. They apologized, saying they didn't want to intrude, just thought if we were hungry we might like to come with them back up to the farmhouse. That way we wouldn't get lost. I was relieved to see them.

Alia, Glass's childhood friend, looked as waif-like as Glass. They were about the same height, but Alia's hair was cut in a wispy pageboy. She wore a tie-dyed skirt and blouse and a thick wool sweater that was unraveling at the cuffs and hem. Except for their haircuts, she and Glass could have been twins. But despite their peach-and-pink complexions and thin, young-girl bodies there was a seriousness about them, even when they laughed. It was as though they had recognized—much earlier than I had—that living was not something to be done casually.

As the four of us headed back up the path toward the

center of the farm, Alia pointed out the window of her room in Kestrel. Glass shone her flashlight on the side of the building and we glimpsed another winged being trying to escape the skewering beam. Glass said that Alia had painted the whole of Kestrel and was already considered one of the community's best artists, though she'd been there only since October. "It's pretty important too," Glass said over her shoulder to me, as she followed Alia up the steep portion of the path. "The murals are their records."

"Records of the visions?" came Houdini's voice from behind me. The beam of his flashlight caught Glass's feet.

"Visions, dreams, desires," said Alia, pausing at the top of the hill. "With the murals we represent the visionary world within the context of the real one. They coexist."

When we reached the kitchen we found it full of people lined up, waiting to fill their plates. There was a vague murmur in the line and the Visionaries looked us over, some with smiles, others with carefully neutral faces. I had the sense that our presence was inhibiting them; as we waited everyone in the kitchen was silent. When it was our turn to help ourselves we were presented with a number of large metal containers resting on several long tables, all steaming with casseroles, grains and roasted vegetables. There were platters of bread and fresh fruit. I realized I was starving. After we'd all helped ourselves, Houdini and I followed Alia and Glass into the dining hall.

The room was big enough to seat all seventy-odd members of the community at once, though at the moment it was only half full. People were scattered at tables around the large hall, and when we entered we sent out another ripple of silence that spread through the room as people looked up, saw us, and glanced at one another. Alia led us to a table against the far wall, and around us the tension in the room gradually relaxed, the conversations resuming as though nothing had happened.

"We've done recruiting in the past, but you guys sought us out," Alia explained as we put down our trays. "People aren't sure how to classify you. You're not exactly tourists, and you're not prospective members." She smiled at Houdini and shook back her bobbed hair. "We've never had a scientist before."

"You know how it is," Glass said to Houdini impulsively. "Some people are afraid of science."

"I know how it is," he said, sitting down beside her.

"But your leader didn't seem afraid," I said, sitting beside Alia. "Quite the reverse."

"She's a scientist herself," Alia said, then laughed. "Not your typical scientist."

"But it's true, it's not just science," Glass said thoughtfully, looking at her friend and twisting a lock of long tousled hair. "Some of the people here don't like me, and I'm from a community too."

"Most people come here to make a new start. They leave their previous lives behind." Alia looked at the tables around us. "Sometimes they don't like anything that reminds them of the past."

"They're mad because Alia still has friends from outside," Glass confided. "They think she hasn't let go completely."

"I'm the newest member, that's all. And they do accept you, Glass. You're a member of East Wind. It's not like you're some lawyer from St. Louis."

"And then there are those people who aren't afraid of the outside world, but just decide they don't like you for no reason at all."

"Glass," Alia protested.

"It's true. What about Mary? She was icy."

Alia's face flushed. "That's different. You know it is."

She looked at Houdini and me and then down at her plate, her cheeks burning.

None of us spoke for a moment, then Glass, looking contrite, apologized. Alia shook her head and smiled with effort. She turned to me. "For what it's worth, we've never had a fellow visionary find her way here without one of us acting as sponsor or guide. Some people are very curious about you, Beth. About your visions and what they mean for our community. Other people aren't sure what to think."

After we finished our meal Alia stacked our plates on her tray. "After dinner we usually build a bonfire. It's nice to sit in the dark and watch the flames." She smiled at Glass. "Sometimes after a day of work and socializing we need to be quiet. Let ourselves be soothed." Glass smiled at her and helped her carry the dishes back to the kitchen.

It *was* soothing. Sitting by the bonfire that first night was one of the nicest things I remember about our stay at the farm. Outside on the lawn people milled around, talking and laughing. Some sat on the grass, singing or strumming a guitar; others lay back, looking at the stars. The bonfire roared in its pit in the middle of the yard and Visionaries came and went, some heading off into the night singly or in pairs, others joining one group or another amid bursts of laughter. Sparks of flame shot up and were carried on the wind for several feet before burning out. The cool darkness at your back, the warmth of the reassuring flames, and the millions of stars crowding the sky. I felt that passionate exhilaration that some nights seem to bring on, when you feel capable of anything. Yet at the same time I was perfectly content. I wanted nothing more.

Alia took mats from a pile by the back stairs and we seated ourselves a few yards from the fire. She introduced us to a Filipino-looking man named Tom, who was sitting near us. He was a beautiful young man, small and dark, whose graceful athleticism you could sense even as he sat perfectly still and upright on his mat. He had been holding a flute to his lips and blowing a few trills on it, not a song exactly, just a fragment of melody, when we first sat down. It sounded lovely against the backdrop of crackling flames and the voices and laughter that dipped and rose in the firelit darkness. Tom put the flute in his lap and leaned over to our group to shake our hands. "Welcome to New Light," he said with a warm smile. Houdini nodded curtly and I felt myself flush a little. I wanted to say something to Tom because Houdini seemed so brusque, but just then a man who'd been sitting with some people a few yards away joined us, wedging himself into the space between us and Tom. He was shortish and stocky in an athletic way, in his late forties, his thinning hair cropped short against his skull. I had noticed him watching us when we first sat down, and now he stood over us stolidly. Tom withdrew toward the fire to give the man space, and in a few moments I heard the trilling fragments of melody again.

"Introductions please, Alia," this man said with a broad smile and a loud voice as he settled himself. Alia introduced us, and the bluff Mark told us how excited many people were to have us there. They needed new blood, he said. We had to tell them everything that was going on outside. "Start with St. Louis, but I want to hear about New York too," he said to me. "It must have been hard to leave." He laughed loudly, adding, "Vision or no vision, New York is still the big apple."

It was unnerving to realize that everyone at New Light knew my bio. Alia looked uncomfortable. She said to me, "When Glass called to ask if you guys could visit I had to tell The Mother what I knew about you. I'm sorry, Beth. It's hard to keep secrets in a small community like this."

"Oh, Beth doesn't mind, do you, Beth?" Eagerly, Mark leaned forward. "Believe me, I understand how it is. I lived in Boston before I became a member of New Light. I was an economics professor, can you believe that? The transition is the worst, going from one world to the other. But once you adjust, you'll know you made the right choice."

As he spoke, a woman approached from another group on the far side of the fire. Her blond bobbed hair burned in the firelight, her long white dress glowed orange as she came up and stood before us. She glanced back at the man who'd been sitting beside her. He got to his feet reluctantly and followed her over.

"I'm Mary, this is Ted," she said, gesturing to the tall man who stood behind her and seemed for some reason uncomfortable. Mary glanced down at Alia imperiously, and Alia, who'd been looking up at Ted, quickly moved over so that Mary could sit beside Mark. Ted continued to stand where he was, gazing down at Mary, as though debating what to do. He had a chiseled jaw like some Western good-guy, except that he seemed gentler than one of them, at a loss as to how to proceed without being indelicate. Mary gave him a sidelong look that seemed petulant, then turned to Mark with a wide smile. Ted came around the circle and settled just behind Glass. He fixed his eyes on Mary with musing but narrowed eyes.

Mary placed one hand on Mark's arm, as though in answer to Ted's look, and gave the burly man beside her another wide smile. Then she turned to Glass. She tucked a lock of blond hair behind her ear and smiled archly. "You look good, Glass. Sorry we didn't get to talk before." Then her smile widened again as she turned to Houdini. "Everyone's excited about the newcomers. You're a scientist, right?"

"A lot of people don't expect people in a visionary

community to be interested in science and technology," Mark said, squaring his shoulders and lifting his chin. "What do you work on, Houdini? Did Monica tell you about our computer center?"

Houdini looked from Mark to Mary appraisingly without replying. There was an awkward pause, during which they looked from Houdini to one another. I said quickly, "She mentioned it. We didn't see it though. It was getting dark."

Mark turned from me back to Houdini, still waiting for a response.

"I've seen your web site," Houdini said finally.

His remark only intensified the awkwardness. Mary looked perplexed and Mark stiffened. He said to me with a show of bluff casualness, "Sounds like Monica was making you feel welcome. Don't pay any attention to her. She's territorial when it comes to The Mother."

"Listen to Mark," Mary nodded, putting a hand on his knee. "He reads people so well. Unfortunately, some of our members will be suspicious of you no matter what. They think you're here to invade us. Just ignore them."

After summoning him over with her look, Mary had studiously ignored Ted. He had come at her peremptory call, then sat all this time watching her in silence, until just now when she put her hand on Mark's knee. At that point I saw him turn his eyes to the fire. But now he looked up again. He spoke thoughtfully, as though unmoved by Mary's flirtatious behavior.

"It's true that some people here are afraid of the outside world. It's stronger than we are." Ted flexed his fingers as though testing this strength. "It's the nature of a community like this. But most of the people here are well-intentioned." He glanced around the circle, his eyes gliding past Mary and coming to rest on Alia. The pretty young woman seemed flustered by his frank gaze and turned her own gaze to the fire.

Houdini leaned forward so that he could see Ted. "Do they think they can hide here from the world?"

Mark gave a derisive laugh. "They can and do. Some of them resent the fact that we do data-processing."

"It's complicated," Ted said cautiously, ignoring Mark. "The community used to be located in San Francisco. We came here three years ago to get in touch with the land and focus ourselves spiritually. We wanted to get away from the outside world. Well, some people felt that meant we should break off all ties with the outside. Others think we're too isolated."

"The isolationists think we can live in a vacuum," Mary declared sarcastically. "They want The Mother to invent a new world for them so they can pretend mainstream America doesn't even exist."

"Both sides get frustrated," Ted said, again ignoring the interruption. "That's why The Mother has called for a balance between isolation and contact. It's just a matter of people getting used to having outsiders among us again." He smiled thoughtfully. "You see, the people who are most opposed to outsiders are often The Mother's most ardent supporters. Like Monica. But unlike many of them, she's not anti-technology. Like I said, it's complicated."

Mark shook his head with a smile and appealed to Houdini and me. "Ted wants to be fair, but sometimes you have to draw the line. I'm afraid the problem goes beyond how these people see—" He broke off, gazing over at the farmhouse. All of us turned. The Mother had appeared underneath the yellow porch light and was coming down the back stairs. She still wore her white robe.

Silence fell as the forty-odd members of New Light seated around the fire realized that their leader was among them. The crickets and peepers sang on; from the forest by East Field path we heard an owl hoot. The Mother crossed the lawn, nodding at people as she came. She stopped before our group and smiled.

"May I join you?" she asked. Everyone stared up at her and she smiled again. She stopped by Alia and Mary and the two women moved apart to let her sit between them. She gathered the folds of her robe into her lap and looked around the circle. "You can tell from the expressions that I don't usually sit by the bonfire in the evening," she laughed. Her glance passed from me to Houdini, then out to the night. "It's quite nice. I should do it more often."

The silence stretched on. "Please," she said. "Continue." Her gaze took in the people in the groups around us. As though this were a signal, the Visionaries turned back to their conversations and music.

Mark leaned forward with a sharp, eager expression. "Actually, we were talking about recruiting."

"We were not," Alia said, shaking her head so that the bobbed wings of her hair fluttered.

"I was about to explain to the newcomers why there's tension in the air," Mark amended quickly. "They felt it themselves."

The Mother smiled. "Of course we should explain that. We must do everything we can to put them at their ease." She touched Alia lightly on the knee. "Go on, Mark."

"I was telling them that some people are afraid of the outside world. But the thing is," his voice grew passionate and he looked from Houdini to me, "if we don't reach out, make an effort to go to different cities, different parts of the country, people aren't going to know what we're doing here. Our message gets lost on the Internet. We have to *show* people what we're about. Let them feel our energy." He turned to the Mother again. "If we don't we're going to stagnate."

With a glancing smile at Mark, the Mother explained, "Mark was one of our best recruiters in San Francisco. Here he hasn't had much opportunity to use those skills."

"I've worked in St. Louis some. I brought Alia here. Remember that night?" he said, appealing to her. "You were in a bad way."

Alia nodded reluctantly. She looked at the fire for a moment, then said in an emotional voice, "You knew." After another moment she gave a half-hearted laugh and tucked the wings of her hair behind her ears. "I guess it wasn't that hard to tell."

"The point is, we can bring New Light's message to people who need to hear it," Mark said, turning to me. "There are a lot more people out there. People who feel lost."

"But there is an argument to be made for the way we've lived the past three years," Ted put in.

The Mother nodded firmly. "Yes, there is. You should know, by the way, that Ted is someone who misses San Francisco quite a bit." She smiled at him, then continued. "The problem we're faced with is one of belief. It's very easy to get distracted by city life, or by the zeal of proselytizing." Her gaze flicked to Mark, then back. "Here, we dedicate ourselves to the visionary life. We're reinventing America. Or going back to an earlier vision of what it means to be American."

"But people *need* to know what we're doing," Mark said. "If we don't tell them, what are we? Just a few people sitting by a campfire."

The Mother looked around the circle as though to let people decide for themselves if that's what they were. Then she said lightly, "Houdini and Beth found their way here. Maybe the people who need to know will find us."

"No!" Mark said vehemently. "We moved here to

create a new life. We didn't wait for one to be made for us. We have to do the work, let people know. It's our responsibility. We can save people. Like Alia."

His vehemence carried on the cool night air and silenced people in the groups nearest us. A log popped. Flames ate at the darkness.

The Mother gazed at him, her expression serene.

"We know that America is corrupt," Mark said, making an effort to soften his tone. "We know it offers us false images—of ourselves as well as the world. It's our responsibility to let people know there are alternatives. They haven't seen the visions. They need to know what they can become. They need to see their own potential."

He gazed fixedly at the Mother, then added, "You can't deny them that, can you? You've said it yourself, it's every person's right."

When she still didn't answer he looked around the circle at the rest of us again. In mute appeal his eyes focused on Mary. She hesitated for a moment, then gave a quick nod. Bolstered by this sign of support, Mark turned back to the Mother.

"It's your destiny. *And* ours."

I wasn't sure what the inflection meant, but it seemed to be at once challenge and plea. It lingered there in the air, even after Mark fell silent, gazing at his leader with clenched jaw. The Mother seemed caught off guard by the intensity of Mark's feeling. It was only a moment before she recovered, but the others had seen her surprise. Alia, Mary and Ted stared, first at her, then at Mark, then finally dropped their eyes to the ground.

Around us people began to rise and head off into the night. Most of them couldn't have heard the particulars of the exchange, but they probably knew the gist of it already—it had the feel of an on-going debate. Mark wanted changes, and he was the kind of aggressively self-assertive man who believed that if other people disagreed with him, it was because they didn't understand his ideas. He was something of a bully, but it was also clear that he meant what he said. He believed in the Mother and her destiny. He cared passionately about New Light and the role it could play in American life.

I looked at Houdini, but he was no longer watching the Mother or Mark or any of the people sitting in the circle. He was gazing up at the sky, at the brilliant stars.

Destiny. It was something all the Visionaries believed in. A desire for some larger meaning in their lives. When Mark used destiny to appeal to and threaten the Mother, I thought to myself, what century is this? Are they for real? And yet, in a way, their belief in destiny wasn't so far off from Houdini's own ideas about how the world worked.

Later that night, after we'd returned to Sparrow, I asked him what he thought of the exchange we'd witnessed. Instead of answering my question, he told me more about the patterns of chaos and how they related to his research at New Light. His intensity had returned: cheeks were tinged with color, lips framed words with unconscious voluptuousness. Perhaps, in his preoccupation with tracing the invisible lines of force that control our lives, he betrayed himself. Perhaps I was seeing Houdini revealed. He followed me into my room and sat down by the window again. He took his chair at my table automatically, as though he had the right. It was flattering and annoying at the same time. He assumed that when he offered up a casual confidence, a glancing attention, I would accept such crumbs from his plate gratefully.

But then, why shouldn't he have assumed these things? I never protested.

We sat at the round wooden table, our elbows sticking to its surface of gummy shellac, while outside the country night was full of unseen life. The chorus of crickets, the rustle of mice, the call of owls, as well as other noises whose origins remained mysterious—these became backdrop as Houdini unfolded more of his theories for me. As for me—I listened raptly.

Strange attractors. That's the actual name that mathematicians came up with. The invisible patterns in chaotic systems require the existence of something they call strange attractors. These quantities—or beings—focus the seemingly haphazard order that chaos theory predicts. In a simplified sense, the Mother or the colony itself might function as a hidden organizing principle that controlled the chaotic pattern, in much the same way that Mesmer or Madame Blavatsky did in their time. If you buy it, the theory helps to explain the seemingly magical power lone individuals have wielded from time to time throughout history—people like Hitler and Napoleon. For some reason they become locuses for these invisible lines of force. They draw events to them and set huge changes in motion. They themselves don't understand how or why.

Houdini believed that all people act without a real knowledge of what motivates them. Even strange attractors like Hitler do not actually *will* events to occur, though they might think they do. They are vehicles for other forces, larger than themselves, that act through them. He gave me an example that he felt illustrated the inadvertence of our behavior and the obliqueness of our motives to ourselves, a study done of epileptics whose connection between brain hemispheres, the *corpus callosum*, had been severed in an effort to stop their seizures.

When the brain is split, information no longer passes back and forth between the two hemispheres. The right and left brains function independently instead of as a whole. In other words, one eye doesn't know what the other eye is seeing. In the study Houdini described to me, scientists blindfolded the subject's right eye, which is connected to the left side of the brain, the side that controls language. Then they showed a written message to the left eye, which is connected to the right brain. The left eye can read, but its brain hemisphere has only passive linguistic ability—it can't form sentences. It could read the message that instructed the subject to get up, go to the sink, and get himself a glass of water, but it couldn't comment on that sentence, to say, oh I'm not thirsty now, or, why don't you get it for me?

Because they were good participants, each subject read the command, got up, went to the sink, drank a glass of water, then sat back down again. At this point the doctors asked them why they got up. You must remember that though the right side of the brain can read, it can't form sentences. It is the left side that's responsible for verbalizing and explaining; it controls all conscious uses of language. But the left side had not seen the message the doctors showed the right side.

Every subject in the study made up a reason for going to the sink. One told the doctor that he got up because he was thirsty, another because she was restless and wanted to take a walk, then saw the faucet and decided to have a drink. Every subject *believed* that the reason they gave the doctors for getting a drink was true. That is to say, none of them could tell the doctors what had actually prompted them to get a drink because their left brains hadn't read the message. The left side of the brain invented a reason because that is its task: to devise rational explanations for behavior. The right side knew the real reason, but the knowledge was not accessible to the left side since the two brain hemispheres had no conduit through which to share information.

What does this imply? According to Houdini, it shows that we have a deep-seated need to explain our behavior. But the rationale we make up may not reflect the real reasons for what we do. All it reflects is our need to explain ourselves plausibly and rationally. What this meant to Houdini was simple. He believed in chaos because he didn't believe any of us could know our own minds.

That night at New Light, as we sat across from each other in schoolroom chairs in my room, the acrid perfume of woodsmoke still sharp in our hair and clothes, I felt for the first time that I was beginning to understand Houdini. He leaned forward, elbows on the table, chin resting on his clasped hands, and revealed himself to me. Outside the peepers and crickets trilled. The white curtains fluttered in the window.

I considered what he'd told me. How, for example, would the left brain explain a behavior that was motivated by an unconscious desire? I mean, was Houdini trying to tell me something, to tell me without having to commit himself to words? Was he confessing, in his roundabout way, that something *had* happened between us a week earlier? He kept his arm around me as we sat on the roof after the vision receded. Above us there was nothing but a normal spring-time sky. Around us, the lights of the city diffused into the darkness.

He had left the party and come to me out there, without quite knowing why. He found me in the spasms of a vision, and without a moment's hesitation he held my body to him. Maybe he hadn't known for sure that I was going to have a vision. Maybe he had felt some inexplicable attraction, and allowed himself to obey it by claiming he sensed I would have a vision. And what he really sensed was our mutual attraction to each other. It beckoned him on.

So here's one explanation of what happened to us that night at Boris's party. The mutual attraction we felt somehow enabled us to intuit what the other wanted most. I collided with Houdini in the hallway on my way to the bathroom, and then I had a vision, as though I were giving him a gift. It was the thing he wanted most, the thing that he was searching for desperately. And in response he produced the thing I left New York in search of...an adventure, something that would rescue me from ennui and indecision, give focus to my life. It was what *I* wanted most—a fantastic, exotic undertaking that was set in motion at the moment I appeared, implying that I was somehow necessary to it.

Does this mean that attraction is really some strange ability to sense what the other needs, in his most secret heart? I want to believe this. Yet at the same time I wonder whether, all along, it's actually someone else's powers of projection that draw us to them. We find the person who can present us with the self we want to be. If this is true, then perhaps the adventure was Houdini's, not mine. I was simply there as a bystander, only pretending to understand the significance of the things I witnessed. And of course the same would hold true for him. The visions I saw would never be more than descriptions to him, banal postcards from a place he'd never go.

twelve

I woke the next morning—Tuesday—to an abrupt knocking at my door. I sat up, feeling waves of shock for a moment, before I realized where I was. The room was cold because I'd left the window open. In the leaves of the maple outside I could see tentative beams of early morning sunlight. "Wait," I called, pulling on the robe Boris had lent me. I opened the door.

Houdini stood in the hallway. He glanced down: I was balancing on the toes of one foot. The floor was freezing. "They don't believe in rugs here," I said, holding onto the doorjamb.

He wasted no time on preliminaries like good morning, just asked if I wanted to shower. His hair was wet and curling around his ears, and he had a small nick on his chin. I lifted a handful of my own hair to my nose and made a face at the still-sharp scent of woodsmoke. "I'll wait," he said and went back to his room. His laptop was open on the table.

The shower in the bathroom at the end of the hall was surprisingly powerful. I didn't realize until I got to New Light how dirty you get in the country. I wanted to stand there and let it scald my shoulders and neck, but instead I gave myself a quick soaping and got out.

"So," I said, as I emerged from my room in jeans and a t-shirt, my hair soaking. "What's the plan?"

I leaned against the doorframe, not quite in his room. He'd made the bed. "Do we meet with the Mother again?" I asked as he looked up belatedly from the computer screen. "Or do you want to interview more of her followers?"

He shut down the computer. "There is no plan," he said. He passed by me without meeting my eyes and headed down the hall.

Fuck you, I thought. Just like that, the intensity and tentative intimacy of the night before had been erased.

We emerged from Sparrow into luxuriant spring-time. Rain during the night had washed the skies the softest blue. Sunshine as thick as honey; a light breeze stirring the still-wet meadow grass; bees and dragonflies drunk among the wildflowers. The air smelled sweet.

Architecturally, the barracks were housing-tract structures, but by the light of day we could see the bird-people and aerial views of abandoned cities that decorated their walls. The images exalted their mundane backdrops; they had a haunting, plaintive quality that seemed very much like Alia. The buildings leaned back in the sunshine with magisterial repose, facing a wide field bordered by shady clusters of oak and maple. The forest that climbed the ridge behind Sparrow was thick and green and shady, though it thinned out toward the top, so that one would have a good view of the farm from the ridge itself. The path we'd followed back from the farmhouse the night before ran north beyond the barracks and ascended the slope to disappear between the trees. It had seemed much steeper in the dark.

We climbed the hill, heading south back toward the center of the farm. There in the sunlight, I realized how big New Light was. There were numerous fields and pockets of forest, all connected by these meandering footpaths. At the crest of the hill were extensive vegetable gardens and, about a quarter of a mile beyond them, two large greenhouses. I identified bright green lettuces and curling sweetpea vines among the rows of tilled earth. There were coldframes for more sensitive plants. Beyond the greenhouses stood the barn.

The sunlight also revealed the importance of the visionary life to the community's inhabitants. Murals decorated many of New Light's buildings. The bird-people were a popular motif, as were images of men and women that seemed straight out of primitive fertility rites. The most provocative of these paintings covered the east wall of the barn. We rounded the bend just past the second greenhouse, and there, in the revelatory light of day, we saw an enormous man and woman, held up above the grass by an explosion of color. If they were meant to be Adam and Eve figures, Edenic in their bliss, their eden had become a Rousseau jungle. They leaned toward each other to touch lips in an ethereal rapture that seemed not to have lost its innocence, in spite of the fact that they appeared quite conscious of their nakedness.

We both halted to take in this sight. It was really quite magnificent, and I turned to Houdini to say so. He was studying the mural as if hypnotized and didn't even glance my way. I wanted to laugh. The artist who had executed it had created something extraordinary indeed, to transfix Houdini like this. But in truth it was extraordinary. Beautiful and at the same time almost shocking in its provocativeness.

As we drew closer I saw that the lovers' bodies seemed to have been taken over by the jungle. Vines laced their flesh, flowers bloomed from crotch and armpit and ear. Indeed, upon closer inspection I realized that some of those vines seemed to grow *out* of the lovers' bodies, as though drawn forth by the tropical forest's wreathing green. Stranger still, these vines were only part vegetable. In addition to leaves and flowers, those curving fleshy stems produced little heads—some human, some animal, and some that were strange metamorphic creatures out of a fairy tale. All the heads seemed to have their own consciousness, unrelated to the adam and eve whose bodies symbiotically supported them. They swung and darted on their stems in a pantomime of independence, wild in their unnamed state, regarding one another with a panoply of ferocious expressions: licentiousness, anger, terror, venality. Their hosts' erotic burn was fueled by the passions of the lush and unruly creatures that lived on their bodies, unbeknownst to them.

I cleared my throat. We had been standing there for so long I was beginning to feel embarrassed. "So what do you think it means?" I said brightly. Houdini seemed to wake up. He looked at me and his face closed. Without a word he strode toward the farmhouse.

Breakfast at the colony was a quiet affair. People sat alone or in small groups, reflecting in silence or conversing quietly. As we entered the dining room with our trays, we saw Glass and Alia by the far window, sitting with two other women. Glass waved.

When we came up Alia was shaking her head. "No," she said. "I just don't see it that way." The curly-headed woman across from her frowned and seemed about to speak but Alia shook her head again. She turned to us. "You're just in time to save us from a pointless debate. Beth, Houdini— Crystal and Tianne."

Crystal said hello and smiled, pushing back several long curls that fell in her face. She was about my age. Her long curly hair frothed around her face like some Renaissance maiden's, and her voice belonged to that image—light and fluting and faintly foreign-sounding. We learned later that she had been raised in Holland but had come back to the US as a teenager. A college friend of hers had told her about New Light, and she left New York where she was working at the UN and never looked back. She wore a woven hemp necklace and bracelets which we discovered were samples of her work. She was one of the community's masterweavers; her basket designs were especially intricate and beautiful. Perhaps it was the quiet focus of her work that made her such a careful listener. When you spoke to her she gave you her full attention, as though she were listening with her whole body to what you said. The effect was a little disconcerting but I liked it. I found I paid more attention to my own words.

Tianne, across from her, said hello too and invited me to sit beside her. I put down my tray, admiring the bright yellow of her dress and headscarf, which burned brilliantly against the rich dark brown of her skin. She looked no older than Crystal, though eventually we learned that she was in her thirties. She was more reserved in her bearing and conversation; she carried herself with a gracious dignity that commanded respect, coming as it seemed to from some deep reserve of experience. She told me later she had worked as a nurse in a clinic in San Francisco before joining the community. She was attracted to New Light because it was so open to different cultures: its members included Americans of many different ethnicities: whites, blacks, Asians, and even people who weren't US citizens—a Mexican woman, an Israeli man, and a Swedish couple. Everyone there had different backgrounds and experiences; these differences were seen as enriching the community. But at the same time they all agreed to let their pasts remain the past. They were here to create the future together.

Both Tianne and Crystal were striking women. They were beautiful, yes, but what struck me was something other than their beauty. They had a vitality to them. I realized then that this was true of most of the Visionaries. Even if they didn't fit conventional standards of beauty, there was something else that made them attractive. A vividness, a liveliness, as though the air they breathed, the visions they saw, made them a little more alive.

"I remember seeing both of you by the fire last night," I said.

"We would have come over but we didn't want to overwhelm you," Tianne said.

"It's a lot to take in," Crystal agreed. "We try to remember how intense it can be when you're first introduced to the community."

"Mark and Mary didn't seem to mind overwhelming anyone," Glass said with a glance at Alia.

"They're both really excitable," Alia said. "They want you to feel welcome. We haven't had any new people here for a while."

"I thought Mary wanted everyone to see that she and Ted are back together," Glass said.

"They've been back together for a while. I told you that before," Alia said sharply.

"You know he was looking at you," Glass replied.

"Mary knew too," Tianne added quietly.

There was a silence. Alia, blushing, looked at me. "Ted and I were...involved. He and Mary had been going out for a year and a half but then they...broke up. You know how these things are. Glass thinks that Mary came over to rub in the fact that they're back together. But it's not really like that. I knew when we got together that Ted and Mary had been involved." She glanced at Tianne and Crystal self-consciously, then said in a dismissive tone: "It's complicated."

"That kind of thing happens all the time," I said sympathetically. "It was the same when I was in college. Everybody slept with everybody else."

"Except that Ted is still in love with Alia," Glass said. "I'm not the only one who thinks so," she added defensively, looking at Tianne and Crystal for support.

"We all think so," Crystal said. "Except Alia."

"But Alia's right," Tianne said to Crystal. "It doesn't matter, for now, anyway. Mary wouldn't have come over to them last night if she didn't feel confident about things with Ted."

"He's still in love with Alia," Glass repeated. "That's

more important." She looked from Crystal to Tianne.

"Not necessarily," Alia said with an unhappy smile.

"And why did Mark come over?" Houdini said, after listening in silence to this exchange.

The women looked at each other.

I turned to Alia. "I was thinking about what he said. How does this recruiting work? You said he brought you here?"

She nodded. "He saw me at The Way Out Club. He knew I would respond." She shrugged as though that were explanation enough.

There was silence. The three Visionaries concentrated on their breakfasts, while Glass gazed at each woman in turn. Finally she met my eyes, her face unhappy.

Houdini said casually, as he began to eat his cereal, "I imagine it would be a powerful position to find yourself in."

We had just finished eating when Monica appeared in the dining room and came marching grimly toward our table. Her mouth was pursed in a sour moue. She came to a halt behind Houdini and Glass and announced that I was to come with her. I was being granted a private audience with the Mother.

"I don't understand," I began, feeling confused, but Houdini interrupted, saying that I would be honored to meet with the Mother. I looked from him to the women around me, expecting to see my confusion mirrored in their faces sympathetically. Instead Alia, Tianne and Crystal beamed at me. They were pleased that the Mother had chosen to honor me in this way. Glass was the only one who seemed to understand my uncertainty. "We'll wait for you," she called as I followed Monica through the dining room and out the door that led to the hall of murals.

She brought me back to the throne room with its

tinkling exotic trinkets. The Mother, looking coolly elegant in her loose white sheath, emerged from the chamber beyond and shut the door behind her. I caught a brief glimpse of a room done up in pale pine, with a white muslin spread on the bed, white cotton throw rugs, and long gauzy white curtains fluttering their hems against the bed posts. The Mother nodded to Monica, who left us, shutting the door noiselessly behind her.

The Mother faced me with a smile.

"Thank you for coming, Beth. The members of this community know they can approach me at any time, but I thought you might need an invitation."

Without waiting for an answer she gestured toward the cluster of chairs and we sat, she on the wicker throne, I in one of the purple armchairs. She focused her eyes on the distance above my head and took several deep even breaths. After a few moments her eyes returned to me. She gave me another one of those serene smiles, and I found myself suddenly irritated.

"Why did you want me to come alone?"

"Ah," she said with a nod. "You were surprised that I asked you and not Houdini?"

I didn't reply and she smiled again. "I wanted to talk to you about your visions. Sometimes it's awkward in front of a third party."

"Houdini was with me the first time. He helped me. It wouldn't be awkward in front of him." It was a lie, of course, and I felt myself flush as I said it.

As though embarrassed for me, she gazed out the window at the purple beech. "I will talk to Houdini, of course," she said finally. "He brought you here. In a sense, as you say, he was the catalyst for your vision. He and I have much to discuss. But first—" Her eyes flickered toward me again.

I was tired of being studied, tired of long significant silences. As though she sensed this she drew herself up and said in a new tone:

"The visionary life is our concern here. Your visions seem unusual, Beth. They may be important to our community. I was hoping you would tell me what made you decide to come to New Light."

The question caught me off guard. The afternoon before, when I described the vision of the monster city to the Mother, I hadn't told her how I had announced to Sarah and Lisa that I was coming to New Light. I omitted any mention of the fact that, in the throes of the vision, I'd said something I now had no recollection of. Yet as I faced the Mother that morning, it seemed to me that she already knew. She had that ability, to seem to know what you were hiding, thereby making you feel that you might as well confess. I glanced nervously at the candles, the brass teapots, the carved heads that seemed to regard me suspiciously, then blurted out the details of that second vision.

It came out in a rush—how I seemed to see an image of Sarah's desire for Houdini, how I was then sucked upward, how I viewed the sorrowing beauty of the dying city from the sky. I described the vision's strangely ironic flavor. She questioned me about every nuance of atmosphere, image, and emotion to be sure she had them right, and it was a relief to tell all, to hold nothing back. She was most interested in the fact that I didn't know what I'd said to Sarah and Lisa, and of course now seemed genuinely surprised by this, and kept returning to it. But when she was finally satisfied that I was telling her everything I knew, she sat back. She held her palms together as though she were praying, while her pursed lips pressed against her index fingers in a meditative kiss.

"The vision spoke through you, Beth. That's very rare," she said finally.

I sat in my purple chair, waiting for more. A long moment passed and my relief began to turn to uneasiness. I remembered Houdini's claim that the Mother had hypnotized me the day before, somehow causing me to recall the summer house that overlooked Long Island Sound. I didn't know I'd been hypnotized then, and with a lurch in my gut I wondered if she had done it again just now, to compel me to tell her the details of the vision. It didn't feel as though I'd been compelled, but maybe that was how it worked.

Across from me the Mother glanced sharply up.

"You have great visionary power. But it's all unconscious. Untrained."

A wave of warmth washed over me from the flattery, but there was suspicion in its ebb. I was annoyed with myself—was I that desperate for praise? I said in an accusatory voice, "Did you hypnotize me?"

She blinked. She folded her hands in her lap and shifted in her seat as though to see me from a new angle. "Houdini said you were in a trance yesterday?"

"Was I?"

"Well, it certainly seemed that way. But I didn't put you there, if that's what you mean."

"Then how did I get there?"

The Mother smiled and seemed to relax slightly. "I told you. You have a great deal of unconscious power."

She crossed her legs and said in a smooth, surprisingly professional tone, "My habits of attention seem to help people focus, Beth. I can't tell you exactly why this is so, but it appears that a trained mind can help an untrained mind explore itself. Of course I can't take you beyond your own desire and potential. In hypnosis research circles, you are what they call a high. You enter trances spontaneously."

I felt oddly vulnerable sitting there before her, the way you do when you describe a symptom to the doctor, trying to ignore the fact that you're sitting there naked while he's completely clothed. I tried to consider the fact of my visions with detachment. "That's why I saw things?"

"Oh no," she shook her head, smiling at my eagerness for an explanation. "The visions are something else entirely. There are correlations between visionary ability and hypnotic potential, but the two are quite different. I'm sure Houdini can explain better than I. He has the numbers."

"I don't understand. I went into a hypnotic trance because you were there?"

"Hypnosis is essentially a state of highly focused attention. Attention that is focused inward. Only a small percentage of the population can switch off the outside world so completely that they're able to enter an entirely mental state. But those that can—people like you—are no longer aware of the information pouring in through their senses. Instead they see images, memories, imaginary scenes. It's like switching your stereo receiver from radio to CD player."

"I saw a place we stayed at when I was a kid."

"It's probably important to you in some way. Most likely it represents some part of yourself you've forgotten. As you listened to me you were able to tap into your unconscious mind, where that part has been stored." She shrugged. "It's interesting. At times it can feel quite fulfilling. But it's basically a parlor trick unless it's developed. You have to develop it, Beth, for it to be the beginning of something else."

"The beginning of what?"

"The visions, Beth." She leaned forward. "They're not simply mental phenomena. They aren't the recycled images of your own mind. They come from outside. They are spiritual experiences given visual form."

I pressed down on the nap of the velvet with my fingertips. I tried to consider everything the Mother had said with an open mind, but it wasn't easy. Or else it was too easy.

I didn't want to be like Sarah and dismiss the group as a cult, but I hadn't thought before about the visions as a part of a system of belief. I hadn't thought that my coming there might mean something to them. I had come because it seemed like the thing to do, after everything that had happened.

The Mother watched me with an unreadable expression, trying, I felt, to avoid influencing me. She waited for me to speak. What had Houdini said on the patio Saturday morning? He didn't want to invalidate my experience. I had the sense that she was trying very hard not to interfere.

"Why did I have the first vision at the party, after I bumped into Houdini?"

"That's an important question," the Mother said. She gazed out at the beech again, as though for guidance. "We believe that coincidence directs us. As I said before, Houdini seems to have been the catalyst." She looked at me. "A way had to be discovered to bring you down here."

"You're saying I was meant to come here?"

"Perhaps."

That was too much. Coincidence, mystical connections—the vision coming to me at the party so that Houdini would tell me about New Light. This is how cults lure you in, I told myself. The Mother figured out what I wanted to hear and handed it back to me. It was humiliating to discover how hungry I was for some kind of direction.

"Why don't you do more recruiting then, like Mark wants?" I asked, folding my arms across my chest. "You can help untrained people like me. Spread the word." I thought of Houdini's mission and added bitterly, "Who knows? Maybe you could set off some huge movement, like Mesmer or the Spiritualists. Think of the power you'd have."

A terrible stillness came over the Mother's face. It cut through me like a blade. She seemed hurt, yet also deeply sad that I would insult her like that, and in silence studied me with her sorrowing eyes. Just then a burst of children's laughter came from the grove of fruit trees that stood near the front of the house. Immediately I felt cynical and mean.

She apologized for offending me. She said that that was exactly why they didn't recruit anymore, and why she hesitated to let Mark go out again. Her face retained that crushed immobility.

"The temptation is always there," she said slowly, her voice emerging from some deep center, as though fighting gravity to reach me. "If we become a community concerned only with increasing our membership, what happens to our spiritual mission?" Her eyes turned to the window briefly, as though looking for the children. I didn't know what to say.

"I didn't mean—"

She held up her hand. "Please. Don't apologize. It's my fault. I told you, your potential—" She broke off and said instead, "I allowed myself to be carried away by the extraordinary nature of your visions, forgetting that your conscious mind is probably working very hard to deny their significance."

The lines around her mouth seemed to deepen as she gazed at me. She shook her head.

"You can't understand; it's too soon. Yet you have to. You're on the threshold of a crisis. One way or another, Beth, you must discover what your visions mean."

We sat there, eyeing each other across the low wooden tea table, in silence. Finally, I asked her how I was supposed to do this. She shook her head. She said she wished me luck. I sat there for a little longer, dumbly, then got to my feet.

She stirred then, as though calling herself back for my sake. "You should ask Houdini. He's a scientist. His approach is different from ours."

I stared. "You think I should ask Houdini to help me

understand the visions?"

She gave me a sad smile. "If his is the voice you can hear."

I suppose the blankness of my look moved her to pity. She added:

"He would not be my choice for a mentor. But you aren't me. I am wary of his approach to the visionary world. He wants to quantify, to control. But perhaps in the end you want that too."

I didn't answer and she added, almost casually, "And then, of course, there's the matter of his belief."

I looked at her blankly again.

"In the visions. Don't you think he believes, in spite of his scientific stance?" There was an odd expression on her face. The pity and concern had been inflected by something else.

"He might," I said, hearing the caution in my voice.

She made a dismissive gesture as though the question were suddenly unimportant. "What about you, Beth? Do you believe?"

I studied her but I couldn't make her out. Whose belief was she really concerned with? Which question betrayed her interests, which was the blind? She smiled with satisfaction at my silence.

The formal end of the interview occurred immediately after that, when the Mother crossed the room and opened the door to the hall. Tom, the flute-player from the night before, entered the throne room. He was dressed in a gauzy light-blue outfit. By daylight I took note of the dark eyes, coarse black hair that stood up straight from his skull, skin the color of almonds. He was only about 5'4", but he really was beautiful.

"Tom will be your guide this morning, " she said.

"Any questions you have about the community, he'll be able to answer."

I looked from the Mother to Tom. He stepped forward and took my hand again, as he'd done the night before. His body moved beneath the gauzy blue cloth with the graceful economy of a dancer, like he was wearing air.

The Mother said, "Tom was chosen to guide you because a spiritual resonance exists between you. Don't be afraid of it. Let yourself follow." She smiled and we were dismissed.

His assignment was to take me on a spiritual tour of the community. He would show me where the community's rituals were held and explain as best he could their meaning. He was so beautiful I found I had to look away, out of fear that I was staring. I was annoyed that the Mother had known I would feel this way, but when Tom set off down the hall of murals, I trailed after him willingly.

"Pretty strange at first, isn't it?" Tom said over his shoulder. I laughed.

"She's usually right, you know," he added, holding the front door open for me. "About the spiritual resonance." He smiled.

He said we would go to the barn first because it was the site of their most important ritual, the vision ceremony. We crossed the fields and when we reach the mural-covered barn, Tom gave the handle a pull and rolled open the wide doors, then stepped inside and flicked several switches. The cavernous interior sprang into view. And there I saw the most lavishly executed, gorgeous and disconcerting of all the community's murals.

As a complement to Adam and Eve on the east wall outside, the interior walls of the barn were also covered with painted men and women. The figures hemmed in the expansive emptiness with crowded life. Each was engaged in some kind of action: one wrestled a boa constrictor to the ground, another was attacked by an enormous pig, a third made love to a bird-woman. Yet regardless of their actions, all the figures stared out at the viewer. The effect was unnerving, especially because their eyes were much too big for their faces, like the kitschy big-eyed art from the '60s. Each figure wore the same dazed expression. I stared at a woman in the middle of the far wall who stood with a rearing leopard in her arms. The big cat's muzzle was intimately engaged at her throat, yet she gazed out at the viewer with a placidness that was somehow soothing and horrifying at the same time.

"This is where we gather to receive visions as a group," Tom said, his sudden voice startling me. He apologized, giving the paintings a glancing smile. "They're overwhelming at first. You get used to them."

"I find that hard to believe," I said. My voice echoing back at me sounded brittle.

Tom said that many things at New Light were difficult to believe or understand at first. To outsiders their life seemed strange, but he was there to help me adjust. He seated himself on the floor in the middle of the huge room and gestured for me to join him.

"It's kind of tough, the first time you meet with The Mother by yourself," he said. "How do you feel now?" I sat down on the wooden floor opposite him and made a face. He laughed. "That bad?"

"She put me into a hypnotic trance yesterday. I mean that's what I'm told. And today I found myself telling her things I hadn't planned on saying."

Tom said that people can't be forced to act against their will when they're under hypnosis. He asked if I'd decided beforehand not to tell the Mother certain things. When I said I hadn't even thought about it, he said that if I had in fact been hypnotized, I probably told her about the vision because part of me wanted help understanding what had happened. But he said it didn't sound to him like I'd been in a trance during that second conversation. I admitted that I hadn't had the same feeling of reverie that I'd experienced when I remembered the house on the Sound.

"Hypnosis is tricky," he said, scratching a knee through the gauzy fabric of his pants. "Sometimes it can be useful—anesthesia, helping you change a habit you don't like, or bringing back memories that have gotten misplaced. But it can't really change you, not unless you've decided you want to change. When I first came here I used hypnosis for a while. It helped me deal with the dreams. Kind of like a clean-up operation."

"Clean-up operation?"

He smiled. "Before I came here I was living on the streets in San Francisco. I even slept with people for money a couple times." Tom shrugged. "The Mother rescued me. It was a matter of life or death, you know? I could have gotten AIDS, I could have been killed. And that's just the physical death. Spiritually—" He shrugged again.

His face was serious yet untroubled. He saw that I didn't know how to respond and smiled again, touching my hand with a light, reassuring gesture.

It was moving. He looked at me without shame, without defensiveness. I wanted to thank him but I still didn't know what to say.

"It's all right," he said softly. "I'm lucky. I survived."

"It's sad," I said awkwardly.

"It was sad, but that time isn't real to me anymore. Now I'm here. And you're here too." He glanced at the silent figures who watched us from the walls, then took my hand with both of his. It was comforting, as though we were declaring, there in that huge room, that we weren't completely alone.

"Like I said, hypnosis is just a useful shortcut. In the vision ceremonies we experience transcendence. We gather to seek Oneness with the Beyond." He spoke with simple earnestness, searching my face. I nodded.

He pressed my hand briefly to his cheek. "We also desire Oneness with each other, Beth. This is what we strive for in community." He paused. "The Mother asked me to tell you about these mysteries because of our compatibility. She thought you would find them compelling, coming from me. It would help you make the leap."

"What leap?"

"Do you find me attractive?"

I laughed, slightly embarrassed. He took it as a yes.

"The vision ceremonies are very advanced. But we also have a practice that strives for Oneness on a smaller scale. We call it the vision journey. It's familiar to most people, and so they find it less overwhelming than the vision ceremony. The passion we experience carries us beyond our isolated selves. Through it, we discover ourselves newly. We are made and unmade."

Tom turned my hand over and ran his fingertips along the lines of my palm. I stared at my hand held in his two. Finally I met his eyes. There was nothing but gentleness in his face.

He said softly, "The passion of the body feeds the passion of the soul. In Oneness there are no divisions." He leaned forward and, with marvelous delicacy, touched his lips to mine.

He didn't insist. It was as though he were learning the texture of my lips with his own. My breath caught in my throat. It was my lips he touched, but I felt the kiss burn through my whole body. His fingers shivered in my hand.

I don't know how long we sat there, lips touching. I say that, even though I realize you can't say such things without sounding ridiculous. But it doesn't matter. I really don't know how long the moment lasted. The sensations, the feeling of intimacy and connection to him, were overwhelming. We sat there in the middle of the empty barn, and when I finally withdrew from the kiss—less a physical withdrawal than a waking up, an emotional disentanglement—he sensed it immediately. He straightened. The movement carried him a slight distance away from me.

"I understand," he said with a gentle smile. He let go of my hand.

Coincident Desire

Tom realized before I did that I had decided, in the midst of that kiss, that I couldn't go on a vision journey with him. I didn't want to face the decision because to do so would mean that the connection between us would be broken, the delicacy of our touch no longer suspending us above the world.

I mean this in all seriousness. The moment was magical: I didn't want it to end. That, even though I knew I couldn't go to bed with him.

Yet why couldn't I? In the past I'd gone to bed with plenty of men I didn't like, men I didn't want to talk to afterward, who weren't interested in talking to me. Not only did I like Tom and find him devastatingly attractive, I also found him spiritually...compelling. Yet I refused, as though I could accept only if my whole self accepted, and, unfortunately, my whole self did not.

Perhaps all of this sounds hard to believe. But really, who doesn't want to have the passion of their body feed the passion of their soul? I can say this: I've never been propositioned in such a spiritual way, free of any weird residual feelings. It was very different, for example, from that kiss in the doorway to Dan's apartment. With Tom I didn't feel ashamed afterward. I didn't have the sense that we were being dishonest. It was this that made me believe what he said about the vision journeys. They *were* somehow spiritual, less about sex than about using sexuality to light up the whole self. The blindness I had come to associate with fumbling dully at someone else's genitals, caught up in the rutting lust, was gone. To go on a vision journey, both parties had to be clear and vivid and light. That's why Tom stopped when he felt me hesitate.

The rules governing the vision journeys were simple. Both Visionaries had to want each other equally. Sexual bullying—like the kind practiced at Oneida—was not tolerated. It was the coincidence of desire that the Mother encouraged; from this flowed all things.

Each member of New Light gave themselves over to these two elemental forces. They believed that coincidence and desire were the secret structuring principles of the universe. And so the Visionaries contemplated them in their murals, paid homage to them in their ceremonies, and chanted to them in the seclusion of noon meditations. When one desire coincided with another, the members experienced reverence and awe. They were in the presence of a guiding spirit.

Because of these beliefs, the Visionaries did not feel it necessary to maintain monogamous relationships. Which didn't mean that exclusive relationships, like Ted's and Mary's, were discouraged: if loyalty to one lover was the desire you felt, you had to follow that course. However, if your partner suddenly decided to follow a different path, you had no one to cry to. You simply had to follow your own desire, provided it was coincident.

I imagined that, as a Visionary, you'd spend a lot of time seeking out coincidences, sexual and otherwise, as you meditated on the shape of your visionary path. But I was told that this would be a violation of the spirit of the journey. The coincidence of desire cannot be denied, but neither can it be forced or fantasized into being. It has to find you. Otherwise its magic, which can suspend you above the laws of physics, social contracts, and friend- and lover-loyalties, would be violated. To accept the gift of transcendent destiny, you had to abide by its rules.

fourteen

The rest of my tour that morning was focused on the practical side of life at New Light. Tom showed me the weavery and milking shed, the chicken coop and greenhouses, allowed me a brief glance into the computer center, with its fluorescent lights, coils of extension cords, and the steady tapping of keys as ten Visionaries stared at their monitors. We didn't interrupt them, but everywhere else we went I was introduced to a number of other members, all of whom smiled graciously, welcomed me to New Light, and then politely returned to their work. A little before noon Tom walked me back to Sparrow, reminding me that no one left their building until the meditation hour had ended. "Then we're all starving," he warned, "so don't be late for lunch." He smiled and touched my hand briefly, then turned left onto the path that led to the east field, to his room in Thebes.

I walked down Sparrow's hallway, past the rows of doors closed on empty rooms, waiting for guests who might never arrive. My sneakers squeaked loudly on the linoleum. Houdini's door was shut; from within I could hear the muted patter of keys. I stood there in the shadowy hall between our two rooms, looking out the back door's rectangle of window glass, onto a patch of daisies and gravel. The white of petals and stones ached brightly in the sunlight.

I went into my room, closing the door behind me a little harder than I had to.

For a moment I stood in the middle of my room, wondering if Tom was meditating about me. I thought about writing in my journal, but instead lay down on my bed and stared up at the coils and matting of the upper bunk. I imagined I felt a strange stillness settle down over the farm, and gather and thicken in my room. Meditation hour, the noon retreat. I tried making my mind a blank but it was no use. Outside the sun was bright; I gazed out the window at the gold leaves and green shadows of the maple tree. A wind passed through the branches and the curled red tips of the leaves shimmered as they moved. I didn't feel a thing.

"Are you sure? What happens if you trust her?" my mother said, appearing before me in her Feeling chair, which was her refuge that year after the divorce. She would seat herself in the overstuffed orange chair with a cup of tea and a bag of Pepperidge Farms Vienna cookies to recover after a bad scene with one or another boyfriend. She'd sit in that chair and feel, sometimes for a few hours, and once she got up she was finished with him. The cord was cut. I was more surprised to see the chair than her; I think it got thrown out when we moved from Stamford. That is, when I moved to my father's, and my mother decided she couldn't live in that apartment without me. There it was, just as it had been when I was twelve, the orange '50s upholstery, the embroidered flowers whose petals I liked to imagine were lopsided wings. I liked that chair because she was always calm then, she would sit there and rest, smiling sadly, talking in a resigned voice about what you could decide to live for. For that brief time we were safe from scenes and emotional upheavals.

"Trust who?" I said, standing awkward and mystified before her, trying to remember which boyfriend it was that she was Feeling, what kind of life she'd chosen most recently.

My mother shook her head and gave me the you-know-what-I'm-talking-about look.

"Who?" I repeated, desperate to make her believe that I didn't know. "Who?"

But instead of answering me she clutched the sides of the chair, and suddenly it began to expand and I panicked, thinking it was going to crush her. Then the scene shifted. I was sitting in Boris's apartment. He was smiling at me, and leaned forward to kiss me, but just as he did so I realized that the walls were covered with the mural people from the barn, and that all of them had suddenly shut their eyes.

I awoke to a knocking for the second time that day.

"I wasn't sure when you'd be back," Houdini said when I opened the door. Chairs, table, lamp, bag, window. I blinked several times, then looked at him again.

"Are you all right?"

"What time is it?"

He looked at his watch. "Twenty after." I frowned and he said, "After twelve."

"I fell asleep," I said.

He sat down at the table. I stood there for a moment, then sat down opposite him. I bent my head to stretch the muscles in my neck and said into my lap, "The Mother thinks you want to control the visions. She said I should consult you if that's all I'm interested in."

"She told me."

I looked up. "Did she tell you about my potential?"

He cocked his head, considering. "She mentioned it. We had an interesting conversation."

The two of them had talked neurophysiology—it turned out that the Mother really did fancy herself a scientist. She used to work in a neurology lab in San Francisco and was, according to Houdini, pretty knowledgeable about brain chemistry. They discussed what happens in the brain when a vision comes on; they even argued about whether a vision could be induced or controlled.

I told Houdini that she had been rather dismissive of the scientific approach during our conversation. He just shrugged.

Annoyed, I said, "Then I suppose you told her about

chaos theory and strange attractors."

He was cool. "We had a very candid talk. As I said, she's been on the research end of it herself."

I looked beyond him, out at the maple. I wasn't sure why he was being so cagey, even more so than usual. But it didn't make sense to me, that she would criticize the scientific angle during our conversation, and then get really into the science thing with him, unless she was trying to feed each of us what she thought we wanted to hear. Or play us against each other.

"How was your tour with Tom?" Houdini said in a different tone.

I felt myself flush. I crossed my legs and clasped my hands across my knee. "You told each other everything, didn't you."

"I should have warned you." He hesitated. "I really didn't think they would try to bring you in so fast."

"What do you mean, bring me in?"

"It's part of their doctrine. They believe sex can be used as a vehicle for transcendence."

"The Mother said I had sex with Tom?"

"She didn't say that exactly."

"What did she say, exactly?"

He looked out the window. "That you and Tom had a spiritual connection."

I sat there, feeling a bit stunned. I couldn't picture the two of them, talking about neurophysiology one minute, and then the next, discussing my visionary-sexual connection with Tom. What was she up to? And had she really assumed that Tom and I would have sex once she declared that we were connected? Was she that confident of her powers?

The whole thing was too weird. What's more, I realized that Houdini was embarrassed. He was looking out the window, his lips pursed, his face stony. It made me like him a little more. I laughed suddenly and he glanced at me with surprise.

"We did," I said. "We definitely had a spiritual connection."

Houdini studied my face. The familiar impassivity returned, but it was different now, relieved. "Good," he said lightly. "So, that part of the plan has been accomplished. You've infiltrated New Light, and now I can find out how the visions work." When I laughed again he actually smiled at me.

We had lunch that afternoon with Alia and Glass and Crystal. Alia had to work her computer shift after lunch and told us she was leaving us in Crystal's care. Crystal asked if we wanted to go to the weavery to see the kinds of work the Visionaries did there. I liked the idea of that kind of work and asked if we could try weaving ourselves, too. She laughed and said that we were welcome to try anything we liked, though she warned that weaving wasn't easy. She turned to Houdini, who was just about to take a bite of a peanut butter sandwich. "But then, it's not about what's easy, is it?" she said to him, smiling. He held the sandwich arrested before him in mid-air, looking at the women as though he'd been caught doing something he shouldn't, but he didn't know what. Crystal, Glass, and Alia all looked at each other, then burst out laughing. "I'm sorry, Houdini," Alia said, covering her mouth with her hand. "You just don't look like someone who's comfortable working with his hands."

Houdini didn't know what to say. He took a bite of sandwich and when his eyes met mine, he dropped them to his plate. There was something wonderful about seeing him so easily embarrassed.

When we'd finished we left the dining hall and Alia headed across the fields. Glass linked arms with Crystal and me, and Houdini followed behind us silently. As we headed down The Briars toward the weavery, Crystal told us that Native American weavers took years to learn their craft, and that the truly great ones had been weaving all their lives. But we would see that it was satisfying just to work with the rattan. It felt alive in your hands, even when you were a beginner. The shoots of redbud and willow took longer to get used to, though they were especially prized because the Visionaries gathered them themselves. She squeezed my arm. "It's so nice to have someone to tell all this to. It's been so long since we've had visitors, people who are really interested in what we do." She glanced back at Houdini to include him, then abruptly faced forward again and said nothing more.

The Briars passed between the farmhouse and the bakery and wound its way through the trees southward, ending up at South Field where the weavery stood. When we emerged into the open I was surprised to see how large the building was, easily bigger than the barn. Like the barracks, it was a prefabricated structure of grey metal, though it was much taller than Kestrel and Sparrow and looked gaunt and soulless without the mural work. Adjacent to it stood a smaller grey shed used to store the cut lengths of willow, redbud, and rattan.

Crystal held open the aluminum door and we passed into a large interior lit by yellow lightbulbs hanging from orange and yellow extension cords. The high ceiling gave the weavery a feeling of spaciousness; wooden partitions about six feet high kept the weavers from feeling too exposed. Several Visionaries were in view, standing before wooden frames, stretching rattan in complicated weaves that would eventually become chair seats and bookcase backs. From the belly of the place we could hear voices, laughter and music. Three men and a woman working at a loom that was half-eclipsed by a partition looked up as we all bunched in the doorway. Then Ted appeared from around a corner, his tall form stopping immediately when he saw Crystal.

"I was hoping you guys would show up," he said, taking in the four of us and glancing around. "I wanted to let you know that if you have any questions I'm happy to answer them if I can."

"Alia's doing her computer shift," Crystal said. Ted nodded and seemed disappointed, but he also seemed to relax. "Can we see what you're working on?" she continued. She spoke to him in a gentle, concerned voice. "His work is so amazing," she explained to us. She turned back to Ted. "I told them they could try it out, but I also want them to see what years of dedication and focus can do. Ted puts his soul into everything he does," she continued. "He's one of our best teachers."

Ted turned red and the muscles in his jaw stood out. He shook his head. "Crystal's work is incredible. She's also very kind, as I'm sure you've already discovered." He smiled at her. "I'm lucky to work with someone as understanding and talented as she is."

There was a pause. "How much business do you do?" Houdini asked.

"Depends on the season," Crystal said briskly. "We get a lot of orders in the spring. Summertime, wicker." She shrugged. "Most people want furniture. But I guess our baskets are starting to get more popular. Yours especially," she said, looking back at Ted.

"My mom taught English on an Indian reservation. I learned when I was a kid," he explained. "I was so lucky. The people I met then—they understood. The good and the bad, you know what I mean?"

Ted led us back through the maze of partitions and looms and tables loaded with rattan. We paused at the thresholds of a few of the weavers' areas and he introduced us to other Visionaries who were also at work. We met Oak, a tall woodsy-looking guy who nodded gruffly at us and bent back over the frame; Kala, a woman in her thirties who was the community's historian; and Marshall, whom I recognized as one of the guitar players by the bonfire the night before. Then Crystal led us around another partition and into the workspace of a plump man who sat crosslegged on a woven mat beside a pile of thin branches. He had a long tangle of hair that fell in his face as he leaned forward and manipulated a willow shoot with his hands and teeth. A reedy whistling music stole softly from the cassetteplayer beside him. Jidd, as he called himself, grinned up at us, spitting out some flakes of bark and flipping his hair out of his face. He welcomed us.

"Did you just gather those?" Ted asked, gesturing toward the pile of shoots.

Jidd nodded, pleased. "Yesterday. I found a stand. It was just north of Sleepy, where we saw the doe with the two fawns?" He explained that Sleepy was their swimming hole.

Ted admired the reedy wood, and Jidd showed us how he split them with his teeth into separate threads.

"That's one more reason you want to protect the environment from contamination," Crystal said. "If your willow is poisoned, you're poisoned."

"We're lucky," Jidd agreed. "We haven't found any signs of dumping on our land. Around here there are stretches of forest that look okay, but then you find out there's a creosote factory down the road."

"I know a woman at Shining Water, a community up in Frederickstown," Glass said. "Lead mines. The whole place is polluted. But it brings in money so no one does anything."

"Sometimes intentional communities can have a positive effect on the townships they settle in. You know, we're a big voting block, and usually there are a lot of committed activists," Jidd told us.

"This is the problem," Ted said. "Sometimes people form communities to escape from the outside. But if you're too insular you can't do anything."

"I can't believe you guys still don't belong to the Federation," Glass said.

"We have to vote," Crystal said. "The Mother's not going to force anyone."

Ted explained that the Federation of Egalitarian Communities was a nonprofit collective entity made up of over 500 US communities engaged in collective living. I was surprised that there were so many, but Glass shook her head.

"Oh no, that's not many at all. There are lots more communities than that. Places like New Light, that don't want to commit themselves to the larger network." There was a silence. Glass looked from Ted to Crystal, then bent to admire the pattern of an almost-completed basket that sat on the floor beside Jidd.

Ted left us to go to the storage shed, and came back with two bundles of rattan. We all followed him to a far corner where he and Crystal worked. He put the rattan down on one of the tables, which also held several frames, some empty, a few half-started, as well as a number of baskets, various tools, and boxes containing beads and dyes and inks. He and Crystal showed us how to soften the stiff lengths in water. They encouraged us to flex and bend our rattan, to get the feel of the fiber's pith.

"It's all in the hands," Ted said, skillfully manipulating a slender flexible stick-like length. "Let your hands listen to it. Find out what it'll do." He trimmed a piece that had been dyed red, then bent it expertly and nosed it between two white strands that had been secured in a frame. "Frame work is easy, it's the baskets that are hard. You have to plan the shape and the different lengths you'll need." He leaned forward and pulled the rattan taut. Easy or not, I admired the strength and deft grace of his movements, as well as his hands' beautiful muscled lines beneath the callused skin.

"And if you want colored patterns you have to dye or stain the rattan ahead of time," Crystal said. "It takes a while to get the hang of the colors. I made a blackberry dye last year, and these are treated with a natural bleach." She held up lengths of vine-like fibers the color of pale ivory that would be incorporated into the half-finished basket on the table before her. "We try to avoid commercial dyes. Most people prefer the natural colors anyway."

Glass handled the rattan easily, and when I commented on this she explained that at East Wind they made hammocks and sandals. "That and the nut butters. Thank god that's enough to support us." She glanced at Crystal. "Sorry—it's just that I wouldn't want to do computer work."

Crystal smiled serenely. "But without it we couldn't have moved here."

I liked the springy feel of the rattan, and liked it even more when I glanced at Houdini, who stood looking down at a chair-seat frame, half-heartedly flexing a length of rattan in his hands. Probably the last thing he'd expected out of this trip was to find himself in one of the commune's warehouses, trying to learn the basics of basket weaving.

"Ah, there you are," a voice called. Mark was standing behind us, smiling, his hands on his hips, belly protruding proudly. Ted greeted him, while Crystal turned the half-woven basket over in her hands, studying the pattern without looking up.

"I found Alia in the computer center. Where are our guests, I said. She said she passed you on to Crystal. I had to track you down."

"We've been learning to listen to our hands," Glass said, holding up a braided strand of red, dusky grey, and ivory rattan.

Mark smiled at Glass, taking the braid from her and wrapping it round her wrist. "I went to Monica. I figured she'd know exactly where you were." He laughed. "I noticed Bert and John and Rennie quit early today."

Ted frowned at the older man, who seemed to think it funny that three Visionaries would leave the weavery rather than face being introduced to us. "You're a detective, Mark," he said.

"Don't get mad at me," Mark said. "I was the one who predicted this. I've been trying to do something about it." He turned to Houdini. "You don't know it but all eyes are on you." He glanced at me and gave me a knowing smile.

"Of course you're special," he added, turning to Glass. "You have honorary Visionary status. No one really minds you being here. Well, almost no one."

"You're over-dramatizing," Crystal said sharply.

"Am I?" Mark said, just as sharply. "Everyone's either excited or terrified. It's the best thing that's happened to us in months. We need to be shaken up. We're too isolated. You guys force us to re-examine our lives." He laughed. "Not that everyone likes that."

"Mark's our gadfly," Ted said.

"Like Socrates," Mark grinned.

"Socrates? You?" Crystal said.

I had a teacher at Charondon who dressed up like Socrates and employed the socratic method throughout the entire month we spent on the Greeks. This and the fact that he was unmarried sparked the obvious jokes among the students. "Socrates was put to death for corrupting the children of Athens," I said.

Everyone looked at me.

"High school. Athens in the 5th Century," I explained
with a shrug. "They didn't want to kill him, they just wanted
him to leave. They were sick of him. He chose to drink the
hemlock. He was making a point." There was a moment of
silence during which, I suppose, everyone considered drinking hemlock to make a point.

"Okay, not Socrates," Mark said.

That night we sat around the fire again. Our group was larger
than the night before, even though the Mother didn't join us
this time. Aside from Houdini and myself, there was Glass
and Alia and Crystal and Tom, Jidd from the weaving shed
and a woman beside him named Mallow, whose long plaits
of hair brushed the ground as she sat. Beside Glass sat
Tianne, the serene composure of her manner inspiring even
Mark, who sat on the other side of her, to make an effort to
behave himself, though it was clear he wanted more attention from her than he could get.

There were too many of us to sit in a complete circle,
sandwiched as we were in between a group of singers to our
left and a straggle of ghost-storytellers who lolled on the
grass and commanded most of the fire's perimeter. I ended
up far away from the center of heat, talking with Glass,
Tianne, Mark and Tom, while Houdini, who was closest to
the fire, sat with Alia, Crystal, Jidd and Mallow. Crystal and
Houdini had gotten into an animated discussion and I was
trying to hear what they were saying, but it was impossible
because the guitarist near me was too enthusiastic. So I
turned my attention back to Mark, who had broken into a
loud voice full of conviction as he declaimed how he knew
someone was a potential Visionary.

Mark explained that he felt a kind of pressure forming around him when he saw someone who was being called.
Something in the atmosphere around him changed, and he

knew he had to go to the Potential and tell them what he saw. There was always a kind of tension at these moments, because though he was impelled to go to them, tell them what he'd seen, they were often resistant. He said that this was normal when someone first felt themselves called. A part of them recognized the call, but they would resist the feeling because they were afraid. They didn't know what was happening to them. It was his job to confront them with the truth, to challenge them to hear him.

Tianne, beside him, shook her head. Firelight gleamed on her dark skin. "It's true that people resist, but you can't force them either. If the person isn't ready to admit they're being called, there's nothing you can do." She turned to me. "Mark was my first contact with New Light. We were still in San Francisco then. We met in a bar. A few days later I came to the community's center, but I decided it wasn't for me. Then they moved here."

"I came back for her," Mark said, adjusting his belly. He smiled at Tianne. "Remember? You told me to get a life."

She shook her head. "I didn't move here for another five months. But in the meantime The Mother and I were emailing. I came when I was ready."

Glass had been following their exchange intently. "But Alia knew immediately that she was called." She looked from Tianne to Mark. "She didn't have any doubts."

"Alia was right there from the start," Mark nodded. "She was ready to come. But some people aren't. Some people are afraid to make the break."

"I wasn't *afraid*, Mark," Tianne said. "It's a matter of timing," she said to Glass. "When the time was right I came."

"But if I hadn't come after you? If I hadn't made you face the challenge of a whole new way of life? You'd still be in California."

"You don't know that."

Glass was frowning. Tom, who had had his flute to his lips and was puffing out faint wisps of sound, put it down and said reassuringly, "Different people have different approaches, Glass. Recruiting is a tricky business—one reason we don't do it much. In the end it's a matter of belief. You have to trust you know what's right."

In the pause that followed I asked Mark how he ended up at New Light. He smiled and said off-handedly, leaning away from me out of the circle: "It would take too long to tell. Mary!"

Half in shadow, Ted and the blond Mary stood engrossed in conversation by the staircase that led up to the kitchen door. Mary glanced distractedly toward us when Mark called her, then turned back to Ted. Tonight she wasn't in control of the situation. She and Ted continued to talk, and after a moment she shook her head angrily. Ted said something else, the muscles in his jaw clenching, and abruptly Mary turned and stalked off into the night. Ted stood looking after her, his face pained.

Crystal got up and went over to him. She put her hand on his arm and spoke earnestly. This time it was Ted who shook his head, but in the end it seemed that Crystal won out. They approached the fire. Crystal continued to talk to him urgently, and as he listened to her and allowed her to lead him forward, Ted's eyes were fixed on Alia. Alia met his eyes, then dropped her gaze to her lap. She looked miserable.

"I knew this would happen," Mark said to Tom. "Poor Mary."

Tom glanced at Mark, then raised his flute to his lips again. Tianne and Glass exchanged looks. It was clear that whatever Mary was angry about, it had to do with Alia. From what I could tell, Alia herself had made an effort to keep away from them, though Mary seemed to seek her out. At any rate, at this point it was obvious that Ted and Alia wanted only to talk to each other.

Crystal led Ted toward the space where she'd been sitting, between Alia and Houdini. She sat him down, exchanged glances with Jidd and Mallow, then came over to sit by Tianne and Glass and me. Immediately Jidd and Mallow got to their feet, said goodnight to everyone, and headed off into the dark. This left Ted and Alia facing each other, with Houdini making the third point in the triangle. Houdini looked from one to the other.

There was an awkward pause. Ted and Alia glanced at each other, then looked away again. With forced cheerfulness Alia asked Houdini how he had liked the weavery.

I stood up. "Come on, Houdini, I'm exhausted," I said.

Houdini looked up at me, then at Alia and Ted. After a measured interval he got to his feet. "I suppose we've had a full day."

I ignored him and told everyone goodnight.

It was about eleven. We followed the Barn path back to the barracks, crickets and peepers filling the silence underneath our footsteps. The air smelled of grass, damp earth, and an occasional sweeter floral scent that wafted briefly past. Scattered along the path were pockets of chill air.

Just beyond the second greenhouse Houdini stopped. He gestured upward, losing the beam of the flashlight in the sky.

"Look at it," he said. He clicked off the light. The fire was a faint glow behind us. I couldn't see his face. Above, stars crowded the sky.

We looked up in silence. Before we came to New Light I'd forgotten you could see so many stars in the country. I was impressed that Houdini would take the time to look at the night sky. I hadn't expected that of him.

"It's so dark," I said.

He didn't reply. I could hear him breathe; I felt the nearness of his body. Around us the crickets trilled. A long moment passed and then, like the touch of a hand on my face, through the darkness I could feel him look at me.

fifteen

Waking at New Light was not like waking anywhere else.
Each morning I opened my eyes just as it was getting light,
luxuriously turning on my back to watch the tree outside
assemble itself. Then slowly I'd drift into unconsciousness
again. When I awoke the second time I felt aglow with the
clarity and lightness of springtime. It was so pleasurable, so
delicate; just remembering it makes me want to go back
there, to wake up into that springtime once more.

Houdini and I ambled into the farmhouse Wednesday morning after a meditative walk. For once I was glad of
the routine of silence. The farm seemed strangely quiet, and
when we got to the kitchen we found it empty for the first
time since we'd been at New Light. We passed through and
pushed open the swinging doors that led to the dining hall,
and looked upon rows of empty tables and chairs, appearing
oddly tentative in the slanting early light. The whole place
was empty. I joked that maybe they'd gone out for pancakes,
and imagined the Visionaries, wearing their colorful robes,
filling the booths and tables of an IHOP in a take-over that
would make headlines in some cow-town local.

The door off the mural hallway opened. Monica,
wearing overalls, a flowered shirt and a grim expression,
entered. She had come to tell us that there was an emergency
council meeting and that no one would be available to act as
escorts for the next few hours. She turned to Houdini. Hadn't
he said the day before that he was interested in the towns and
county surrounding New Light? Monica suggested that we
take a drive, familiarize ourselves with the area. The nearest
town, Elkhead, was about eight miles away.

Houdini said that this was exactly what he'd wanted

to do, and asked how long the council would be in session. Monica gave a stony shrug. She added coldly that we could help ourselves to fruit and bread, then folded her arms across her chest and waited for us to go. We went. But in the end she relented. As we passed through the swinging doors she said that the Mother would see us after lunch. The echoing emptiness of the dining hall broke up the tightness in her voice, exposing how frightened she was.

Bewildered, Houdini and I went back to Sparrow to get the car keys, and on our return, walked by the barn for the third time that morning. Monica stood in front of the closed double doors, waiting for us to pass. She was still standing there as we drove away.

It wasn't yet nine as we headed down the long dirt road toward civilization. Houdini spread the map in his lap and pointed to a green spot that he said was the farm. He suggested that we head west and do a wide circuit of McDonald County to get the lay of the land. We could check out Elkhead on our return loop. I gave him a sidelong glance. He seemed focused only on the logistics of our excursion. He didn't even comment on the fact that the Visionaries had kicked us out.

We passed through a tunnel of green trees, then hit pavement. We were out. The road unwound through the green light of forest, whose soothing coolness was interrupted occasionally by the shock of sunlight on pasture. The trees and fields here looked no different from those belonging to New Light, and yet they were different, in some ineffable way.

It was strange, that drive. We followed twisting roads over hills, through stands of conifers and hardwoods, down into the fertile valleys of quick streams. We passed lone houses standing forlornly at the edge of the pavement. Then a sudden steep rise would present a view of ranging forest, or a breathtaking sweep of land. It was lonely, beautiful country.

The pine trees rose up, and the land rose up, and I took the curves fast so that butterflies fluttered inside us for a moment, before they were squeezed in the fist of gravity again. Mostly we were silent. We didn't speculate about what had happened, overnight, to disrupt the community. We simply let the land flow past us. After a while there was something companionable about our silence.

We drove west, paralleling the county line, until we reached the border between Missouri and Oklahoma. Then we headed south, and about ten miles from the border with Arkansas picked up Route 90, and traveled east again. We passed through forlorn little towns with names like Ginger Blue, Noel, and Jane, lonely little places that hardly felt lived in.

It was several hours before we ended up in Elkhead, the town eight miles south of New Light. The town was one of McDonald County's metropolitan centers, population 512. We passed a scattering of houses along the county road, then a small strip of stores in the town's center. I pulled up in front of The American, a grocery store with tar paper on the front. Next door stood a barber shop, and farther on a hardware store-cum-bait-and-tackle, gas station, and, across the street, Freda's Diner. The town, constructed when the twentieth century was still young, seemed to have faded over time, avoiding change by being banished to the collective uncon-scious of its citizens. But over time, Elkhead's storefronts, sidewalks, and streetlights began to blur. The townsfolk got their haircuts and ate their chicken-fried steaks, while the Platonic essence that was Elkhead wavered and thinned.

A church on the corner advertised a barbecue. There was a fun-fair coming in July to a place called Low Bluffs. A man and a woman sitting in lawn chairs on the sidewalk stared at us.

Outside The American was a pay phone. I called Boris and got his machine. I said that we had arrived safely Monday afternoon, had some interesting conversations with people yesterday, but that this morning something strange had happened. I didn't know what was going on yet, but we were fine. I would call him again soon.

Inside, I found Houdini standing in front of the store's tiny dairy case. He held a bottle of water, a bag of bruised apples, some Sunshine crackers. He picked up a block of mild cheddar with something sticky on the wrapper and handed it to me. "We might as well have lunch," he said. On the way up to the check-out I grabbed Sun Maids, Chips Ahoy, and a long tube of slim jim. We set our pile on the counter. A man in suspenders and a button-up white shirt straining at the belly looked us up and down.

"Goin' on a picnic," the man said. His face wore no expression, as though the heaviness of his cheeks weighed down his mouth.

"That's right," Houdini said, smiling. "Beautiful countryside you've got here."

"Yeah," the man said non-commitally. "You oughtta be careful. People round here don't like folks parkin' themselves on private property."

"We'll be careful," Houdini said in a respectful voice. "God given right to protect your land."

"Mmmhmm," said the man, picking up the apples and turning them over in his hands. "You all from that commune farm?"

"Pleasant View?" Houdini asked brightly. "It's what brought us down here, but no, we're not from there."

"You have friends there?"

Houdini laughed as though this were unthinkable. "No, no." He flexed himself against the counter and lowered his voice. "We're trying to find out what's going on there. I've been sent to investigate."

The man eyed Houdini dispassionately; I, on the other hand, could barely conceal my surprise at this performance. But the man seemed to warm to Houdini. "They've got some different ideas."

Houdini looked grave. "You could call it that. I have to admit I'm concerned. People don't often consider the effects an experimental community can have on the local culture."

The man folded his arms across his chest. "You got that right. Nobody came and asked us what we thought."

A heavy woman who had been sitting out of view behind the counter now heaved to her feet. "You know what they're up to?" she said excitedly, shuffling toward us. "You say you're investigators? Are y'all from the government?"

"Is there a problem?" Houdini asked in a concerned voice.

"You know what they are, Frank," the woman said to the man as though he'd tried to silence her. "He won't say it, but we all know." The corners of Frank's mouth turned down stoically and she continued. "They're devil worshippers. They have orgies, they dance around bonfires in the night and call the spirits to them. The kids spied on them. We don't let them go no more, after what they saw. So a few of our men, you know, they went down to investigate. They got some kind of laboratory where they make their potions and what all."

Frank looked at us tight-lipped, severe. "We stay out of their way, and they don't come here. They know how we feel. There's been a skirmish or two, and they called the sheriff down. Got an injunction."

"It's not right, them comin' here. This is our home, they walk in like they own the place."

"They own that farm, Helen."

"I don't care if they do," Helen said furiously. "Can't y'all arrest them?"

"I'm afraid your husband's right," Houdini said. "There's nothing the law can do."

The woman turned away, muttering. Her husband rang up our purchases in silence. As we gathered up the bags he said, "You see, we're a community here. Folks are afraid these people will change things. If you turn up anything that could help us, we'd sure appreciate it."

Houdini nodded. I smiled weakly as I picked up a bag. Outside we didn't look at each other until we'd stowed the groceries and climbed back in the car.

"'They own that farm, Helen'," Houdini said, with what was almost a smile.

We left Elkhead's strip and drove on through heavily forested land. Neither of us spoke. Hot sun beat in through the windshield; air rushed through the car. We each stared straight ahead of us. I was still trying to reconcile the man I'd glimpsed in the grocery store with the Houdini I knew. I suppose he was adding the information he'd gathered there to everything else he'd discovered about New Light. Yet after our tour through McDonald County and our conversation with the proprietors of the American, New Light seemed very far away. I found myself wondering again what Houdini was doing down there in southern Missouri, and what I was doing there with him. The whole trip suddenly seemed fake, as fake as his impersonation of a federal investigator. It was all a put-on, a joke, things we'd invented on a long car trip to while away the time. A passing fantasy that would, eventually, grow boring.

When it did we'd lapse into silence again, conversation beaten down by the endless forest, all that green becoming more and more monotonous. We'd begin to feel irritable, hemmed in by trees and useless sunlit fields that cradled ponds between reed-lipped banks. Then we'd see a notice of land for sale. We'd talk about buying it to build a summer place. Suddenly Houdini would brake (he'd be driving), and say that the investment could pay for itself if we developed the lot, and built, say, a water-slide, or a miniature-golf course. We'd talk about construction, loans, taxes, then we'd have sex right there in the car. Later on that night would come the fight in the restaurant, him telling me to suck his dick, me telling him to suck his own dick, and the hours of silence on the ride home.

We had our picnic in the car and headed back to New Light. It was about three when we pulled into the lot. Monica was waiting on the porch again. "How does she know?" I murmured, as we followed the path across the small field to the house. Houdini looked back at me.

"The Mother is waiting," Monica said in a terse voice, passing quickly into the house.

There was no bother with ceremony or atmosphere for this interview. As soon as we entered the Mother turned away from the window, her face haggard and urgent. "Thank you, Monica," she said, and Monica hastily withdrew. The Mother gestured us toward the cluster of armchairs. She followed us over, and rather than taking the high wicker throne she seated herself with us, in a third velvet chair that had appeared.

"You're wondering why we asked you to leave this morning," the Mother said. She rubbed one clenched hand along the velvet nap of the armrest. "You think no doubt that it was secretive of us. An act of bad faith."

Houdini and I exchanged glances. The Mother dropped her hands into her lap and enveloped them in the folds of her white robe.

"Something happened last night. I'm—we're all at a loss to explain it. Nonetheless, it happened. We must go forward. We must deal with it." She spoke these words to herself, not us, her gaze getting lost for a moment in the middle distance.

With a shake of the head she brought herself back.

"Glass left in the middle of the night." She raised one hand to forestall questions. "She left because...she had to. So she said. Something happened; she wouldn't say what. It upset her. All we know is that she and Mark had sex."

"Are you saying Mark raped her?" I managed, shocked.

The Mother's expression was pale and fierce. "She *wouldn't say*. You must understand—she refused to tell us what happened."

"But why would she leave unless Mark—"

"Something happened to upset her," Houdini interrupted, looking at the Mother. "You're saying that's all you know." The Mother nodded and he looked at me.

"You think she got lost in the woods?" I said sarcastically.

"She called some friends at East Wind," the Mother said. "She woke Alia to say goodbye. That's when she said they'd had sex. Alia was distraught. Ted came to wake me."

"So Alia and Ted spent the night together," I said, putting it all together. "Which left Glass alone. Where was she supposed to sleep?"

"Alia had given her the key to a room in Sparrow. She didn't use it. She and Mark were...talking...by the fire. No one noticed anything out of the ordinary. Then Glass went back with him to his room." The Mother's face was expressionless.

"He coerced her?" I said.

"She wouldn't say," the Mother repeated wearily.

"So you held the meeting in the barn to decide what to do," Houdini prompted.

"Yes. We had to decide on a course of action. Mark denies having done anything wrong." The Mother smoothed the folds of her robe. Her tone became more reserved. "Nothing like this has ever happened. We were all at a loss."

This I found hard to swallow. "Your belief system is based on sex. You tried to set me up with Tom. You're telling me you've never had misunderstandings?"

The Mother drew herself up. "Our belief system is *not* based on sex. The vision journey is an important ritual for us. But it's voluntary. What Mark did has nothing to do with the community's beliefs."

"But you knew that Mark was predatory. It was obvious. I saw him yesterday all over Glass, telling her she was an honorary Visionary. Last night he went on about how he had to challenge people who were too afraid to answer the visionary call."

The Mother tossed her head. "So you say now. Were you disturbed by his attentions to her yesterday?" She gazed at me narrowly, then added: "Anyway, what he said was true. Think of your own resistance."

"Is sex part of the recruitment strategy?" Houdini asked quietly.

She hesitated slightly. "Only if both parties are willing." She turned to me again. "Did you feel *any* coercion from Tom? Was it in *any* way a violation?"

I gazed over her head at the throne that rose up behind her. I had to admit that it wasn't.

She nodded. "Of course not. The vision journey is sacred to us. It cannot be coerced. What Mark did—*whatever* he did—has nothing to do with our rituals." She gazed at me without moving, her face severe, unshakable in her convictions.

Houdini folded his arms. "What happens now?"

She turned to him. "Mark has been sentenced. He will be shunned by the whole community until he recognizes what he's done. At this point he refuses to admit his guilt. He claims Glass left without making any accusations because she wanted to be with him at the time, and only afterward changed her mind."

"And what about Glass?" I said bitterly.

The Mother looked at me. She gave a cool shrug. "What can I do? She left. She's not a member of this community. She's free to do as she pleases."

On our way out we passed through the kitchen. Members preparing the evening meal glanced up at us, then dropped their eyes. The only one among them that I knew was Mallow, Jidd's friend, but she was grinding pepper into an enormous cauldron of soup with the utmost care, as though it demanded all her concentration. When we got outside I told Houdini I wanted to find Alia, but just then someone hailed us from the direction of the bakery. Tom appeared between the trees.

He came toward us quickly and asked if we'd talked with the Mother. I said we had, and that we were going to look for Alia.

Tom frowned. "Didn't The Mother tell you? She won't talk to you. She's gone into retreat. She's formally withdrawn from all social interaction."

He explained that the Visionaries had instituted this practice of retreat so that people could create space for themselves during times when they felt overwhelmed by the constant proximity of other people. When one Visionary declared he or she was in retreat, no one could take offense when this person didn't speak to anyone. It seemed a smart policy, since the nature of life on the commune was so intensely social. But when Alia had announced at the meeting that morning that she was withdrawing, the Mother tried to talk her out of it. She said the Visionaries should reaffirm the connections of community at this time. Alia was too upset to listen. She said she needed to be alone.

"She feels guilty," Tom said. "She blames herself for being selfish and going off with Ted, leaving Glass by herself. Ted feels terrible too, but of course Alia won't talk to him either."

"What about Mark?" I demanded. "Why isn't anybody doing anything about him?"

Tom seemed surprised. "We are doing something. We're shunning him."

I was disappointed and angry. "That's punishment?"

Tom glanced at Houdini, then put a gentle hand on my arm. "We don't know what he did, Beth. Only he knows. The shunning will force him to confront himself eventually."

I couldn't be mad at Tom. I knew he cared. And he believed that they were being fair. But the whole thing upset me.

sixteen

Houdini and I sat by ourselves in the dining hall that night. The room was less than half-full; people ate their meals quickly and left. It seemed that no one felt like being social.

I kept thinking of Glass, calling her friends at East Wind in the middle of the night, then having to wait for them to drive the hundred plus miles to pick her up. Had she woken Alia so that she wouldn't have to wait alone? Or did she sit there by herself, the smell of Mark's sweat on her skin ensuring that she wouldn't forget even for a moment what happened?

But what did happen? No one knew. I remembered what Tom said. And really, how could you punish Mark, especially when there was no one to accuse him.

As Houdini and I walked back to Sparrow after dinner—it had to be close to nine o'clock—we could see the lights of other walkers bobbing about, some continuing on ahead of us toward the barracks, others branching off to take different paths. Seeing those lights made me lonely. Everyone is isolated now, just like Alia, I thought. It was infectious too. Houdini and I didn't say a word that whole walk back to Sparrow.

Back in my room I sat at the table and tried to write in my journal, but I had trouble concentrating. My attention kept wandering toward the open window, where the curtains shivered slightly and crickets chorused loudly through the windowscreen. Finally I turned off the table lamp and sat in the darkness, looking out. The moon had risen and the faint glow it cast lit up the field outside.

There was a soft knock at the door.

Houdini stood in the hall. "I thought maybe you'd

gone to sleep," he said. He was framed by the fluorescent light behind him, bleeding palely from the doorway to his room.

"I was enjoying the moonlight," I said, not moving from my seat. "What time is it?"

"About ten."

He shut the door behind him and joined me at the table.

"How are you holding up?" he said after a pause. I could just make out his features in the moonlight.

"She left in the middle of the night. We didn't even get to say goodbye."

"I know. I find it disturbing too." It was odd; there in the dark I could tell that he meant it.

"I just assumed you were in research mode. It didn't seem to matter to you."

"You and I express these things differently."

"We experience them differently, too," I said.

"Isn't that inevitable?"

Of course, I thought. Inevitable. It's all inevitable.

"I guess I'm just mad still," I said finally, trying to be fair. "Especially at the Mother. Tom said that what happened with Glass and Mark is everyone's responsibility now, and I can understand that. But the Mother refuses to admit there might be a fundamental problem here."

Outside, a lone firefly blinked three times. Houdini said, as though it were simple, "The vision journey is important to their belief."

"I *know*," I said, thinking of that kiss with Tom in the barn. Then I stopped, struck by how little I knew of Houdini's prior involvement with this community, or others like it. I imagined him sitting on the floor as some beautiful young Visionary drew light fingers across his palm, then leaned in for a kiss that would make them both tremble. Around them the painted figures held their breaths. I blurted out, "Have you ever—?"

"No." He didn't laugh.

By not looking at him directly I could make out his features, in the same way that you can see stars better when you don't look at them straight on. Something to do with peripheral vision and the way we see light in the dark. He had a hawk-like profile, the sharp nose and brow gleaming faintly in the moonlight. The darkness made it easier, I realized. Encouraged, I asked:

"How far would you go—you know, to learn about the visions and all of that?"

"What do you mean, how far?"

"I don't know. Do you want to have a vision? Would you be willing to join them, temporarily I mean, to find out what they believe?"

"You're thinking of what Sarah said about being a participant observer?"

"You said it's better not to remain detached. It seems kind of hard to know what the visions are like if you never have one."

There was a pause. After a moment he turned his face away from the window, toward me, and what little I could see of his features before was now lost to darkness. When he didn't answer I gave a little laugh. "I guess you said you weren't susceptible."

"No," he said quietly. "Unfortunately I'm not."

His answer caught me off guard. I didn't know what to say, his voice was so naked, and so this time I was the one who broke off the moment when I turned to the window. Outside the field had grown more luminous. I could see the moon now through the branches of the maple. The grass glowed with a ghostly silver sheen that I supposed was mist. Then I blinked. Something flickered in the darkness beyond the barracks field. In the distance, partially obscured by the trees, lights were moving in what looked like a procession.

"What is that?" I said, leaning closer to the screen.

"What?" Houdini leaned forward too. Heads almost touching, we both looked out.

About half a mile to the west of where we were, another path led up to the ridge from the parking lot, running parallel with the barracks' path. The raised moving lights flickered in the wind along this route, then climbed up the steep hill. It was a spooky torchlit march. The flames stretched into long thin streaks, almost disappearing, then resolved again into rounder brightness.

"What are they doing?" I whispered.

We watched the line of torches in silence. Why were they heading into the woods at this hour? I remembered what the Elkhead couple had said about the nighttime rituals.

"Do you think it has anything to do with Mark?" I whispered again.

Beside me Houdini shook his head. But I couldn't just sit there. I slid my chair back and grabbed my sneakers from underneath the table. I pulled them on and started lacing them up.

"What are you doing?" Houdini said.

"Monica said the curfew was at midnight. It's not even eleven yet." I stood, retrieving my flashlight from the bed and checking its light. My heart was pounding. "You don't have to come."

Outside the field glowed eerily, though underneath the trees it was still quite dark. The procession of torches that had passed along the western path had climbed the hill and disappeared. I shone the flashlight along the barracks' path, toward where it climbed the ridge. "They'll see us," Houdini hissed at me. I clicked off the light. "We'll be able to see them from the top of the ridge," he said.

I started forward, along the path that headed up toward the ridge. My jeans were soon soaked. Each time we came out from under the cover of trees I felt strangely naked, there in the moonlit darkness.

We had only climbed halfway up the hill when a man's voice called out above us. I gasped and Houdini put his hand on my shoulder.

"Who's there?" the voice called.

"Ted?" I said.

There was a pause. Then Ted's voice said, "Oh. Hey, Beth." I could feel him hesitate. "You guys are supposed to be in your rooms."

There was a strange feeling of suspension in the silence that followed his voice. Then the crickets started again. I said, "But we saw lights." Houdini squeezed my elbow in support or protest.

In the dark Ted hesitated again.

"You want us to take another drive around the county?" I was surprised at how bitter my voice sounded.

A light bloomed up the hill from us, and Ted was the shadow that hugged it as it descended. When he reached us he seemed uneasy.

"Are you standing guard?" Houdini asked.

"Mark's been a little upset. The Mother didn't want him disrupting the ceremony."

"Us too?" I asked. Ted didn't answer.

"Which ceremony?" Houdini asked.

In the diffused light from the flashlight's beam I could see Ted chew his lip uncertainly. He looked around, as though someone might be there in the darkness, watching. "It's the fire ceremony. It's—for purification."

I glanced toward Houdini but he remained silent. I

said, "I'm not trying to break the rules, Ted. I just want to understand. I'm—we're both as upset as the rest of you by what happened."

Ted considered this in silence, then abruptly turned. "Come on," he said over his shoulder. He headed up the ridge.

When we reached the top the path leveled off and we walked through tall grass along the ridge's edge. The trees thinned out and we could look out over the farm spread below us in moonlight and shadow. It was unrecognizable: greenhouses shining like ghost palaces, the dark earth giving birth to lurking shadow creatures.

The ground along the ridgetop was uneven; at one point we crossed a little wooden bridge over a stream. As we came to the head of the western path we saw another dark figure also standing guard. It was Oak. He and Ted held a brief exchange, then the two of them turned their backs on the farm and led us forward, following the route of the procession. Here the western path was nothing but a faint trail through the grass. It continued through a fringe of trees into a large cleared space about the size of a baseball field. The grass had been mowed earlier in the spring but had since grown up again. It was now about two feet high.

As we approached we could see the glow of the fire, and when we emerged from the brake of trees we saw the Visionaries as well. They were seated in a series of concentric circles on mats around the blaze. Torches had been stuck in the earth at intervals along the circle's perimeter. Ted shone the powerful beam of his flashlight toward the gathering and people turned. The Mother got to her feet. She left the center of the circle to stand between us and the seated Visionaries.

The grass was silvery, and the wide expanse of field, with the fire burning at the center, was framed by silent trees. Shadows seemed to flicker and shift in the periphery, but when you looked there was nothing.

The Mother watched us, head back, shoulders squared, as we approached the circle's perimeter. Her gold halter sparkled in the firelight. All eyes were on us.

"Beth. Houdini." She didn't sound pleased.

"They were on the barracks path. I didn't know what to do with them," Ted said.

The Mother nodded. To us she asked, "Why have you come?"

I looked at Houdini. He met my eyes, then glanced at the rows of watching faces lit by firelight. It was eerie to stand there before them, people we'd seen eating lunch, doing chores, laughing and singing together, now gazing up at us, many of them with antagonistic expressions. I saw Alia on the outermost ring sitting with eyes lowered, Tianne nearer by, easily identified among the jean-clad people by her yellow-and-orange kaftan. If the Mother threatened us, would they come to our defense?

Houdini looked back at the Mother and cleared his throat.

"It was me," I said, before he could speak. "It was my idea. I saw the torches. I wanted to find out what was going on."

The Mother tilted her head and gave an inquiring half nod.

"I was upset about Glass. I was...curious. I wanted to know. I wanted to find out what was going on."

"I take responsibility," Houdini said. "Beth is upset because of what happened with Mark. She feels close to Glass."

The Mother folded her arms and gave him a cold look. "How can you take responsibility for how Beth feels? Isn't that rather presumptuous?"

Surprised, Houdini shut his mouth.

"Beth's presence here means that she's been called," the Mother said, turning to the seated Visionaries. "She was called down to New Light, not once but twice, and then she was called from her room to the fire circle. To us, seated here in the darkness." She faced us again. "You're here because you need us, Beth. Just as we need you. It's as simple as that."

There were murmurs from the Visionaries in the circle, while the Mother studied me. After a moment she spread her arms wide. The Visionaries fell silent.

"We assembled tonight for the purification ceremony. A terrible deed has shaken our faith as a community. We came together to renew that faith." She lifted her arms straight over her head, reaching up to the sky as though in supplication or demand. There was something adamant about the gesture.

She let her arms fall to her sides. "Now, instead, from out of the darkness we are joined by the strangers who have walked among us for two days."

She turned her eagle gaze on me again.

"It is not the purification ritual that we must perform tonight. We are in the presence of something new. We are being called."

The murmurs of the Visionaries were louder this time. The Mother gestured for us to seat ourselves on the few empty mats that waited on the outside edge of the circle.

"Tonight your role here will be revealed," she said. "But to understand that role, you must first understand what we're doing here, all of us Visionaries, seated before the fire with our backs to the darkness. More than that—you must understand why all of us came to New Light."

She paused, looking around at her audience. Then she began to walk around the circle, speaking in a singsong voice over the heads of her followers. Those with their backs to her looked straight ahead, into the flames. Those on the opposite side of the fire watched her with rapt faces.

She intoned:

"We find ourselves in the middle of life. Surrounded by people we can only know in passing. We are all caught up in the struggle. Trying to survive."

She moved in rhythm with her speech. From time to time she paused to look down at someone, or out at the darkness, then resumed the pacing, the rhythmic chant.

"Darwin was a seer as well. He spent the last twenty years of his life in bed. He was doing penance, though he remained an apostate to the last. His inner self rebelled against the vision of the world he had imagined into being. But he had to give us this vision. If not him, then Wallace, who had come up with the theory of evolution independently. It was time; the vision was waiting to be presented to humanity."

On the far side of the circle she stopped, allowing her gaze to sweep over us all.

"It was time for us to see our burden, to face our perpetual struggle against one another. To understand that we weep for our world and then turn around and do our neighbor harm. That is our world. We are weeping for ourselves."

She began to walk again, in her white robe becoming the moon swinging coolly around the earth, the earth turning hot cheeks away from the sun.

"But we have no choice. We're trapped. We must live, and as a result, others cannot. This is the vision that Darwin the seer, the tormented prophet, revealed to us. This is the image of ourselves that drives us to despair, even when we deny it, even when we aren't aware that it is always before our eyes. It haunts our dreams at midnight; it confronts us starkly in the harshest light of day. We spend our lives trying to banish it to the shadows."

I felt stealing over me a terrible sadness. It seemed to emanate from her; I watched her turn sorrowing eyes from her people to the dark night that surrounded us. When she fell silent, the world of shadows beyond the fire circle ached back at us her lament. Hers was a burden that belonged to all of us. It was a terrible one, yet she was willing to shoulder it alone. I was grateful to her, and at the same time longed to roll in the grass until the sadness was smothered.

She spread her arms.

"The ritual of the fire circle forces us to confront these facts of our own nature. We call to the dark parts of ourselves to come forth so that we can see them. To do so is to suffer. But no engagement of the visionary life can deny these elements. To do so would lead to madness."

She let the word linger, then gave the slightest shake of her head. She straightened. Her face in the firelight flickered with hope.

"At New Light we own the dark part of the self, in order to discover the light. We looked into that darkness today, with Mark. It is necessary that we face it down. With Darwin we embrace science's revelation of our true natures, but unlike him we do not give way to despair. Science can take us beyond that." She laughed suddenly, her voice suddenly light. "But to do so, it must turn to the ancient wisdom that for so many years it has tried to destroy."

Her voice became matter-of-fact again as she explained it to us. "The eastern mystic undergoes a rigorous training of attention. So much so, that he is actually able to control his own brain, to selectively change its electrical and chemical activity. Some claim that the devotee of meditation can sustain an inward focus that, over time, actually changes the brain's structure. You see? They invent themselves. They are at once the products of evolutionary process, and conscious shapers of that process."

On her face was an expression of quiet joy. She said softly: "This is the doorway. We have found it."

She was irresistible. I looked at her and loved her.

Because of us, because of me, the Mother did not hold the fire ceremony that night. She chose instead to honor the fact that Houdini and I came forth from the darkness to appear before them. That we gave ourselves up to them.

Actually I can't speak for Houdini. I don't know if he gave himself up to her or not. But I know that I did. How else can I describe what happened as I listened to the Mother's speech? It was the same feeling I'd had during our first meeting, when I found myself drifting into that memory of a family vacation on Long Island Sound. The Mother talked about Darwin, our competitiveness as a species, our attempts to deny it, and I found myself captivated. I was startled out of that mesmerized state only at the end, when the Mother announced that we'd found the doorway, then lapsed into silence. Those of us listening seemed to let out a collective sigh, expressing satisfaction, a sense of peacefulness. I too sighed, feeling content and relaxed, and then I turned, out of reflex, to Houdini.

His expression was different from everyone else's. His eyes were narrowed with concentration, not relaxation; he looked like a man who was trying to solve differential equations in his head. It startled me out of the moment. Self-consciousness came flooding back—all of a sudden I woke up to what was happening. I had been sucked in once again. I was pissed.

I think now that the anger was actually resentment—I regretted losing that brief peace I'd experienced while the Mother spoke. I felt cheated. Of course I blamed it on her. I sat there feeling outraged that I'd been taken in by more of her cant. I was as malleable as the Visionaries, sitting there under the phosphorescent light of the fungus moon. Did they really think that the future of human existence was going to be revealed to a bunch of yahoos sitting around a campfire in the rural Ozarks?

But I was also angry at Houdini. Sitting there, seeing the tight concentration on his face, I felt abandoned by him. He was detached and cold and distant, and he was probably studying me along with the rest of them, as though I too were one of the yahoos. Perhaps, as far as he was concerned, the moment I fell prey to the Mother's fervor, during that first interview two days ago, I became one of them.

Perhaps. But it's possible that, underneath it all, there was something else bothering him. I mean, it makes no sense for him to abandon me because I was susceptible to these trance-like raptures. Wouldn't it be more likely that he had distanced himself because his plan had worked: because the Mother found me interesting, because she'd singled me out? Even though it gave him the in he wanted, on some level it had to rankle. Yes. The fact that it was me, not him, that she acknowledged. My visions, my feelings. My decision to leave the barracks and find out why they were sitting in a field in the dark.

But it wasn't over yet. The Mother stood there, ruddy and flickering in the firelight, lost in a reverie. Around her people gradually reoriented themselves. My body felt strangely itchy —I wanted to run off into the darkness and disappear beyond the fire's perimeter, to leave the Visionaries blinking in their stupor, bewildered to find me gone.

But then the Mother stirred again. She raised her head and looked across the fire, directly at me, then spread her arms wide and laid her head back, as though offering her throat to the glittering moon. It was a striking pose. She became both omen and sacrifice. Her white robe glowed and flickered. Moonlight and firelight fought to claim her.

A long time elapsed before she let her head fall forward again, to stare into the dying flames of the fire.

"I understand now," she said. Her voice had dropped into an alto register and reverberated in the dark. "It's all clear." She let her arms fall to her sides and announced in a hoarse voice:

"Beth is the missing link."

Then she drooped. She staggered to the left a few paces, and Visionaries sprang up to catch her by the arms and guide her down to the grass. Monica rose immediately to her feet.

"The ceremony is over," she declared. "The Mother must rest."

Because the Mother collapsed after her announcement, I didn't realize right away how completely my status in the community had been changed by what she said. I noticed glances from the Visionaries as Houdini and I walked back to the barracks, but I assumed they were looking at me with sympathetic curiosity, as mystified as I was as to what it all meant. What was the Mother talking about? The missing link? Houdini and I retraced our steps along the edge of the ridge, behind a few people who lived in Kestrel. To our left Alia walked alone through the taller glass, hardly a person at all, reduced to a solitary bobbing light. I felt sorry for her because I had seen her face as we left the fire and she looked utterly alone. But I was too preoccupied by the Mother's words to think of Alia for long. I turned to Houdini, hoping he'd want to talk about it, but he shone the flashlight ahead of us and walked fast, making conversation impossible.

When we reached Sparrow and went squeaking down the echoey linoleum hallway, I realized I was exhausted. I went into my room and kicked off my clammy sneakers.

Houdini stood behind me in the doorway.

"She gave us quite a performance," he said. There was an edge in his voice, as though he were angry about something.

I sat down on the bunk in my damp jeans. I didn't look up at him. I couldn't believe how tired I was. My limbs felt like lumber.

"She's chosen you," he said, the words knife-like. "You're part of the community now."

I looked up, feeling suspicion prick me through my exhaustion. "What do you mean?"

"I saw the expression on your face. You went into a trance."

Another wave of exhaustion rolled over me. "It wasn't what you think," I said, and began to arrange the blankets on my bed.

"No?" he said. Then he laughed. "No. But now you're the prophet."

I looked up at him. For a moment he didn't say anything, just studied me with a look that had become measuring and cool.

"I think you should be careful," he said finally. "We don't know what it means to be a prophet here."

Then he turned away, pulling off his shirt in one eloquently disdainful gesture as he crossed the hall, revealing muscular arms, smooth back, a brief, possibly imagined outline of brown nipple. I looked down at the pale yellow coverlet. Both of our doors stood open, and from across the hall I heard the faint creak and jingle of bed springs.

The fusion of the mystical and the scientific is an essential feature of the New Age movements Houdini studied. Two seemingly incompatible kinds of thought, brought together into a new harmony. In fact, this kind of fusion has been a feature of esoteric traditions throughout history—astrology, rosicrucianism, alchemy—all evidence the same impulse. Charismatic leaders promise their followers a world in which the mystic and the scientist can marry their knowledge. The mystic gains empirical credibility, while the scientist is released from the tedious burden of fact.

I suppose the desire for a fusion of such complete opposites begins with a longing for what we've lost—some imagined primitive past when the universe was mysterious and magical, when a god might reach down and take a man or woman by the hand. We half-remember the time when collective beliefs made it possible for spirits of water and earth, fire and air, to assume human form and communicate with us. We could be destroyed or saved, depending on our response to their words.

But the longing felt by New Age visionaries for a magical relationship to the universe is fueled by more than nostalgia alone. These groups also want their mystical beliefs to be ratified scientifically. They are proud of their analytical inheritance, proud of the interpretive faculties that have allowed us to penetrate cells and stars, black holes and atoms. They desire a magical communing with the universe that can be measured and proven.

Franz Anton Mesmer, one of Houdini's favorite strange attractors, is a good example. In 1773 Mesmer believed he had discovered magnetic fluid, invisible energy that bound everything in the universe together. He could feel when a person's magnetic fluid had become congested, and by applying his will, could cause it to circulate freely again. In this way he cured sickness, restored energy, alleviated depression. He was convinced that his ability to manipulate this invisible magnetic energy would have dramatic spiritual and psychological effects on the human race. We would be liberated not only from physical and mental illness, but also from conventional thinking and other social ills. His discovery would be the means of reuniting us with the natural world we'd become estranged from, enabling us to live in an ancient, and so, new harmony.

Many people believed Mesmer's claims. He sent his patients into strange trances in which they saw visions, heard voices, felt relieved of terrible burdens and the sorrows of a lifetime. His disciples felt they'd been transformed. The universe became incandescent and meaningful, and their own lives took on a beauty and a shape that corresponded to that incandescence, shared its meaning. Suddenly, life was revealed anew. The richness it contained was shocking and illuminating.

Mesmer was glad to have touched people's lives, but he wasn't satisfied. He was a social revolutionary, true, but he also wanted to be recognized for his scientific explorations. Perhaps he even hoped for a bit of homage from other scientists. He applied to France's Academie of Sciences to receive credit for his work. He set up demonstrations to provide proof of the existence of magnetic fluid, wrote letters, and persuaded supporters to do so as well, all so that the reigning scientific authorities would acknowledge him.

Mesmer never received the recognition he craved. However, he did take pre-Revolutionary France by storm with his new science. If the men of the Academie didn't believe him, the populace embraced his theories with hysterical enthusiasm. And among his converts he numbered quite a few people who considered themselves Enlightenment men (in the scientific sense, though the New Age one is applicable too). One of these was the Comte de Montlosier. The Comte spoke for many disciples when he explained that Mesmer's appeal lay in the fact that he had introduced his followers to a deeper, more profound kind of science, one that left room for religious and philosophical beliefs. Mesmerism, the Comte believed, would "change the face of the world."

All of this provides context for the Mother's ideas about Darwin and human evolution. Her idea was fairly simple once you disentangled it from its dramatic setting of night field, bonfire, hard cold moon remotely luminous. In fact, her message was in many ways quite similar to Mesmer's own. She believed that we would find our way forward with the aid of science, but a science different from the one currently practiced in most research labs. This was why she focused on Darwin.

The father of evolution suffered from a mysterious illness, one that left him essentially bedridden for the last twenty-odd years of his life. The Mother believed that this illness was a psychosomatic expression of the anxiety Darwin experienced. He had proposed a theory that completely reinvented human beings' relationship to the universe. It was arrogant and incendiary. It defied every authority represented by church, state, and social tradition. He was the rebel, and you must understand that the Mother loved a rebel. She drew us to Darwin's bedside, forced us to feel the heat rising off his flushed skin, made us listen to his swelling hysteria as he wept and swooned.

Simply put: she accepted that we are products of evolution, and accepted that we compete to survive. Darwin was right. But he wasn't right when he assumed that we were passive receivers of our evolutionary heritage. He reached this conclusion, the Mother claimed, because he was so traumatized by the act of breaking with the beliefs that had shaped him. He was a prophet of the new order, but like Moses he couldn't go to the Promised Land himself.

But we can. Thanks to Darwin, we can harness our understanding of evolution, put it to work for us. We can choose the ways in which we will evolve. We can create the human race anew.

So that's it. Mesmer and magnetic fluid, The Mother and evolution. The mystic pretending to be the scientist. The strange hybrids that are born in these millennial times. Implicit in all this is an argument about the nature of human desire. The power of fantasy.

But I must confess something. The reason I used Mesmer to illustrate the mystical-scientific fusion is not because his beliefs accord so well with the Mother's own. No. It's because, as I sat there in the dark, on a straw mat in the wet grass, watching the Mother's face catch the firelight and sensing the shadows at my back stealthily creeping nearer, I felt something. I can't explain it. Nor will I defend it. Simply: for a moment, I believed. I was mesmerized. I felt uplifted and astonished and exhilarated.

I, like the others, had been transformed.

eighteen

That Thursday morning witnessed a strange role reversal in Sparrow. For some reason the events by the fire had released something in Houdini. That morning he walked into my room—I was still half-asleep in bed—nervously talkative. He wondered aloud about the significance of the events by the fire, what the Mother wanted, how the community would treat me now. He asked me how I felt, what I thought about her attentions, whether I was ready for another round. I, on the other hand, remained distant and silent. I didn't want to talk about the scene up on the ridge, or the exhaustion I felt when we got back to Sparrow. I lay in my bed thinking about the unsettling dreams I'd had—I couldn't remember them, but I still felt uneasy.

All of this uneasiness was made worse when we got to the farmhouse for breakfast. Everyone stared at us. The whole room fell silent. We carried our trays to a table by the far window. I felt more uncomfortable than I did our first morning there.

We were half way through our cereal and coffee when the Mother made her appearance. Smiling, she came over to our table. She sat down without ceremony, as though the three of us were old friends. She seemed immensely pleased with herself. She asked me how I'd slept.

Her manner was irritating. I took another bite of cereal before admitting I'd had bad dreams.

This didn't seem to surprise her. She asked me if I remembered the dreams. Curtly I said I didn't, then asked why everyone was staring at us.

"Because your status has been revealed." She said it as though it were obvious. She surveyed the roomful of silent

Visionaries, then waved her hand. Reluctantly people turned back to their breakfasts.

"I told Beth last night that you've made her your prophet. She didn't believe me." I detected an undertone of defiance in Houdini's voice and realized he still felt the sting of the reprimand he'd received from the Mother the night before.

"I like to think of her as a messenger," she replied, looking at me as she spoke. "But prophet, messenger, it's more or less the same. It's who she is. Why else would she receive the visions?" She glanced at him. "It's why you brought her to us."

"Of course I claim no responsibility," Houdini said. He sounded annoyed. The Mother smiled.

"Of all people, Houdini, you should understand. It's a simple question of balance. What's the relationship between the aminergic and cholinergic systems in her brain? Is it different from most people's? My guess is that Beth has an unusual degree of control over her thalamus. Of course she doesn't know she's exerting that control. And so it seems involuntary to her."

The Mother sat, smiling and still, watching Houdini's reaction to her words. He became immediately alert. He sat up straighter and began to flex the fingers of his right hand abstractedly.

He asked the Mother how much control she wielded over her own thalamus, whether she could raise her cholinergic levels through an act of will. The air seemed to crackle between them. They had forgotten about me as they began to discuss the relationship between the thalamus and these levels of cholines and amines, which, they explained, regulated consciousness. Our state of consciousness depended on which of these chemicals was flooding the brain—if amines were predominant, we were awake and alert; if acetylcholine was present in force, we were in a dreaming or hallucinatory state. From what they said it seemed it was also possible to modulate between these two chemical extremes, to get unusual admixtures of chemical-conscious states. But what caused one or the other to predominate? And what did all that have to do with the thalamus? I was lost.

"Would you mind telling me what you're talking about?" I interrupted finally.

It was painful for the Mother to tear her gaze from Houdini and return her attention to me, the visionary messenger. She had been flexing herself for a debate over the nature of my neurophysiological state. Turning to me was nothing less than a let-down. She bridged the awkward moment with a laugh.

"It's as I said. You don't know yourself. But we know you. You're the messenger."

From the explanation that followed, I gathered that the Mother saw me as a kind of spontaneous mutation. I had a raw ability to receive visions—without training or the benefit of an orienting spiritual framework—which meant that my brain had evolved in some unusual way. What I had done by accident the Visionaries were to accomplish through conscious evolution. I was like Homo erectus or the Neanderthals, or the mother-Eve that Leakey discovered in Africa. I was a living fossil.

But at the same time I was also a mystical cypher. The Mother claimed I had been sent to them from the outside world—as though the universe, growing impatient to see the Visionaries evolve into a higher form, decided to nudge them along. And so I appeared before them. I had received the visions so that they would be able to know me. This was my role as messenger. I brought word to them from the world. It was time they took their rightful place in it.

I felt as though I'd been appropriated, sitting there in the dining room, listening to these ridiculous claims. It's strange enough to be told you're an evolutionary link, an accidental mutation or experiment of nature. But to be called an...unwitting...emissary on top of that leaves you feeling a bit overwhelmed. Nor did it matter what *I* thought. Whether I accepted my status as evolutionary messenger-prophet or not was irrelevant. The Mother knew who I was. Everything I said or did could be interpreted as fulfillment of that identity.

Yet if it didn't matter what I thought, whether I accepted my identity or not, why did the Mother press me so? Why did she turn resolutely to me, insist that for my own sake I recognize my power? For the next half hour she lectured me on the significance my presence had for the community. New Light would be changed dramatically, she said, and I was the key. They needed my help. But to get my help, evidently the Mother also needed Houdini's.

"What could we use to persuade her?" she said to him musingly, her confidence that it was "we"—her and him—perfectly assured. He was spellbound. He listened to her raptly, Houdini, the man who was impervious to hypnotism and charismatically induced trances. She turned musingly to me, not seeing me at all. "What about Spiegel's evidence that the cortex can be altered at will during hallucination? She needs to believe that there's a scientific basis to all this before she'll accept it."

I got up from the table. The two of them looked at me in surprise. I told them I wanted to meditate on my new status. I left them there together.

I didn't know where I was going. I was thinking of Mark and Glass, and how effectively everyone's attention had been diverted from that saga to this new one. I remembered how lonely Alia had looked the night before as she left the fire and headed back to the barracks by herself. I knew she had chosen that isolation, but that didn't mean she didn't want to be rescued. I considered going to her, but in truth I was too preoccupied by my own situation to be of any help to her.

I found Tom in the weavery. Jidd was there, as well as Oak, a woman named Marcia and another man named Sea. Also, two of the three people who had fled the weavery two days before to avoid being contaminated by our presence. Everyone stopped what they were doing when I came in. I did my best to ignore their stares and asked Tom if I could talk to him.

We returned to the sunlit world and followed South Field path toward the east. Grasshoppers took flight as we walked, keeping just ahead of us like courtiers leading a procession. Dragonflies hung in the air to inspect us, then darted away. The sky was very blue, the sun not yet hot. For several minutes we walked like this. He didn't ask me what was wrong, and I wasn't sure that I wanted to know how he saw the events of the night before. But in the end I did ask. Tom continued to look off toward the line of woods to our right without answering. When we came to North-South path, where the trail was too narrow to walk abreast, I stopped.

"So you believe it," I said. "You think I'm the messenger."

He looked at me for a long moment, then asked quietly, "Is it the idea that you've been singled out that bothers you?"

I looked over at the trees. I shook my head without answering.

"I don't think you're a prophet in the Biblical sense," he said. "But I do think that anyone can be a prophet if the time and place are right."

"That's not what she was saying. She called me the messenger."

"I know her language is hard to take sometimes. But it's actually necessary. It helps to formalize things. You need ritual, especially out here. Otherwise you have no order. It'd be all too easy for each of us to spin off into our own private worlds. Like Mark."

"I understand that. I really do. But why me? I feel like she's doing it deliberately. Like she wants something from me."

"She does want something. The Mother feels you have things to teach us. I don't find that so hard to believe."

"No. It has to do with Houdini. It's like they're diagnosing me. Like I have no say in the matter."

He looked at me. His eyes were the color of dark chocolate, beautiful and secret. "You have a say, Beth."

Probably Tom understood better than I the spirit motivating the Mother's declarations. But at that moment the only thing I could say with certainty was that I trusted him. Even though what he said upset me, I believed in his sincerity. I believed in his ability to evaluate people. I suppose I felt a kinship between us. He had told me stories about being a prostitute, and I had told him that, in a way, waitressing wasn't so different. In both professions your job is to serve the customers. Eating, drinking, having sex—they're all basic human drives. When people do these things they reveal themselves.

Tom and I went back to his room in Thebes. It was a calm place, full of plants, hand-built furniture, intricate rattan wall-hangings. It felt like him. He sat me down by the window, in a rough chair with a chunky wooden frame and woven hemp strands for back and seat. He touched me on the shoulder once, to reassure me, and promised to be right back.

When he left I ran one finger along the twists of hemp that wrapped around the wood frame of the seat. I blinked several times to clear my eyes. It was the simplicity of the chair, and the clean lines of the room with its plants and woven hangings and wooden furniture. Some of the pieces were homely and clumsy, while others showed signs of the growing sophistication of the craftsman. It was all right here to lean your head back on the wood of the headrest, to look out the window at the field grass waving in the breeze and the line of trees beyond, and think of nothing at all.

About ten minutes later Tom came back with Crystal, Tianne and Ted.

"Oh, Beth," Crystal said, coming immediately over and hugging me. A wave of curls brushed my face. Tianne, more formal, took the chair beside me and put her hand briefly on mine. Ted sat on the bed next to Tom and told me how sorry they all were. They should have thought how I might feel, how overwhelming it was. Tom gave a brief nod. "I brought them so you'd see," he said.

Tom wanted to show me that my friends didn't treat me any differently since I'd been named messenger. Some of the Visionaries might stare, but it was only because they didn't know me. They could only watch from the outside as my relevance to them changed. It was natural that they'd be curious.

The others agreed with this. But Crystal wanted me to remember one thing more. The key to the law of coincidence lay in its dual nature, she said. It wasn't just that I was a messenger, there to guide New Light on its path. New Light was also there for me. I too was being given a message that would lead me forward and show me the way.

When I left Tom's room an hour later I felt calmer. I understood what they meant. From their perspective, it made sense to let the Mother deliver her pronouncements, even if

I chose not to accept them in the end. This attitude reflected something fundamental to the Visionaries' outlook. Their concern was not that they might be duped, but that, through inattention or cynicism, they might miss a chance to learn about themselves and their place in the world.

I respected their philosophy. It was gentle and spiritually sincere, even if they did wear silly robes and sit around a fire in the middle of the night waiting to be visited by visions or purity or whatever it was. They forged a life that was different from the American norm. Who wouldn't want that? Yet in the end that was what made me resist the Mother the most—the fact that I did want what she offered. To be the chosen one, the cherished daughter whose importance is finally recognized. I can't help but believe that the intensity of the longing is an index of how fantastic it is. In the end, no matter how much we're loved, we all feel we should be loved more.

I found the Mother and Houdini by the barn standing with a group of Visionaries. They were watching Alia, who stood spread-legged on a ladder scaffold fifteen feet above the crowd. Her face and hands were black with charcoal. She was sketching a new mural on the barn's north wall. Everyone was watching, eager to see what she was creating. It was her first act of communication since going into retreat. It meant that she was returning to them.

The Mother and Houdini stood side by side. I looked at New Light's leader, but I wouldn't let my gaze stray beyond her face to meet Houdini's eyes, even though I felt him looking at me. Above us Alia rubbed out a line and redrew it, then leaned back to take a look at her progress.

There on the side of the barn, larger than life, stood the Mother. Her back was to the viewer. Her arms were raised. The panorama Alia was sketching seemed to spill from the Mother's regal head. There was a sun in the east, a moon in the west, and stars overhead in a sky that would eventually grade from brightest blue to the darkened tones of night. Winter and summer would exist alongside each other. On the same tree, leaves would sprout and fall.

Kala, up in front, glanced around. "All time exists in the present moment," she called, gesturing authoritatively toward the landscape that was beginning to overlay the barn's silver wood, as though anything to do with time became her charge.

The Mother nodded her approval. Then she looked at me. "You're ready now?" she said, as though she had known as soon as I walked up that I had let go of my resistance. I wanted to tell her that I was calm not because of her, but because of the Visionaries who'd befriended me, Tom and Crystal, Tianne and Ted. But there was no point. For a moment we regarded one another. Then she nodded and looked up again at the mural and Alia.

"Thank you for this gift, Alia," she called.

Alia shook her head modestly. "It just came to me," she said. Her smile was vibrant.

The Mother turned to the others. "Alia has given us the sign. Tonight we hold the vision ceremony."

I allowed myself to look at Houdini. His eyes met mine with a coldness that was like winter coming on. I turned away and shut him out. Above our heads Alia was adding some trees

That night there was no dinner. Houdini and I stood inside the entrance to the barn, watching the Visionaries prepare for the ceremony. We didn't have much to say to each other. I could see him taking mental notes on all the activity, and his particular interest in the painted figures lining the walls. He kept glancing behind us at a woman who was being embraced by a huge bird. Its head lay on her shoulder and it had enfolded her body in the bright whiteness of its wings. She stared out at the viewers with an expression of pleasant surprise.

People called and conferred excitedly as they readied the space for the visions. Crystal, Kala and Sea set out pillows on the floor, while a woman named Suzanne and her son, Apollo, placed a candle and a book of matches before each pillow. From outside came a steady trickle of members into the barn. Everyone wore their colored robes. Apollo, stopping before us, looked down at the crumpled front of his robe and told us it was yellow like the sun.

After an interval of fluttering robes and last-minute seat changes, the seventy-four members of New Light, minus Mark Ryder, had settled themselves on pillows arranged vaguely in concentric circles. The New Light children were on best behavior and looked around eagerly; this was the only ceremony they were allowed to attend. In the center of the innermost circle an empty space had been left for the Mother. There was also a corridor about three feet wide left open to allow her to pass.

Monica emerged from the barn to stand beside Houdini and me. She didn't scowl at us this time, but she didn't acknowledge us either. Her eyes were on the Mother, who now approached down the path from the farmhouse. The white robe glowed in the last light of evening, like the painted bird's wings.

She nodded graciously to Houdini and me as she entered, and touched Monica on the shoulder. Monica drew herself up proudly beneath the touch. She even managed to look at us.

"Where shall we sit?" I asked. The Mother smiled.

"You have places up front. Don't they, Monica?" The woman looked lovingly at her leader, nodding.

We approached the aisle that led to the center of the inside circle. I saw Tianne and Tom seated in the outermost ring. They smiled at me as we passed up the aisle. Around us the seated Visionaries watched us with curious eyes. I felt underdressed in my jeans. The barn's spacious interior was lit by muted spotlights, like the ones in the church I went to, growing up, and the wide empty air of the room resounded with the crowd's murmurs and whispers, which seemed to carry up to the ceiling and then hang there, the coincident voices of desire become disembodied and independent.

The Mother led us to the innermost ring where two pillows waited for us. Kala politely drew the green folds of her robe into her lap to make room. Houdini sat beside her, I next to him on the aisle. I made a quick survey. Behind us was a woman named Sandy with a man I hadn't met before, and across the aisle Suzanne and her son. I glimpsed Ted and Alia sitting behind Crystal a few rows back, and Mary, looking sullen, in the row behind them.

The Mother swept up her robes majestically and took her place in the center of the circle. The room fell still.

After a quick glance at her audience, she made a careful circuit of her stage like a pilot checking out her control panel before preparing for take-off. When she returned center-stage, she let her eyes sweep over the silent Visionaries once again, this time attending to the emotional atmosphere in the barn. I glanced uneasily around and the painted figures along the walls looked back at me impassively.

She spread her arms. "I welcome you," she said, turning in place so that she greeted the whole room.

"We welcome you also," the Visionaries replied in unison.

She nodded. She clasped her hands.

"We come together today to receive Beth's message.

The vision ceremony will guide us."

"We await guidance," came the reply.

My cheeks burned at the mention of my name. I managed not to look around, but I felt many eyes on me.

The Mother nodded again. "Beth is a Visionary, but she has not come to join us. She is not yet reconciled to her visionary self. Each of us has stood with her on the border between the spiritual and the material domains. It is a no man's land, yet people live there. They are neither believer nor skeptic, neither guided nor abandoned. Perhaps our belief may help her to find her own."

It was then that I began to suspect I wouldn't be watching the ceremony like someone sitting in front of the TV. The Mother had something planned for me. I was very aware of Houdini to my left, his stillness.

The Mother raised her eyes to the lights that illuminated her from the rafters and called out: "We offer up to the One our many! To the unity of spirit we offer the division of the flesh!" and the Visionaries echoed back the refrain.

Then she came forward and held out her hand. There was nothing I could do. Her palm was cool and dry and made me realize how moist my own was. She smiled at the alarm in my face and led me to the center of the stage. She had me sit. We faced each other, with the candle between us, and she pulled out a small box of wooden matches from the folds of her robe. She struck one and held it to the wick. Someone in back turned down the lights, and dusk fell in the barn.

Seventy-three matches scratched and flared in the room, and seventy-three candles sputtered and brightened. The Mother intoned: "By this light may we learn to see. By this light may we find our way. By this light may the truth be revealed." Everyone, except Houdini who had no candle, stared intently into a flame. The room twinkled in the artificial evening.

"We are the recipients of two kinds of sight, outward and inward," she said. "The outward vision sees the world and other beings, and registers love and hate, desire and fear. It is the vision of separateness.

"The inward vision sees the world of spirits. It recognizes the vast interconnections that link all beings, all phenomena, in the interaction of non-locality."

The Visionaries looked into the candle flames, and I looked at Houdini. He gazed at me steadily. I felt a little reassured.

The Mother gathered her robes and stood again.

"We are here to welcome Beth into the Visionary Company. We welcome her and we walk with her, into a world that is always new, yet always familiar, the world within the world, where the inward and outward visions meet. We bring our individual visions together here, to blend, to join, to become one in the great union of our discovering selves."

Some of the Visionaries had developed fixed, glassy looks. Others continued to look into the flames that burned before them, lighting the way, but one scratched a leg, another pushed hair back behind an ear. The Mother walked around the perimeter of the center circle, leaving me alone before the candle. She faced outward toward her flock, speaking again in a rhythmic sing-song, rehearsing what they all knew by heart.

"I have come to you as the Mother, to help you give birth to your spirit. We've each been confused, unhappy, lost. We looked around ourselves desperately, blind to the fact that we couldn't see the world within the world.

"To give birth to ourselves anew, we embrace the drive into thanatos, that annihilating plunge. We face the negative visions we carry inside ourselves, and in doing so we are released. We are free to affirm life, eros, the journey into desire and love, the joy of communion and brotherhood. It is this that the fire ceremony celebrates."

Her words were spoken with ritualistic richness. They poured like liquid chocolate in the dark room. Each person lent their will to the Mother's words, and in doing so made those words resound more deeply and convincingly. It was impossible not to feel her power, just as it is impossible to convey it here. She passed around and around the circle, her very body testifying to the ardency of her vision. People started to sigh softly, to keen and exclaim, and these murmurs of satisfaction augmented her power.

I looked around the room full of entranced people and beyond, to the inspirational paintings hovering like ghosts in the shadows. It all led up to this. All the conversation, all the props, all the preaching—it was mere preparation for this moment. Would we accept her spiritual authority? Would we open our minds to the possibility of another way of seeing? Or would we defy her, refuse to be led, deny the visionary moment. I looked at Houdini again. In the dim light I saw him shake his head slightly. Beside him Kala's eyes were glassy and unseeing. Farther back I could see Mary casting furtive looks around her. Our eyes met and she dropped her gaze.

It all led up to this—and I felt nothing. I came here in good faith, to find out what she meant when she called me the messenger. Yet it seemed I was impervious to her effects after all. Around me the Visionaries sank one by one into the trance that all of them seemed to crave, while I rejected the ceremony, rejected the Mother's co-option of Freud and Darwin, rejected her image as spiritual mother.

I don't know if she was dissatisfied with how the ceremony was proceeding. It was the only vision ceremony I've attended; I have nothing to compare it to. Gasps and soft cries of pleasure floated through the twilight interior, but there were still a number of members who glanced up at her from time to time, or craned their necks to look at me. She had been pacing the circumference of the inner circle when suddenly she faced me again.

She came closer until she towered over me in her white robe. The candlelight threw strange shadows across her face. I swallowed nervously and she frowned, then squatted before me. She looked intently into my face. I didn't know what she wanted. From time to time her gaze shifted beyond me, to Houdini.

Something wasn't right. She seemed to think one of us was resisting her. She looked from him to me, gauging which of us was responsible for the tension and refusal in the room. She licked her lips. When she spoke again, her voice had gone slightly hoarse.

"Occasionally we have trouble achieving the vision. It can be blocked by disharmony. Unresolved feelings. When that happens we need someone to lead the way. A person who becomes the point of focus, like the candle flame."

It had to be me, of course. I was the messenger.

"We use that person to build a bridge between worlds. Our focus flings her forward, and she draws us after her."

She looked at me as though she were waiting for an answer. Around us the Visionaries were silent. Houdini was silent. I wanted to know what it meant to be flung forward. Was she planning to offer me up like a sacrifice to the gods of disharmony? Was this what she had planned? So that, even as she sat me down in front of the candle and told us that bedtime story of thanatos and eros, she knew that in a short while she would rise from her cumbrous squat and hold out her hand to me, while, overhead, a huge murky shadow of a hand blotted out the ceiling?

I felt nothing, as I said. My rebellion against her was instinctive, but it was also confined to what the Mother would call my inward vision. I didn't want to be rude to her; I didn't want to trumpet my mental freedom. I took her hand and stood. She turned her gaze to mine.

And then I almost fell backward. It was shocking, the wave of desire I felt coming from her. Even more shocking was the overpowering desire I felt in myself. A moment ago I had thought I was resisting. Now I saw that all along I had been part of it, unbeknownst to myself. Maybe that's why she wanted me to stand before them and meet their collective gaze—because I was entranced and thought I was free.

Everyone in the room seemed to be surging toward everyone else. But of course, no one moved. There was a roaring in my ears, yet the room was completely silent. I was baffled, terrified, exhilarated. And underneath it all, I felt her, directing and modulating the flow. She looked into my eyes, her hands squeezed mine, she seemed to shudder as the feeling of unity took over our separate selves. I was fenced in on all sides by Oneness.

I fell back before the power in her eyes, but at the same time something struggled inside me, a kind of tickling feeling in my head, like what happens when I'm really hungry and devour a hunk of Swiss milk chocolate. Sugar wings beating like moths, their magic powder brushing my neurons and setting them on fire.

Then, suddenly, the intensity of her demand was deflected from me. It was like someone stepping in between you and a bonfire. Houdini had joined us, taking my left and her right hand in his own, so that the three of us were linked. A current coursed through our bodies, around and around, snapping, sharp. I had a visual impression of colors passing through our bodies like a circuit of electricity.

We were transfixed. No one was the leader, no one the follower, because we had entered into some strange electrochemical state of suspension. Each time the influence of one of us seemed to engulf another, the third stepped in and changed the balance. It was an essay on the very nature of desire. No one could focus on more than one person at once. I looked at Houdini and felt him tremble. The sensation was sweet, but almost immediately the Mother intervened, and suddenly I realized I was in her thrall. Then Houdini, by staring at her, caused her attention to slip from me and then she was overcome. So it went, around and around.

The end was like overdosing on Halloween candy. There was a short-circuit, a fizzing. The lights went out in our minds, the desire and the aggression and the empathy all shut down. We were each alone again. The Mother breathed raggedly, looking down at the planks of the floor with a sagging expression. I, too, felt my eyes dragged down, and stared at the scuffed outlines of the fitted wooden sections with an apathetic relinquishing, as though the floor, ground level, had conquered me, and I wanted nothing more than to give myself up to it.

Then I remembered Houdini.

The effort required to raise my eyes to look at him was exhausting. I almost gave up. When I finally managed to focus on him, I saw that he was staring at the Mother with the same fixed gaze she and I had turned on the floor. His eyes were on her face as though nothing else in the world existed. He reached out. He touched her on the wrist.

Then he seemed to shake himself. He turned to me. He held out his arms, stepped toward me, and pulled me to him.

Which is how it happened that we became lovers. An indirect result of the vision ceremony. So perhaps it was a kind of sexual visionary encounter, such as they practiced at New Light. I can't even remember the trip from the barn back to Sparrow, how we stripped, or who pulled the mattress onto the floor. But I do remember lying there, the two of us holding each other.

The taste of his mouth was a revelation; it was the thing I had known about, without knowing that I knew, ever since we stood on Boris's patio together. Familiar, so familiar. Perhaps that's why it wasn't like other first encounters. I still wince when I remember the awkward grinding sex Kevin and I had, the first night we slept together. This was nothing like that, nothing like anything I'd experienced before. But then, Houdini and I had been pumped up by the vision ceremony. We were awash with the residue of so many desires—not only the Mother's passion, but the cascade of visionary longing that spilled forth from every member in the room. I'm a little ashamed, looking back. Was it the vision ceremony? Or was it Houdini and I, alone, embracing? I don't know.

But I accept that the vision ceremony was necessary to release us into that embrace. I was moved, I realize in retrospect, by the sheer force of the Visionaries' desire to be lifted up, taken beyond the limits imposed so beautifully by the body, to be flung into the chaos of transcendence. Houdini and I rode that desire like a wave, which carried us somewhere we'd never been before. To defy the limits that bound us and them, the Visionaries had to concentrate on a focal person—myself, and Houdini when he joined me. They flung us forward, and we provided them with the fact of our fusing. Our separate lives became parts of a whole. Houdini and I functioned as the sacrifice, sent out to propitiate the gods, not of disharmony, but of some chaotic new form. The Mother was the bow, we were the arrow, the community's ardent longing the bow string. She strung that longing onto her, pulled it taut, and shot us into the darkness.

And in doing so, she answered the question he must have put to her, at some point or other, over the course of

194

their conversations. Neurophysiology, the role of the thalamus, the problem of controlling the visions. All that was only
part of the larger question that brought him to the Wash U
medical school in the first place, and from there to Boris's
apartment, and finally down to McDonald County in the ass
end of southern Missouri. It was the simple question of a
pattern. The possibility of a secret order lying hidden beneath the chaotic swirl.

From out of one darkness, we moved into another. As
I said, we found ourselves, after the ceremony, face to face on
the mattress. We were both kneeling. Was this what the
Mother intended? For the two of us to be embracing? In the
back of my mind I doubted it. But I didn't stop to think about
it. His naked body was more beautiful than I could have
imagined. Clothes interrupted the pure lines, the curve where
back turns into buttock, the strangely private transitions
from ribs to belly to groin. I drew my hand along the slender
muscled flesh and discovered another trompe l'oeil landscape. I traced the underside of jaw, brushed fingers over
lips, skimmed the sculpted cheekbones. The tips of my fingers nestled in the soft place just behind the ears, where
Houdini kept his heat.

He lay down on the mattress and looked at me. I knelt
there, feeling held by his eyes. For a long moment he simply
stared. Then he reached up and brushed my lips with his
fingers. My mouth opened involuntarily. His hands moved
over me, my skin beneath his skin tingling, even after the
touch was gone. The dark weight of him drew me down.

That was when he moved back and looked at me in a
different way. And for a moment I faltered. I saw myself
described. I saw that all along he'd wanted me too, yet at the
same time he thought of me as a kid, an amateur. On the patio
in St. Louis, down there at New Light: such vivid, complicated desire, which never would have been realized if we'd

met under any other circumstances. He would have been a man I talked to for a night. We held each other's bodies only because we had come there, because the Visionaries and their ceremony had released us.

That was the source of the pain that was also part of the lovemaking. I've never had a sexual encounter that was so revealed or intense, yet all along I knew that, without the Mother's instigation, we would never have burned together, more completely naked than either of us had ever been. I didn't want her to have any part of that moment between us. I wanted it to be just Houdini and myself, so that as we lay there, after, with a thin sheen of sweat covering our bellies and chests, we could look at each other, saying nothing, in the perfect silence of understanding.

Mystery

Who was Houdini White?

To be honest, I don't think I really wanted to know. Not then, and maybe not even now. I told myself that the question was too complicated: there was the man who had held me against him as the vision raked my body, who spoke passionately of patterns and chaos; and then there was the other man, the one who was mocking, cold, even cruel. I could never predict which man Houdini would be.

So I say. And yet, that morning after the Mother had proclaimed me the messenger, when I refused to talk or look at him, it wasn't the complexity of the question that made me turn away. It was that I couldn't bear to watch him enter that passionate mode, talking about me with the Mother. I knew that, in his excitement, he'd forgotten who I was. I became a research subject to him, one more New Age phenomenon he'd discovered at New Light.

But after the vision ceremony all that changed. A new Houdini was revealed to me, a man who could make love, lie quietly in the dark, hold my hand. In the space of a moment the distance between us was erased. The Mother became nothing more than the instrument of our union, while the Houdini of passionate and chilling extremes became a myth I'd invented. This new Houdini had a quietness that included me; he allowed me to feel his vulnerability. He was tender, cupping my chin and kissing my eyelids gently; telling me in a whisper that I was beautiful. When I asked him what he was afraid of, he answered: that question.

Of course he told me everyday things too—things that lovers tell one another to anchor themselves in each other's minds.

For example, his real name was Hayden E. White—E for Ellen, which he disliked and so pretended the initial stood for nothing, just served to distinguish him professionally from a historian who shared his name. He picked up the name Houdini in grad school—if you say Hayden E. fast, it sounds like Houdini. Plus he had that Eastern European bone structure (I was not the only one who found the look so devastatingly attractive—he'd slept with a number of women as an undergrad, when he still had time for such things). The name stuck. At the corporation where Houdini worked, the nickname was respected as a kind of visual or conceptual pun, a witticism, something absurdly droll yet true. In addition, Harry Houdini's reputation fit well with Houdini White's own cool style.

After we had lain for a while, side by side, in silence again, Houdini asked if I remembered telling the Mother that I hadn't slept well after the fire ceremony. He asked if I really didn't remember what I'd dreamed. I told him I didn't.

He was silent again. Then he said he'd asked because he too had had an uneasy night, but that unlike me he'd remembered his dream. This was unusual for him. He wanted to describe it to me, but I had to understand: the kinds of dreams he had were probably not what I would call dreaming.

Explain, I said.

He said he didn't dream in pictures. Just words. Voices, writing, text.

No images? I said, trying to imagine it and failing.

Just words, he said.

But that night it had been different. In the dream a voice kept saying, "You see, we must pay attention to the image, not the words that describe it." But of course there weren't any images, just the words, glowing in old-fashioned LED. All this wasn't so very remarkable, in Houdini's opinion. What was unusual was his *awareness*, in the dream, that he couldn't see anything but the words. That had never happened before.

I listened to the even sound of his breathing. We lay on our backs, my legs draped across his. I tried to conjure it, but I just couldn't imagine not seeing pictures in your dreams. It seemed eerie and somehow wrong; I mean, if he had been blind I could understand, but he wasn't blind. But then I had to wonder why the idea of imageless dreams was so upsetting to me. Why was I recoiling, was it just because the idea was foreign to me? So I asked him what he thought the dream meant. He didn't answer. His breathing was even and deep and I thought he had fallen asleep. I turned my head to look at him and found that he was watching me. Then he told me he didn't believe that dreams have meaning.

twenty

When I woke up the next morning, he was gone.

At first I thought he'd gotten up early and gone across the hall to update his notes. I stood on the cold linoleum and knocked. When I got no answer, I tried the door. The room was empty.

My watch said eight-thirty. We'd been up before seven every morning; it was possible that he'd gotten restless or hungry, waiting around for me. I knew he would be eager to hear the Mother's reaction to the vision ceremony. That's what it was, I decided, deliberately not letting myself entertain any other possibilities. Instead my mind returned to the night before. I wondered how he saw what happened. Perhaps he was even a little embarrassed this morning. The intensity of our exchange did seem kind of unnerving by the light of day.

But then I found myself thinking about the vision ceremony itself. That too was unnerving. I hadn't seen any visions, at least nothing like the ones I'd had prior to coming to New Light. But the palpability of the desire I'd felt coming from the Mother, and the odd locked-in sensation as the three of us were caught in that strange current that felt like electricity. Had our desires been revealed to one another?

It felt like desire, but as I thought about it I concluded that it wasn't sexual, or not only that. A hunger perhaps, but that too is a physical metaphor that puts limits on the feeling and so misrepresents it. Whatever it was, it took me over. It was something outside of me, yet it also came from inside. It was as though I were being formatted by this electrical charge to produce an answering charge. Which perhaps was how the Mother thought she could fling me forward in the first place, to use me to create a bridge between this world and the next. She called up the most intense longing from somewhere inside me, and used it to drive me forth into the unknown. Except Houdini intervened. He entered the circle and changed the valence of her power. And now where was he?

I opened the outer door and left Sparrow's coolness for the bright morning light. Opposite, on Kestrel's walls, Alia's aerial people flew in lonely sorrow over their deserted cities. Beyond the path, the barracks field was alive with bees and dragonflies, yet I felt a strange air of stillness overlaying the farm. The sky's blue was electric and trees shifted in the wind like members of a crowd whispering together. The beauty of it all pained me. That was my first clue.

No one was working in the gardens or greenhouses that Friday morning as I passed. This was unusual; by New Light's standards it was already mid-morning. Someone was always weeding or digging by now, before the sun got hot.

I passed the barn and came in sight of the farmhouse. There, on the lawn where the bonfires had been held after dinner, were around thirty people, milling about. I could hear their voices as I approached, drowning out birds and the dull hum of insects. When they saw me they quieted. Feeling nervous suddenly, I came to a stop between the barn and the purple beech, as though the big tree would shield me if I needed protection. The Visionaries conferred, then Crystal separated from the rest and came toward me.

For a ludicrous moment I felt like the villain in a bad western as she approached, her frothy hair blowing in the wind. The others watched her. About ten feet from me she came to a stop, an uncertain look on her face. A small cold dread blossomed in my gut.

She asked me how I felt that morning, in a stiff,

formal way. This is ridiculous, I thought, and forced myself to walk the ten feet that separated us. Impulsively she put out her hands and gave mine a squeeze, then told me not to worry, it would be all right. I was mystified. I asked her what she was talking about, what was going on. I asked where the others were, Ted, Alia, Tom, Tianne. She said they were needed elsewhere. Needed how, I asked. She hesitated, then, in a voice that tried bravely to sound comforting, she said that people were upset, that they were trying to figure out what to do. I looked at her blankly.

Crystal hesitated again. Finally she said, her voice almost wistful: "Houdini has gone to The Mother. He's with her now."

I didn't understand fully what that meant, right then. I looked up at the windows that faced onto the lawn from the Mother's suite. The shades were down. Had they ever been pulled before? I couldn't remember. I felt a curious foreboding, one completely different from the dread that was making my stomach cramp up. I looked again at the cluster of Visionaries standing by the back stairs.

The pursuit of transcendence had carried them so far from the American life I knew. I realized I had no idea what this pursuit meant to them. Did they really believe it? Did they fall asleep each night, sustained by their attempts to discover a deeper way of seeing? Did they wake up, having dreamed that they'd achieved this transcendence, to find that they could live with their failings and their hope, strengthened by the visionary life?

"They've been in there for hours," Crystal said. "Something's happening."

It was useless to ask what was happening, or how they knew, though I did ask. I tried to dismiss the Visionaries' expressions of foreboding. I wanted to argue with them, to point out that it wasn't remarkable that Houdini and the Mother were closeted together. The Mother often met with people for hours, conversing, exhorting, fantasizing about visions and evolution and alternative states of consciousness. Why was this different? I wanted to remind them that this was her role as a visionary leader, to guide, to instruct, to challenge, to inspire.

"Last night wasn't a typical vision ceremony," Crystal said gently. "I know that you and Houdini had nothing to compare it to. You had no way of knowing." She took my arm and we began to walk, heading across the field, away from the house and the others.

"Maybe it was the strain of holding both of you in her focus simultaneously. That's what some people say. But I don't think so. The three of you became connected, Beth. We all felt it. We were drawn along behind you. But it was different this time. We always seek to approach Oneness, but it's a matter of each of us coming together, becoming part of the great whole. This time our visions were chaotic. We were aware of our many consciousnesses, joined but at the same time separate. It felt crowded, like a bus station. I can't explain it better than that. Do you understand?"

I frowned. I thought I understood what she was saying, but at the same time I knew that I didn't. We passed the bakery, the laundry; all the buildings were quiet.

"You mean that something went wrong? It wasn't supposed to be like that?"

Crystal didn't look at me. She let go of my arm, gazing abstractedly up at the tree tops, as though trying to come to a decision. "It's hard to say," she said finally, turning the woven bracelet that encircled her wrist. "It was somehow unresolved. Too many feelings in conflict."

"What does this have to do with Houdini?"

She met my eyes but I felt the evasion. "We don't

know," she said.

I couldn't imagine what she wasn't telling me, what it was she feared. Did she think the Mother had lost her abilities? That she had abandoned them? Or was it worse than that? "You're telling me she did something wrong? That she abused her powers somehow?"

Crystal stopped walking. She looked at me with grave concern and said in a solemn voice, but proudly: "The Mother is a focusing lens. We are the Believers. She channels our energy. She brings us together. We're sincere in our belief, but we can't maintain that unity without her."

I could see, through the break in the trees ahead of us, the earth descending in waves of green and gold toward the darker forest. I had a sudden urge to go there, to take refuge beneath the trees.

"Without her we exist apart," Crystal said. "But without us she has no well of belief to draw from."

I didn't say anything. I didn't trust myself to answer her adequately. They recognized that the Mother could join them together, and maybe they were even willing to sacrifice their independence to help her do this. In doing so they made it possible for her to exist, to be the lens that brought them all into focus. All right. It was their choice. But what did that have to do with Houdini?

Crystal gazed through the trees toward the forest, toward the hills that rose beyond in the east, and didn't answer the question that I didn't ask. Instead she said simply: "He came up from the barracks very early. Monica said it was a little after five. He ran. He banged on The Mother's door until she let him in. They've been in there ever since."

I don't think I believed that any of it was really happening, at first. The idea that Houdini left my bed in a kind of panic and went to the Mother for illumination, or for refuge, seemed absurd. But as the morning dragged on, and the door off the mural hallway remained firmly shut, it became harder to deny.

Meanwhile the rest of us did nothing. No one had the courage to knock on the door, find out what was really happening, even though the community had essentially shut down. Of course I wasn't about to knock myself. It wasn't my place, and anyway I didn't want to be the one. I felt that this whole situation was their fault, though I couldn't say exactly how. What made me angriest was discovering that every member of New Light seemed to know what had happened between Houdini and me after we left the vision ceremony the night before. They sympathized with me for being left just as they had been left.

Later that morning I ran into Tom on the lawn by the kitchen stairs. I was glad to see him, but it soon became obvious that he was as preoccupied as the others by the Mother's absence. He kept talking nervously about the effect the withdrawal was having on everyone. It was true; very few people were doing their work. In the distance I'd seen people wandering forlornly off through the fields, and come across others sitting by the side of a path, as though they'd simply dropped, unable to go on. Tianne, who was the community's nurse, had to treat several cases of anxiety, and in the end many Visionaries retreated to their rooms. Still, a number of people came up to me as I stood with Tom by the stairs, to ask in plaintive voices what Houdini wanted from the Mother. A woman named Sandy even asked if, as the messenger, I could tell them if they'd angered the Mother in any way.

"I'm *not* the messenger. I never *was* the messenger," I exclaimed. "Why would she be in there with him if I were the messenger?"

Sandy seemed confused by my anger. "This is part of

what she meant when she said that Beth sees but doesn't believe?" she asked Tom. He shook his head quickly, then reminded her that no one knew what was happening; they all had to wait and see. He guided her away, said a few words, and returned to me.

I asked him to explain. Instead of answering, he gazed over my head up at the farmhouse, as though he could see through the walls into the Mother's suite, and thereby ascertain her will. That silence hurt me as much as Houdini's desertion.

In the end I fled. I decided I couldn't bear waiting it out with them, it was too depressing and weird. I walked quickly over to east field, to the path in the woods Ted had pointed out, which would take me to the community's swimming hole.

The path was well-worn. It curved through trees and undergrowth, leading into a cool shadowy world. As I moved farther away from the bright fields of the farm I felt myself relax and realized how tense things were there. Slanting sunlight, leaves newly unfurled, and all around me a recognizing hush. After ten or fifteen minutes I heard the sound of water, which grew louder as the path cut down toward a creek and briefly ran parallel with it. I came out in a half-clearing of moss and rock. Rounded boulders overlooked a wide bend in the creek. Farther out from the bank the current churned in the depths beneath a surface of green quartz.

It was good to sit there, on the bank, and let the river carry me beyond myself. I've found that time weighs heaviest right before something is about to change. You feel crushed, flattened by the weight, but you have to go through that feeling before you can move again. I learned this when I was very young, during the years of heaviness in New Haven, before the divorce was announced and there was release. After that came the tiny apartment in Stamford with my mom. The walls pressed in on me, school was a joke, while my mother, as she put it, struck blow after blow for freedom from a repressive, paternalistic society. Then it was my father's place in Greenwich after he'd got custody, and those painful conversations at the dinner table with him and his wife. Finally I landed at Charondon, the private school my grandmother found for me, which specialized in "understanding and developing the gifted and troubled student." My childhood was a series of weights that increased, almost to the point of being unbearable, and then suddenly were lifted. Replaced by some new weight.

I sat there by the creek for several hours that afternoon. It was soothing. A robin called from a tree behind me; a breeze blew across the creek. I lifted my hair to catch the coolness—a lovely flickering against the back of the neck. On the far bank the young cottonwood leaves stood out with vibrancy against the pale branches. Low bushes uncrumpled thin tissues of green. Ants crossed the great plain of rock, shadow-fish pecked at the surface of the air. The water was the house of their breath. It caught the sunlight.

When I came out from beneath the trees it was late afternoon. The sun hovered above the small mountain to the west. I headed back to Sparrow, but instead of going to my room where the physical evidence of last night's encounter awaited me, I continued up the barracks' path to the top of the ridge. I walked along till the trees thinned out and I had a good view of the farm. The gardens beyond the barracks' field wove neat patterns of green and black beside the greenhouses whose glass walls stunned the eye with insatiable brilliance in the late afternoon sun. Incredibly, there was no movement—no human movement—anywhere I looked. I had to assume that Houdini and the Mother were still closeted away in her rooms.

I sat down on the grassy slope of the ridge to wait for night. To my right the sun set in swelling crimson and orange tones. Long deep shadows unfolded in the growing dusk and slowly consumed the valley. The fading light in the air seemed to shiver. Birds flung themselves into the sky. I watched as the farm was delivered into darkness.

"What are you doing?"

The sharp voice out of the evening's vague dissolution made me jump. Mary stood about fifteen yards away, regarding me suspiciously. In the dim light I knew her only by the shining blond of her hair, which even now fell in a perfect wave. She came closer.

"What are you doing up here?" she demanded.

I disliked Mary because I liked Alia. At the same time I felt a twinge of guilt about it. There was something caustic about Mary, which I tend to respect in a person. But chances were I wouldn't have liked her even if I had respected her, so I didn't feel too bad.

"Nothing," I said.

She glanced down at the farm spread out below us, then back at me.

"Nothing?"

"I'm just watching this day end."

She surprised me then by laughing. "It's not over yet, Beth." Then she glanced down at the farm again and told me I'd better come with her.

We crossed the dusk field, heading toward a stand of pines about thirty yards away. Lights shone faintly from beneath the trees like a fairy congregation. Except I could hear voices. I made out Mark's above the others, speaking in excited, ringing tones. Mary called out to them and there was silence.

As we neared the trees I could see several flashlights resting on the ground, their adjustable shades fixed so that they illuminated the darkness like old-fashioned lanterns. Fifteen people stood in a circle around the lights, eyeing me suspiciously as we came up. Most of the people in the ring I didn't know, or had only met in passing. I recognized Marshall from the weavery, a woman named Kerry who was one of the bakers, Ring and Oak, who lived in Thebes with Tom and Tianne. And then of course there was Mark. So much for the shunning, I thought; the Mother withdraws for a day and chaos is unleashed.

Mark held out his hands to me, looking a little too much like a priest. "Beth," he said. He put one hand on my shoulder. "Welcome."

"She wasn't spying," Mary said. "She told me she was waiting for this day to end." She laughed again.

"Of course she wasn't spying," Mark said. I moved my shoulder slightly and he let his hand fall. "You didn't even know about our group, did you?"

"No." I looked around the ring. "Is this a rebellion?"

This time it was Mark who laughed, his expression hard to read in the soft yellow glow from the lanterns. "That's a good question," he said. "Is this a rebellion?" He looked around at the others. They laughed too.

"I don't think that's the word we'd use," he said, turning back to me. "We're worried about what's happening to the community."

"You're worried that the Mother has disappeared with Houdini?" I couldn't help sounding incredulous. If the Mother hadn't disappeared, I doubted any of the Visionaries would be standing here with him. Mark would still be ostracized by every member of the community.

He ignored my tone. "We think our leader has become unstable. Take last night. Audrey coerced you into a vision union, and abandoned the rest of the members. She's neglecting her role as leader. She's letting herself be ruled by personal desires."

"Audrey?" I said.

"The Mother," Mary said archly.

"The one we *used* to call The Mother," Mark corrected, folding his hands and resting them on his belly. "We don't accept her authority anymore. She has a name like everyone else."

"Audrey," I said again.

Mark waved the name aside impatiently. "Something's happened to her. We can't stand by, waiting until she destroys us completely. The community needs direction. I'm the acting leader. We know there are at least twenty others who aren't *blindly* loyal to...to Audrey. But they need to be reassured. They need to see that we're not a destructive force."

Those assembled listened to him, nodding. I detected a few uncertain glances, but if Mark noticed them he gave no sign. "She abandoned us," he said again. "That's why she's still in there with him. She's chosen the outside world."

Mary smiled at me. "Yesterday it was you, but not anymore."

I didn't like her expression. "I don't know what you're talking about," I said.

"Audrey sensed a rival power in you," Mark explained. "She saw that you were the sign of the waning of her influence."

"Wait. I'm no longer the messenger, instead I'm the sign of your group's ascendancy?"

Mary said, "After you and Houdini left the barn last night, Audrey told us that the rituals had to evolve. She said you and Houdini were brought to us as a living parable. The balance between positive and negative energy in the community is out of whack, but you guys could help us rebalance it. She called it shared dreaming. You have visions though you don't believe, and Houdini believes but he can't let himself see. But together you transcend your limitations. You have the power to make things happen."

I stared at her. She'd recited the Mother's latest proclamation with another mocking smile, as though she expected me to defend my former status.

"It's an obvious attempt to account for her interest in Houdini," Mark said. "Last night she found out she couldn't use you as she planned. So she decided to use him instead." He put his hand on my shoulder again. "She's afraid of you. Join us, Beth. Together we'll make New Light new again."

The colorless fleshiness of his face, there in the lamplight, repelled me. I hadn't liked him before, but I didn't remember feeling repelled by him. Was it suspecting that he'd somehow forced himself on Glass, or had he really changed? It seemed to me that whereas before he'd been enthusiastic and self-confident, now he'd become almost imperious. He spoke and moved as though he saw himself on a stage. I looked around the circle at the others. The group of rebels seemed to huddle there, surrounded by black shadows and jutting branches. They stared at me, some fearful, some defiant, some with a shadow of something else in their eyes. They were all serious though. As far as they were concerned, their world hung in the balance.

I shook my head, not knowing what to say. Immediately Mark took a step back, interpreting my gesture as a refusal. His mouth hardened. He said coldly: "It doesn't matter, Beth. Do what you like. But everything's different now. You'll see."

When I returned to my room in Sparrow there was the mattress on the floor, the tangle of sheets and confusion of blankets. I put the bed back together, then sat down at the table. The ironic appropriateness of the Mother's latest pronouncement was too bitter not to contemplate. Shared dreaming. It was perfect for Houdini. Exactly what he needed to rescue him from the verbal hegemony his left brain exerted over his dreaming mind. But what made it truly impressive was the fact that it fit so well with the rituals and beliefs of New Light. It was the perfect invention: it explained the Mother's interest in Houdini, and gave the community a new focus to distract them from the disastrous events of the last few days. At least it could have done that, if the Mother hadn't chosen to close herself off with Houdini, and let all hell break loose.

And in doing that she betrayed herself. She betrayed her personal interest in the handsome scientist who had appeared at New Light. In that I agreed with Mark. To her, perhaps it seemed like fate, like Houdini had come in response to her summons. He was perfect. He could appreciate her knowledge of neurophysiology; he understood her charismatic powers; he recognized that she was a strange attractor, destined to change the course of American history. And, of course, he needed her. I was sure that he had described his imageless dreams to her during one of their private conversations, and she seized upon it. It made sense—he told her about corporate interest in developing motivational techniques, about his research, and about his forays into the complexities of chaos. Maybe she promised him a vision. Or maybe she decided to go in on a business venture with him. Perhaps she was tired of living in the backwoods. She wanted to see the world, wanted to wield some real power.

I looked out the window into the darkness. I couldn't help it. I imagined Houdini holding her the way he held me.

Then there was a knock at the door. Heart pounding, I jumped up to open it, and there stood Alia, holding a cloth-covered plate. Her face was flushed and alive, locks of her hair defied the pageboy cut in tousled disorder, and bits of her unraveling sweater trailed from her hem and sleeves and collar. She looked wonderful. I assumed she'd just come from being with Ted.

My expression betrayed me, I think, because she smiled uncertainly and asked if this was a bad time. I invited her in. She put the plate on the table and sat down in Houdini's chair.

"I brought you some dinner. You didn't have lunch?"

"I wasn't hungry." I sat down. She had brought me a sandwich and fruit and cheese. I realized I was starving. I thanked her and started to eat.

"We were kind of worried," she said. "Tom felt bad that he wasn't there for you earlier, when you needed him."

I swallowed a bite of sandwich and told her that they all had enough to worry about. I was fine.

She shook her head. "You've been through a lot, Beth. You and Houdini went on a vision journey without even knowing what was happening to you. And then he's gone when you wake up? That's so traumatic."

I asked her how it was that everyone knew Houdini and I had been together the night before. She said it had been obvious what was happening. It was the way we looked at each other, the way we held each other after we came out of the trance. She was silent a moment, then said gently that though the vision journey was an important part of their community's rituals, it could bring up a lot of intense emotions. Since neither of us had ever had such an experience before, we were especially vulnerable.

I considered this. "So it's a real thing," I said reluctantly. She nodded sympathetically.

I had to ask about Mark and Glass. Did she think that Glass had been vulnerable too, overwhelmed by the emotions? Or did she think that Mark had done something wrong?

Alia hesitated. She said that the journey was different

every time; you couldn't predict what would happen. But no, it didn't seem like Glass's style to freak out. That's why Alia had blamed herself at first, for leaving Glass alone and for being too preoccupied with her own drama to be there for her friend.

"You have to know the whole story," Alia said. "Ted, Mary, me. About a year ago, before I joined New Light, Mary and Ted were having problems. They broke up and got back together a number of times—you know how it is. Well, they were back together when I first arrived, but after a few months things got rocky again. So they decided they would allow themselves to go on vision journeys with other people. If either of them felt drawn to someone else they would follow through on the desire. Just to see."

"That's when you and Ted got together?"

She nodded. "About three months ago. Mary did it too. With Mark. I don't know how it went, but she came back to Ted afterward. She wanted to work at it some more. Ted wasn't sure what to do, but he wanted to be fair." She shrugged.

"But he'd fallen in love with you."

She blushed. "We both wanted to be fair. Mary had a hard time before coming to New Light. Her husband moved in with her best friend. They weren't even divorced. This is hard for her, Beth. I'm not pretending that we're friends, but I can understand how she feels." She looked down at the plate of fruit and cheese as though trying to gauge the sympathy she could feel for Mary, then shook her head and looked back up at me.

"Anyway, Glass met Ted the last time she was here. She liked him. She thought he and I were right for each other, that the vision journey brought us together." Alia paused. "You know, right, that Mark and I were together before I came here?"

"That's how he recruited you."

Suddenly Alia looked like she was about to cry. "It wasn't bad. I know it might sound fucked up, but I had been in so many shitty relationships, and to have this man who held me all night—god, it was totally affirming; he was so tender and amazing and kind. And then he wanted me to come down here and be part of his family? It was incredible. I don't think I would have trusted him if he hadn't shown me."

I put my hand on hers. She smiled and shook her head and gave a little laugh. It was in that instant, between Alia's moment of exposure and her recovery, that I saw how much was at stake for the Visionaries.

I said tentatively, "And you think Glass went with him because of that? Because she wanted to have what you had with Ted?"

Alia took a deep breath and sat up straighter. "I don't know. When I went into retreat I was doubting everything— me, Mark, the ritual, New Light itself. I thought that maybe we were living some kind of delusion. Our visions, our hope for a life that wasn't about consumerism and possessiveness and self-assertion. Maybe you can't escape those things. Maybe you have to give in and accept that human beings are selfish and aggressive and cruel. That's what I thought. There was Mary, so upset she said terrible things to Ted and then just walked off; and Ted and me, falling in love with each other without even thinking how it would affect her. And then Mark thought he could force someone into having a vision journey? We were all acting selfish. I mean, think about it. You guys come down here and The Mother is interested in you and so everyone starts taking sides? I decided I didn't believe in the visions anymore. I was going to leave New Light."

The silence in the room weighed heavily on both of

us. She looked at me, then down at the cheddar and plums that sat forgotten on the plate. "And now?" I asked in a low voice.

She nodded. She smiled bravely. "I realized it's not about being certain. I didn't see that until I started making some drawings in my room. Like the one I sketched on the barn wall. The drawings just came, and that's when I realized it's about having faith. Trusting each other."

I frowned, thinking about Glass trusting Mark. Alia knew.

"I tried to reach her at East Wind but they said she couldn't talk. I called again yesterday and they said she wasn't there. I called her sister's but I got the machine. Until I hear from her what happened, I can't be sure. The Mother's right. Mark needs to face what he's done. But we can't judge him."

"I think he's judging you," I said. I told her about my conversation with Mark, Mary, and the other rebels.

She nodded soberly, but said it didn't matter. "We knew that something like that was happening." She shrugged. "It doesn't change anything. We're here because we don't want to settle for mainstream America, not because it's easy to make another life."

I found myself growing impatient. "Alia, the Mother has abandoned you guys to go on some vision-retreat love-fest with Houdini. Some of your members are out wandering the fields like lost souls, others are rebelling. New Light is falling apart."

She smiled sadly at me. "The rebels have lost their faith, just like I did. They have to go through it. Nothing is ever perfect, Beth. In a community you have to make compromises. Sometimes people are dissatisfied."

"But the Mother is *in there* with Houdini. They've been in there all day. The rebels have a point. She's making things up as she goes along – about me, him, why we're here. It's all about maintaining her power."

"You mean shared dreaming?" Alia said.

"I can see visions but I don't believe in them? Whereas Houdini believes but he can't see?"

Alia frowned. "In a way it makes sense. The Mother said you two had to confront each other before you could deliver your message to New Light. She couldn't know what that message was until you actually confronted each other."

"But doesn't it seem a little convenient? There's always some new twist."

Alia looked at me soberly. "The Mother said we need to start thinking about our relationship to the world, not just about New Light's immediate concerns. Through shared dreaming we'll invent the world around us, rather than focusing only on our own potential. We'll enter history."

"History. She got that from Houdini."

"We've learned things from both of you."

"And meanwhile your community is disintegrating. Shouldn't the Mother do something? At least the rebels aren't afraid to say what they think. The Mother's abandoned you."

Alia picked up a plum and cradled it in her palm. For a moment she didn't answer. Then she said softly, her face expressionless as she stared down at the plum, "You're right. I think she should do something."

She looked at me. She put the plum down.

"I know what they say sounds true. But I'll tell you what I really think. The rebels may be right—but I think they're wrong in *spirit*. Maybe The Mother's caught up in something. Maybe she's excited by some pattern she's seeing with you and Houdini. But even if what she's *doing* is wrong, in spirit she's right. She's our leader, Beth. We have to wait."

Belief and Seeing

– Why did the Visionaries come to Missouri?
– Because it's the show-me state.
(A riddle told to me by Apollo.)

New Light's land spreads out over 647 acres, across field and forest, over stream and valley, up ridge and hill. The Ozarks countryside, from Missouri to Arkansas to Oklahoma, is haven to many alternative communities, each one with its own vision of existence. Life in these places is strange to those of us coming from outside. We enter a world of seekers who have retreated to invent their own America. And it is a new world.

After Alia left that night I remained sitting on my bunk. I felt how ardently the Visionaries wanted to deliver themselves. They fought fiercely to keep cynicism and possessiveness out. I sat there in their midst and saw that it was necessary for them to believe as they did if their community was to exist. Otherwise its visions and hard work, its lovemaking and faith in self-knowledge, wouldn't be possible.

But how did it all relate to me? Was the Mother right, in some strange way, about Houdini and myself? When she said he couldn't allow himself to see, did she mean that he lacked—or perhaps feared—imagination? What then did I lack, or fear? The ability to commit to the concept of community? To the idea that visions reflect a reality we can't otherwise see?

But belief isn't a matter of ideas. It's not intellectual at all—it has to be a living thing, something you feel. So I asked myself, what did I feel, there at New Light?

I wasn't certain. A lot had happened since we'd arrived. And it all began with that first interview, when the Mother brought me back to my family's vacation house by

the Connecticut shore. It was an important moment, and I
had forgotten it. Perhaps the memory's return also brought
back something that had gradually become submerged as I
grew up. Some passionate longing, framed by the blue distance of pre-dawn.

Ever since we'd arrived at New Light I had felt different somehow. There was something extraordinary about the
way the Visionaries lived. Even that night, as the community
spiraled out of control, I could still feel the intimacy Alia and
the others shared, their concern for one another. I couldn't
help contrasting it to my own relationships. Who had I
loved? My parents, Boris, Kevin, Dan. A few others. But none
of those relationships were very successful. Only with Boris
did I feel a true connection—the feeling of knowing and
being known—and I had barely kept in touch with him over
the last three years.

But none of this made me soften toward the Mother.
If anything, it made me angrier at her. She had watched me
wrestle with myself, had seen that I was vulnerable, and
exploited me. In retaliation, the child that she called back
rejected her. And in turn she accused me of not believing.

Of course, her relationship with Houdini was nothing like the mother-daughter pantomime she and I acted out.
Houdini was 36 years old, a grown man. Though he was eight
or nine years younger than she, he wasn't too young. He was
attractive, accomplished, enigmatic, and his needs were very
simple. That whole "inability to see" thing. It was the Mother's
forte. There were concrete things she could do that would
help to compensate for the rather ordinary deprivations of
his upbringing. Deprivations that were not unlike the ones I
had suffered.

That's my concession to the Mother. She was right to
link us. Houdini and I were not so different after all. We were
each unfinished in a tragic though ultimately run-of-the-mill

way. Hayden White was the son of a cardiologist and a corporate lawyer. As he told me during our brief night of intimacy, he spent most of his childhood in boarding schools. There was no Hungarian grandmother, no colorful family history. He was expected to be at the top of his class, and later to succeed dramatically in a career. These things he accomplished. The rest of life—the stuff that doesn't make it onto the resume—was trickier. I mentioned that he had a lot of sex as an undergrad. But by his junior year he'd stopped sleeping around. It was too complicated. The women he slept with always wanted more. Of course he was never in any danger of succumbing, but fending them off still took up time: screening his calls, avoiding public places, staring in silence when they tracked him down and demanded an explanation.

But if the Mother was right about our similarities, was she right about him too? What was it exactly, aside from his dreams, that he couldn't see? Was it the larger pattern that every life becomes a part of, when it begins to intertwine with others? Or was his blindness more specific? Was he unable to see the new pattern that had been created in history when his own life intersected with the Mother's?

Mark said everything had changed at New Light. And Alia had acknowledged that he was right in criticizing the Mother, even if she claimed he was wrong in spirit. I decided then that Alia was protecting the Mother because she couldn't bear to face the truth. But I could. I saw that now, when the Mother was defied—by the rebels, me, anyone—she no longer cared. She had other things to think about.

It was a question I never thought to ask. Who accompanies the Mother on the vision journey? Whose dreams does she share?

twenty-two

The next morning, Alia, Ted and I walked up to the farm-house together. We were all wondering whether the Mother and Houdini had finally left her rooms but no one voiced the question. I suppose we already knew the answer. The farm felt deserted. The whole way up to the farmhouse we saw only two other people, both disappearing down East Field path. As we walked on past the barn I imagined that, except for Houdini and the Mother, the three of us were the only people left at New Light. Everyone else had fled, leaving the place empty and abandoned, a silent testimony to the death of desire and belief, to the primacy of the needs of two individuals over the needs of the whole. The absent pair were closeted away, enjoying their secret pleasures, but they could manifest themselves at any time, like some kind of living revenants. We might glimpse them strolling off down a leafy pathway or disappearing around a corner. There but not there, they would preside: New Light's ruling shades.

It was a relief then to find about thirty people break-fasting in the dining room. We sat down with Crystal, Tianne and Tom, who were happy to see us. People were hunkering down, withdrawing into smaller groups of close friends. There was a watchful, guarded quality to people's conversa-tions, a heavy hooded look on every face. A fine tension sang in the air like wind humming through telephone wires.

I wasn't immune. I felt the tension and the heavy, hooded feeling. New Light was changing before our eyes—its mood, the structure and rhythm of its life. Yet no one knew what the Mother's withdrawal *meant*. The community had been shaken loose from its framework, and members found themselves in free-fall, but they didn't know how they'd gotten there, or where and when they'd land. No one could say anything for sure. And so Monica kept providing food and drink for the sequestered ones, and the whole community kept waiting for a sign to come forth from the silent hallway.

I spent the morning helping Tianne and Crystal in the infirmary, then went to the kitchen after lunch to help Tom and a few others prepare dinner. No one talked much. We had grown numb over the course of our wait.

But that afternoon something happened to alter the emotional valence at the community yet again. Later that Saturday, six days after Houdini, Glass and I arrived, the outside world came knocking at New Light's door a second time. By which I mean, Boris and Ty pulled into the dusty parking lot, a few hours before sunset.

They came to save me. Glass had called Boris and told him what happened. She came over to his apartment and he convened an emergency meeting, calling in Ty, Lisa, and Sarah. Not having heard from me since Wednesday, they decided that I might be in danger. Boris and Ty left St. Louis that Saturday morning and drove straight through, doing, Boris claimed, 90 or 100 the whole way, and would have arrived earlier except that they got lost.

Apollo and Jenna, a girl of six, had been playing out by the purple beech and had seen the car turn in and head toward the farmhouse. They came running to the kitchen, where we were making dinner. All of us hurried down the back steps and around to the front of the farmhouse. And there in the lot were Boris and Ty, clambering out of Boris's Volvo, looking around with dazed expressions. I ran down the path to the lot and threw myself into Boris's embrace.

I sat with them under the beech. Tom joined us. He had suggested to the Visionaries that they should all leave us alone for a while, but as everyone turned to go I asked him to stay, explaining to Boris and Ty that he was my friend and had taken care of me. Tom smiled and sat down with us. I saw Boris's eyes linger, but he was too worried to allow himself to admire Tom and instead turned back to me. He kept asking if I was all right. He'd been convinced that New Light was some kind of weird sex cult, despite Glass's insistence that this wasn't so.

It was so strange to sit on the grass, there at New Light, and gaze into their faces. Boris had had his hair buzzed, so that it was just a fringe of blond on the top of his head. Ty was as steady and calm as I remembered. Just looking at them gave me some distance from the events of the past few days.

Boris confessed that Glass had called him because she felt guilty for leaving New Light without saying goodbye, not because she was really worried about me. She thought I would be okay, but when pressed said that if they really wanted to come down to act as moral support, it wouldn't be a bad thing. I asked what she said about the incident with Mark. Boris shrugged. She hadn't told them much either, except to say that both she and Mark were at fault. Sarah and Lisa were outraged at this, but Glass remained firm. Sarah and Lisa had driven with her back down to East Wind, hoping to persuade her to file charges. They would come on to New Light after they dropped her off.

We spent the next several hours catching up. I tried to explain what had happened at the farm since Glass's middle-of-the-night departure. It wasn't easy, even with Tom there to back me up. We told them about the shunning, my temporary elevation to the status of messenger, and Houdini's subsequent disappearance with the Mother. We tried to account for the rebellion. I left out my interlude with Houdini.

Boris took all of this in, then shook his head unbelievingly.

"Houdini has holed up with New Light's spiritual leader. This other guy Mark is rebelling against his mom. And while he's gathering his troops, she's off doing the nasty with Houdini, who it turns out is a scientist-turned-guru?"

"How are you?" Ty asked.

"You mean how is she as an ex-visionary messenger," Boris said.

"I've been better," I admitted. I looked from one to the other, then gave in and told them about my vision journey with Houdini.

Boris couldn't believe it. After the way Houdini had behaved, was I insane? Then he began to berate himself. He had known the state I was in when I left. He should have tried to stop me. Tom interrupted this in a kind but firm voice.

"I don't think you understand, Boris. It was a vision journey."

Tom explained, simply and candidly, what happens on a vision journey, and both Boris and Ty listened in silence, at once fascinated and a little taken aback. "You take a risk," Tom concluded. "You expose yourself to someone in a completely unselfish way. You love them. It's different from our debased notions of sexual engagement. It's not a one-night stand. You're transformed." He smiled gently at Boris. "We've been taught to fear these things."

Boris actually blushed. He looked from Ty to me, then back at Tom. Above our heads, the leaves of the beech swayed in the late afternoon sunlight.

I took them on a tour of the farm before dinner, while Tom went back to the kitchen. The sun was going down, and I was reminded of my own first view of the place, last Monday. It seemed like a long time ago. I led them down the barn path past the greenhouses, then cut down Cow Path toward the east field. It smelled pretty ripe as you passed the cow shed, but I didn't feel like going down to the barracks.

"I like the vision journeys," Boris declared as we came out onto the slope above east field. "They're straight out of gay culture." It was a typical Boris about-face in attitude. It was one of the things I loved about him, his willingness to contradict himself.

"I'm sure Beth's glad you approve, man," Ty said.

We stopped to look up at the deepening blue of the sky to the east. "I am," I said. "I'm so relieved."

"I can change my mind," Boris said. "You have to admit, it's a bit much at first. And I still don't trust Houdini. Look at him, in there with the leader. They really haven't come out for two days?"

"I think he's having a spiritual revelation," I said. "You know he dreams in words? No images."

"My god." Boris stared at me, then turned his eyes to the dark line of forest, trying to imagine that kind of dreaming life. "Have you ever heard of that before?" he asked Ty.

Ty shook his head. "No. But I don't do dreams."

"I wish you'd been there when the Mother was talking about neurophysiology," I said to Ty. "I don't even know if she's for real. Houdini seemed to think she was."

"Houdini's a talented researcher," Ty said.

"Yeah, but maybe he'd already been taken over by her," Boris said. "Maybe she hypnotized him. She fed him his own knowledge of the brain."

"He told me he can't be hypnotized," I said.

"Don't make things worse," Ty said to Boris. "She couldn't fool him that way. He would know."

"You can only be hypnotized if you want to be, right? Maybe unconsciously he wanted it. He wanted an excuse to believe in her." Boris smiled in triumph.

Ty shook his head, dismissing Boris's speculations,

and the three of us stood there on the hilltop, while around us east field relinquished its light to the sky. Several moments passed before Ty looked at me thoughtfully. "The neurophysiology of the vision state," he said. He looked at me musingly. Then he turned his eyes to the horizon.

It was a relief to have them there. I loved Alia and Tom and the others; I trusted and respected them. But I didn't realize until Boris and Ty showed up how lonely I had felt. It was hard being the only non-Visionary in circulation; it was even harder not knowing what was going on in the Mother's private rooms. I was especially grateful for their presence that evening at dinner.

The atmosphere in the dining hall was tenser than ever. It was the second night of the Mother and Houdini's withdrawal. The strain was becoming unbearable, and the Visionaries now had the added stress of these new outsiders, my friends. Their appearance had increased the hostility felt by some of the members toward people from the outside. We felt it as soon as we walked in. Everyone in the room turned and stared. Tom, Alia, Tianne, Crystal and Ted were sitting by the far window and waved to us; we ran the gauntlet of stares to their table and I introduced Boris and Ty.

I thought the meal would be unendurable, but almost immediately all attention was deflected from us. Mark and the other rebels walked into the dining room.

No one had seen most of them since the day before. But after I had left to take Boris and Ty on the tour, Tom said Oak and Ring showed up to help prepare dinner. He guessed the rebels must have been pretty hungry.

They sat by themselves against the far wall, barely acknowledging the other Visionaries. With their arrival the atmosphere in the room had taken on a new charge. People conferred excitedly with their allies, then cast suspicious looks around them. Some Visionaries seemed angered by the rebels' presence, while others—the ones who resented out-siders—seemed almost sympathetic. Across the room, several people at different tables began arguing. The level of antagonistic factionalism was almost absurd, except that it was too real to be absurd.

We had just finished eating when Monica, two tables away from us, stood, her expression grim, her hands grip-ping the edge of the table in front of her. She cast glowering looks around the room until silence fell, then announced that a meeting would be held in the barn afterward, to decide what the next course of action would be. It was a meeting for Visionaries, she said, flashing a look at our table, then added, Faithful Visionaries, with a look at the rebels.

Mark sprang to his feet.

"We hold our own meetings," he declared in a defiant voice. He looked around at the room full of the faithful with the expressive disdain of a Roman general toward the about-to-be-conquered. "We are no longer the *receivers* of wisdom, passively waiting to be told what to do. We discover our own truths! Vision is not given to the passive. *It must be seized.*" The last sentence was uttered with equal emphasis on each word. It was a threat. He walked out of the room, Mary in step to his right.

But the effect wasn't quite as dramatic as he'd in-tended. When Mark spun on his heel and exited the dining room with his lieutenant, most of his supporters clambered to their feet and followed. But Oak and Marshall hadn't finished eating. They looked down at their plates and dog-gedly shoveled the last forkfuls of noodle salad into their mouths, then rose and hurried out.

The room was absolutely silent for a moment; then everyone started talking at once. "This is our cue," I said, getting up. "I think we should leave you to your meeting." Ty thanked Tom and the others for their hospitality, and Boris did likewise with a slightly wistful expression. Alia promised to meet us at Sparrow later, after they'd found out what Monica had planned.

"Beth," Alia called out then, as we were walking away. "Don't forget that we're your friends!" She glanced defiantly at Monica, who had been watching our leave-taking.

I smiled at the five of them. They looked worried, despite their attempts to be reassuring. Boris, Ty and I left the dining hall and walked back through the night to Sparrow.

We spent the next hour or two doing Q & A. They wanted explanations and I did my best to provide. I sketched the Visionaries' characters and their differing attitudes toward outsiders; I explained about the power of the vision journey and the difficulties between Alia and Ted and Mary; I tried to outline the Mother's philosophy and did my best to describe what the vision ceremony felt like. Ty was especially interested in questions of the Visionaries' belief, and Boris joked that Ty had wanted to come down here less to rescue me than to find out about visionary religion.

When the five Visionaries returned from their meeting we all went to Alia's room in Kestrel. The interior ceiling and walls were decorated with more of Alia's bird people. Her room had a fluid feel to it, silks and beads splashed everywhere, brightly-colored pillows lapping like wavelets on the bed and chairs and floor. Alia dropped onto the mattress and put out her hand to Ted. He took it and settled himself wearily beside her.

The meeting hadn't gone well. Monica had declared herself the leader of the pro-Mother faction, and had insisted as the first order of business that they expel the outsiders, meaning Ty, Boris, and me. Tom and the others weren't the only ones to object. Jidd had made the point that even if they did kick us out, Houdini still would have been there, keeping them from the Mother.

"Monica kept trying to do The Mother's gestures," Crystal said. "The raised arms, the whole 'Hear me!' thing."

"It was annoying," Tianne agreed. "Even Mark has it down better than Monica."

"She also tried to blame what he did on you guys," Alia said.

"What he did with Glass?" I asked, surprised.

Tianne shook her head. "The rebellion. She said he was proof of the infection. He didn't realize it but he was rejecting the corruption you outsiders introduced."

"He was being shunned," Boris said incredulously, unable to keep quiet any longer. "Of course he's going to try to get out of it."

Tom shrugged. "According to Monica he's our weakest link. He's become interested in power and status, things you guys brought with you when you came."

"We had to leave finally, it was so outrageous," Alia said. "Everyone was arguing, the whole thing was out of control." She sighed and rested her cheek on Ted's hand.

He put his other arm around her, saying, "But it's serious, too. We know that Monica was being ridiculous, but people don't know what to do anymore. What Mark said at dinner freaked people out."

When Ted fell silent a pall seemed to settle over the Visionaries. They stared at the floor or into the middle distance with exhausted expressions. Ty and Boris and I looked at each other. If they hadn't been there, witnessing the Visionaries' synchronized sorrow with me, I know I would have been freaked out too. The presence of other outsiders enabled me to find the moment of joint mourning simply weird. Where was the magician who had enchanted them?

How could they be so perfectly in synch, such that, even as they suffered the loss of coherence in their community, they unconsciously testified to its continued and living force? Proclaiming its power to connect them, each to each, even in their grief.

"What about the Mother?" Boris said suddenly, thrusting into this silence. I could tell he was upset by the pain on their faces. "Why is she doing this to you? Does she even care what you're going through?"

Tom, who was sitting on the floor beside Boris, was the first to come back to us. He drew his knees to his chest and clasped his arms around them, as though made cold by what Boris was suggesting. He said in a low voice, "Does she care? We have to believe she does. As to why–?" he shrugged. "She's human. Maybe she's distracted right now. Maybe she doesn't know what's happening to the community. Or maybe she's testing us." He added this last reluctantly.

Boris raised his eyebrows. "I am a jealous leader, you shall have no other leader before me?"

Tom looked disturbed. "She has the power to bring us together. She's like a focusing lens. Without her we blur. That's why the community is spiraling out of control now."

Boris didn't answer immediately. He looked at Ty and me, then around the room at the others. When he turned back to Tom, his brow was creased in concentration.

"You're all connected. You have to trust that." He considered this, then added: "If you don't believe in her, you're definitely screwed. Though you might be screwed anyway."

His dark eyes serious, Tom nodded.

"You live through faith," Boris said.

Tom looked at him.

There was a long silence in the room. I thought that the Mother was less a focusing lens than a mirror the Visionaries used to see themselves. Right now she was excited by Houdini, by the challenge of civilizing him, and so she concentrated her reflecting power on him. Yet if my own experience was any guide, Houdini wouldn't be able to satisfy her. His identity was founded in the disguises he wore; he could no more reveal himself to her than the Visionaries could hide. Yet the Mother could not survive without such offerings of revelation. If she remained too long away from her people, eventually she would begin to tarnish and stain, and finally, reflect back empty space. While their lives fragmented into chaos, because they could no longer see who they were.

At about eleven we dispersed. The group of us said goodnight to Ted and Alia, and for a moment stood facing each other in the hall, unresolved as to what to do next. Thebes, where Tom and Tianne lived, lay on the other side of the farm in the southern field. Crystal lived near there, in a single dwelling she called By. It was a long walk through the dark.

Tom told Crystal and Tianne he would catch up with them. The two women, with sidelong glances at Boris, kissed Tom goodnight, then glanced from him to Boris again and smiled. Then they both hugged me and headed down the hall. Ty, Boris and I stood with Tom.

"It's the kind of night no one wants to spend alone," Tom said, gazing up at the ceiling above us, where one of Alia's winged beings flew moonward in exalted lonely solitude. With a jolt of understanding I glanced after Crystal and Tianne, who were just disappearing through the door. They were holding hands.

I turned back to Tom. He and Boris now looked at each other in silence. Boris, almost a foot taller, stood gazing down at the small dark man with something like wonder on his face.

"So much beauty here," my closest friend said finally, in a voice I hadn't heard in years. "Just to be destroyed."

"No," Tom said firmly. "We won't let that happen."

They looked at each other for another long moment. They made a beautiful pair, I had to admit. Nonetheless, I was a little surprised. When had this happened? What else hadn't I seen? I looked at Ty to see his reaction, but when his eyes flickered to mine he just smiled.

The tall pale man seemed to hover before the small dark man, as though suspended by the latter's dark eyes. Finally Tom looked at me.

"A long night ahead of us. Are you all right, Beth?"

I gave a quick nod and he smiled. He turned back to Boris. "I live over in Thebes. It's different from the barracks. Would you like to see my room?"

Which left Ty and me.

We went to Sparrow. I thought it would be strange to bring Ty into the room I had shared with Houdini for a night, but it wasn't. I turned on the light by the window and realized that it seemed like that night had never happened. I couldn't even feel Houdini's presence anymore.

"Boris and Tom," Ty said musingly as he sat down at the table.

I sat down also. "I think they make a good couple."

Outside moths clung to the windowscreen, and a long sticklike bug crept slowly upward. I looked at Ty. It was incredible, I realized suddenly, that he was there sitting across from me. Too much had happened too quickly for me to take it in. "It's hard to believe you guys are really here."

"I know," he said. "Boris wanted to come down here ever since you left on Monday. Then when he heard what happened to Glass—"

"He was worried," I interrupted. "I know. I haven't

been a very good friend to him."

Ty didn't seem surprised by this confession. He also didn't seem to think it worth much comment. He said mildly, "You do what you can."

We were both silent. Ty leaned back in his chair, that mild expression still on his face. It was gentleness, I realized, an awareness that we all fail one another, but that we also forgive one another. I looked out the window. "He knows I love him," I said finally.

Ty smiled. "I'd say it's pretty clear how the two of you feel about each other." Then he hesitated. "Boris was worried because he thinks you throw yourself into situations to punish yourself. To make yourself unhappy. Do you regret coming down here, Beth?"

I scraped at the gummy varnish that caked the table, not looking at him. "You mean, do I regret what happened with Houdini."

Ty was silent.

I looked at the varnish under my nail. "No," I said, so firmly I surprised myself. I looked up at him. "No. I guess I don't."

Ty nodded, his expression still gentle. I could see that he understood. Not regretting was, for me, a strange new feeling. "That's good," he said quietly.

"Is it?" I said, still wondering at the strangeness of it. Then I found myself smiling.

He smiled too. "It is," he said.

twenty-three

As I sat there across from Ty I realized a number of things.
Contrary to what the Mother had said about me, I did have
belief. I believed in Ty, sitting across from me; in Boris, who
was finding love on the other side of the farm as Ty and I
spoke. I believed in Tom, Alia, Ted, Tianne, Crystal. I even
believed in the stars' tingling rapture, which, inexplicably, I
actually got to feel one night as I stood on Boris's patio. That
too was something that happened. It was part of who I was.

Ty gazed at me, his chin cupped in one hand. Beside
him the white curtains stirred in a slight breeze; and the stick
bug climbing up the screen caught a back leg in a strand of
spider web and paused to flick the leg until it was free. Yes,
I thought, these are the things I have faith in.

At New Light metaphors were literalized. The community was a haven in the wilderness; and the Mother was
the civilizing spirit that tamed the wilderness within. By
introducing you to the visions she pointed the way out of the
dark thicket of your own monstrousness, toward a brighter
place. Ever since we arrived I'd felt her trying to redirect my
gaze. But seeing alone was not enough to get you there. To
put it another way: I felt that she wanted to change the *nature*
of my seeing. And not just mine. She wanted to change the
way all of us saw the world, so that we'd no longer simply
accept things as they presented themselves. Truth hid behind
the appearances. This was even true of the visions themselves: they were numinous, ungraspable. They led us on to
some vaguely-glimpsed place, whose meaning the Mother
would translate for us. This was why Houdini's blindness to
the visions was preferable to my simple acceptance of them.
And this was why, in the end, the visions themselves weren't

enough for her. They didn't leave a record. They didn't change the face of the world. Only we could do that, only we could make the visionary world a real one.

In the Mother's eyes I was still wandering in the wilderness.

But I believed something different. My take on things didn't make her vision untrue, but it also didn't fit into her framework. I believed—I believe still—that the visions just *are*. They're there, all the time, if we want them.

I looked at Ty and in a rush one of my earliest memories came back to me. I was three or four, lying under the coffee table in our living room. My mother was vacuuming. I lay on the rug and felt the throb of the machine's roaring motor. A plume of hot air blew against my side, and goosebumps shivered outward from that hot point underneath my shirt. For a moment I was transfixed. I have no memory of anything else. Only that brief moment of exaltation, played out against a backdrop of rug, table, vacuum. That feeling has been preserved.

Most of those childhood exaltations get forgotten. We exist half in, half out of such states for years, and then we grow up and put them behind us. Yet until our adult identity takes over, we are continually permeated by these strange moments of entrancement. Perhaps it's a sign of our gradual development—slowly we build up our defenses against the dangerous outside world. We grow warier, tougher. We learn to survive. Yet the trancelike thrall I remember so vividly seems to me also a way of knowing—and surviving—the world. A talismanic way of trying to save ourselves. We survive as children by bringing the outside into us, so that it can't kill us without killing itself. And sometimes, when we're grown up, we get a brief glimpse of that vanished way of existing. Who we were before language. Before thought. That's what the stars and the ascension above St.

Louis were. A brief return to another way of knowing.

Ty and I had been sitting together in companionable silence for some time. He gazed out the window at the night pressing in on us. His ear was a pool of shadow, the dark rim of it shimmering. His hair was cut so short it told the shape of his skull.

Boris had said Ty studied how the eye saw color. As I looked at him sitting across from me, I imagined him in the neuro lab standing over a microscope. I saw him examine the magnified cells with the same concentrated expression that he now turned on the warm May night: part fierceness, part cautious joy. He was a man who could move between realms, from the rapid staccato of the darkness cells firing wildly in the visual cortex, to the dark night at the screen, relieved only by moonlight. I glimpsed his metamorphic power. He could translate experience between realms.

The imagination was fleeting. I blinked, expecting the odd intimacy of the image to dissipate as well, but it didn't. I continued to feel that, just for a moment, I'd seen into Ty's life. I want to say I glimpsed who he was.

A new kind of silence unfolded itself beneath the trill of crickets. After a long moment I cleared my throat and asked him if he used microscopes in his work. Ty cocked his head. He nodded.

To see a vision is not an inherently communal experience. It can isolate the receiver; it can make her feel separated from other people's experience. But with that said, I have to point out that no one would really be offended if I said I saw the stars unobscured by the earth's atmosphere. They might not believe me, but that disbelief would be the extent of it. Maybe John Glenn would be annoyed, maybe he'd say that I couldn't have *experienced* the naked stars unless I'd gone up in space like him. And that would be valid; Glenn should protect the purity of his experience. He doesn't want some earthbound person who didn't train for years to casually say she saw what he saw. I accept that. But astronauts aside, in the end the stars are free game.

But a person? Even empathy can be dangerous. The empathizer assumes a certain knowledge of the other, and her motives can be obscure to herself. Yet mine was a feeling of suddenly *knowing* Ty.

Outside the window the crickets paused, then started up again.

"Why did you ask whether I use microscopes?" Ty asked.

When I hesitated he shook his head. "It's just that it was funny. I was wondering whether the eye actually registers something when you have a vision. We have evidence that in the act of looking, the cells in the visual cortex take on the physical shapes and patterns of the things they're seeing. I wondered if the optic nerves would register vision-images."

That's what he said to me. Coincidence? Or something else, something obscure, that connected us as we sat in the darkness together?

I told him what I'd been thinking. I said I'd imagined him looking through a microscope, studying the way we see darkness and light. I said (my heart beating like the wings of some fantastic being straining to lift herself beyond the limits of the earth) that I'd had the feeling that I knew him.

I met his eyes. He frowned. After another pause he said, "Do you think you do? Know me?"

I didn't answer. He said, "Let me tell you about myself."

Ty had gone to Howard. In his sophomore year, as part of a history project, he began to research his family line. There were very few records, but thanks to his grandmother, who remembered stories she'd heard as a little girl, he traced his mother's family back to 1816 when one of their forebears had been brought over from West Africa. There was very little information: a few church and plantation records, a great-great grandfather who'd escaped north and then enlisted to fight in the Civil War. In the end Ty felt overwhelmed by the blankness of his past. It made him feel bitter, not only because slave owners and traders had caused husbands and wives, parents and children to be separated forever, but because he himself felt bereft. He'd been cheated of a clear sense of his own history, and so of himself. Suddenly there was nothing behind him, shoring up his past. His people and their beliefs, loves and fears had been swallowed up long ago by the impenetrable dark. He told me this, yet I couldn't see a trace of the bitterness in his face. He described in a calm voice feelings I couldn't imagine, and the calmness itself seemed the product of a very living history, one completely different from my own. In a way it shamed me. My knowledge of my heritage went as far back as my grandparents.

In his frustration, Ty decided to practice the beliefs of the Yoruba. He thought in this way he could honor the ancestors whose lives were darkness. He had stopped going to church when he left for Howard, and thought that perhaps by turning to an African religion he'd discover a spirituality he felt he lacked.

He laughed. "The Yoruba have a saying that describes me. They say you can't wake up someone who's pretending to be asleep." Eventually, he saw his conversion as a show-offy gesture, especially because it had pained his Baptist family. It seemed to him an attempt to rewrite the past, not discover it. But in spite of this, he didn't want to forget it entirely.

"I don't want to repudiate the gesture I made then," Ty said. "It explains who I was. I thought by an act of will I could connect with a past that was a mystery to me. I could somehow change what had happened. But it was anger too. I wanted to protest. I felt like my family, a lot of black people I knew, were playing by the rules, never daring to think that what happened to us as a people wasn't just wrong, it was unacceptable. You know how you are in college. Everybody has to drop everything the moment you discover how unfair the world is. Everything I saw then was true, but I was mad at my parents for not feeling outraged too. My dad said to me, son, you've got to have enough anger in you for a whole life. Don't use it all up now."

After I'd heard his story, my moment of incandescent insight fluttered away like ash. But it didn't matter. The one led to the other. The shadow-Ty of my imagination, the real Ty across from me, both were necessary. The first, in being displaced by the second, also revealed him. I felt moved again that he and Boris had come all the way down to New Light to make sure that I was okay. I reached across the table and put my hand on his.

He picked up my hand in his two and turned it over. He brushed my pale palm with his dark fingers, then looked up. "You have beautiful skin," he said.

I smiled. "So do you," I said.

He didn't let go of my hand. "Tell me something about you. Something that changed you."

"You mean from college?"

"Whenever. Anything you like."

So I told him a story about my own father. It was the day we drove up to Vassar. We stopped and had lunch on the way, and when we arrived my father unloaded my suitcases. After we carried everything up to my room, he turned to me, his face guarded, and for a moment I felt like another piece of luggage. He pecked me on the cheek stiffly and told me it would be nice if I did well. Then he rubbed his hands together and said he'd better get on his way.

I walked him back to the car and watched as he climbed in with sudden agility. He gave me a little wave as he backed the car up. It was the little wave that did it. Something broke open. His jaunty little goodbye trilled the end of responsibility and blame. My father drove off into his own life, relieved to leave me behind.

I turned around and started walking. I remember my first view of the campus vaguely. It didn't feel real. Buildings of ivy-smothered stone, aloof pines, returning students going through the motions of ecstatic reunion. I thought, oh god, it's Charondon all over again. The airless complacency of the privileged. I felt like I was suffocating.

But then I took a deep breath. The past had waved me on. What happened now was up to me. I clenched myself around that thought until it seemed to me the most austerely beautiful thing I'd ever come across.

When I'd finished my story Ty and I sat again in silence, but it was different now. We had stopped speaking, but we continued to listen. I brushed the smooth skin of his index finger with my own.

Then Ty turned to the window. What made him turn? Did a moth flutter its wings, did the moon clear a branch and ever so slightly brighten the night field? If one of us had been talking still, would he not have turned? With the possible result that the very history of New Light would have been changed?

But he did look out the window, then half-tilted his head and leaned closer to the screen.

"What is it?" I said, leaning forward too, though I think I already knew. Across the field lights flickered. Flames grew slender and long and the procession moved forward.

I turned out the light. The field beyond the window

glowed mistily. The leaves on the maple were silvery-faint and stirred in the dark. The moon was full, or almost.

"It's the Mother," I whispered. "She and Houdini must have finally come out."

"What're they doing?" Ty asked.

"I think they're holding the fire ceremony."

"What happens there?"

"We didn't get to see it. They say it's some kind of cleansing ritual."

I could feel Ty across from me in the dark. I could make out the glimmer of his eyes, his white shirt, but his expression was invisible. He stood up.

"What?" I whispered.

"Let's go see. There won't be any guards tonight." His fingers brushed my elbow. He said, "You want to find out what happened to Houdini."

We climbed the path to the ridge. The night was lit up; the moon was almost full. Each time Ty and I came out from under the trees our moon-shadows trembled faintly before us like mice in the open. When we reached the top we turned left and struck out over the field, heading away from the ridge and the path that followed alongside it.

Our shadows now hovered to our right, as though trying to persuade us to take a different course. Ty and I didn't talk; we just glanced at each other from time to time for reassurance. We crossed the little stream a ways up from the wooden footbridge, then climbed up the far bank to a cluster of pines. From there we had a view of the bonfire. We were fifty yards away. About forty people—Monica's pro-Mother faction—sat grouped around the flames in a large circle. Absent were the rebels, as well as Tom and the others. Beyond the circle, at regular intervals, stood tall torches that streamed and flickered in the breeze.

I made out Houdini, sitting with his back to us. For a moment his profile was outlined by the blaze as he turned to say something to the Mother, who sat beside him. Monica hovered on the Mother's left.

It was difficult to gauge how Houdini had fared after his two-day sequestering. As far as I could tell he seemed fine: he sat erect, and looked around the circle alertly. I rested one hand against the scraggy pinebark; Ty stood beside me. The wind was at our backs. When we changed position needles crunched faintly underfoot.

After a few minutes the Mother stood. She faced away from us; we could hear the rhythmic rise and fall of her voice, but we couldn't make out what she was saying. But it caused the members of the circle to bend their heads meditatively.

I touched Ty on the shoulder, then began to creep forward over the pine-needles in a half-crouch. When I came to the grass I went down on my knees and began to crawl. I could hear Ty behind me. The long grass swished loudly and I dropped to my belly like they do in army commercials. About twenty yards away from the circle I stopped. The wind continued to blow but I could make out the Mother's words.

"– why else would it happen this way? And through this test we will know ourselves better. But not just our visionary selves. We must also know our darker selves now, because we have seen what they can do, how they can subvert our own most desired ends. Defying the vision. Deifying the dark."

Ty came up beside me. We both lay flat, and unless someone knew to look for us, I didn't think we'd be seen. At least not till they got up to leave.

"Hayden, you begin," the Mother said. There was a surprised murmuring from the Visionaries, as though protesting the inclusion of the outsider. I could see the Mother, who was standing very erect, scan the faces of the people seated around her. "He has much to teach us," she said. She looked back at Houdini. "But right now you are still struggling against yourself. You must purify your desires, Hayden."

So, I thought, the Mother was ordering Houdini to begin the fire ceremony. What this entailed was still unclear to me. How did they confront the dark parts of themselves? Was the Mother testing him, hoping to elicit a confession of some kind? Maybe she wasn't satisfied with what she'd learned over the past two days. On the other hand, maybe it was a formality, something she was doing to force the other members to accept Houdini's presence among them. Ty and I exchanged looks. The Visionaries watched Houdini in silence.

He let the moment stretch out. Then he looked up at her and said calmly, without apology: "I can't."

The murmurs were louder this time, led by Monica's honk of triumphant outrage.

The Mother stared down at him for a moment without speaking. If he failed the test, would she reject him? I wondered if the two of them were engaged in a power struggle.

"As I told you before," she said. "You speak the dark parts of yourself. Your fears and ambitions, your competitive desires. Any kind of conflict you feel is owned here. This is not a confession so much as a statement. You must acknowledge the existence of the dark elements that are part of you."

Ty looked at me uneasily. We lay in our flimsy camouflage, heads poking up through the grass. Houdini didn't move or speak for twenty seconds. I counted.

Then he stood, and the Mother nodded and sat down. I could see the burning reflection of the fire on his face as he gazed down at her.

"I can't do what you ask," he said. He looked around

the hushed circle.

"I don't believe any of us can know our own motives. I could make up a story for you, but that's all it would be. Even if I told you what I came here for, you'd be dissatisfied. You'd always suspect there was something I wasn't telling you. If you kept at me long enough it's conceivable you'd convince me of it too, and I would search for something dramatic enough, dark enough, to satisfy you. But you'd always want more. There would always be something else I was hiding."

"You just tell us why you came. We'll decide if we're satisfied," Monica called derisively.

Houdini paused for just a second but when he spoke his voice betrayed no emotion. "I came to find out whether you believed in your own rhetoric. I was fascinated by the legends that circulate about you. Not to mention the claims you make on the Internet. Visionary clarity. Revelations. How to confront your desires and face who you really are." He shrugged and looked at the fire again. "I came to find out what historical need you're unconsciously serving."

The Mother stood up. She folded her arms and for a moment they stood face to face. Then Houdini nodded deferentially and seated himself again. She gazed down at him.

"You disappoint me, Hayden, but I'm not surprised. You're still afraid to see where your journey has taken you. You've been fighting it ever since you arrived." She looked around the circle.

"It's foolish to reproach the seeker who refuses to see. Nor are we blameless, that we can find fault with him." She studied him again. "I say you're afraid to see where you are, but can't that be said of all of us? Look at us now. We are all fallen from the heights. Perhaps I expected more of you than I should have, but perhaps, briefly, the community spoke through you."

She spread her arms. "We must remain open! We must be willing to recognize enlightenment, no matter what form it takes! Hayden is right. We are in the midst of a dark time. And so I remind you: to assume our newly evolved forms, to create history through shared dreaming, we must know ourselves.

"As the leader, I must assume responsibility when the members of the community fall into darkness and confusion. I will speak into the circle now. I will face my own darkness."

A peculiar hush fell, as though the whole night grew suddenly quiet. The wind dropped, and the darkness crowded in until it became denser and more shadowy. Even the moonlight seemed to waver and take on a duskier hue, as though it were a brownish milk bleeding from the sky.

I was reminded of the uneasy dreams I had after we sat around this fire the last time. No specific images, just the feeling of something frightening. Beside me Ty reached over and put his hand on mine.

The Mother spread her arms again and began to chant in a jagged rhythm.

"I look into the mirror.

"I see the shadow looking back.

"I raise my eyes to the bright vision.

"I see only darkness."

She spoke these statements and responses in different registers. The first was her normal high alto, but the respondent part was deeper, more resonant and disturbing. Then she began to increase the pace of her speech.

"In me the darkness grows furious! It pants and heaves! It crouches at the soul's door.

"—I see, I see. In the ecstatic night the darkness gathers you to it and holds your lips to its breast. Who doesn't open her mouth and suck?

"—And then it's inside. Sleep, sleep. Let the dreams open their doors.

"—Oh it hurts! And, oh! the precious pain. You are delirium it screams in you; the body jerks and spasms and promises everything if it is abandoned to the solace of unconsciousness. Sleep! Sleep! The heavy dreams drag you down."

The litany went on for several minutes. It was bizarre enough to be chilling, stagey enough to seem surreal. When she finally stopped, the sudden echoey silence made the fire blaze more brightly. It lengthened into a tall narrow column of orange burning. The Mother began feeding it sticks as though in response to its call. A nightmare atmosphere hovered over us in that field. It was dread and sorrow and a terrible pressing weight.

She resumed her monologue but her voice had changed again. It was hard and cold. She laughed briefly, a cold, sharp sound in that shadowed darkness.

"Mark. Small child stuffing chocolates into its mouth. They make him ill but he eats every one because he is jealous of other people's pleasure. Then he shits in the box and puts the lid on.

"Houdini. Ah Hayden, I feed on you, as you feed on me. Oh how delicious, when we taste ourselves in each other's mouths."

The fire devoured the sticks the Mother fed it, while the black skies seemed to consume moonlight and stars, swallowing all that was bright, except for the fire's light, which burned with a flame that grew more and more emphatic and proliferated the darkness it spread across the world. She named other people; she continued her disparaging, biting assessment of their inner hearts. She mocked Monica for being jealous and following her like a dog; she criticized Ted for being weak, Mary for being possessive, Alia for being afraid of her own desire. And as she spoke her followers lifted their arms in the air, waving them in time to that ugly fractured rhythm. And all the while, Houdini sat looking from face to face, as though he were fascinated, or afraid.

Finally the Mother turned her back to the flames. She glanced down at Houdini, then squared her shoulders and faced outward, training her eyes on the night. It seemed as though she was staring directly at us. We could see her face perfectly now. Her expression was completely calm.

"No, Hayden, with you it's not chocolates. Nor do you get pleasure from denying others theirs. Yours is the most precise of pleasures, cold and abstract, and very orderly. Oh yes, I know what that desire is. I can give it to you."

She didn't move but I understood why Houdini got to his feet then. The menace in her voice; the way she seemed to come nearer, without moving. He got to his feet and took a step backward. That was all, but that was all. He broke before the onslaught. He stepped aside.

But the Mother didn't even notice her victory. She continued to stare out at the darkness, out toward us, where we lay hidden in the grass. Ty and I gazed at her with alarm. She didn't see us, I swear, yet she stood with her back to the fire and addressed the dark.

"And Beth. Oh Beth, you make me burn. Perhaps you are the emblem of our destruction. Its messenger. You carry the vision of the community's demise to us, from the outside world that would destroy us."

I was as mesmerized as the Visionaries. There was no hypnotic trance, no altered state, just the thing you dream about, the Kafkaesque sentencing, while molasses coats your limbs so that you can't move. Beside me Ty pulled on my hand, then pulled again and harder to rouse me, but I couldn't convince my eyes to look away. I didn't want to stop the experience.

But Houdini stopped it. He stepped forward, and his movement shattered the moment. The Visionaries lowered their arms partway, so that their hands made two fans on either side of their faces.

"What." The word the Mother uttered was icy. She looked at him with savage indifference.

"Cleansing?" Houdini asked casually. That show of indifference astounded me. It required phenomenal self-control.

"To be cleansed. To know," the Mother responded, her voice resounding with mesmeric power. "The innermost self must not hide its truth in shadow. To know all!"

He made a small movement with his head. A slight impatience. Maybe boredom. "Violent fantasy?" he said. "Purging? A bit dated."

She drew herself up. "*You* can tell *me*," she said in a majestic, scornful voice, seemingly untouched by his ironic tone. "You know what you've been and who you've worked for. You know what you've done to people."

Houdini hesitated and she laughed. "But in a way, once again, you're right. Usually it is, as you called it, a festival of violent fantasy. But my visions are too powerful even for me to control. I saw New Light, and so it was. Now I have seen the destruction of your friend, and so it must be."

Ty yanked violently on my hand and I staggered to my feet. He was trying to back up and pull me with him but I jerked my hand out of his and the force of that sudden movement sent me stumbling forward. The Visionaries, Houdini, the Mother, all turned on us in surprise. There were screams and exclamations. The Mother took several steps toward us. She was still in the grip of whatever thing held her, and through her held us and the sky as well, casting us all in a deep otherworldly darkness that was like one of my visions but didn't belong to me.

Houdini bounded to the Mother's side as though he were afraid she had some ray gun and was going to zap me out of existence. I looked straight at him, ignoring everyone else.

"The visions and the darkness?" My voice was angry. I thought in surprise, I'm angry.

I said, "The shared dreaming amendment, to make people think they're evolving?" He shook his head as though in warning, but I ignored that too. "Is this your historical force, your brilliant pattern out of chaos?"

But as I spoke my voice became smaller and more remote until it was a tiny sound in the midst of a cacophony, a jumble of noise that was perhaps like the voices of the earth heard from the top of the tower of Babel. But there was no tower, and these weren't human voices. Sound had taken on a viscosity, and the fields and the trees, the fire and the people around me, each emitted a particular note or sequence of notes that, added to the whole, became a music. My furious repudiation of the Mother and Houdini dwindled; I was still saying something but it no longer mattered. Ty had his arms around me, and the Mother rushed toward me. Houdini started after her in belated motion. The notes she gave forth were mournful bass tones, while Ty's music surrounded me with the lilting delicate trickle of a harpsichord. In contrast, Houdini's music reached me remotely, and it wasn't even music, more a series of odd techno-blips. I found myself a bit suspicious suddenly of this music of the spheres, the fact that most of the sounds were familiar in an ironic way: the orchestral counterpointing the industrial, the urban trying to assert itself over the natural. But I had no more time to reflect on this because then the Mother was upon me, she had thrown herself at me, and Ty tried to pull me behind his body but wasn't able to stave her off because of the confusion caused by my own struggle with him, as I pulled away and fought to be clear of his restraining, saving hands. And then she had me, she had flung her arms around me, she was clinging to me, weeping.

The Osage Oranges Fall to the Ground, and the Ants Avoid Them

It's sunny as I sit here writing. A wind-filled autumn day. The blue of the sky through my window seems brittle and distant; it's thinner and older than the tender blue of spring. A matter of seasons: so much less is possible at this point in the calendar. Autumn is the time for reflection and review, to order the past and prepare for the long dissolution of winter. Autumn explains the world, after spring has invented it and summer has wantonly used it up.

That vision I had there in the field left me suspicious, as I said. Ty as a harpsichord? Houdini as the little blipping sound that radar screens make in war movies? Yet at the same time there was something majestic about it. The confusion of sound became all I knew, in the way that hearing a foghorn close to its source can take over your mind completely. The experience was a little like going to an Andrew Lloyd Weber show. You know those actors leaping around in cat suits are absurd, yet you still get chills.

That first night at Boris's party, Houdini told me there's a look you get as a vision is coming on. He said later that he made that up. It was the excuse he invented to explain why he'd followed me out onto the patio. He didn't want to admit that he had been impelled on the strength of desire alone. But the question he wouldn't answer was: what desire? Desire for what?

This is the problem. How can you explain desire? What is it? How is it quantified?

Obviously I was angry at Houdini. That came as no surprise to anyone but myself. But I was angry not because he left me after our night of passion. In a way that night existed in a place that was separate from everything that had preceded or followed it—St. Louis, the Visionaries, Boris and Ty coming to rescue me. I didn't expect what happened between us to translate back into everyday life. I was angry for a different reason—because he had gone along with everything, hearing testimonies of visions, avowals of belief, yet had never once risked himself. I felt he had cheated. He was fundamentally dishonest. Yet, after the vision faded away and I continued to stand there with Audrey's arms around me, I found I no longer cared.

That third vision was strange. I had only a limited experience of visionary phenomena, but nonetheless it struck me as odd. It wasn't visual, first of all. And second, it was even more ironic than the ascension over St. Louis.

I decided it was a response to what happened to Audrey during the fire ritual's cleansing. My vision, my aural emanation, had been influenced by her descent into the darkness of herself. Yet the irony made me uncertain how to interpret it. Those mournful bass notes, like the cello concertos by Bach, were so evocative, yet when they were combined with Houdini's radar and Ty's rippling harpischord, the effect was almost campy. But the campiness didn't detract from the vision's seriousness. I was moved by it. Which meant I was also moved, in a curious way, by Audrey's descent into violent fantasy.

I was moved because what we had witnessed Audrey perform there by the fireside was actually an act of *anti-* transcendence. Her refusal to scale the lofty heights of the soul brought me nearer to believing in her than any of her insights or her charismatic allure. It elicited in me a feeling of sympathy and trust where the earlier talk of coincidence and visions and transformation of self hadn't. I felt she had bared herself to us. By exposing her egotism, arrogance, and furious lack of empathy, she was making an admission. There was no attempt to efface the violence and ugliness of her soul. At that moment Audrey went to a place most of us never go. She certainly showed up Houdini. She let pretence drop. It was humbling. I felt that if I were to avoid ending up like Houdini myself, risking nothing, then in response to the Mother's gesture I couldn't offer up anything less.

She embraced me. And I thought, what does this mean to me? Do I care about her, or about any of the people here? Do their fears and hopes matter to me at all? I came here for reasons that were largely selfish. I came to this community so that I could stand in this field and silently scream out my name, among all the other voices screaming their own.

To feel the weight of someone embracing you, someone who weeps at the violence she promised you. To feel the weight.

twenty-five

Houdini and Ty watched uncertainly as the Mother gripped my arms and held me to her. The fire had entered her body: I felt the burn lick me. The last chords of the night-symphony faded away. I stood awkwardly, cupping her elbows with my hands.

The other members of the fire circle swarmed over the dark grass after their mother. The fire popped and burned against the moonlit dark by itself.

Kala ran to the Mother and put her hands on her back. In her face shone the echo of the older woman's sorrow.

"The fire circle is dangerous for her," she said in a soft voice. "Her visions are so intense. For a moment she believes they're real." She stroked her leader's head and crooned to her, as though the Mother were a little girl. I felt the Mother's grip relax spasmodically. She released me and drooped with exhaustion, looking at the ground.

I felt an inexplicable tenderness for everyone there.

Kala explained with dignity that the cleansing ceremony could be frightening, but that afterward the members knew themselves in a way that could only be experienced, not described. They went *through* the dark part they'd confronted, and came out beyond it. Normally the Mother acted as anchor for them in this process. She was there for them, and they knew they wouldn't get lost in that place.

"When she needs to walk the fire circle, the whole community participates, and we help her find her way through," Kala continued. "But now we're fragmented. We weren't strong enough to anchor her." The Mother looked up at Kala with a strange, urgent expression. Kala nodded, adding, "She fought it though. She wouldn't hurt anyone.

She would never allow herself to will your destruction."

The Mother turned then to the people surrounding her. She raised her hands in weary benediction, then folded them beneath her breasts, her head bowed. The group had been waiting for this signal. They bowed their heads too, then dispersed in small groups and pairs. Some headed back toward the farm, while others went to quench the fire. As the crowd cleared, we saw Monica.

She stood half-way between us and the fire, chastened and bereft. Beside her a torch sputtered. In the lurid light her face looked like a marble mask of grief. The Mother roused herself again and murmured something to Kala, who called out. Monica came forward, her face downcast. The Mother raised her hand and rested it heavily against Monica's cheek, and Monica burst into tears and embraced her. The rest of us looked away. In the awkwardness of the moment, Sandy and a few others busied themselves with prising the torches from the earth, while Kala and Sea shoveled dirt onto the fire. Meanwhile Audrey walked away from us all, and stood facing north toward the dark forest.

I turned from the spectacle with an abruptness that made Ty and Houdini look at me. Suddenly I had to get away. I began walking fast, back toward the clump of pines where Ty and I had stood watching the fire circle. The night was dark and cool and private, and I fled into it as though it could drink me up. I was vaguely aware of Ty and Houdini following.

The moon was hard and tiny, high up in the sky. We stumbled over roots and pine cones, and slipped and stuttered down the stream's uneven bank. We came to the field Ty and I had crossed earlier. At the far end, trees gathered up the dark beneath their unmoving forms.

Perversely, I felt a flood of sudden elation, there in the open night. I walked fast, the grass shushing against my jeans. The trees and field whispered intimately, the wind's touch was delicate and mysterious. I lifted my chin and shook back my hair, feeling it spill down my back. Overhead the stars burned like cold bright chips of light on velvet.

None of us noticed anything unusual. I had no lurking suspicion that inside the shadows hid other, more dangerous ones. The ambush was at the field's end, beneath the trees, at the head of the path before it dipped downhill toward the barracks. They hid behind sycamores that wept their skins in the autumn and grew them back in the spring. I was grabbed from behind—which meant that I walked right by them—and as I struggled, I glimpsed figures wrestling with Houdini and Ty. Then a pillowcase was thrust over my head, twine bound my arms to my body, and I stopped struggling so that I wouldn't suffocate. With the pillowcase over my head, my heart thumped loudly in my ears; then fingers waggled through a slice in the fabric at my neck, coming to rest against my collarbone briefly. A voice told me to breathe.

We were taken on a forced march. I didn't know the direction, except that it wasn't downhill, toward the farm.

I had recognized the voice as Gavin's, though he tried to disguise it. I called out to Houdini and Ty and Gavin in his throaty kidnapper voice told me sharply to be quiet. I heard Houdini's and Ty's muffled responses, and another hard voice telling them that if they didn't shut up they'd be knocked out. We were led, stumbling, through long grass. I walked with my head down, to keep my mouth as close as possible to the slit in the pillowcase.

The blind march was long. Eventually my initial terror was replaced by numbness. We were propelled along in silence, and now and then the men who had me by each bound arm thrust me forward impatiently, so that I tripped.

They had to catch and steady me. We climbed a grade, crossed another field, then passed through trees. It was an old forest: I could feel the trees' great stillness, the towering mass of them, from inside my cotton cocoon. It was hard going for all of us there—my captors couldn't walk abreast of me, and with less guidance I tripped more often over sticks and stones. The guards cursed and steadied me, and I heard exclamations a ways off from the other men too.

I suppose my sense of time was also blinded by the pillowcase. We walked and walked, and imprisoned with me was the weeping face of Audrey as she sputtered in my arms. But after a time I saw brightness through the white weave. At first I felt relieved, but then the glow filtering through the fabric became more frightening than the long march through field and wood. My knees locked up. If my keepers hadn't supported me, I would have fallen to the ground.

"Put them in there," a man's voice said gruffly. There was a zipping sound, then the twine was removed from my arms and I was told to bend down. I was prodded forward, then found myself scrabbling over the nylon lip of a tent. I fell forward onto a blanket and clawed the pillowcase off my head.

I gulped breath in the airy darkness. The sides of the tent glowed faintly blue from the fire a distance away. In the dim light I saw nothing more than the outlined head of the man who zipped us in. I made out Ty to my left, and Houdini beyond him.

We sat in the dark without speaking. Ty breathed deeply; Houdini flexed his shoulders. Now and then an elbow was silhouetted against the blue wall. I kneaded my arms and resisted the urge to curl up in a ball on the thin blanket.

I don't think I was in shock, but I was too exhausted to take in the implications of the kidnapping. I sat there dully, listening to a mental echo of that rippling harpsichord that had been Ty's music in my aural swoon. Then I found myself blinking. It occurred to me that yes, there was something anachronistic about the kidnapping, as anachronistic as that harpsichord's brittle rain of notes. I had the sense of actions being translated, not accomplished in their original vernacular, as though the whole thing were an elaborate performance, someone's melodramatic *idea* of a kidnapping.

I inched closer to Ty. "Vision must be seized," he said softly, repeating Mark's threat in the dining room. The three of us considered this statement, framed by the tent's nylon silence. After a moment Houdini asked Ty what he was doing at New Light. Ty said he was rescuing me. He gave a short laugh.

I remarked crisply that a lot of things had changed after Houdini disappeared with the Mother. But it sounded bitter and I was annoyed with myself. I asked him if he'd found out anything during his retreat that could be of use to us now. I meant it to come out brisk and business-like, but to my ears again I sounded vaguely reproachful.

There was a pause. In the faint blue tentlight I could see Houdini shift, but it was too dark to see his face. He was a blank to me: there in the tent all expression was in the voice, and he didn't choose to speak.

I fingered the thin wool blanket. The chill of the earth seeped through. I said to myself, we have been kidnapped and are being held hostage in a tent. What possible good we'd be as hostages I failed to see, and then it occurred to me that perhaps we weren't supposed to be hostages. In which case our captors were insane, and we were at their mercy.

"We have to do something," I whispered.

We tried to come up with a course of action, but it was difficult since we didn't know why we were being held. We continued to speak in whispers. Houdini said this was clearly a bid for power on Mark's part, and that we couldn't risk antagonizing him. We didn't want to make our captors feel they had to prove themselves.

"But what do they want with us?" Ty hissed.

Steps passed us and we held our breath. The tent's confined space pressed on my eardrums as I strained for sounds, even after there was no sound but crickets, and the distant pop of the fire.

"This is about the Mother, not us," I resumed. "Mark tried to get me to join them yesterday. Maybe I can find out what they want."

.   I crawled over to the zipped-up tentflap. What would happen if I simply unzipped it and emerged? Would a gang of rebels surge over and wrestle me to the ground? It was hard to take the situation seriously, until I remembered the grimness of the forced march.

I called out tentatively, "Excuse me? I'd really like to talk to someone about what's going on here. Hello? Is anybody there?"

There was no answer. After a moment I said in a loud voice that I had to pee. I heard footsteps moving closer and voices conferring.

Someone approached the tent with a flashlight. The flap was zipped open and there stood Mary. She motioned me out. When I stood up and started to stretch, she gestured peremptorily with the flashlight toward some bushes. She accompanied me. I squatted and she shined the light briefly on the swirling puddle, then handed me a tissue. When we returned I made out Mark waiting in front of the tent. Light from Mary's flashlight gleamed on the curve of his head.

He gestured for me to come with him, and Mary fell into step on my right. Several people lay on the ground in sleeping bags. When we reached the fire Mark squatted beside it, but when Mary moved to sit down too he stood again and asked her to leave us alone. She gave him a defiant look. Mark stroked her arm and spoke soothingly into her ear, and in the end she turned abruptly away.

He watched her go, then turned to me with a smile.

"I would apologize for the inconvenience, except I'm sure you see it's necessary," he said, seating himself. He was pleased with himself and gestured toward the ground beside him. I sat down but I didn't speak.

He shook his head at my stubbornness. "Beth. Surely by now you see that Audrey leaves us no choice. We must find a way to retaliate."

I thought of the woman who had bared herself to the darkness, exposing her inner ugliness. I couldn't imagine Mark doing that. "Against what, exactly?" I said.

"She has abused her power. We're her playthings."

"If you hate her so much why you don't just leave?" I asked, trying to sound reasonable.

"No! *She* has distorted the nature of the visionary quest, not us!"

He sounded a bit crazed.

"What do you want with the three of us?" I said cautiously.

He nodded eagerly. "You and Houdini have exposed her weakness. She's become obsessed with you. She admitted that you're the sign, the prediction of her downfall!"

He had been spying on the fire circle, too. He had probably watched Ty and me crawl through the grass. I was suddenly afraid. And, as though he smelled it, he pursed his lips and leaned in closer. There was something hungry in his look, at once sexual and abstract.

"You don't understand us. You think you do, and that's why you don't. We see beyond the surface. The vision journeys? We become more than ourselves. You know nothing of transcendence. You and Houdini think we're a bunch of freaks."

"That's not true."

"No? And Houdini, spending two days with The Mother. The scientist. He just wanted to see a vision. That's why he brought you along—because you saw them. Because it would make Audrey jealous. And it worked. She spent two whole days with him. Holding him against her, smoothing his forehead with her cool fingers, suckling him with her dried-up tits."

I was afraid to move, afraid to say anything that might set him off. Mark breathed raggedly through his mouth, his face inches from mine. Finally, keeping my voice soft, I said: "I don't understand what you want."

"You don't understand? She can do it. That's why she's the leader. If I could enter the visionary state without her, I could save this community." He leaned back a few inches to see me better, his face heavy and slack. "Help me. Help me have a vision right now."

"I don't know what you're talking about."

"Help me," he insisted, leaning closer again. He grabbed my wrist.

I tried to pull away but he was strong. "I can't," I said.

"Of course you can. You have natural ability. That's why Audrey picked you for the vision ceremony. But she was using you. You and I will enter the state together, and we'll both be transformed. I have experience, you have ability; together we'll discover a completely new state. Visions, coincident desire." He put his other hand to my cheek and touched it lingeringly. "Don't worry, Beth—I'll help you too."

I shuddered. He disgusted me, but I steeled myself. "Like you helped Glass?" I said lightly, meeting his eyes.

His expression went flat. His fingers bit into my wrist until I gasped.

He released me. He stuck his chin out.

"Well, I don't know what we're going to do then." His voice was slow and hard, meant to sound musing. "We need you and you won't help us. I don't know what we're going to do."

When I remained silent he called out and a man appeared from behind a tree. It was Oak. He acted as though he'd never seen me before. He motioned for me to rise, then waited for orders. Mark was too angry to speak. He just handed Oak a gun.

I was delivered to the tent.

When I crawled back inside, I found that while I was gone Houdini had stopped talking. No explanation—he just wouldn't say anything. Ty and I both tried appealing to him, asking him what was wrong, even demanding that he speak, but Houdini had become a mute hunched form staring at the glowing blue wall. I suppose he listened to my report, but he didn't turn around even when I repeated the part about the gun.

We tried to sleep—at least Ty and I did. It was a restless night. I'd start to doze off but as soon as I felt myself slipping down, I'd panic and wake myself up again. I would have sworn I didn't sleep at all, except that I opened my eyes to Houdini shaking my shoulder. The bright blue tentlight of morning suffused us in a fishtank ambience. Ty was sitting up, rubbing his eyes. Houdini still wouldn't say anything, but at least he acknowledged our existence.

It was only moments later that the tent flap unzipped, and Mary ducked her head inside, telling us tersely to follow her. She had the gun now, and let it rest with showy casualness against her hip. We were allowed to stop at a cluster of bushes, where I squatted and Ty and Houdini considerately turned their backs to me. No tissue was passed out now.

Mary was annoyed, and this showed itself as impatience toward us. When I asked if there was anything to eat she snapped at me irritably. Ty commented that it was a while since we'd had any water. She motioned us forward without a word.

She stopped us just outside the clearing where I'd talked to Mark the night before. We weren't yet allowed into his presence. The fire was still burning. I think it was a symbol, like the gun. Probably it referred to the fire circle ritual and represented the rebels' defiance of the habitual politenesses of daily life. But instead of examining their own flaws, which was the purpose of the fire ritual, they were staring hard-eyed at New Light's failures. They were impatient of the concessions of communal life. They wore dangerous-looking expressions and prowled the small camp, with its lumped sleeping bags and designated piss bushes, as though the rocks and trees might turn traitor. Their stances of slouched defiance declared there was no going back.

Their resentment made them bigger than life. They let us feel their disdain for us, with our petty hunger and thirst, before handing out water and bars of nutrigrain. They chewed their own bars savagely, as though they were haunches of meat, and felt reassured by their own outrage at their bodies' need. They knew what martyrdom required. Not a relinquishing of self or a sense of humility, but simple infuriated denial. They were like movie stars. The whole scene was surreal.

After we'd eaten Mary gestured with the gun for us to precede her. We filed into the clearing, and there was Mark, sitting on a rock by the fire, trying to look regal and outlawish. Mary had us sit by him, then she squatted and stared fiercely at the flames, pointedly ignoring the rebel leader. I think her coolness made him nervous. Every now and then he threw a glance her way, then glared at us in annoyance. But as soon as the rest of the rebel clan drew close to the fire, Mark resumed his role.

"Well," he said. He looked at us with folded lips, trying to use the Mother's trick of making silence her ally, but ruined it by sneaking glances at his audience to gauge the effect. Mary still wouldn't look at him. Finally he cleared his throat and held out his hand. She stared at the fleshy palm, then lifted her eyes insolently to his. Several seconds passed, then she looked away with disgust and handed him the gun.

The transaction reassured Mark. He held the gun as though it were a wine glass, letting it rest on his thigh. "Well. Tell me, Beth, have you reconsidered?"

"Reconsidered?"

"I told you I wanted you to help us enter the vision state." His eyes went flat again, warning me not to contradict him.

From the fire came a snort of laughter.

Mark froze. "Mary has her own opinions," he said menacingly. The gun flashed. "Why don't you tell us what you're thinking, Mary? Rather than sit there snorting like a little pig."

"You don't know what you're talking about," she said. "Beth can't help you. It's an ability Audrey has. Why can't you just accept that? I told you before, we can develop our own visions. It *won't* be the same, but that's what you said you *wanted*."

"We don't have to settle for less," he returned, clenching his teeth.

"You could have Houdini hypnotize you," I said. "Maybe you can find the vision state yourself." In response Mark glared at me. Something flickered beneath his gaze and I was afraid again.

He said icily, "I wouldn't let Houdini hypnotize a dog." He turned back to Mary. "We *will* have our own

visions, and they *will* be different. We are not dependent on
Audrey." He got to his feet, brandishing the gun. "And we're
not dependent on Houdini, with his science and his tricks.
You think you're too good for the fire ceremony." He looked
down at Houdini, who returned his gaze impassively. "Who
do you think you're kidding? You think we don't know what
you're up to?"

Mark's face was contorted. Houdini didn't speak,
and the silence infuriated Mark further.

"You can't say anything because you know I'm right.
You come here, treat us like we're some experiment. Who do
you think you are? You think we don't know what you've
been up to? You disappear for two days with Audrey. Then
you have the gall to mock her. To mock all of us."

The gun in Mark's hand caught the morning sunlight
as he waved it about. Houdini's eyes never left Mark's own
but he still didn't speak. And suddenly I was struck by how
bizarre all of this was. Suddenly it was as though I were
witnessing the morning's events from a long way off. There
stood the rebels, angry, uncertain, upset, in the midst of
springtime's gentle green. The women looked tousled and
dazed, the men unshaven and haggard, and all of them were
covered with dirt and ripe with the smell of militance and
wood smoke. Yet I couldn't believe that any of them really
wanted this. They had no idea what was happening. And in
the meantime the violence that had been pent up in Mark for
the past five days was about to spill out. His face was
contorted. He needed an object for his fury, and Houdini was
giving it to him, sitting there in silence, as arrogant and
insulting as he'd been when he came to Boris's the morning
after the party.

It was inevitable. Part of the pattern.

Inexplicably, and just as suddenly, I was very much
a part of the events again, not distant from them. I called out

to Mark. I don't know exactly what I was going to do—I had an idea I could offer myself to him, or distract him by making him mad. But he didn't even hear me. The rest of us didn't exist. All he saw was Houdini, who had told Ty and me, earlier when he was still speaking, that we should above all else not antagonize Mark, not make him feel he had to prove himself. The two men stared at each other, the gun raised between them.

And then the Mother stepped out from the bushes on the far side of the clearing.

twenty-six

Her appearance was perfectly timed. There she stood. Everyone in the clearing was silenced. The violence that had threatened to overwhelm us instantly drained away.

We were left feeling stunned and a bit limp. It was all we could do to take in the fact that there she was, the Mother, the subject of all of our disputes, the cause and object of Mark's angst. After all, isn't that what it came down to? Mark was angry because she'd turned her face from him. The Visionaries were in an uproar because she'd forsaken them for Houdini. I myself had felt the effects of her influence. Her face sputtered in the darkness when I closed my eyes.

As I said, her timing was perfect. Mark and the rebels; Houdini, Ty, and myself; we all gaped. The Mother stood before us in the overcast morning light, glowing in her white robe like an apparition. She was like one of Harry Houdini's spirit-envoys: the dream-mother returning. So palpably among us in thought had she been a moment before that her sudden appearance in flesh produced an ancestor-response, the prickly superstitious fear-and-awe evoked by the shaman. I managed to resist the impulse to sink to my knees.

But the strayed Visionaries were less stalwart. The Mother gazed at us solemnly from twenty feet away, and as one they stared back. Several rebels looked like they were about to cry; Oak, Ring and a few others wore expressions of undisguised relief. Mark was so overcome he couldn't speak. The gun dropped from his hand.

Mary bent quickly and picked it up.

From the bushes behind the Mother more people appeared. First Crystal and Tianne, then, remarkably, Lisa stepped out from the shrubbery. I guessed that she and Sarah had arrived that morning, only to find out from a hysterical Boris that we had vanished. That is, if Boris and Tom had even emerged from their love fest. I tried to imagine the hell Sarah had raised when she and Lisa hadn't found any of us. If one of them had to accompany the Mother, I was relieved it was Lisa, whose sensible kookiness made her remarkably tolerant.

Beside me, Ty murmured in my ear, "Everybody wants to get in on it." And looking at the four women standing defiantly before us, that was exactly what it felt like—that this interlude with the rebels had become glamorous and exciting, so much so that the rest of the Visionaries wanted a piece of the action, so as to make sure the bad guys didn't get all the lines. The whole scene felt absurd. A nervous laugh bubbled up inside me.

"He didn't mock us," the Mother said to Mark in a gentle voice. "One cannot mock what one doesn't understand."

She smiled. There was something undeniably luminous about her.

"We are a community, Mark, even in our dissent. You yourself just admitted that." She held out her hands to him. He stared back at her, longing and uncertainty mingled in his expression. He wanted to go to her.

"Nobody move," Mary ordered.

She looked like she might've been sleepwalking. Her eyes were glazed, and her voice created a sudden, eerie silence around it. She gestured toward Lisa with the gun and asked me who she was.

Audrey responded before I could, her voice soothing. "This is another friend of Beth's. When she and the other outsiders found out about the kidnapping, they were going to call the police. I told them I thought we could come to a settlement without endangering anyone. They wanted to be sure. So I agreed to bring one of them along. This is Lisa. Mary has the gun, Mark is standing next to Beth. That's Ring, Mona, Gavin and Belim behind the fire; Oak, Marshall and Kerry to their left; Bloom, Janet and Lara on the right. Behind them, John, Rune and Jason."

Mark had pulled himself together as she spoke. He was tough and in control again. "Are you finished introducing everyone?" he said coldly. "You were stupid to come here, Audrey. You're playing right into our hands."

"I'm in your hands completely. Let the others go. I'll stay here voluntarily and we can avoid a run-in with the police."

Lisa glanced at us worriedly as Mark and the Mother faced each other. I gave her a weak smile, and beside me Ty nodded, to let her know we were all right. Then we turned our attention back to the spectacle that unfolded before us. Mark stood glaring at Audrey, but he seemed too self-conscious to really seem outraged. After all, this was exactly what he had wanted all along. This was why he'd staged the rebellion and then the kidnapping—to attract this kind of attention from the mother who had neglected him. But did he know that? I had to admit that Audrey at any rate seemed to understand what was going on. She played her part admirably. How soothing she was. How calm, how gentle, how kind. Who could resist her? It was hard to believe that this was the same woman who'd described Mark as a small child shitting in a chocolate box. The same woman who vowed to destroy me, then embraced me, sobbing.

All eyes were on her. And that, of course, was something Mark couldn't stand.

"What makes you think we *want* you?" he said defiantly, his voice trembling.

She shook her head. "I'm sorry, Mark. I understand how upset you are. We are bound, remember? You are alone only when you reject us."

"Oh really? I'm not alone." He looked around at the others. "All of us are sick of you and your lofty presence. You have to run everything. Every time I turn around, people are deferring to you. They ask you if they should have sex, for god's sake. What the hell, they can't decide who they go to bed with? You're controlling them."

"That's not true."

"Isn't it? Look around. I'm not the only one who thinks so."

Silence followed his words as the rebels gazed shame-facedly at their leader or down at the ground. Mark was right, they were all out here because they were somehow dissatisfied with life at New Light. But all of their complaints were different. Mary was pissed at Ted and Alia. Oak, like Mark, thought they should recruit more actively. Lara and Belim and Bloom thought the Visionaries were being alien-ated by all their computing work and wanted to develop more natural products like the woven bookshelves, which were big sellers these days, especially among yuppies. In contrast, Gavin, who kept up their hardware, was angry because Monica controlled the computer center and treated him like a repair man. None of them really agreed.

Nonetheless, Mark smiled coldly, his eyes flitting over his followers' faces. "They're all with me, Audrey. Doesn't that tell you something? Once the others are broken of their dependency, they'll join us too."

The Mother regarded him calmly. She said in a quiet voice, "You know I don't tell people what to do, Mark. I offer advice if they consult me."

His face contorted at her words. "Why should anyone trust you at all? You abandoned us!"

It was a howl. The rebels looked at Mark in dull surprise.

"I never abandoned you," she said. "You didn't have faith. That's always been your failing, Mark. You always want proof."

He looked desperately around at the rebels. "I do have faith! That's why we're out here! You're the one looking to make a deal with Houdini. *You* want the outside world. You're bored with us!"

Audrey stiffened. She said quickly: "I told you I was searching for a new path for us. We can evolve. We can change reality through shared dreaming. The visions we live for will be written in the face of the earth, not painted on the side of a barn!"

"We've heard it all before," Mark said. "The pronouncements, the new ideas. You manipulate people."

"*I* do?" Audrey said in a cold quiet voice.

Mark faltered. He said defensively, "You trick them. People come to you for help and guidance." He breathed in raggedly and cast his eyes around at the audience. "What about Mary? I've been here for her, not you. She was unhappy with Ted for months. She wanted to be free but felt obliged to stay with him because of you. Tell her."

Mary looked suddenly self-conscious. The Mother said quietly, "That's not true, is it, Mary?" Mary looked down at the gun in her hand. It seemed to lower of its own accord.

"What about me?" Mark said, his tremulousness suddenly swallowed up by fury. "You made everyone shun me. But you weren't *there*. It was just me and Glass. You decided to punish me because you knew I was a threat to you. You were jealous. People were starting to listen to me."

The Mother looked at him steadily. She said, her voice compassionate now, "I know the shunning was hard, Mark. But everything I do is intended to bring the outer vision into coherence with the inner one. You had to face yourself. You want power over others. But instead of confronting that in yourself, you pressured Glass to do what you wanted. You convinced yourself that she wanted to go on a vision journey with you, so that you could avoid facing your true motives. You can deny it to us. Can you deny it to her face?"

From out of the bushes appeared Glass, with Alia at her side. There were gasps, followed by a hush. Crystal and Tianne left their positions beside Lisa so that they stood shoulder to shoulder with Glass and Alia, forming a solid wall of women confronting the rebel camp, each eyeing Mark stonily.

Once again I had to admire the Mother's flair for the dramatic. Glass and Alia had been hidden in the bushes the whole time, waiting for their cue to emerge.

"Can you deny it, Mark?" Alia asked bitterly, one arm around her friend.

Glass's face was troubled. She looked at Mark without speaking. After a moment she dropped her gaze to the pine needles at her feet.

At this point Lisa, who shouldn't have been there in the first place, who knew nothing of New Light or its practices, could no longer contain herself. She had been listening doubtfully all this time to the Mother, but it was Mark who made her explode. "I don't know anything about this community, who's in charge, or what kinds of crazy sex games you play. But you forced yourself on Glass, and then you kidnapped my friends. Nothing you say can justify that."

Mary turned to Mark. She didn't speak, she just looked at him.

"It was a vision journey," he said to her, spreading his hands in appeal. "Wasn't it, Glass? I thought if I could show her what it was like she would join the community. I was trying to help her. We were talking about the visions and she said she'd like to have one. She thought our community was based on beautiful ideas. You said that, Glass! You told me that East Wind doesn't practice communal spirituality. She belonged here but she couldn't decide. I was trying to help her see."

Mary stared at him. "You forced her?"

"No! She was afraid. She wanted to, but she wasn't sure. That's what she said. That she didn't think she was ready. But she *was* ready."

"All this time you've been telling us how unjust your punishment was," Mary said. "You lied. Glass didn't want to have sex with you."

"No! What I said was true. The Mother thinks she can control our lives!"

"You prick," Mary said. Without blinking she lifted the gun and fired. The bullet hit Mark in the thigh. He staggered backward and fell next to the fire, gasping. Blood began to soak his pantleg and he bent over the wound in shock. Mary stared at him as though transfixed. Then she looked around at the rest of us. We were all frozen, the rebels wearing expressions of horror and disbelief, the rest of us suddenly aware that we were afraid of her. Mary's expression didn't change. She tossed the gun at my feet and turned and walked off through the trees. The gun bit into the dirt in front of me and and sprayed pine needles and crumbled earth onto my sneakers. I stood looking at it stupidly until Ty snatched it up. Then everyone was moving and talking at the same time. Mark had started to scream.

It was the Mother who got Oak and Belim to carry Mark out to where the truck was parked, at the edge of the forest. It was she who drove him to the county hospital, while Tianne cradled him against her and applied pressure to the wound. Later, when she and Tianne came back from the hospital,

Tianne told us that Mark had lost a lot of blood but was going to be okay. The Mother didn't address her followers then. It seemed that she had spent herself in dealing with the crisis. She went straight into the farmhouse and shut the door behind her.

Throughout the whole episode and its aftermath, Houdini never said a word, not even when we came straggling out of the forest and saw Mary, weeping like an icon at the edge of the trees. Houdini went over to her and mutely put his arms around her. For a moment Mary didn't move, a crude statue made of wood, until suddenly she crumpled and clung to him. He held her for a moment, then drew her toward the group of us who stood watching: myself, Ty, Lisa; and Crystal, Alia and Glass. We stared with what must have been stupefied expressions. None of us spoke as we waited for them to join us, cocooned as we were in our exhausted separateness. The six of us let them catch up and then all of us trailed after the rebel faction, as they returned in shame to the land of visions and light.

twenty-seven

And so the rebellion at New Light was quelled. The violence Mark had threatened was turned on him, with Mary as the agent.

Most of the Visionaries felt that Mark was to blame for what happened out there in the woods. The shooting, they said, had been his punishment for forcing Glass to have sex with him and then refusing to acknowledge what he'd done. The other rebels each played a role in the melodrama, but even Mary was innocent in comparison. She had turned to Mark after her relationship with Ted had soured, and he had told her that the two of them were meant to be together. This happened on Wednesday afternoon, the day after he had had sex with Glass; the same day the shunning had been declared. Mary believed what he said—that what happened with Glass was a vision journey gone awry—because she wanted to avoid facing her own sorrow. And so the two clung to each other, sympathizing with one another's need to deny what neither could face.

The only one who challenged this neat assignation of blame outright was Glass herself. She disagreed with those who claimed that Mark had brought on his own punishment, because she said that he was not solely responsible for what had happened between the two of them. She refused to call what he did rape. She claimed that, in the end, it was her decision to sleep with him: she decided he needed to have sex with her more than she needed to refuse him. This made Lisa angry. She told Glass hotly that that didn't matter; Mark was still guilty of forcing himself on her. Glass agreed. But she said it was also complicated.

The way Glass told it was this: They had talked for a

while by the fire. Mark genuinely wanted her to join the community, and she was interested. They went back to his room together after the fire died down and there he told her excitedly about life at New Light. She had heard most of it already from Alia of course, and in the end said that she wasn't ready to leave East Wind. In response Mark said that he would show her how wonderful this life could be. He would prove to her that New Light was where she belonged. Together they would go on a vision journey, and be mutually transformed. They would emerge from the experience as new beings.

Glass was flattered, but the fact that Mark had also recruited and gone on a vision journey with her friend Alia made her a little uncomfortable. She said she wasn't used to the open attitude toward sex the Visionaries had. Affairs at East Wind could get incestuous too, but it wasn't a part of the rhythm of life there. She didn't want to do it.

In response Mark began to beg. He told her how lonely he was, and how he longed to make a connection with someone from outside to spread the word of the visionary life beyond the confines of the New Light community. He confessed that the vision journeys were a way of recapturing the intensity you felt upon first joining, when the Mother was very attentive toward you, when you realized that your place in this new world was important, that you were irreplaceable. That's what the vision journey could give you, he explained, the feeling of being cherished. The feeling that, to someone, you were important above all others.

As she listened to this Glass felt sorry for him. Maybe Mark sensed that. Suddenly he stood up and told her she was afraid to transcend. He told her she lacked faith. He was trembling. Glass stared at him, taken aback. Then he put out his hand and touched her cheek. She didn't resist or encourage him, she just looked at him. He dropped his pants, and in a few minutes it was over.

I think she was proud of her decision to take responsibility for what happened. And whether we agreed with her or not, what could any of us say? She had been there.

The eight of us trudged through fields and along forest paths back to the farm. We walked slowly, the rebel group always just in view ahead of us. Oak and Bloom held hands, Ring wept quietly and was supported by Lara and Janet. Among our group, Crystal, Alia and Glass led the way, followed by Lisa, Ty, and myself. Trailing about twenty-five feet behind us came Houdini and Mary. We crossed the upper fields in mournful silence and finally caught up with the rest of the rebels at the ridge.

Their sad band was looking dazedly down at the farm below. Oak kept shaking his head; Ring and the others just stood and stared. From below we heard a noisy commotion.

We came up beside them and then, like them, gaped at the scene spread out over the field below us. There, advancing toward us along the barn path, was the whole of New Light. Every Visionary had come out to greet the wayward ones, even the children. People danced and sang; some played instruments; others leapt about joyously, flinging colored scarves into the air. It had been decided that the rebels' return would be not a defeat but a celebration.

Dumbfounded, the rebels continued to stand there, until suddenly Lara broke into a run. Soon all of them were careening down the slope after her. Alia and Crystal laughed and ran after them. We outsiders stood in silence and stared at the chaotic celebration in disbelief. Glass stood with us, frowning down at the celebration. And behind us, forgotten by her fellow Visionaries, stood Mary.

It was a time of rejoicing. Rebels and faithful hugged each other and wept, as though the Mother and Mark had become symbolically joined by the moment of violence. There were apologies, reassurances, testimonies of faith and love. Some people were whooping and laughing, others raised tambourines in the air or performed country jigs. Jenna, the little girl who had announced Boris and Ty's arrival, kept darting in and out, opening and closing a red umbrella, the other four children following after her in a small swarm.

There was something appealing and at the same time shocking about the display. Boris and Sarah made their way through the mass of celebrants and climbed the path to join us on the ridge. As we watched the riotous festivities they explained that the Mother had stopped briefly on her way down from the rebel camp to give word to the others about what happened. I understood that, after the past two and a half days of tension, the Visionaries were terribly relieved, yet all I could think was: this is how they respond? Their community was host to several acts of violence, and the only thing that mattered to them was the fact that the rebels weren't rebelling anymore?

"Mark's been shot by Mary," I said, as though the fact itself was in dispute. I looked at Ty and Lisa, then turned to Sarah and Boris, who had just reached the top of the ridge.

"You guys are okay?" Boris said, panting and wiping his brow as they came up beside us. "I can't believe any of this." He glanced down at the crowd of Visionaries. Tom was hugging Alia and Crystal.

Sarah, slightly breathless from the climb, shook her head. "Thank God you guys are all right. This place is crazy. This morning they were talking about disbanding the community. Now look at them."

Glass had been watching the Visionaries in silence. "It's not crazy," she announced suddenly. "They're relieved. They've been so worried. It's just how they choose to express themselves. Would you feel better if they stood around and told each other how terrible it is that Mark got shot? They know how terrible it is."

We stared at her. She descended the hill to join the celebrants.

Glass was right, I suppose: the Visionaries saw the shooting as an explosion that led to the healing of New Light. The act of violence was necessary, or more precisely: the act of violence simply *was*. There was no changing it. The only thing the Visionaries could control was their response to it. And so the festivities continued, the participants wending their way slowly back to the farmhouse lawn. The scarf-fliers ran ahead, silks rippling in streams of gold and purple and green behind them. Next came the musicians and singers, the loudest of the rejoicers, followed by the dancers and the children, and finally, bringing up the rear, those who talked, some with laughing enthusiasm; others earnest, their pleasure more solemn.

We followed. When we got to the farmhouse lawn we seated ourselves on the edge of the gathering, near the front of the house by the purple beech. The celebrations continued, and as we watched I realized that, at least in one sense, Glass was right. Despite the rather frenzied nature of the Visionaries' rejoicing, there was something quite serious about it too. There was a formality to its spontaneousness. Every now and then there would be a lull in the singing or dancing, and people would pause and look around at each other, their foreheads creasing momentarily, a shadow of uncertainty in their eyes. Then someone would step forward into the silence and determinedly take up the mantle of celebration again. The others all smiled at each other and joined in again with enthusiasm.

Throughout the festivities Mary remained apart. She stood with her eyes downcast, Houdini beside her, on the far

edge of the lawn by East Field path. And none of the Visionaries tried to approach her. From time to time someone
turned a face full of fear or sorrow to her, but no one tried to
draw her into the circle of warmth.

What was there for us outsiders to do? We sat on the
grass and watched, we discussed the events of the last few
days, we talked about how weird it was, to be sitting there on
the grass talking, while the Visionaries celebrated twenty
feet away. After we'd analyzed the kidnapping and the
Mother's negotiation tactics to death, Sarah and Lisa turned
the conversation to Boris's love affair. Sarah leaned back
luxuriously, resisting Boris's attempts to change the subject,
especially after Tom ran up and planted a kiss on Boris's
cheek, then danced off again.

"Boris," she said. "I've never seen you like this."

"Sarah," he said warningly.

"Yes? Do you know you're glowing? And you haven't
made a single sarcastic comment, even though the rest of us
have gone on and on about how weird all of this is."

"Sarah, don't."

"I'm *not*. I think it's the best thing that's ever happened to you."

Boris looked over at Tom, who was being swathed in
silks by Alia and Glass. The women giggled as they wound
him round and round with a fringed purple strip. Tom held
his arms out, but he was laughing so hard various silks kept
flying loose and frothing about his face. Boris sighed and
leaned back too, briefly resting his head on Sarah's shoulder.

"Glass was wrong. They are crazy. And I envy them."

When the truck turned down the rutted drive a few hours
later, the revelries were still going on, though they had
calmed considerably. The pitch was less frenzied now, but
the celebrants had amazing stores of energy. Several contin-

ued to sing and dance, their voices now loud, now murmurous, their movements vigorous and charged, then rapturously slow. Others sat in the grass more quietly, exchanging confidences, renewing severed bonds. Their relief at finding their community restored gave the occasion the feeling of a holiday.

But as soon as the truck appeared between the trees it was clear that, all along, even while they celebrated, everyone had been waiting. A hush fell as the truck disappeared into a declivity, then reappeared closer to the house. The Visionaries unwound silk from their necks and shoulders, pulled dried grass from their hair. Slowly they approached the front of the house, where we outsiders stood.

The Mother and Tianne pulled into the parking lot. The truck braked abruptly and we could see Tianne, in the passenger side, lurch forward and back. She glanced out at the crowd, then turned her face back to the Mother, who was invisible behind the glare on the windshield.

They sat there in the truck for some time. I suppose it was only five minutes, maybe ten, but it felt much longer to those of us waiting. The Visionaries' attention seemed to stretch and grow taut. We could hear the rise and fall of the two women's voices through Tianne's half-open window, but not what they were saying. No one on the lawn stirred.

Then the truck door on the far side of the cab squeaked open, and squeaked again as the Mother slammed it shut behind her. Tianne got out from her own side and followed the Mother. We all stood in silence as New Light's leader crossed the sandy lot, her eyes on the ground. The white robe hung from her arm, catching on tall grass that fringed the perimeter. I'd never seen her in safari shorts before.

Tianne followed her as though she wanted to say something. She glanced at the crowd, her expression unreadable, then back at the Mother. And all this time the Mother never once looked at us. It was as though she didn't even know we were there, so immersed was she in her isolation. The skin beneath her eyes was pouched; her face looked like it was made of parchment. There was something terrible about her exhaustion. She had spent herself utterly for her people. She was scraped bare and dry. In the silence we heard the wood creak as she climbed the front stairs. She opened the screen door and disappeared inside.

Tianne followed her to the foot of the stairs. She stood staring up at the door as it banged shut behind the woman who kept New Light whole.

There was a baffled silence. Finally Tianne turned to us.

"Mark will be okay. He lost some blood. They gave him a transfusion. The Mother insisted on donating her blood. He wept when I told him it was hers."

There was a silence. Tianne described Mark's interrogation by the sheriff. Mark said that the shooting was the result of a lover's quarrel, that the gun had gone off by accident. He refused to file a complaint or give the woman's name. He told the sheriff he had done everything in his power to drive her crazy, so should he blame her when she got so upset? And when he was questioned as to what he'd done, he said, "You know. Sex stuff." The sheriff had turned away in disgust.

There was another silence. In the quiet I could hear the breeze stirring the leaves of the beech. I glanced up and noticed that the undersides weren't purple but pale green.

Monica said into the silence, "What happened to her?"

Tianne's expression became more somber. She said nothing, only shook her head.

The mood on the lawn had inverted starkly since the truck pulled up. The atmosphere of celebration had vanished; the crowd now floundered in airless misery, everyone turning to his or her neighbor in a hopeless quest for understanding. I looked at Ty and Boris, at Sarah and Lisa. We felt the Visionaries' desolation press down on us.

Then a murmur spread through the crowd of the faithful. Seventy-one people seemed not to be speaking so much as emanating sound. It was an aching, wordless vibration; it swelled and rose like the beating of wings, like a wind that gathered us up in it.

As a body they turned, seeking solace. It seemed to me I felt the Visionaries' joined minds: seeking and faltering, bumping from here to there, then sharpening, focusing, scenting relief. The aching cry seemed to expand and fill the air around us, drawing us toward the other end of the lawn, where Houdini and Mary sat forgotten.

"Oh God," I said to Ty. I remembered the helpless nightmare feeling of the fire circle. He gripped my hand.

"Beth," said Lisa, "what's happening?"

"What's going on?" Sarah echoed, looking at the crowd that had turned their backs to us. Boris was straining to see where Tom was, though he didn't move from his place next to Ty. He couldn't have, even if he'd wanted to. We all stood there, feeling overwhelmed, not knowing what to do.

Yet the fact that all of us spoke to one another, that we were afraid of what was happening and communicated this fear to each other, reassures me now. Of course it's evidence that what I felt was real, and that scares me, but it shows the spell wasn't unbreakable. We voiced our shared distress at the feeling of doom that was humped over the farmhouse lawn, as electrically threatening as a massing thunderstorm. We rejected it. We were afraid.

Still, as we gazed at the two outcasts, I continued to feel whatever it was I felt. I was impelled toward Houdini and Mary, as though all life would stop if I didn't get to them, face them, stare into their eyes.—and do what? I don't know.

"Come on," I said. I led them around the edge of the crowd, which had so far done nothing more than look and keen. We hurried forward, positioning ourselves between them and the man and woman who sat on the grass, mutely, without moving.

Houdini and Mary sat there, apart from us, alone and undefended. They presented themselves to us. They had been waiting for this all along, only we couldn't see it. Or were too afraid to see it. They were offerings, the already-dead. They had been waiting, patiently, passively, for the sacrifice. And we were the ones who would give it to them.

The feeling was the underside of the communal spirit that inspired New Light. The individual had to be sacrificed to the group in a gesture that was at once symbolic and practical. The community had priority over the isolated self. Those individuals who threatened it had to be destroyed. This was the source of that electric fear that had caught us up, in that terrifying fascinating compelling suspension of ourselves.

Sometimes I'm afraid that I could still feel it, now, if I let myself.

Then, as my friends and I stared at the two victims—with the mob of Visionaries rumbling behind us like an eighteen-wheeler, as though they were slowly building speed—then, just then, the Mother appeared at the top of the kitchen stairs.

She had donned a fresh robe. The gold halter was back. Colored silks fluttered from wrists and hair.

She raised her arms.

Her presence shattered the mob. The Visionaries, all of us, were banished back to our individual selves. I know we stood there, stock still, blinking, but I was left with the impression of us milling around like sheep, baa-ing confusedly.

"Are you all right?" Ty asked, his hand on my shoulder.

"*What* is going on?" Boris muttered, eyeing the Visionary leader.

"More theatrics," I said, my voice shaky and defiant, as though I thought I could erase what had happened.

Though of course nothing had happened. Aside from our mad dash from one end of the crowd to the other, no one had moved.

The Mother looked out over the faces of her children and nodded solemnly. Then she came down the stairs and walked slowly past us to where the outcasts sat in their mutual silences, one protective, one abject. We watched.

The two looked up at the Mother as she approached. Mary immediately cast her eyes down again. The Mother stopped in front of them and began to speak in a low voice. We couldn't hear what she was saying, but Mary got to her feet and stumbled away. Houdini watched her go, then turned his eyes back to the Mother. Or rather, to Audrey. She said something else and waited for him to speak. When he didn't, she turned and followed Mary. Houdini was left alone on the grass.

Audrey caught up with Mary and held out her hand to the younger woman. Mary whirled away from her and shook her head violently. Audrey said something and Mary stood there, immobile and unyielding, eyes on the earth. Audrey waited. It was a pantomime acted out for our benefit: the Mother reclaims the lost soul and brings wholeness to New Light. She waited, her tired face resolute, until finally Mary's resistance slid off her like a load of melting snow slipping down a roof. She still looked at the ground, but suddenly her whole body seemed lighter. The Mother spoke gently to her and Mary nodded. Together the two left the lawn, cresting through the field of long grass. They walked toward the east.

Houdini remained sitting where he was. He looked at all of us without expression, then turned his face to the northern fields.

twenty-eight

To my right stood the pastel-yellow farmhouse. To my left, Barn Path, curving past the mural-covered barn and out toward the greenhouses and gardens. The cropped grass of the lawn ruffled slightly in the breeze. It was a placid, lovely place. It didn't look like the backdrop for violence and terror.

As the Mother and Mary crossed Center field and disappeared from view, the Visionaries on the lawn began to mill about in a lazy, aimless sort of way. We were all a bit dazed, as though we had just done the emotional equivalent of the Ironman. Tom threaded his way through the crowd to join us; behind him came Glass with Alia and Ted in tow, and after them Tianne and Crystal, arms linked.

None of them seemed disturbed. They looked tired, which was understandable after the hours of celebration and the exhausting trials of the last three days. They did not seem self-conscious. The hint of sacrifice in the air, the surge of bloodlust that left a metallic taste in the mouth, all that was gone. No one looked guilty, no one seemed afraid of what had almost happened. Of course, nothing had happened. Nothing at all. I reminded myself of that.

I couldn't stay there. If nothing had happened, then it was me, it was my own violent fantasy that I had imagined playing out on the farmhouse lawn. Which was worse than falling prey with all the others to a collective nightmare. I mumbled something about being back in a little while and started walking. Boris and Sarah called after me. Ty frowned. Lisa took a few steps. I waved them all away and they got the message. They didn't follow.

I wasn't sure where I was going. I headed toward the parking lot, thinking perhaps I would just keep walking, right off New Light property. But instead I stopped in front of the farmhouse.

I remembered our arrival, last Monday, how Monica stood on the porch in her purple robe, frowning down at us. I remembered how strange my first glimpse of the mural hallway had seemed. As then, so now, I thought. I climbed the stairs, opened the screen door, and stood on the threshold.

It was too dark inside to see any of the images clearly. I felt behind a curtain and found a light switch. And there were the visions, revealed in all their disconcerting colors and shapes by a dusty, dull-yellow bulb. They looked better by candlelight. The electric light uncovered the awkwardness of execution, the violations of perspective and form, the mistakes that had been clumsily painted out.

I went down the hall and tried the throne-room door. It was open.

I hadn't been there for days, not since my private interview with the Mother. It felt strange to be there by myself, especially knowing that she and Houdini had spent two days in the suite. The shades were still down. At the far end of the chamber the door to her bedroom stood open. I averted my eyes, examining instead the sumptuous furnishings of the throne room.

It may seem surprising, yet the room felt even more fantastic without the Mother there. It wasn't anything obvious. I think, with her there, one couldn't fully appreciate the rather labored exoticism of the place. Her presence was the main event, it dominated the mosaics and stained glass, the inlaid tables and silk curtains. All of these things were intended as backdrop, but with the star gone, the set was laid bare.

The first time I'd been there I felt I had walked into a parlor of empire spoils. In a way that was right, but in the diffused white light that came through the shades I saw that these objects didn't belong to the collection of any emperor. They were a strange hodge-podge, carelessly assembled: a Hindu altar with a hand-made Ozark banjo leaning against it; chunky blue-glass Mexican candleholders resting on a large Arabic dish, its intricate Moorish design filmed with wax; fancy Czech lace that had been soiled by a Tibetan incense burner. The objects told no story, or none that I could see. They simply bespoke an omnivorous hunger for that which was unfamiliar.

Yet despite the arbitrary feel to this collection of objects, as a whole it worked. It was fantastic, it was strange. You weren't left with an impression of imperial ambitions, or of someone's carefully cultivated taste, carefully displayed. The collection presented the things of this world in order to take you beyond this world. It was in service of the mystery.

The mystery. That was what she offered. The promise that, inside each of us, our true selves carried on their existences, independent of the lives we were forced to lead. We could fight our battles, fall before our adversaries, but meanwhile a tiny ember of belief, a faith in something we couldn't put into words, burned on. Many of us spent our lives ignorant or afraid of this thing. Yet it persisted. It was there.

Sometimes sensing its presence would lead us to do things we couldn't explain. We'd break with people we'd been intimate with for years, for no apparent reason. We'd find ourselves cradled in the arms of strangers. We did things that embarrassed or frightened us, driven on by a sense of possibility, an inkling of revelation whose meaning eluded us.

I thought of my mother. It was the strangers who drew her. She entered into love affairs with a savage abandon that terrified the people who witnessed them, myself included. Terrified us, and left her bereft. But of course I couldn't allow her the right to that feeling, because, after all, she brought it on herself.

My father was different. He was sustained by the secret life he lived in his car, driving from one role to another. He was truly himself only between destinations. He went from corporate exec to dutiful father, afraid of the daughter he couldn't understand; then from father to distant husband, married to a new wife who didn't upset him. That car life of his freed him, just as much as my mother's savagery freed her. That is to say, not at all.

How we fight to keep from knowing what we know.

But the inevitable always wins. We do what we must. The mystery eludes us, yet drives us on; that much I had learned. And so I turned toward the doorway that led to the Mother's private bedroom.

From where I stood I could see the white bedspread. The gleam of floorboards, a creamy rug. I approached the threshold. This room was very different from the exotic waiting room for the faithful. This room was all in white, so that the Mother would feel her spirit lighten as soon as she walked through the door. It was austere in a pleasing way: floor-length white drapes made of cool-looking cotton, matching spread and rug. The simple fabric complemented by the pale oak of floors, walls, furniture—small bureau, table, two chairs. Simple and harmonious. Reflecting back the Mother's private self.

I returned to the throne room. I sat down on one of the wine-colored velvet armchairs, facing the wicker throne, and imagined the conversation the Mother and I would have.

So, I had finally come to her. She would stand on the threshold, taking in the fact of my being there calmly. She could tell I was prepared to be open, and that I hoped for some conversational candor on her part in return. But then she glanced around: the exotic backdrop was no longer appropriate. We needed to meet as equals, with the sky above us, the earth below, the sunshine illuminating our two faces.

We left the farmhouse and followed the western path to the ridge. But at the top we didn't head toward the site of the fire ceremony. Instead we took the path that ran along the edge of the ridge. The grass rippled in the warm wind.

"I have many questions," I said.

She smiled at me. "Most of them only you can answer."

I bowed my head. A breeze kissed my face. "But I also wanted to ask you about Houdini," I said.

She looked at me, then turned her eyes to the east. Maybe she walked with her hands behind her back, in a meditative pose, her eyes caressing the landscape. I wanted her to be familiar with every tree on their land, every hill and ravine and river.

"He's going to be all right, isn't he?"

"Is that a question or a threat?" she asked in an amused tone.

"A question."

"Is that the real question you want to ask?"

At first I said I didn't understand what she meant. I protested. But finally I had to concede. "I want to know what happened between you," I whispered.

She nodded. She came to a stop at the same spot where, two days ago, I had sat and looked out over the farm. The end of the first day they had spent together.

"You had to ask before I could tell you," she said. "You had to be willing to know what happened to him."

Then she explained that Houdini had fallen in love with me. He discovered this the night we made love. It wasn't a state he could tolerate; he fled the scene like a criminal. (To her description I added an allegorical figure of personified

Guilt that pursued Houdini as he fled. It wore the guise of a horrible demon whose eyes were black holes, sucking light.)

"I held him," she said, meeting my eyes electrically. "For hours. And then we talked. It almost seems like we talked for two days straight, though of course that's not the case."

She described the scene to me. How she seated herself in the center of the white bed, arranged her robes around her, and went into a light meditation. Houdini stood and watched her. He watched her go deeper, deeper, and finally he knelt in front of her, held his hand under her nose, felt the faint even breaths feather against his fingers. Then he began to kiss her. All over her body. He became the small point of consciousness inside a frenzy of kissing, and the whole time she continued to meditate, unmoving, the light regular breaths her only response. After he'd exhausted himself, he curled up in a ball before her. He fell asleep, and dreamed that he was Christ in his desert, Mohammed on his mountain, Siddhartha during his fast. The images were so vivid, he forgot who he really was.

The Mother came out of meditation. Houdini lay there, remote, eyes closed, and she began to brush her fingers lightly across his brow. These are called Mesmer's strokes; they are intended to help one enter the trance state. But she drew her soft fluting fingertips from brow to cheek, from cheek to jaw, down neck and along collarbone. He rolled onto his back, slipping from sleep into a different state, deeper and deeper. The Mother continued to cover him with Mesmer's strokes, sending him to the center of the trance state, until he climaxed and cried out terribly.

"He was afraid of the release, you see," she told me. "The transformative power of sex." She smiled. "It sounds tawdry in the telling: yes, I masturbated him, yes, this is what we do at New Light, but that isn't how he experienced it. That isn't what it *was*."

How did he experience it, I wanted to know. But instead of answering she suggested that I tell myself a story. "What kind of story?" I asked, and she said, "What kind of story do you want to hear?"

I said: Sometimes I think that it's the act of trying to tell who he is, who he was for me, that causes me to lose him. Each telling takes me further away from a knowledge of that indefinable, elusive essence that is *Houdini*. I want to tell this because I still believe that in telling I'll begin to see who he was, who I was, but I feel more and more that the words solidify some hard and heavy form in my head, while the lightness, the swift and fleeting glimpse that was heat, ache, and echo, and meant Houdini to me, becomes thinner and more insubstantial. Who knows? Maybe that's what I really want.

(None of this is accurate. My image of Houdini doesn't conjure up lightness, nor is he heat, ache, or echo to me, whatever that means.)

She said: Houdini is everything you say he is; he is also many more things you can't see, and even more you could never imagine.

She added, as an aside: Each version must have its visionary complement.

Then she waited. So I imagined the story I'd tell myself. I called it:

First Voyage of the Uninitiated

Houdini and Beth woke to find themselves on a beautiful island, surrounded on every side by the bluest of seas. The white sand beaches sang to the waters, the delicate fronds of the palms caressed the winds that blew softly from the south.

In that place they were confused as to which was sky and which was sea, both were so blue, and of such resonant hue. One was the mirror of the other. "We can swim in the sea," Houdini and Beth said to each other, "and if we close our eyes so that we don't see where sea ends and sky begins, we'll be able to keep swimming right up into the sky, and then we'll be flying though we'll think we're still swimming."

So they decided to try this plan, but they were unhappy thinking that they wouldn't know they had successfully left the sea and entered the sky and were flying, since in order to fly it is necessary to fool the swimming body by not letting it realize it is making a transition from water to air. So they decided that one of them should go into the water and swim, and the other should wait on the shore and watch, so that they would know they had been successful, had tricked the sky and their bodies, and so were able to fly.

Houdini said, "I will go into the water, and I will swim and swim with my eyes closed. You stay here on shore and watch to see if I rise." Beth crouched on the sand like a small earthbound creature, and Houdini slowly (there was something majestic about it) peeled off his clothes. Beth said: "The creature waits crouched on the sand mournfully, seeing before her the years washing chastely over herself." She didn't actually say that, but in retrospect, looking back on that moment before Houdini walked into the sea, she always put this observation in her mouth.

Majestically Houdini strode into the sea, and the waters closed around him. He struck out with a steady stroke (he had a fast crawl) and Beth had a sinking feeling. When she eventually saw him, very far away, moving up the rim of the sky, she sighed and looked around her, at the rotting coconuts lying among the palm roots, the scrappy dirt, the sand flies biting her ankles. She sat down with her back against the trunk of a palm, which was knobby and fibrous and uncomfortable, and thought that if this vision had belonged to one of the sainted women visionaries from the past, such as Margery Kempe (who made her body into a chaste temple), she would be happily uniting with God by now in transcendent bliss. It may not have been sexually fulfilling in our modern sense, but then, what is.

The door opened. For real this time. Monica strode busily into the room, looking like a den mother and interrupting my play-vision, then came to an abrupt stop when she saw me. She stood, staring. Her mouth opened but she didn't say anything. Then she looked over her shoulder. The Mother, who just then followed her in, likewise stopped short in surprise.

Monica turned back to me. "What are you doing here?" she asked. I was surprised because she didn't sound outraged. I felt myself turn red. The Mother looked at me, at Monica, then at neither of us. She stepped around her assistant and went over to her wardrobe. She unfastened the gold harness, unhooked the white robe, then hung them both up.

"Would you mind bringing me that coffee you mentioned?" the Mother said to Monica. "I need to sit down." She crossed the room and lowered herself into the purple armchair beside me. Monica looked from the Mother to me, then turned without comment. She closed the door behind her.

Monica's mildness made me feel oddly exposed, as though the entire fantasy had been written on my face, there for her and the Mother to read. Our little chat, the desert isle, Houdini swimming up the sky. It's humiliating when your own imagination turns on you. The Mother leaned back in her chair and crossed one ankle over the other. Neither of us spoke.

"That wicker chair isn't very comfortable," the Mother said, nodding to the throne. "Jidd and the others made it. One of their earlier efforts." She shrugged and smiled. "It was a nice gesture."

I couldn't meet her eyes. I looked at the chair and said something about its being regal.

The Mother laughed. I looked at her. She got up, tugged on the shades in each of the three windows, and sent them shooting up. The stained glass hangings clinked against the window panes. She stood at the last window for a moment, looking out at the scene on the lawn, then sat back down beside me.

"Why aren't you outside with your friends, Beth?"

I didn't answer. This wasn't at all the tone I'd imagined our conversation taking. She waited, then smiled in a kind of bored way and turned her eyes to the window.

I felt humiliated. "I came here to ask you something," I blurted. She turned her eyes back to me.

"Yes?"

"What happened out there? On the lawn?"

She was ready to be interested. "What do you mean?" she asked, leaning toward me and resting her chin on her hand.

"Did you do it? Were you in control?"

Now she frowned. "What are you talking about?"

"Sacrificing Houdini and Mary."

She raised her eyebrows skeptically, then laughed.

I didn't care. I glared at her. She stopped laughing.

"I think we're all exhausted, Beth. Violence has a strange effect on the people who witness it. We're all feeling the strain."

"That's not what it was."

Her expression altered slightly. Her lips twitched. "No? Tell me."

It was suppressed amusement, I realized. She was sitting there, laughing at me. It was unendurable. "What about Houdini?" I flashed.

"What about him?"

"He hasn't said a word since last night."

She glanced toward the window as though wondering how long this was going to take.

The anger surged freely in me. It was a relief in a way. "You spent two days with him in here. You abandoned your community. And now you don't care what happens to him?"

She looked at me impatiently. "Hayden is finally looking inside himself. For years he's refused to do so, but now he can't escape. Of course he's going to withdraw. He has to re-evaluate his whole life."

I wanted to ask her what things he had to re-evaluate, what life he'd led. I wanted to know if he'd condemned himself, and if she could grant him absolution. At the same time I knew that such questions, even if they weren't ridiculous, became so when spoken aloud. Aside from the fact that Houdini would resent my asking.

"I don't think it's necessary to withdraw in order to re-evaluate your life," I said stiffly.

She gave me a cool look. It was the first statement of belief I had made to her, and even this one had been made in the negative. I tried again.

"I believe people can change. I believe we can find new ways to live our lives. Find new meanings."

The Mother watched me. I couldn't read her face. "Do you," she said softly.

"I do. I was thinking about staying here for a while. I could learn more about what you do. About the visions, looking inside yourself. I don't know if I believe in them the way you do, but I want to understand myself more."

The Mother turned her eyes to the window. She didn't speak. Then she glanced at me again.

"Have you talked this over with Houdini?"

I frowned. "I told you, he stopped talking."

"Did you try?"

I was silent.

"You might ask him what he thinks. You did want to know how he's doing. It's the easiest way to find out."

Then she turned back to the window again. That was it. She had nothing else to say to me. I waited, but after a while I felt ridiculous, sitting there, so I left. I met Monica at the door. She carried a tray with a coffee pot and some cakes with pink frosting. She just looked at me.

I walked back down the long mural hallway that forced you to remain too close to its images. Here a penis turned into a vine and wrapped around the man's hand as he held it out, there a woman bent down to look at the upside-down landscape blooming in her stomach. You could never see the whole wall. It occurred to me that maybe the violations of perspective would be rectified if you could step back. Maybe the ugly mistakes and the awkwardness would disappear when you looked at them as part of a larger whole.

twenty-nine

That was my last conversation with the Mother. I didn't know what to make of it. I certainly didn't feel anything had been resolved. I found this frustrating: I thought I'd earned some honesty. I didn't expect to be shown the secrets of my soul, but I did expect her to be more forthcoming. Four days ago she had called me the messenger who was brought to New Light from the outside world. She said that my presence mattered to the community, that I was a part of their destiny. I felt she owed me *something*.

Which is why I suppose I deserved what I got.

I was walking down the mural hall, feeling the flush of embarrassment still on my cheeks, when the door at the end of the passage that led outside opened. Slanting bars of sunlight lit up the dusty interior and made the electric light blanch. A figure stood silhouetted in the doorway. It was Houdini. I was not reminded of how he came to me out on the patio that night at Boris's party.

He shut the door behind him and the hall was dim again. Had he come to find the Mother, and was surprised to find me coming out of her room?

"Monica just went in," I said.

He frowned. I realized how much I hoped he had come to find me, not the Mother. We faced each other, there in that hallway. It was the first time we'd been alone since the night we'd slept together.

"I wanted to apologize," I said awkwardly, wondering if he'd speak to me.

He put his hand out to the mural, index finger extended toward a painted snake whose outstretched tongue seemed to lick him. He said casually, "Why would you apologize, Beth?"

He sounded exactly the same as before. I faltered for a moment. I knew I was angry, or had been angry, but all I felt right then was guilt. That sacrifice scene with its unspoken violence still haunted me. I had to apologize.

"Out there on the lawn. I'm not sure what happened."

"I wouldn't let it worry you."

"You don't think it was real?"

He laughed. "What happened? You came over. The Visionaries stood and looked at us. It was nothing. Your imagination got going."

"It was more than that."

He smiled. "You're worried that on some level you wanted to punish me? That you wouldn't have seen the Visionaries as a mob if you didn't have the same feelings deep down in your soul?"

"Don't make fun of me."

"I'm not."

His expression didn't change but I could tell he was serious now. We looked at each other in silence and suddenly I recognized the man I had made love to three days ago. It felt much longer than that.

"She couldn't let you stay, Beth. You don't want what she gives these people."

I stared at him. How had he known I would ask to stay? I myself hadn't known. And how could he know she wouldn't let me?

"You're curious," he said. "You want to understand. In the end your curiosity would corrode the community. You'd bring out everyone's latent questions. Their fears. Their boredom."

I continued to stare. I couldn't believe he'd thought that much about me. Briefly I saw him as I had in my fantasy, one arm extended in that wave-cresting stroke, steadily swimming up the side of the sky.

"Did you find your order underneath the chaos?" I asked, trying to say something brave and adult.

He smiled at me as though I were joking.

"I'm serious," I said, realizing that I was. "It would explain things. The chaotic effect works on us too. We're moved along trajectories we can't see. We can't understand the greater order. It's like the mural on this wall—we're too close to it. If we could step far enough away from ourselves, we'd see it."

It was his turn to stare. I walked part of the way toward him.

"That's the mystery. That's the secret all these people come here for. We're all obeying principles of order that make no sense in terms of our individual lives. Our actions only become logical if they're seen in light of some theory of history, some glittering chaotic abstraction. Something we can't see. If we could see it it would take the form of a vision, a mystical communication from some other world. It would *feel* like transcendence. We'd have the sensation that life as we know it has suddenly ceased to exist."

He continued to stare at me. A frog looked out from the mural, just level with his head. It seemed to be flying, its splayed legs pointing in four different directions. It glowed a poisonous blue, and the color vibrated like a piece of sky around the orange spots dotting its back.

I waited. Finally I said lightly, "Don't tell me you've stopped talking again."

He smiled but still didn't say anything. I realized I wasn't going to get an answer.

"Why did you stop talking last night?" I asked him, then smiled. "I'm just curious."

"I don't know," he said.

"You won't tell me?"

He shrugged. "I'm telling you. I don't know."

Baryshnikov could never look as foreign as Hayden E. White. I believed what he said.

"You stopped being an observer," I said. "For the first time you felt involved in what was happening. And that paralyzed you." My voice didn't shake at all.

He didn't answer right away. He studied my face, then looked up at the mural on the wall. He cleared his throat.

"Maybe it was wrong to bring you here, Beth. I didn't consider how you'd be affected." He took a step back, still looking up at the mural, and added casually: "As Sarah said, it meant different things to us."

I saw Ty sitting across from me at the table, telling me about the Yoruba. I remembered the feeling I'd had, that I knew him. Houdini looked at the mural wall, up toward the ceiling, where a ship with sails full of wind set forth.

I said to him, "What do you mean?"

He dropped his eyes. He might have been looking at the poisonous blue frog in front of him, or he might have been looking at nothing at all. He said, "Everything I did here, everything that happened. It was all part of my research. I had to find out everything I could about the visions and their keepers. It was the only way I would even come close to understanding how these altered states of consciousness work."

I let his words sink in. Then I said, my own voice matter-of-fact, "You're saying nothing else happened to you here."

He hesitated, but finally he did look at me. "You saw the visions, Beth. I never did."

Of course it was an evasion. I recognized this even at the time, despite how upset it made me. But it didn't matter whether it was true. The fact was he said it, and now there was nothing else to say.

It was annoying because there were so many questions I didn't get to ask. For example, why was Houdini's curiosity acceptable to the Mother, while mine was not? And what did they really do in there for two days? Why were they so ill-at-ease with one another when they came out?

Unfortunately, once Houdini said to my face that nothing had happened to him at New Light, it was suddenly impossible for me to remain there talking to him any longer. So I left. I walked calmly past him (I hope I looked calm), out the door, and down the front steps. I didn't know what to do then, so I turned the corner to see if anyone was still on the lawn. And there were my friends, where I'd left them, sitting on the grass in a big group. Boris and Ty. Lisa and Sarah. Tom, Glass, Alia; Ted and Crystal and Tianne.

They were talking quietly, calmly, about the day, about the farm, about whatever came into their heads. After everything that happened, there they were, faithfully carrying on.

Tom, who was sitting between Boris and Ty, smiled over at me. He called and, as I approached, shifted toward Boris to make room. I sat down, though I was agitated and would disturb the quiet mood of the circle.

"Did you talk to her?" Alia asked, eagerness in her voice.

"What did she say?" Glass asked. "Did she tell you you should stay?"

I looked from one to the other and didn't respond. My hand was resting on the ground and Ty covered it with his own. I glanced at him. He left his hand there.

"We were hoping you'd want to spend some more time with us," Tom said. "All of you." He looked at Boris.

I didn't tell them I had asked her if I could stay. I

wasn't even sure if I'd been serious. The anger that I hadn't been able to feel while I was talking to Houdini suddenly surged up and I laughed.

"Stay? After what I've been through?" I shifted and Ty withdrew his hand. I was sorry about that, but it couldn't be helped. I folded my arms across my chest.

Everyone regarded me solemnly.

"That's why you should stay," Crystal said simply. "Because of what you've been through."

How pious and good they all were. How devoted. They'd trusted that things would work out in the end, and so they'd been rewarded. Now they sat on the grass like pleased children, clutching their lollipops tightly, their pleasure edged with only the faintest of fears that the candy might be taken away again.

"She's just a woman, you know. She's not your mother, or some spiritual leader who can heal you of your childhood traumas." I looked around the circle angrily. Yes, and like children they met my anger with confused, hurt faces.

"You're upset, Beth," Sarah put in soothingly. I glared at her because she was being kind. Since when had it been Sarah's impulse to play peacemaker? Was she trying to keep things from becoming ugly, so that Boris wouldn't feel he had to choose between me and Tom? Of all times to join the converted. I turned to Lisa, expecting that, as always, she could be counted on to oppose Sarah. But for the first time Lisa didn't rise to the occasion. She sat looking thoughtfully at me, at Sarah, at Boris and the Visionaries. She even managed to look wise. I thought, oh god, her too.

Then, to my surprise, Boris rose to my defense. Boris, who in St. Louis had agreed with Sarah in opposing my trip down to New Light, and who had then, upon arriving here, done an abrupt about-face, falling for Tom, the Filipino Adonis.

"She's not *upset*. Look what she's been through. Some serious shit has gone down here." He looked at Tom and hesitated, for a brief yearning moment appealing to his Visionary lover to understand. But Tom just regarded him dully, his face emptied out by surprise.

Boris shook his head in mute apology. "I understand how you guys see it. This is your community. But your leader makes Beth into a visionary messenger, then disappears with Houdini? You have every right to be pissed," he said to me firmly. "She used you." His eyes slid back to Tom and their eyes locked. Then Tom looked away.

For a long moment no one spoke.

"It's true," Alia said finally. She fingered the frayed edge of her cuff. "You have every right to be angry, Beth."

"I'm not *angry*," I said. "I just want to know what *happened*. Earlier, when the Mother came back from the hospital. After she went inside, leaving us standing here. We all turned to Houdini and Mary." I looked around the circle again. "I want to know what each of you felt."

The Visionaries looked at each other and again no one spoke. I turned to Ty.

"I felt something," he said slowly, his forehead creasing. "I don't know what exactly. It made me uncomfortable."

I nodded. I looked at Tom.

"The Mother would never let anything happen," he said, meeting my gaze unwaveringly.

"But what? What was it?"

"What do you mean, what was it? Nothing happened," Crystal said, distressed.

"She means, was there something violent in it," Ted said quietly, his jaw muscles standing out in relief. "Right? Isn't that what you're talking about?" I looked at him. I nodded.

"She allowed us to act it out, Beth," Tom said quietly.

"It's like the fire circle. We have to experience the darkness of the soul, to see what's inside us. We would never do anything. But we have to know."

I looked at Tom and the others. I believed that they wouldn't commit a crime. It was a ritualized performance, invoked, then thwarted, by the Mother. A thing whose moral valence I couldn't judge. It was too foreign. It belonged to another world, as did their willingness to participate in the ritual, secure in their faith that the Mother would stop them when the moment came.

I had admired Audrey for what I called her courageous self-exposure, there at the fire ceremony, when she had let all of us see the ugliness of her inner heart. It would be tempting to put on a noble face all the time, to allow yourself to be admired. And so I had admired her because she wasn't admirable. Because she'd allowed herself to be human.

But now I wondered. Was she really so courageous, behaving that way in front of all of us? Or had it been an indulgence, something base and selfish that I should regard quite differently? Chilling and awful, not admirable, not brave. Because what if, in entertaining such fantasies, we somehow excuse them? Make their existence more acceptable? What if acting things out in that way causes us to lose sight of the real consequences of the things we do?

"It's like make-believe here," I said abruptly. "You're playing a game."

Ty and Lisa and Sarah looked at each other, their expressions disturbed. Boris glanced uneasily at Tom, then dropped his eyes. None of the Visionaries replied.

"You have to accept responsibility for yourselves!" I said angrily. "It's your *lives*, for god's sake."

Tianne, her face calm, her faith unshakeable, said quietly, "We know, Beth. That's why we're here."

Tom turned to Boris. He said lightly, "I don't suppose there's any chance of you staying now." Boris didn't look up.

"Tom –" I said.

"It's okay, Beth. This isn't right for you. We understand. And you can always come back if you change your mind." He glanced at Boris again. He smiled brightly.

"Tom –" I said again. He looked at me in silence. "I asked her. I asked if I could stay. She wouldn't answer me."

Tom just looked at me.

Ted said, "Do you want to stay?"

I glanced at Ty sitting beside me, then up at the farmhouse, glowing softly in the late afternoon light. "I justdon't believe that this is the only kind of community possible."

Tianne glanced at the others. "We were talking about this when you were inside. It's something we all have to deal with. How do you sustain a communal movement in this country? How do you survive when you live outside the mainstream?"

"Not everyone needs the Mother," Alia said. "I mean,that kind of structure. There's a lot of different communities. Like East Wind."

Glass said tentatively, "I can't really picture you there, Beth. No visions."

I had to laugh.

"We're brought up to be individualists," Crystal said. "No one wants to make concessions. One way or another, you have to find a way to make that possible."

Tianne nodded to her lover. "You have to take yourself apart if you're going to live in a new way. Examine everything."

Her eyes traveled to Tom. He stared at the grass infront of him. His face looked thoughtful and sad.

"She's not an egomaniac," Alia said. She pushed up

the sleeves of her sweater. "She can be very disinterested. But she's human, too. We're all human."

"Are you staying?" I asked Glass.

She shrugged. She shook her head ambiguously. She looked like she might cry. I knew how she felt.

"Tom," I said again, desperate this time. "I want to thank you. For everything."

He looked up at me. I wanted him to smile, to reassure me that everything was okay, that he'd be all right. I couldn't unsay what I'd said because on some level I'd meant it. But I wanted him to forgive me.

It cost him, but he managed a smile. "I told you, Beth. You can always come back."

Then his eyes flickered beyond me and we all turned. Houdini had stepped around the corner of the house and was standing thirty feet away. I don't know how the others felt, but I resented his presence there. I felt he had no right to come to us. I wanted to blame him for what I'd said to these people I'd become friends with, but of course I couldn't. I said what I said because I needed to. Because Houdini was right. I didn't really want what they had to offer. I admired it, I appreciated it, but it wasn't for me.

There was nothing insolent in Houdini's stance. He stood there awkwardly, his hands hanging by his side. His expression seemed...not quite wistful, not sad. Concerned maybe. He didn't come any closer; he just stood there, gazing at us as though he wished he could join us, but knew that was impossible.

"I just wanted to say. Have a safe trip back."

Then he nodded and disappeared. We heard his feet on the steps, then the screen door slam.

It's not enough to stand at the edge of a ridge and look out over the valley of your desires. The kind gaze of morning may edge each tree and building with beautiful light, and you may feel pure in your wanting them, but even at noon, when the shadows have been all but vanquished, you know what's waiting. *Samsara*. The wheel—life's endless cycle of desire and dissatisfaction.

The doctrine is Buddhist, the logic simple. We desire something and feel unhappy because we can't have it. But ifwe do get it we aren't satisfied. Instead, we desire something new, and feel unhappy because we can't have it.

Samsara is not completely antithetical to the beliefs of the Visionaries. With the fire ceremony the Visionariesstrove to break the cycle of desiring and examine the hidden nature of their wants in order to purify them. By confessing the dark side of their longings, they were able to celebrate those longings again with renewed vigor. Like the Buddhists, they acknowledged the cyclical nature of our desires, but unlike them, the Visionaries didn't feel trapped.

The Buddhist solution to samsara is enlightenment, attained by rising above desire's snare, letting go of the earthly self and its perpetually insatiable longings. Perhaps they're right: it's not the object of desire that we crave, but something else, something elusive that can never be captured, no matter how ardent the pursuit. Even coincident desire ends in dissatisfaction.

Yet accepting samsara is not easy. It scores its devotees with its difficult beauty. The exhausted individual must admit she longs for the solace of non-being, which will free her from the endless dissatisfaction that is her lot. And there's a catch. If you remain in the world, buffeted about by temptation and longing, you can't really escape. You must withdraw to *Sangha*, the community apart, devoted to the higher life of contemplation.

We left New Light that Sunday evening, after saying goodbye to the friends we'd made there. The sky was full of color as we drove back up I-44 to St. Louis, all of us outsiders, in a caravan of cars. Of course, Houdini stayed behind.

I felt strangely calm as we headed back. Ty, sitting beside me, understood that silence was what I needed. I realized once we got on the road that it was a relief to leave New Light, and though some small part of me must have been sorry too, it was buried, at least temporarily. Upon our return to St. Louis I followed Boris's advice and got an apartment. It's down on West Pine, a few blocks from his, within walking distance of Duff's, where I wait tables.

Rents are cheap here—I can get by working only three or four shifts a week. The rhythm of life is slow and easy. It'swhat I need—time, the space to think. Mostly I read: nineteenth-century spiritualists, American communal movements, things to help me understand. Sometimes I go out with Boris, Lisa, and Sarah to see Ty's band, or to attend lectures such as "Religions of the East: the Inner Millennium," or "Modern Spirituality: the Quixotic Quest for Order." Then we go to a coffeeshop and argue over whether any of these speakers could found their own charismatic movement.

The calm that I felt as we left New Light was a relief. The exhaustion of desire. I felt numb, and that was easier than facing the tumult. The numbness lasted for almost a month. It broke in early June when I received an envelope inthe mail.

There was no return address but the postmark said

San Francisco, and inside was an article from the McDonald County Bulletin, a nosy little weekly that reported every thing that happened in the county's townships. The article, dated May 18th, was on the shooting. It read:

A man was hospitalized at Mercy County General yesterday after a gunshot wound to the thigh. The man, Mark Ryder, is a member of New Light, a radical commune whose practices may include fornication, group sexual acts, and bizarre pagan rituals. Mr Ryder admitted to sexually tormenting the woman who shot him, and refused to press charges. The woman, who has not been identified, is also a member of the radical group. Mr Ryder has been released from the hospital, but was told to be available for further questioning.

Concern in the community over this most recent example of degenerate and dangerous behavior on the part of New Light members continues to grow. Frank and Helen Abustin, proprietors of the American grocery store in Elkhead, Mo., reported that they have met several times with Federal investigators who are looking into the goings-on at the commune. "We won't rest until we get those degenerates out of our county," Helen Abustin told this reporter. "We're a community here," Frank Abustin added.

The article fussed on about the Visionaries, but there was nothing else in the envelope. I assumed it was from Houdini, but there was no greeting, no message, nothing to explain why he sent it to me. The lack of explanation infuriated me.

But after a while the anger drained away, and I began to wonder if he even knew why he sent it. I tried to imagine how he would interpret the write-up. Was it the first step in the historicization of New Light, evidence of the early effectsof the community on the outside world? Or was he being ironic, acknowledging the community's insignificance, admitting that it couldn't qualify as a strange attractor amid the chaotic sprawl of Visionary movements, which make up one strand of the history of the American will to believe?

And so the article became just another a mystery. I got used to living with it, and continued on with my real life, talking over old times with Boris, developing friendships with Lisa and Sarah and Ty. I made a few friends at the restaurant too, though I didn't go out drinking with any of them. The months passed. The heat of summer finally broke in mid-September and was replaced by mild cool days, blue-skied and sunny.

Then, two days ago, I received a second anonymous missive with the same San Francisco postmark. It arrived almost five months after the first. Inside was another articlefrom the McDonald County newspaper, this one dated October 5th. The article reported, rather smugly, that the inhabitants of the New Light community had taken every-thing from the farm that wasn't nailed down and left the county. They just disappeared—no forwarding address or anything. They abandoned the gardens, left the farmhouse and barn, packed up their warehouses, trucks, and trailers and took off.

I know from my reading that such disappearances aren't unusual for communities like New Light. Probably there's a lawyer somewhere who is managing the sale of the property. Perhaps the Visionaries had been planning the move for months, scouting about for a new site that would provide a more harmonic setting, a better place to evolve their new forms and dream the world into visionary accord. Even as I write this, the Mother and her people have probably resurfaced somewhere else, to start again.

Did he send it to taunt me?

There's no way of knowing, of course. I can speculate, but I can't know for sure. But it doesn't matter. The article brought all of that to the surface again.

I confess that it made me restless, thinking about everything that happened at New Light. It got so I couldn't even read. I needed the world, not words describing it. So I took the metrolink downtown and got off at the stop for theArch, at the Eads Bridge station. I exited onto the street from a staircase lodged in one of the bridge's support pillars.

As I looked up at the enormous iron struts, with their criss-cross of girders as intricate as filigree, I decided that James Eads must have been a fanciful man. His bridge, which was completed in 1874, stretches like iron lace across the Mississippi. People came from all over to marvel at the feats of engineering the bridge displayed: its supporting piers, which reached bedrock via a system of air locks; its 520-foot central span, at the time the largest in the world. The story of its construction is also marvelous. Some of the town officials didn't want a bridge spanning the Mississippi, so they cameup with specifications for height, length and weight-bearing capability that they thought would be impossible to meet. Yet Eads was able to design a fabulous bridge that met the specs. After seven years of construction the bridge that had been an impossibility joined the two sides of the river. It was hailed as the symbol of St. Louis.

I crossed the street and climbed the stairs to the Gateway Arch park. About a quarter mile away, the silver legs of the Arch gleamed liquidly in the sun. It's true what they say—the Arch does draw the viewer to it. By the time you reach it, you're compelled to touch the scored silver of its sides, which are warm and seem to throb faintly beneath your hand. I understood why the Arch replaced Eads Bridge as the city's symbol of itself. Like the bridge, the Arch is a fantastic structure. Completed in 1965, it was designed by Eero Saarinen, and stands 632 feet in the air. The constructionentailed building the two legs up section by section, using engines on tracks that could be hooked onto the sides of the segments already set in place. It was another virtuoso engineering feat. It took 6 years to complete, and the mortality stats predicted that 14 workers would die before the project was completed. But no one died, a fact the park rangers view as a minor miracle.

I bought my ticket and waited in line for a pod-shaped elevator behind a family of three. The four of us rode up together. The little girl about seven or eight shrieked when our pod lurched to the right, and was hushed by her mother, who then smiled at me apologetically. I smiled back:as we rose up the center of the north leg, I felt my own stomach go. It was like riding in Willy Wonka's great glass elevator. The pod moved sideways and then diagonally as it traveled up the Arch's curved leg. The father looked a bit green by the time we got to the top.

When the elevator opened onto the lookout bridge, my legs went too—I climbed the deck's rise feeling all rubbery. Then I stooped before the little window-slice that lookedout onto the miniature city.

It wasn't the aerial vision from my ascension over St. Louis. Below lay a city whose highways and streets receded into the suburbs in a perspective of haze. Buildings looked like toy models, cars were the size of computer chips from the '70s. I was vaguely disappointed. It would have been pretty spectacular to find out that the vision of the dying monster-city was in fact the view from the Arch.

In fact, the real view was kind of a let down. I looked through a smudged, very small pane of glass onto a circum-scribed panorama. From the east side I could just glimpse Eads Bridge, and that too was disappointing, warped and blurred by the thickened edge of the glass in the viewing window. I wasn't sure which symbol I preferred, the out-moded emblem of utility, bridging the east and west, or the spectacle of the Arch, soaring above the city, but serving no useful function as far as I could see. I leaned closer to the window, trying to identify my building on West Pine. After a moment I closed my eyes.

That's when I saw my vision again. The same mystical beast, superimposed on the more mundane outlines of the city; the corrupt fertility of the earth, straining against the sky which reined it in. Above it burned stars—brighter, with my eyes closed, than they had been even in the vision on Boris's patio. I waited, and sure enough, beneath the murmured exclamations of the other viewers, rose the ghost of that swelling symphony I'd heard after the fire ceremony, a music that accompanied all motion, every beating heart andfiring nerve cell. I stood above St. Louis and contemplated my visions, which were not visions at all, but the living images of an invisible world that mysteriously kept its own time. It lived inside me and inside all of us. There but not there. I opened my eyes again. There but not there.

It's autumn, the time of year for recollection and review. Just this week the leaves started to change. Outside my apartment stand two sugar gums, a maple, and a rusty sycamore. Some of the leaves are still green, others have turned. Crimson, peach, watermelon. The variegated effect on the maple and sugar gums is lovely; behind them, the big sycamore in its rusty olive-drab sounds a bass note. Part of the endless cycle.

Tonight I'm going on a date with Ty. It's our first night out alone, without the company of our friends. I thought I'd be nervous but I'm not. He told me he has a surprise for me, he's going to take me someplace in St. Louis I've never been. He said I'd like it. I asked him how he knew. His voice smiled over the phone as he said, "Oh, I know."

I walked into the bedroom to get ready, and the slanting sun through the window gilded the maple leaves with a narrow edge of light. I moved my head so that the sun wasn't in my eyes, and saw that the maple's crown is bare now. It has introduced pumpkin and pale lemon into the spectrum; these burn softly against leaves the color of brick and moss. I stand before the cold glass and trace the patterns.

Annette Gilson was born in New Jersey and educated at Bard College and Washington University in St. Louis, where she got her Ph.D. She lived abroad and in New York City for several years, and is currently an associate professor of creative writing and contemporary literature at Oakland University in Rochester, Michigan. In addition to her fiction she has published poetry as well as essays on contemporary authors insuch journals as *Modern Fiction Studies* and *Twentieth Century Literature.*